Wonderland

Written By

Tommy Kovac

Illustrated by

Sonny Liew

Disney PRESS

New York

Printed in Singapore

First Edition
1 3 5 7 9 10 8 6 4 2

Library of Congress Control Number on file.

ISBN: 978-1-44231-0451-3

Visit www.disneybooks.com

Table of Contents

Chapter One

Impostor!

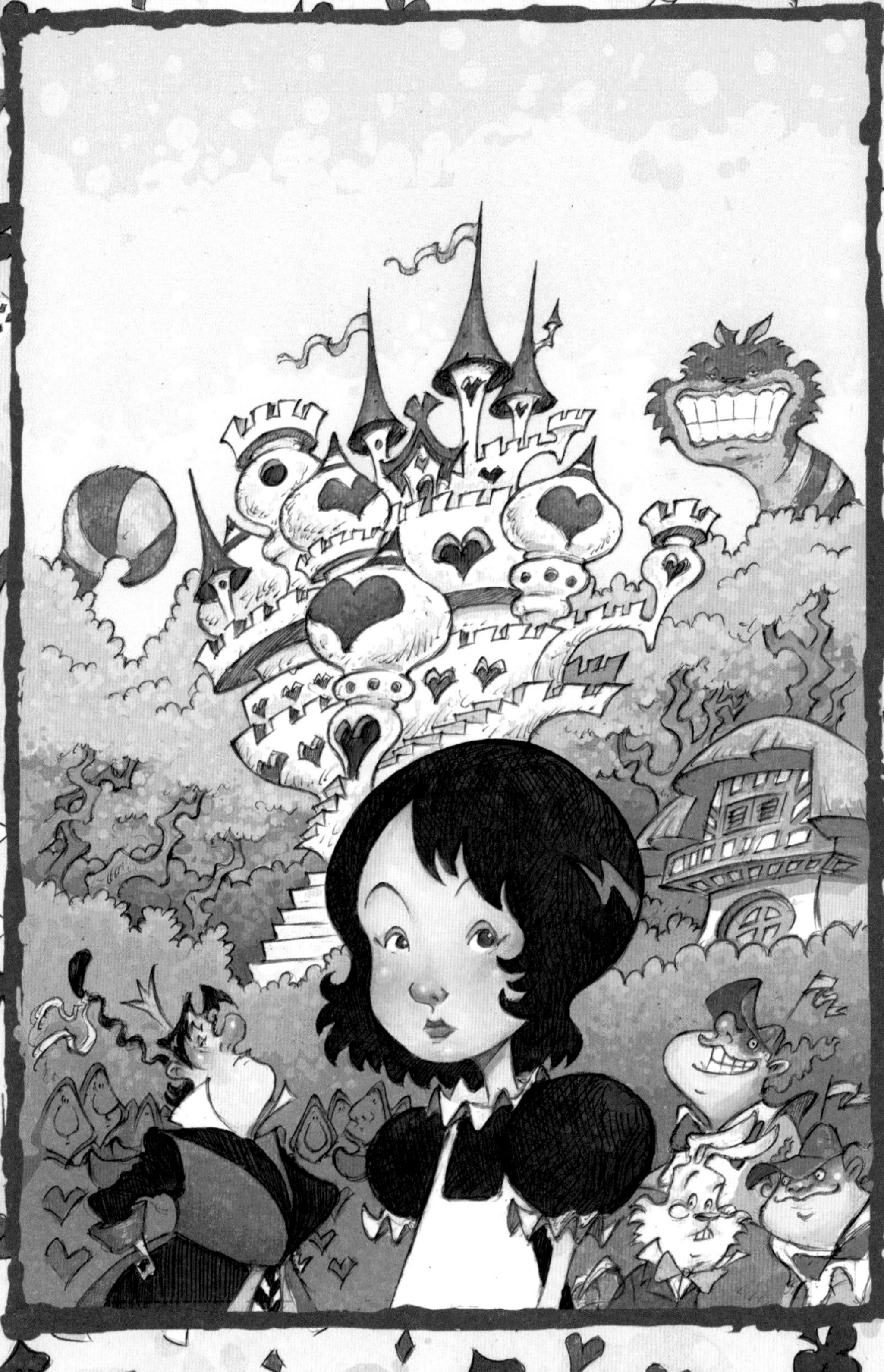

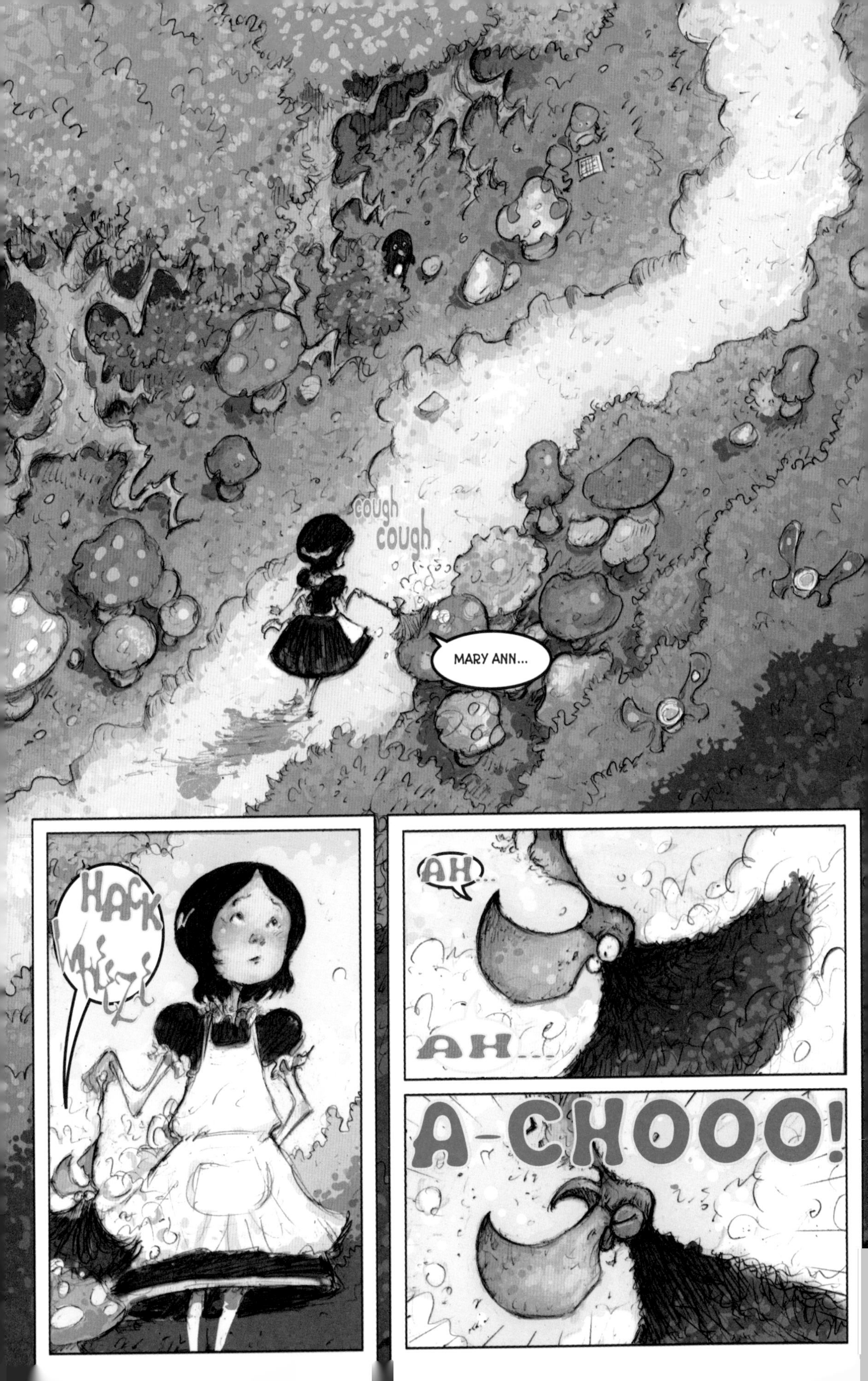
cough
cough
MARY ANN...
HACK
WHEEZE
AH...
AH...
A-CHOOO!

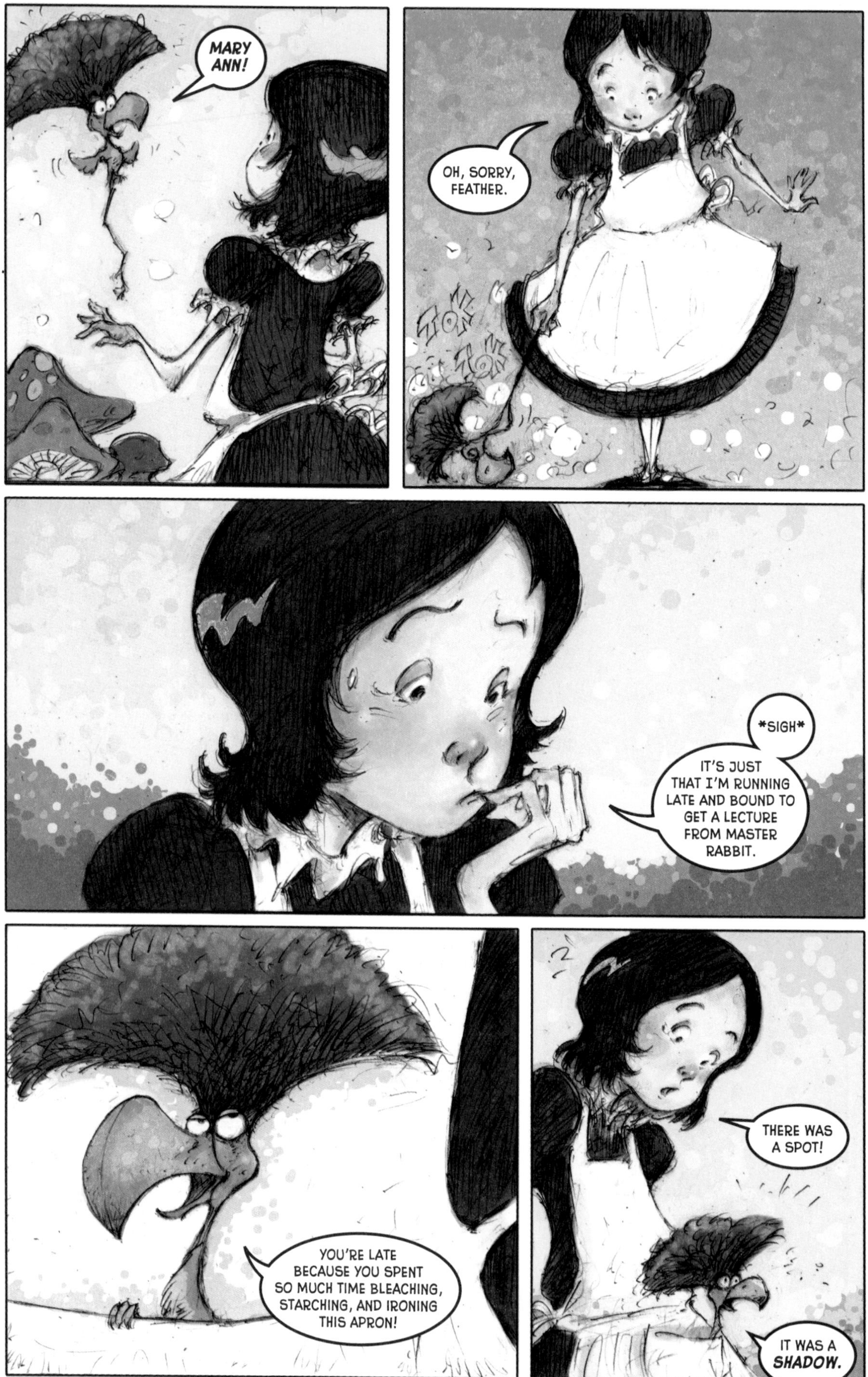
MARY ANN!
OH, SORRY, FEATHER.
SIGH
IT'S JUST THAT I'M RUNNING LATE AND BOUND TO GET A LECTURE FROM MASTER RABBIT.
YOU'RE LATE BECAUSE YOU SPENT SO MUCH TIME BLEACHING, STARCHING, AND IRONING THIS APRON!
THERE WAS A SPOT!
IT WAS A SHADOW.

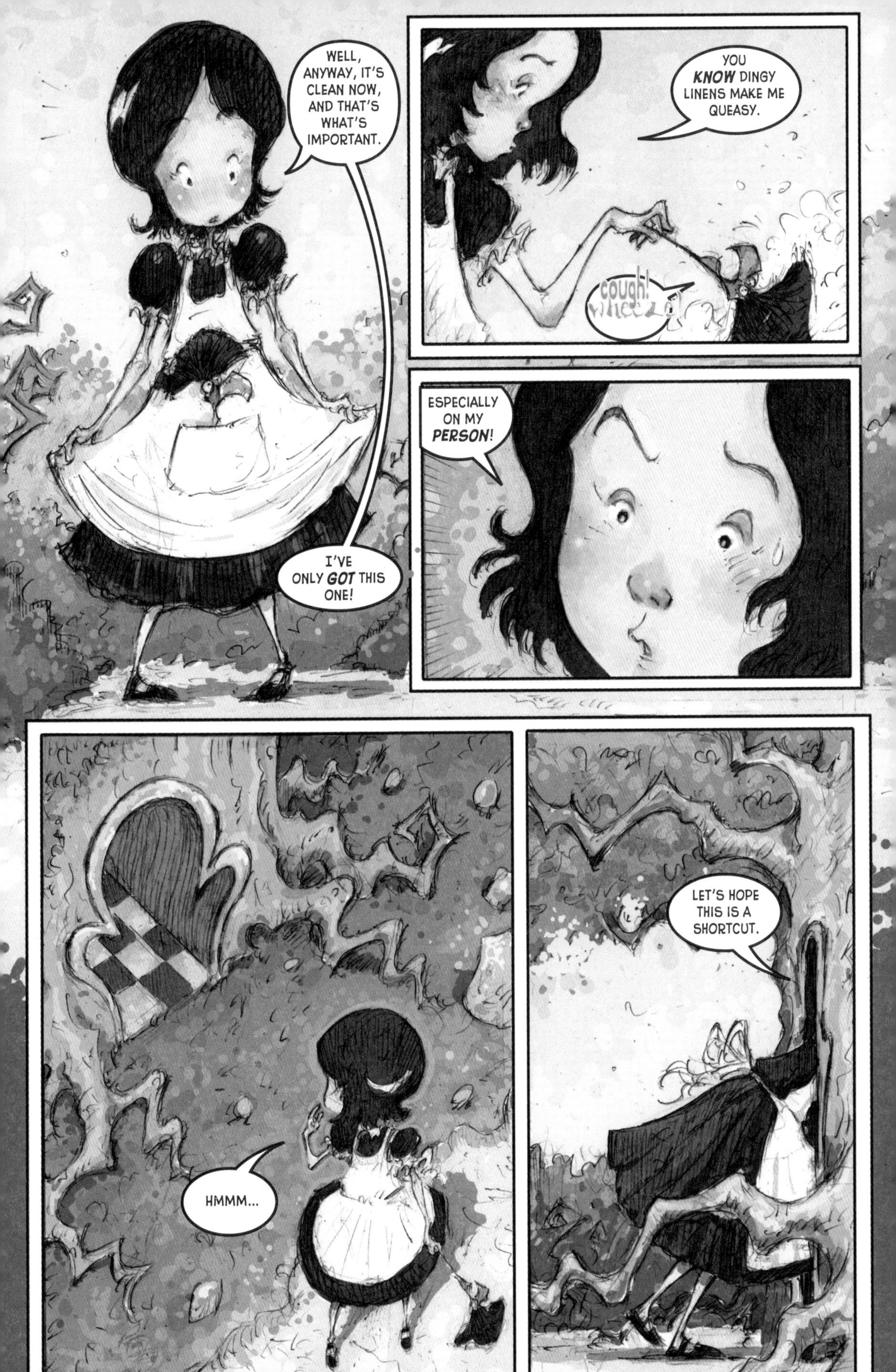
WELL, ANYWAY, IT'S CLEAN NOW, AND THAT'S WHAT'S IMPORTANT.
I'VE ONLY GOT THIS ONE!
YOU KNOW DINGY LINENS MAKE ME QUEASY.
cough!
ESPECIALLY ON MY PERSON!
HMMM...
LET'S HOPE THIS IS A SHORTCUT.

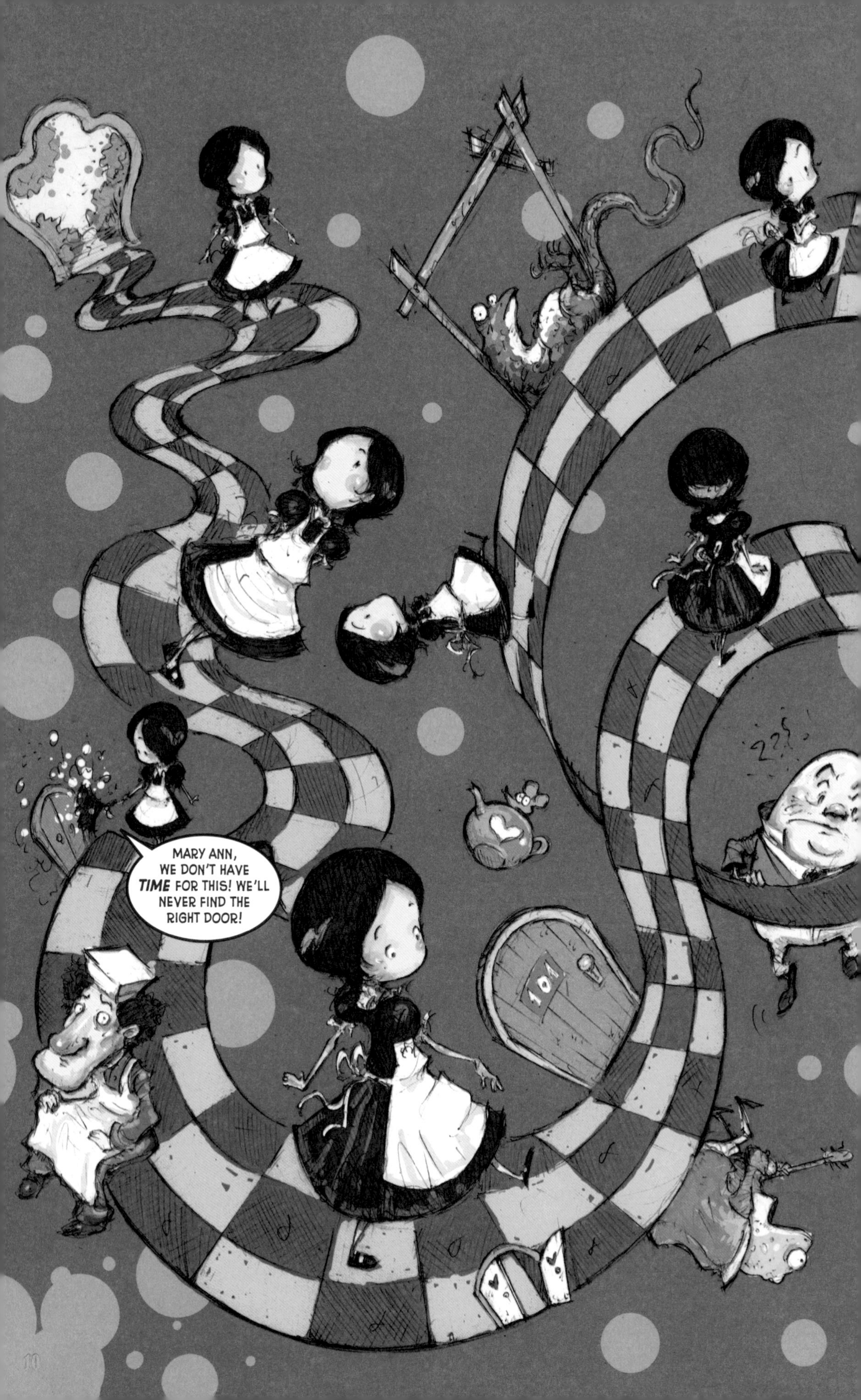
MARY ANN, WE DON'T HAVE **TIME** FOR THIS! WE'LL NEVER FIND THE RIGHT DOOR!
101

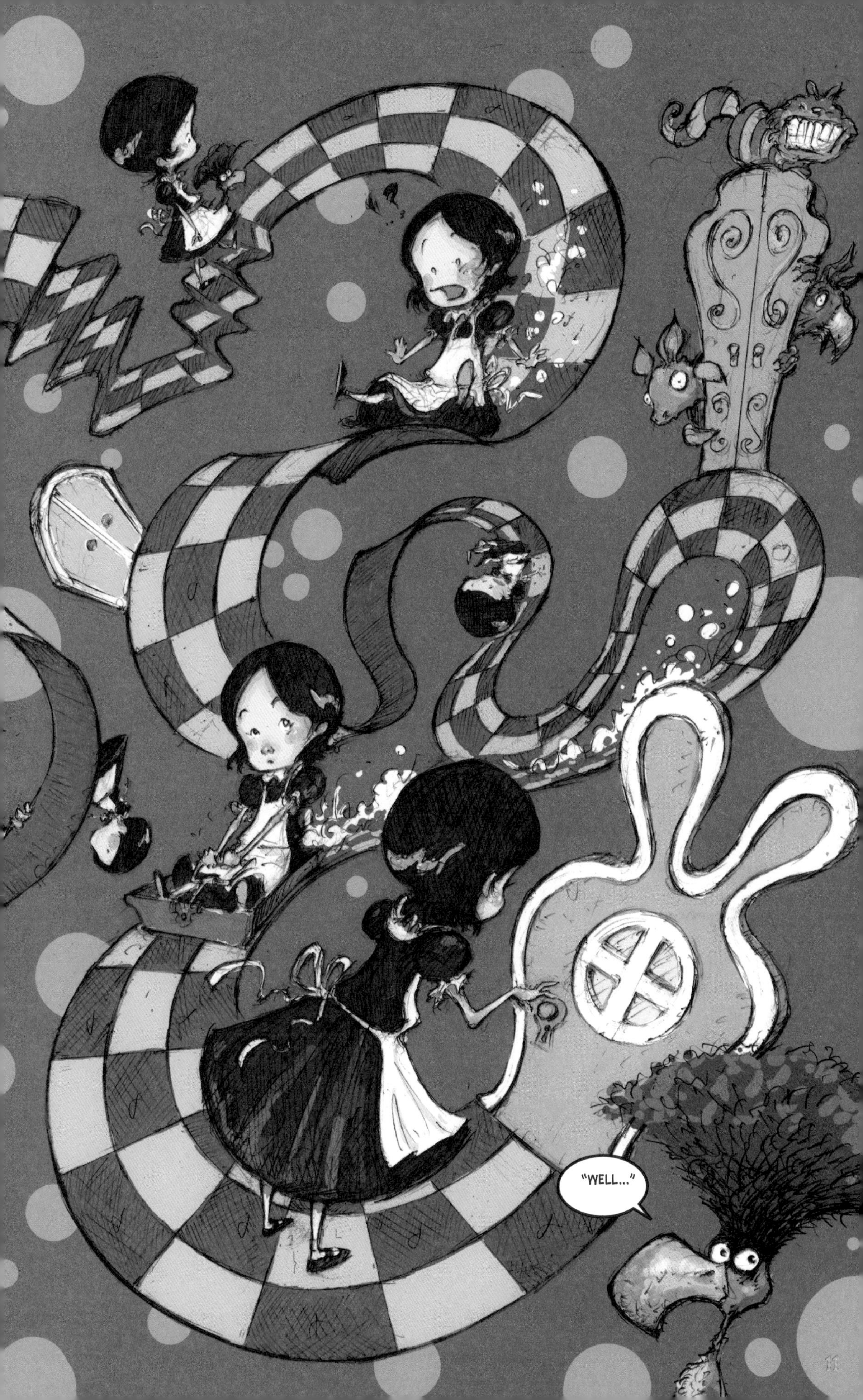
"WELL..."

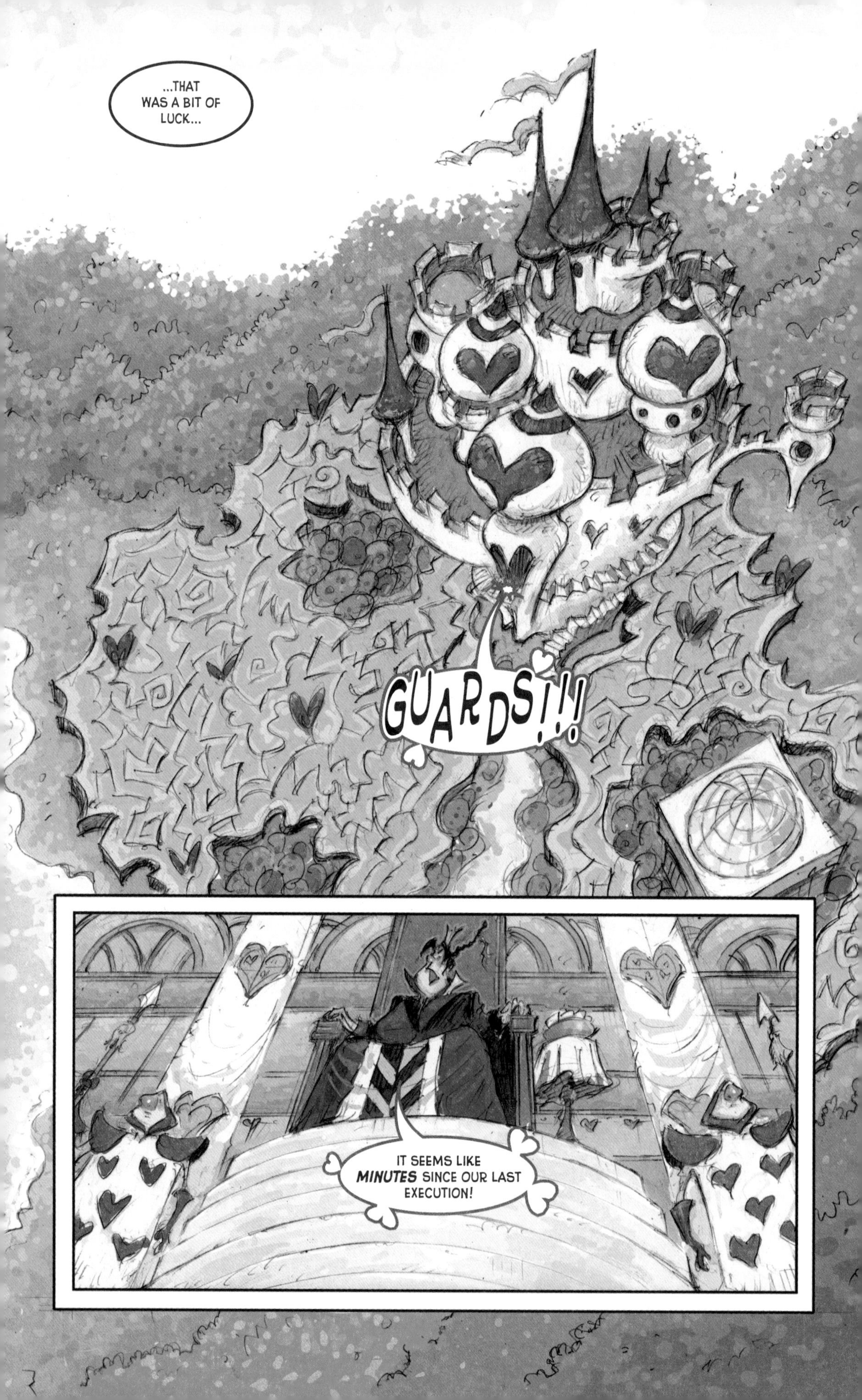
...THAT WAS A BIT OF LUCK...
GUARDS!!!
IT SEEMS LIKE MINUTES SINCE OUR LAST EXECUTION!

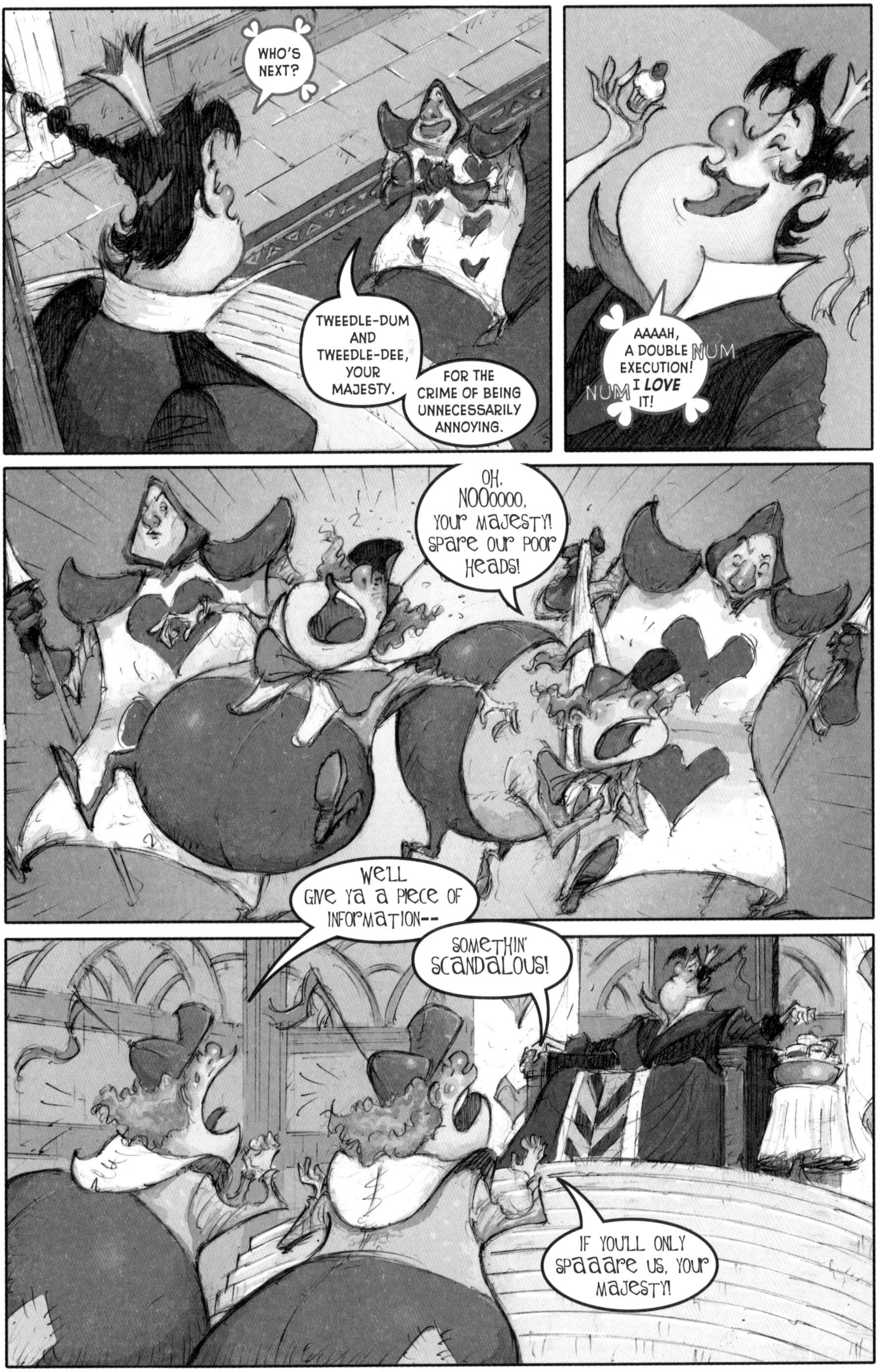
WHO'S NEXT?
TWEEDLE-DUM AND TWEEDLE-DEE, YOUR MAJESTY.
FOR THE CRIME OF BEING UNNECESSARILY ANNOYING.
AAAAH, A DOUBLE EXECUTION! I LOVE IT!
NUM
NUM
OH, NOOoooo, YOUR MAJESTY! SPARE OUR POOR HEADS!
WE'LL GIVE YA A PIECE OF INFORMATION--
SOMETHIN' SCANDALOUS!
IF YOU'LL ONLY SPAAARE US, YOUR MAJESTY!

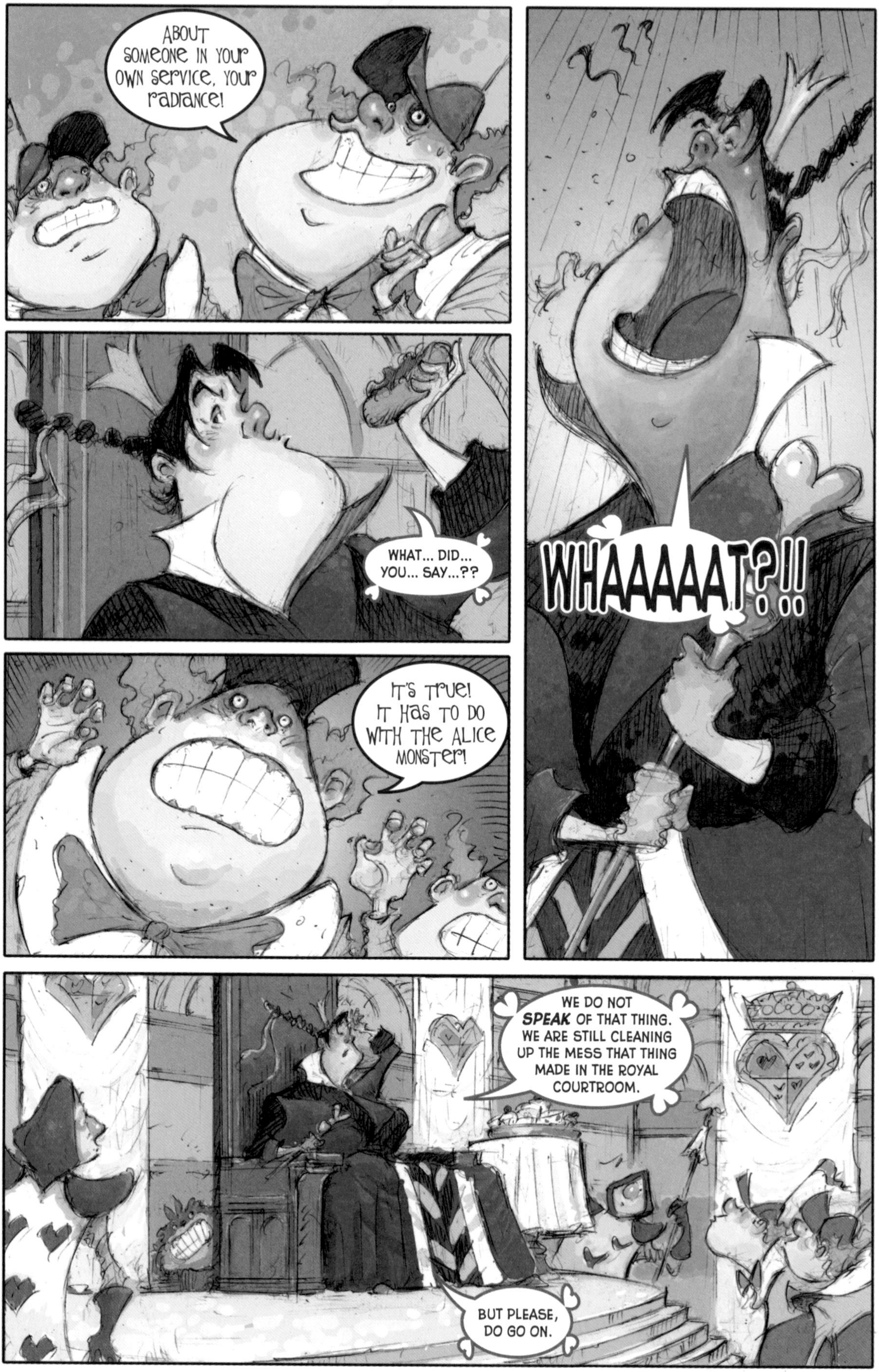
ABOUT SOMEONE IN YOUR OWN SERVICE, YOUR RADIANCE!
WHAT... DID... YOU... SAY...??
IT'S TRUE! IT HAS TO DO WITH THE ALICE MONSTER!
WHAAAAAT?!!
WE DO NOT *SPEAK* OF THAT THING. WE ARE STILL CLEANING UP THE MESS THAT THING MADE IN THE ROYAL COURTROOM.
BUT PLEASE, DO GO ON.

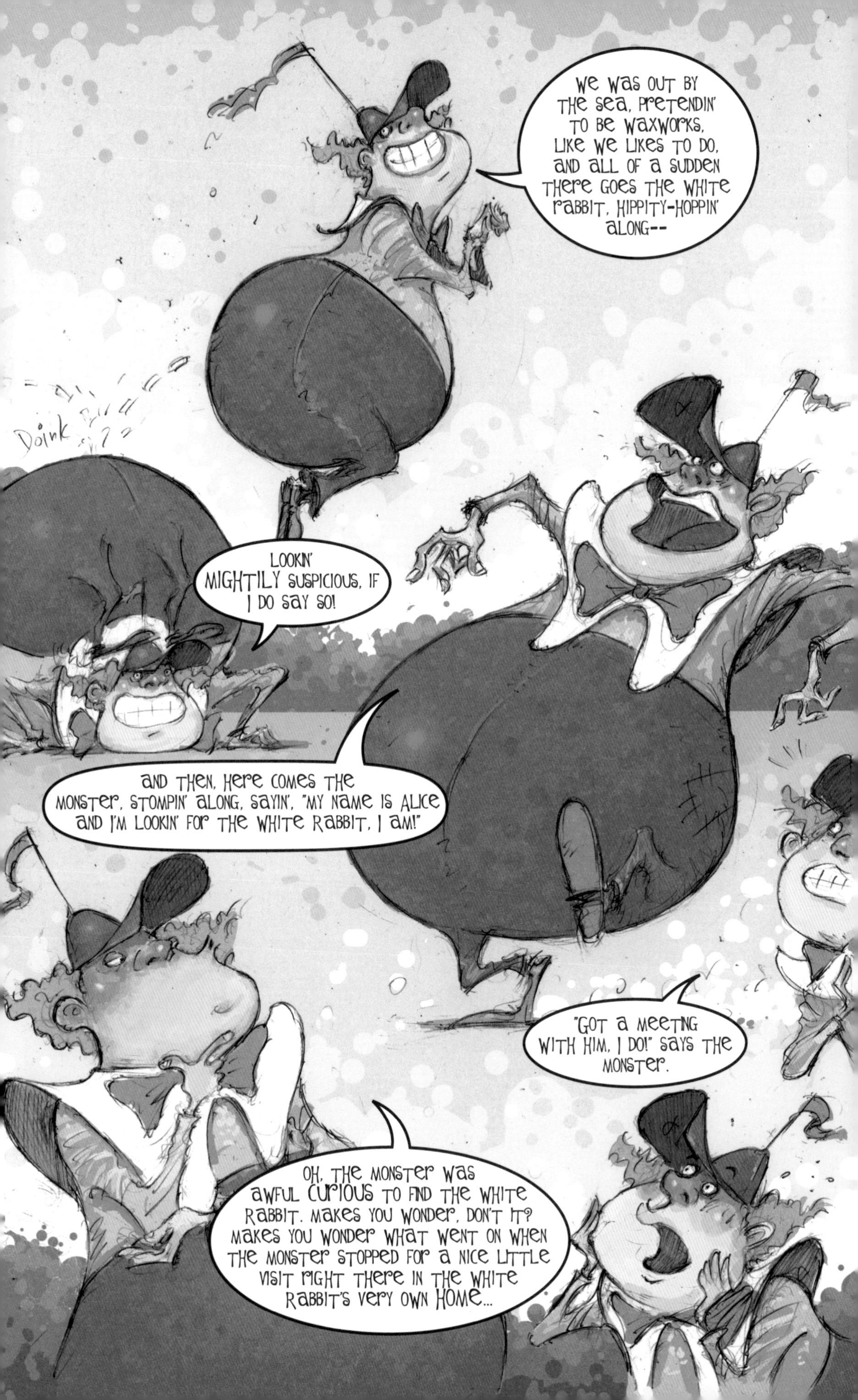
WE WAS OUT BY THE SEA, PRETENDIN' TO BE WAXWORKS, LIKE WE LIKES TO DO, AND ALL OF A SUDDEN THERE GOES THE WHITE RABBIT, HIPPITY-HOPPIN' ALONG--
Doink
LOOKIN' MIGHTILY SUSPICIOUS, IF I DO SAY SO!
AND THEN, HERE COMES THE MONSTER, STOMPIN' ALONG, SAYIN', "MY NAME IS ALICE AND I'M LOOKIN' FOR THE WHITE RABBIT, I AM!"
"GOT A MEETING WITH HIM, I DO!" SAYS THE MONSTER.
OH, THE MONSTER WAS AWFUL CURIOUS TO FIND THE WHITE RABBIT. MAKES YOU WONDER, DON'T IT? MAKES YOU WONDER WHAT WENT ON WHEN THE MONSTER STOPPED FOR A NICE LITTLE VISIT RIGHT THERE IN THE WHITE RABBIT'S VERY OWN HOME...

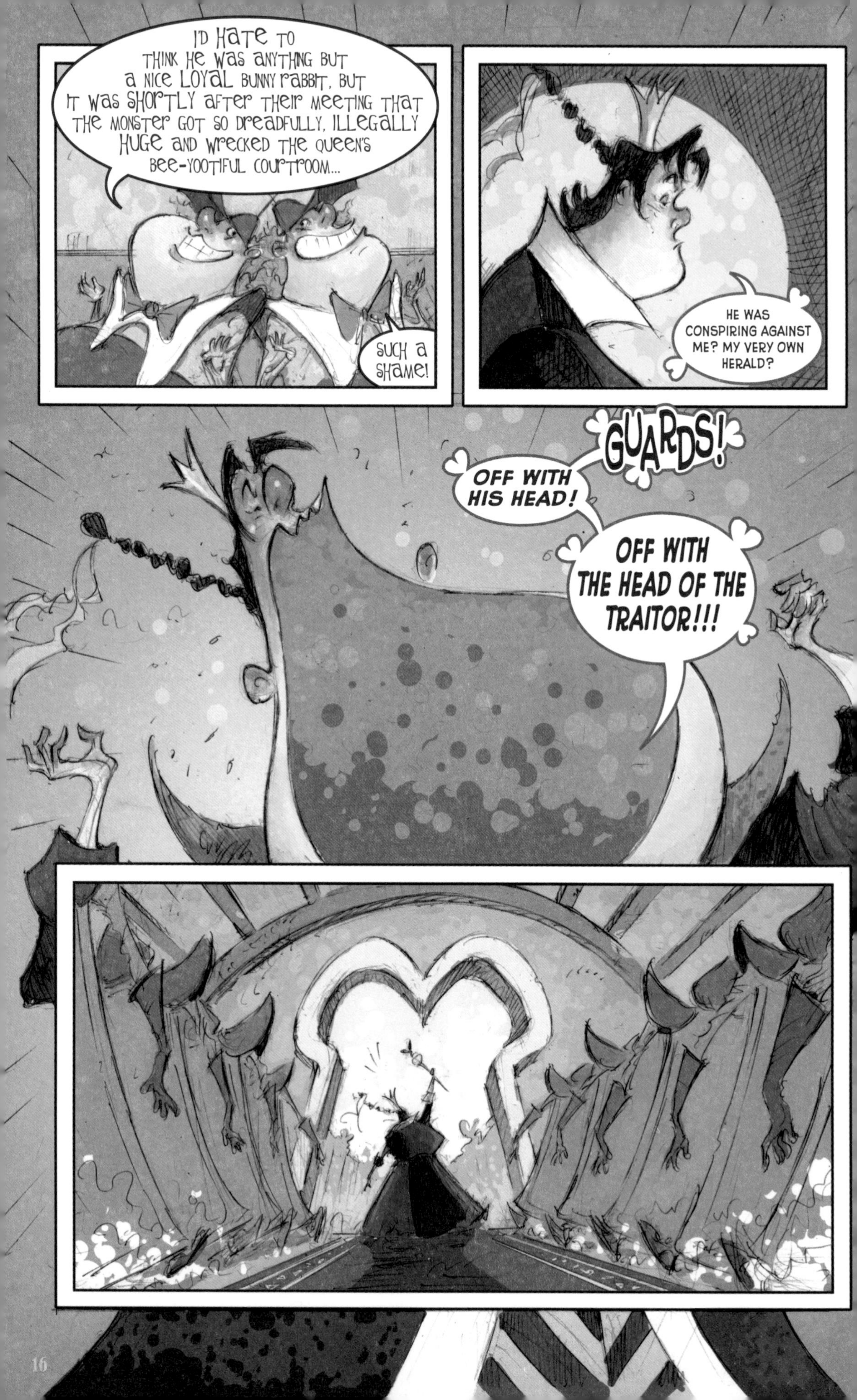
I'D HATE TO THINK HE WAS ANYTHING BUT A NICE LOYAL BUNNY RABBIT, BUT IT WAS SHORTLY AFTER THEIR MEETING THAT THE MONSTER GOT SO DREADFULLY, ILLEGALLY HUGE AND WRECKED THE QUEEN'S BEE-YOOTIFUL COURTROOM...
SUCH A SHAME!
HE WAS CONSPIRING AGAINST ME? MY VERY OWN HERALD?
GUARDS!
OFF WITH HIS HEAD!
OFF WITH THE HEAD OF THE TRAITOR!!!

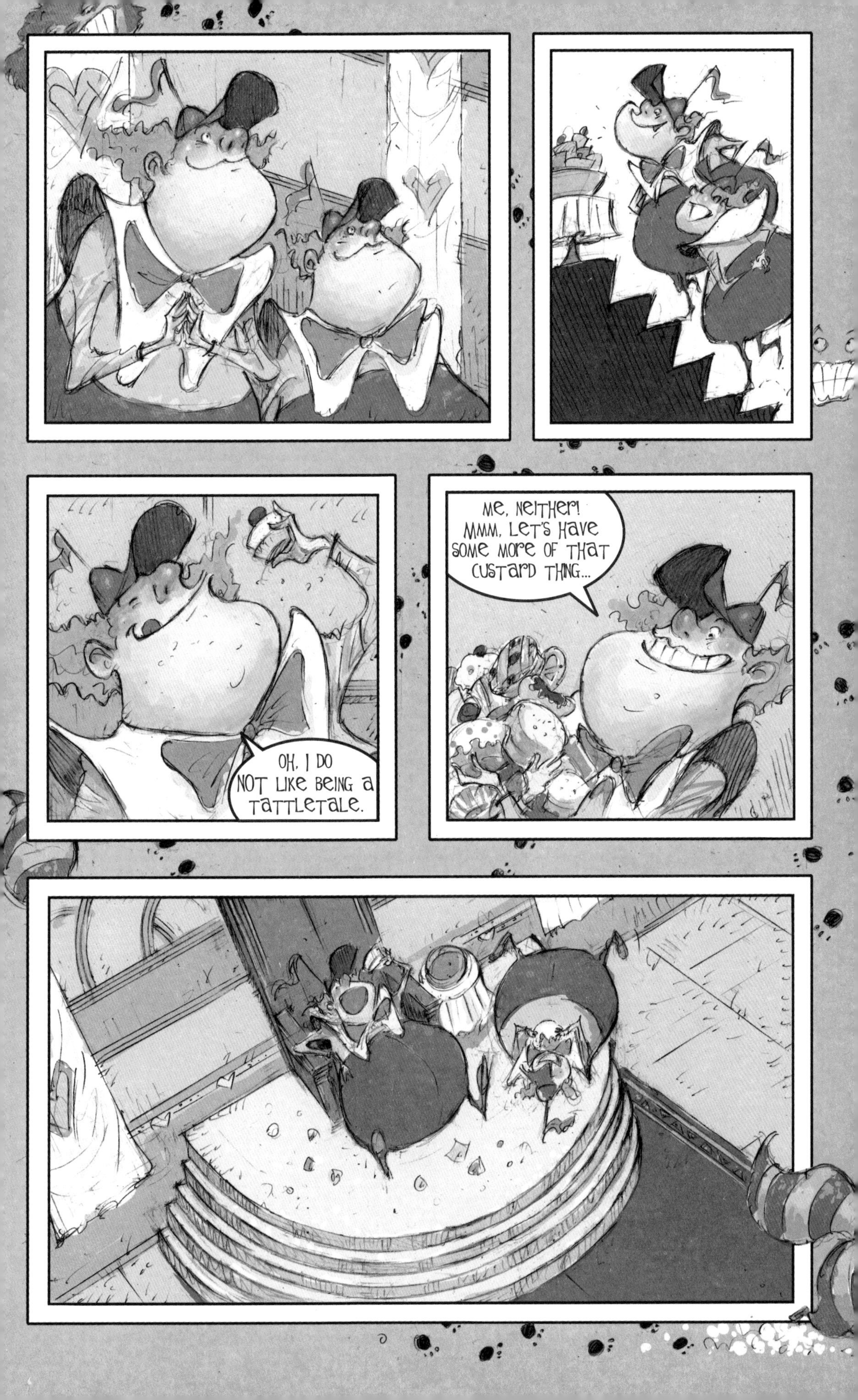
OH, I DO NOT LIKE BEING A TATTLETALE.
ME, NEITHER! MMM, LET'S HAVE SOME MORE OF THAT CUSTARD THING...

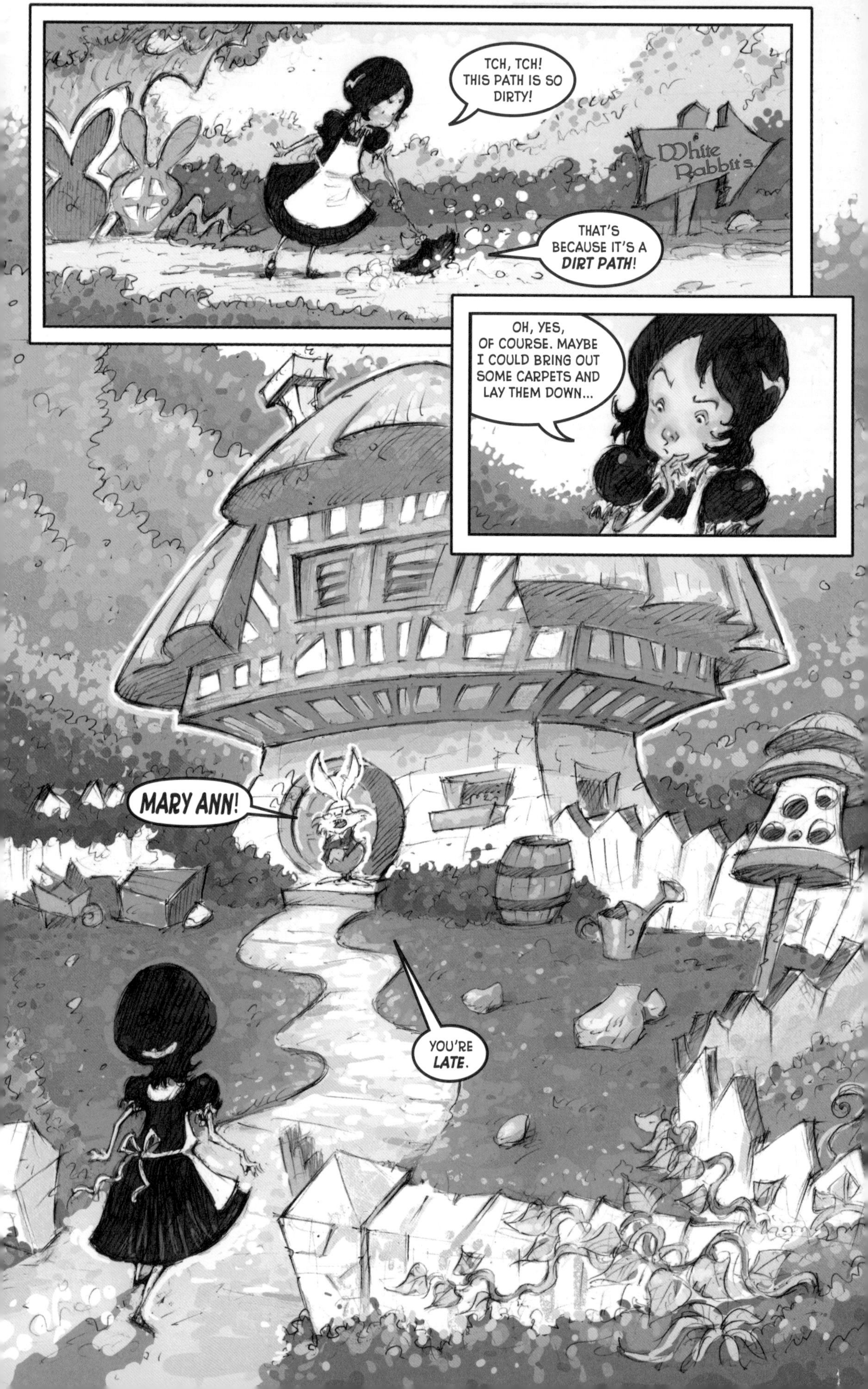
TCH, TCH!
THIS PATH IS SO DIRTY!
White Rabbit's
THAT'S BECAUSE IT'S A **DIRT PATH**!
OH, YES, OF COURSE. MAYBE I COULD BRING OUT SOME CARPETS AND LAY THEM DOWN...
MARY ANN!
YOU'RE **LATE**.

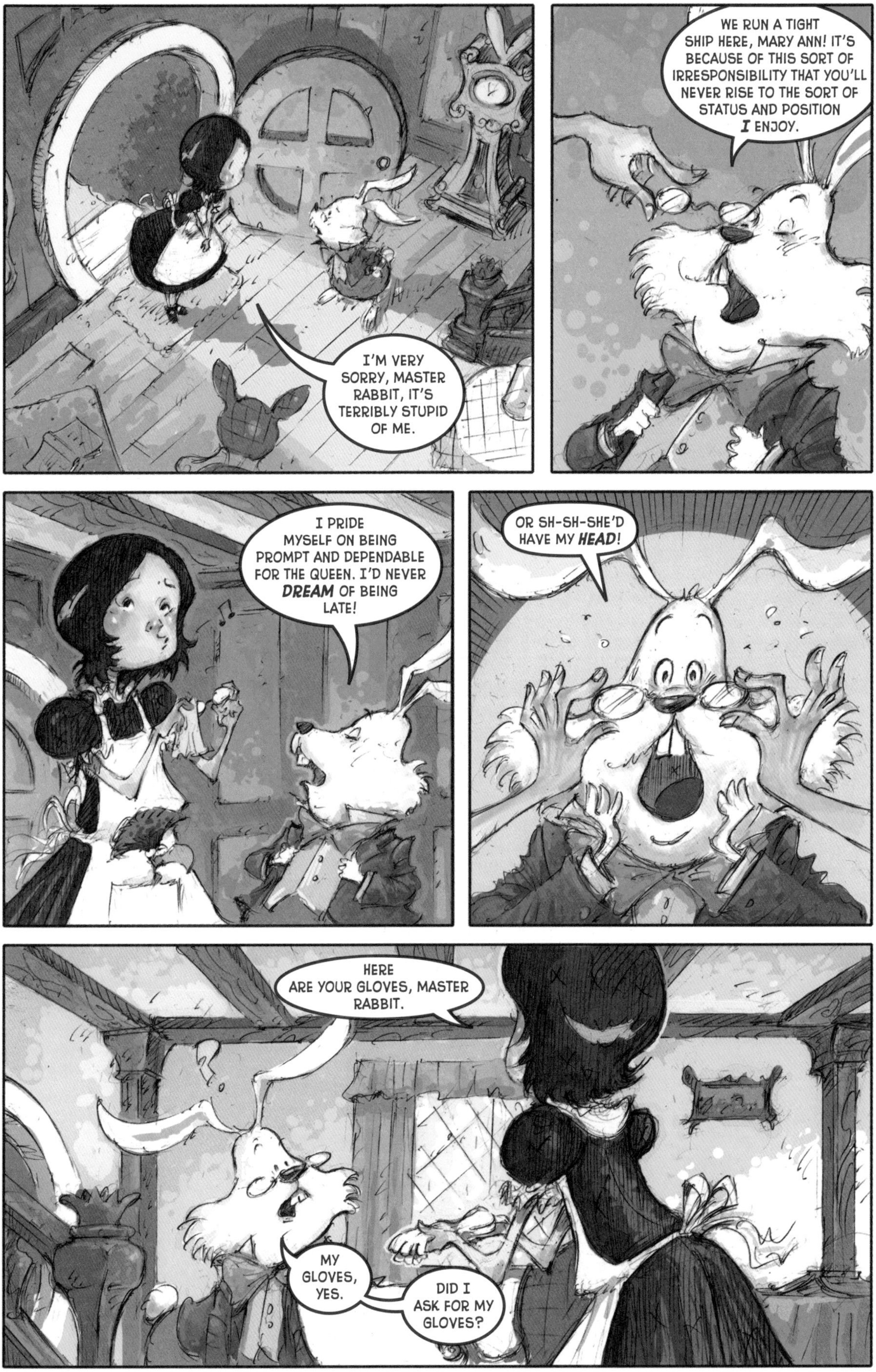
I'M VERY SORRY, MASTER RABBIT, IT'S TERRIBLY STUPID OF ME.
WE RUN A TIGHT SHIP HERE, MARY ANN! IT'S BECAUSE OF THIS SORT OF IRRESPONSIBILITY THAT YOU'LL NEVER RISE TO THE SORT OF STATUS AND POSITION *I* ENJOY.
I PRIDE MYSELF ON BEING PROMPT AND DEPENDABLE FOR THE QUEEN. I'D NEVER *DREAM* OF BEING LATE!
OR SH-SH-SHE'D HAVE MY *HEAD*!
HERE ARE YOUR GLOVES, MASTER RABBIT.
MY GLOVES, YES.
DID I ASK FOR MY GLOVES?

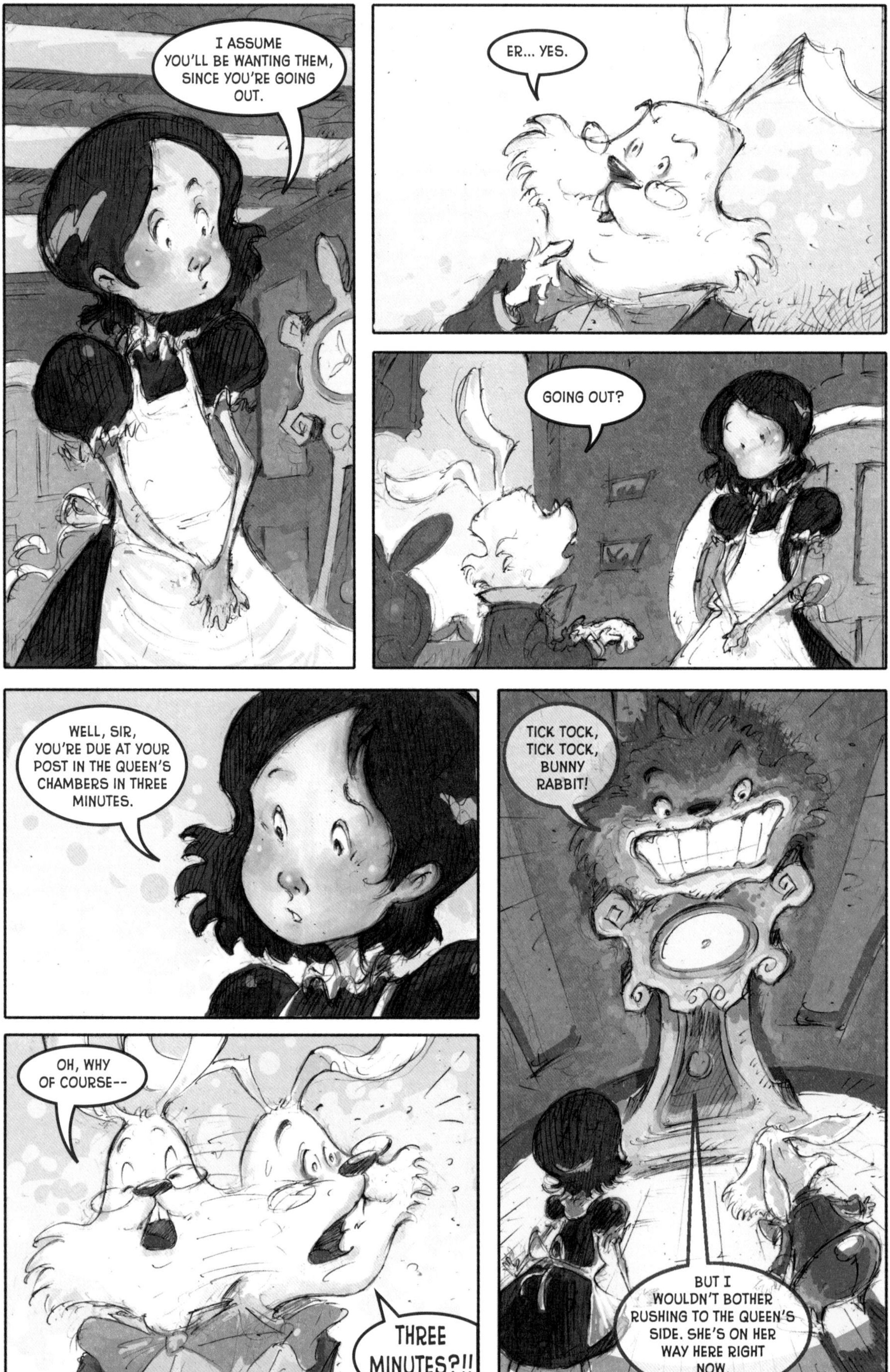
I ASSUME YOU'LL BE WANTING THEM, SINCE YOU'RE GOING OUT.
ER... YES.
GOING OUT?
WELL, SIR, YOU'RE DUE AT YOUR POST IN THE QUEEN'S CHAMBERS IN THREE MINUTES.
OH, WHY OF COURSE--
THREE MINUTES?!!
TICK TOCK, TICK TOCK, BUNNY RABBIT!
BUT I WOULDN'T BOTHER RUSHING TO THE QUEEN'S SIDE. SHE'S ON HER WAY HERE RIGHT NOW.

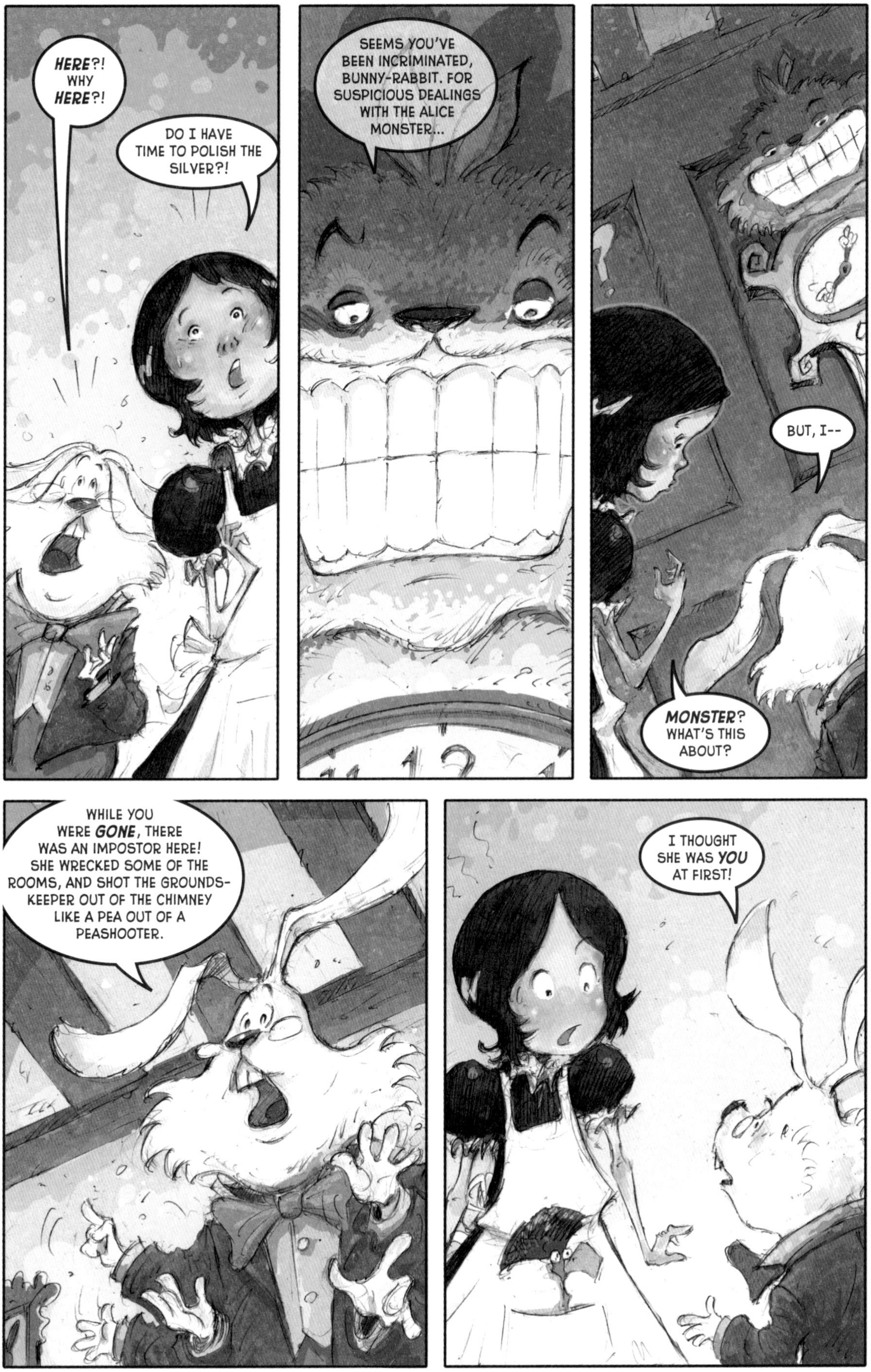
HERE?! WHY HERE?!
DO I HAVE TIME TO POLISH THE SILVER?!
SEEMS YOU'VE BEEN INCRIMINATED, BUNNY-RABBIT. FOR SUSPICIOUS DEALINGS WITH THE ALICE MONSTER...
BUT, I--
MONSTER? WHAT'S THIS ABOUT?
WHILE YOU WERE GONE, THERE WAS AN IMPOSTOR HERE! SHE WRECKED SOME OF THE ROOMS, AND SHOT THE GROUNDS-KEEPER OUT OF THE CHIMNEY LIKE A PEA OUT OF A PEASHOOTER.
I THOUGHT SHE WAS YOU AT FIRST!

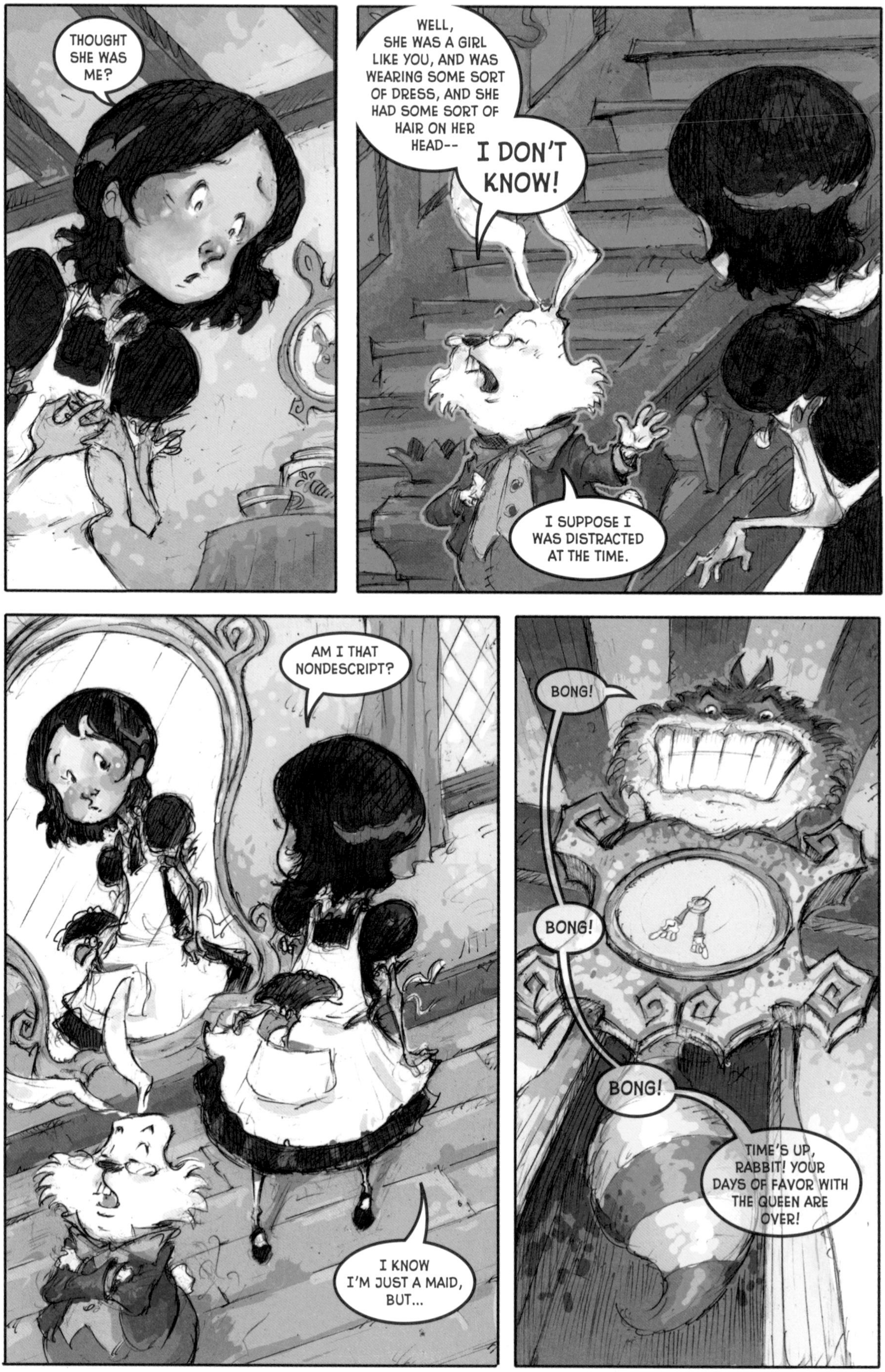
THOUGHT SHE WAS ME?
WELL, SHE WAS A GIRL LIKE YOU, AND WAS WEARING SOME SORT OF DRESS, AND SHE HAD SOME SORT OF HAIR ON HER HEAD--
I DON'T KNOW!
I SUPPOSE I WAS DISTRACTED AT THE TIME.
AM I THAT NONDESCRIPT?
I KNOW I'M JUST A MAID, BUT...
BONG!
BONG!
BONG!
TIME'S UP, RABBIT! YOUR DAYS OF FAVOR WITH THE QUEEN ARE OVER!

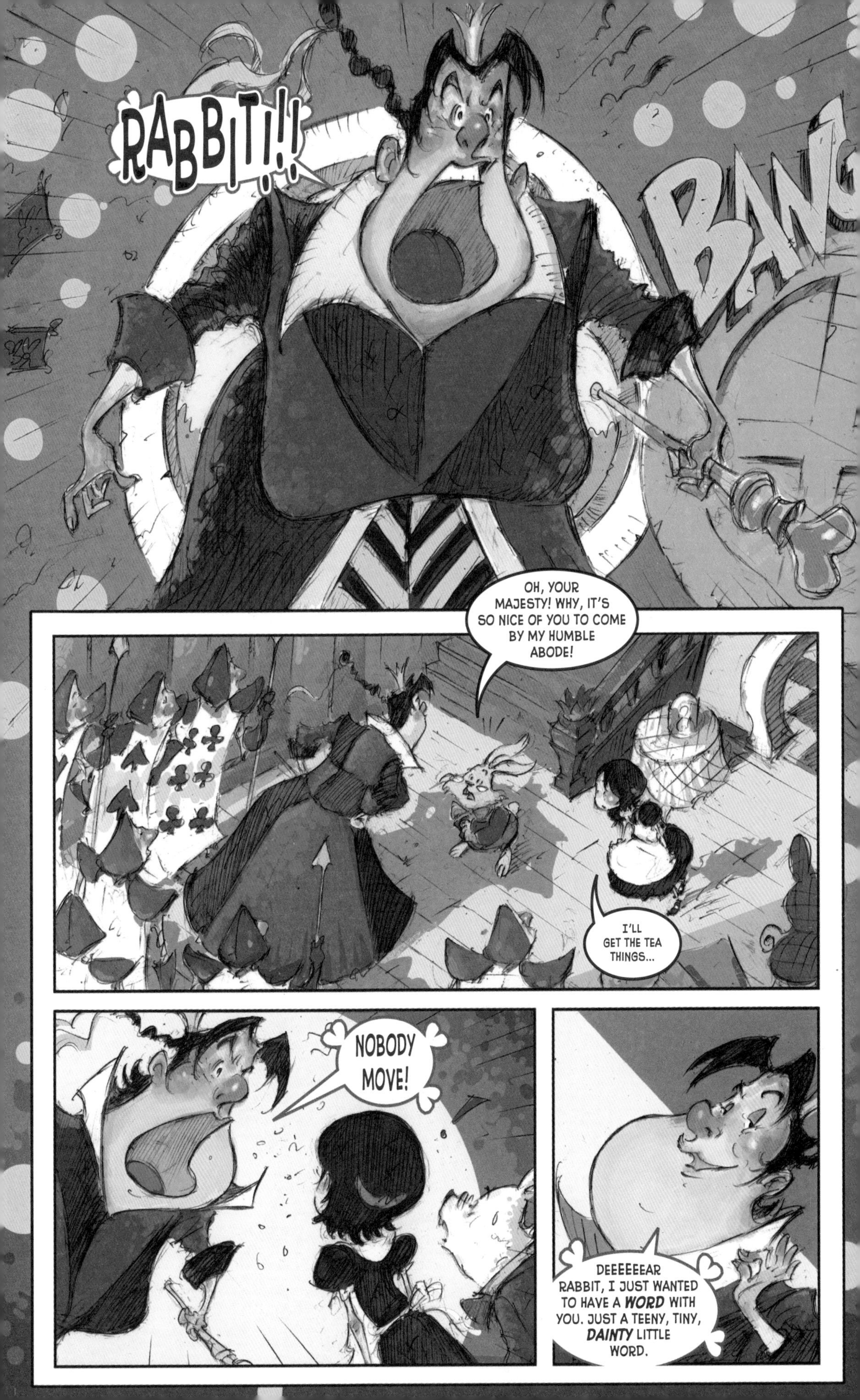
RABBIT!!!
BANG
OH, YOUR MAJESTY! WHY, IT'S SO NICE OF YOU TO COME BY MY HUMBLE ABODE!
I'LL GET THE TEA THINGS...
NOBODY MOVE!
DEEEEEEAR RABBIT, I JUST WANTED TO HAVE A **WORD** WITH YOU. JUST A TEENY, TINY, **DAINTY** LITTLE WORD.

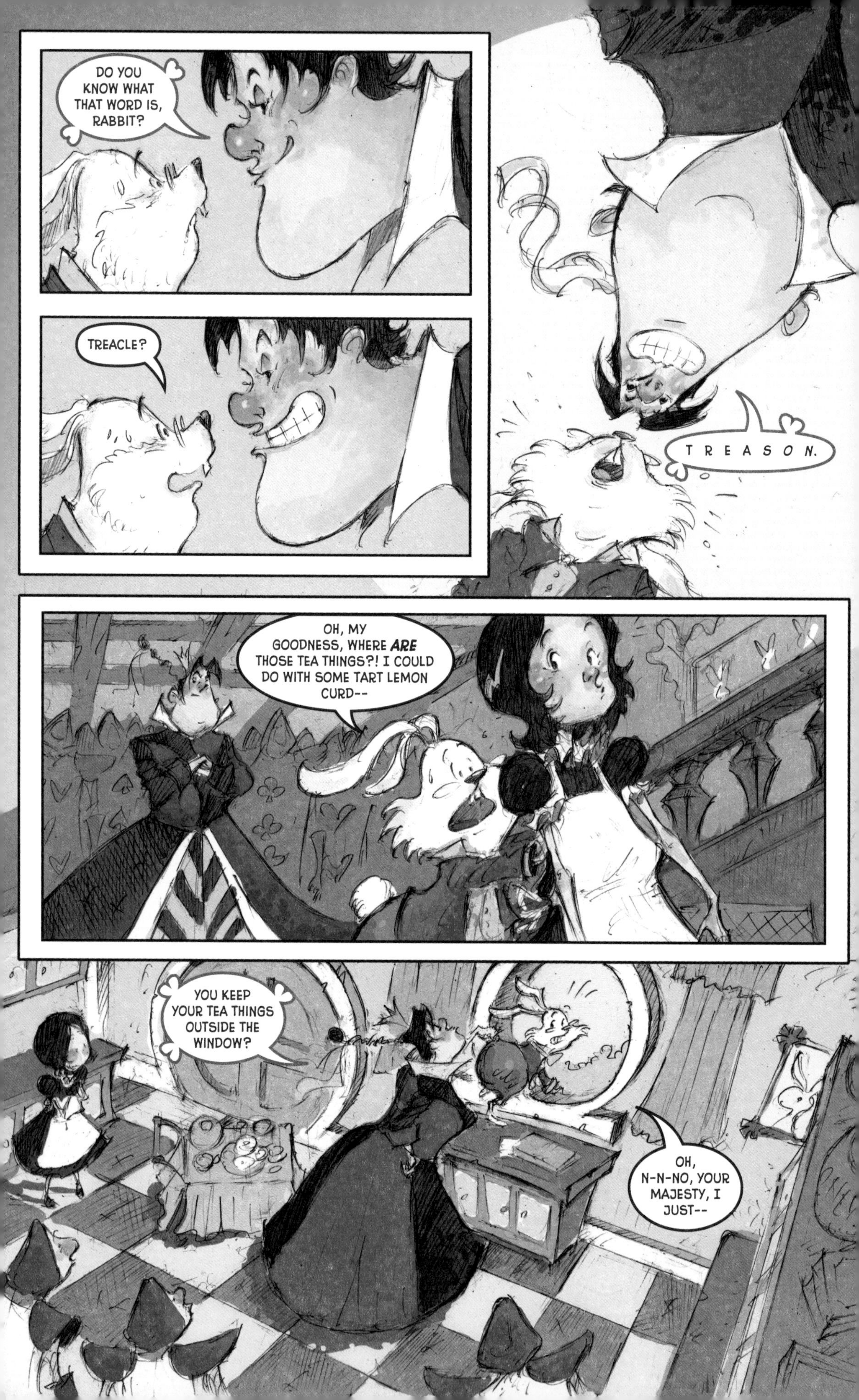
DO YOU KNOW WHAT THAT WORD IS, RABBIT?
TREACLE?
T R E A S O N.
OH, MY GOODNESS, WHERE ARE THOSE TEA THINGS?! I COULD DO WITH SOME TART LEMON CURD--
YOU KEEP YOUR TEA THINGS OUTSIDE THE WINDOW?
OH, N-N-NO, YOUR MAJESTY, I JUST--

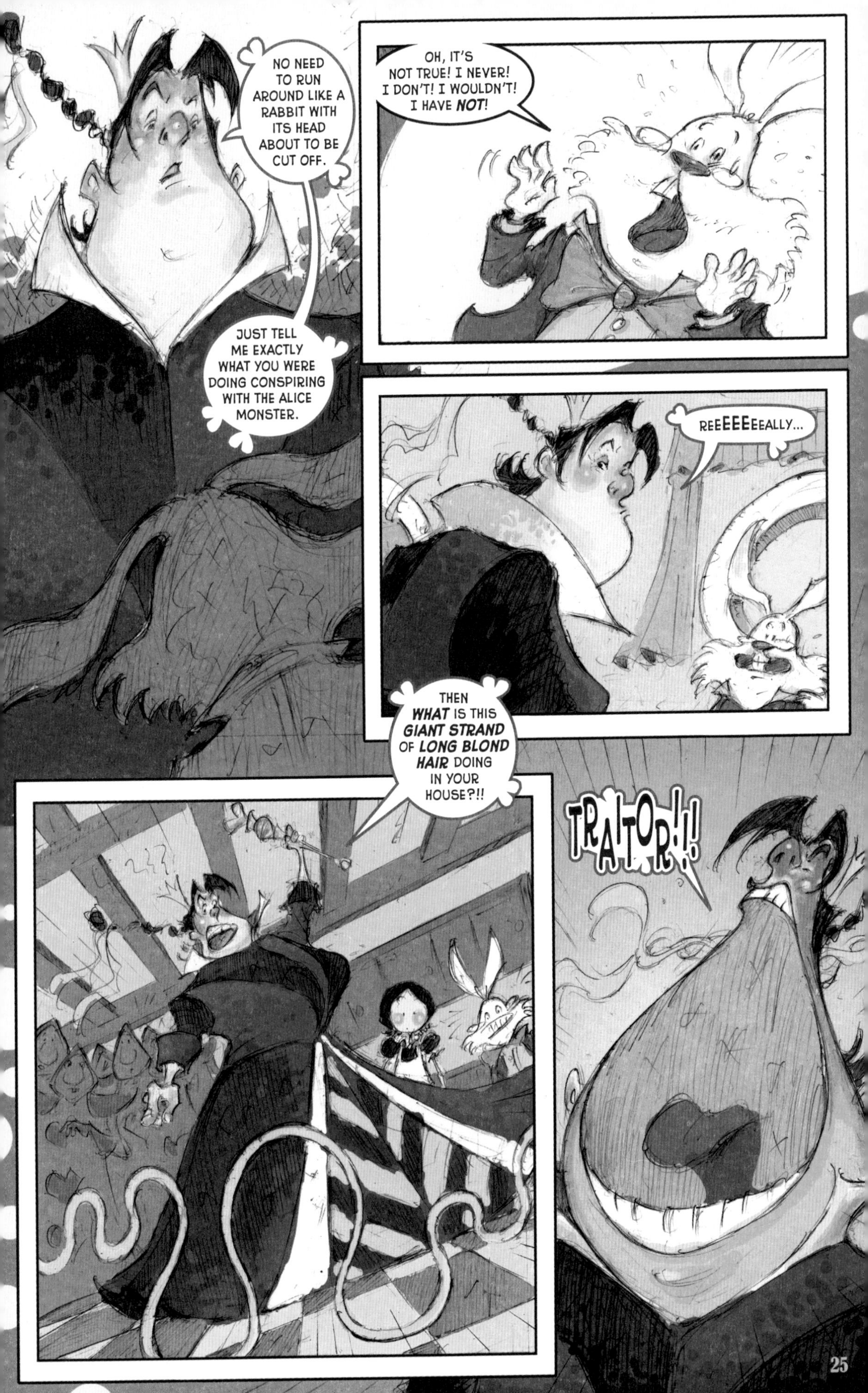
NO NEED TO RUN AROUND LIKE A RABBIT WITH ITS HEAD ABOUT TO BE CUT OFF.
JUST TELL ME EXACTLY WHAT YOU WERE DOING CONSPIRING WITH THE ALICE MONSTER.
OH, IT'S NOT TRUE! I NEVER! I DON'T! I WOULDN'T! I HAVE NOT!
REEEEEEEALLY...
THEN WHAT IS THIS GIANT STRAND OF LONG BLOND HAIR DOING IN YOUR HOUSE?!!
TRAITOR!!!

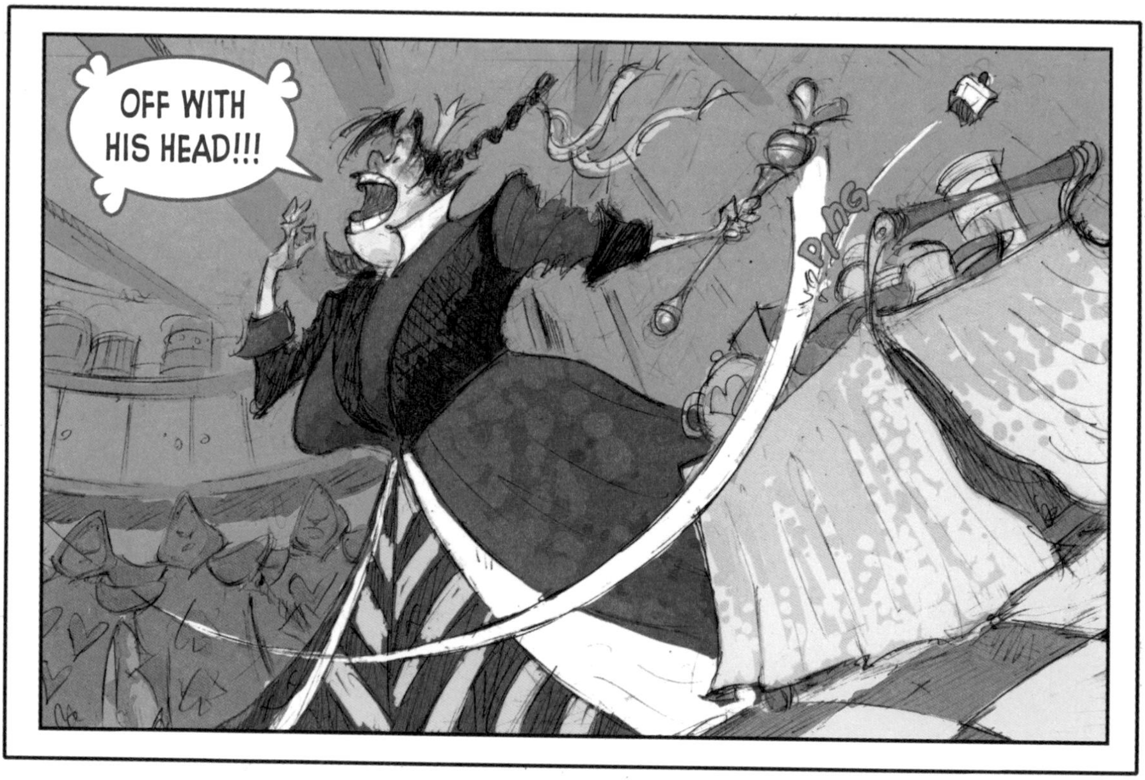
OFF WITH HIS HEAD!!!
PING

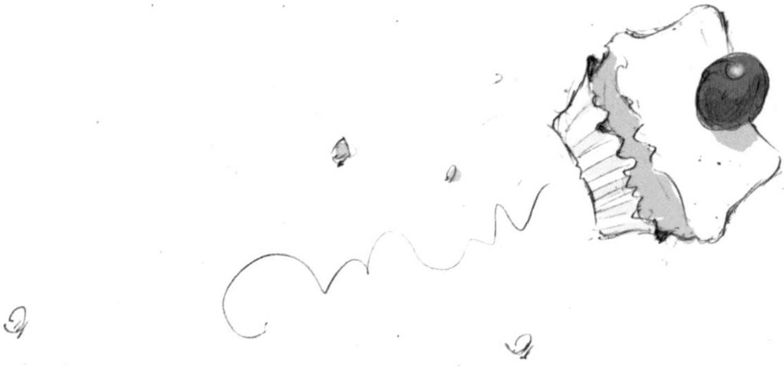

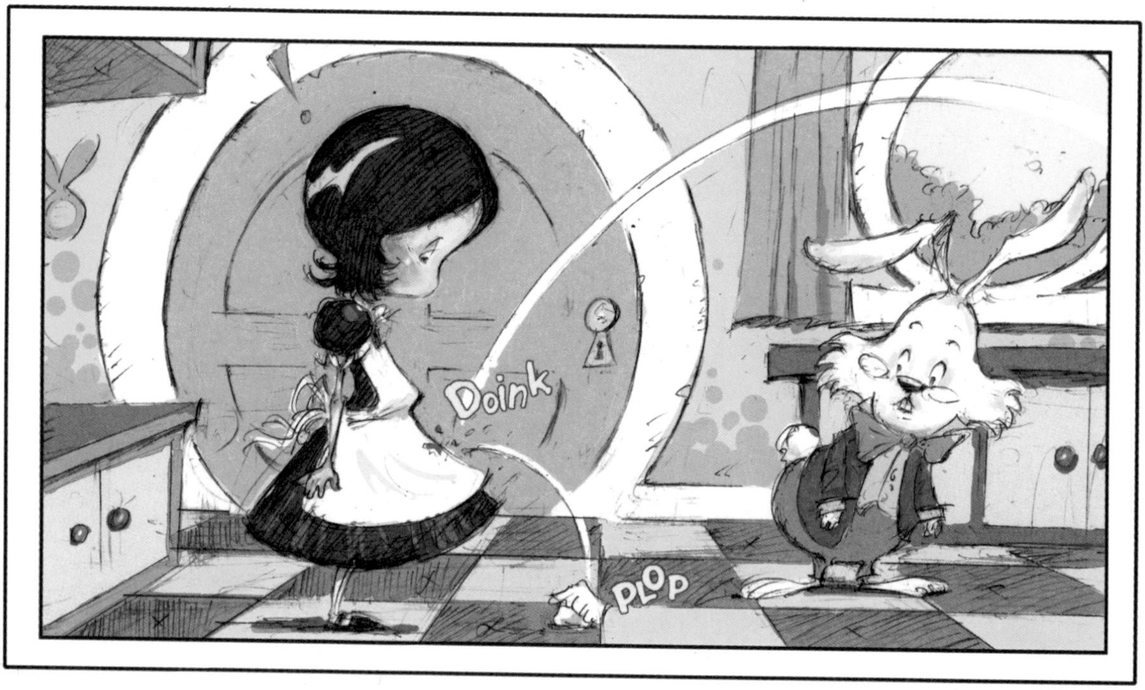
Doink
PLOP

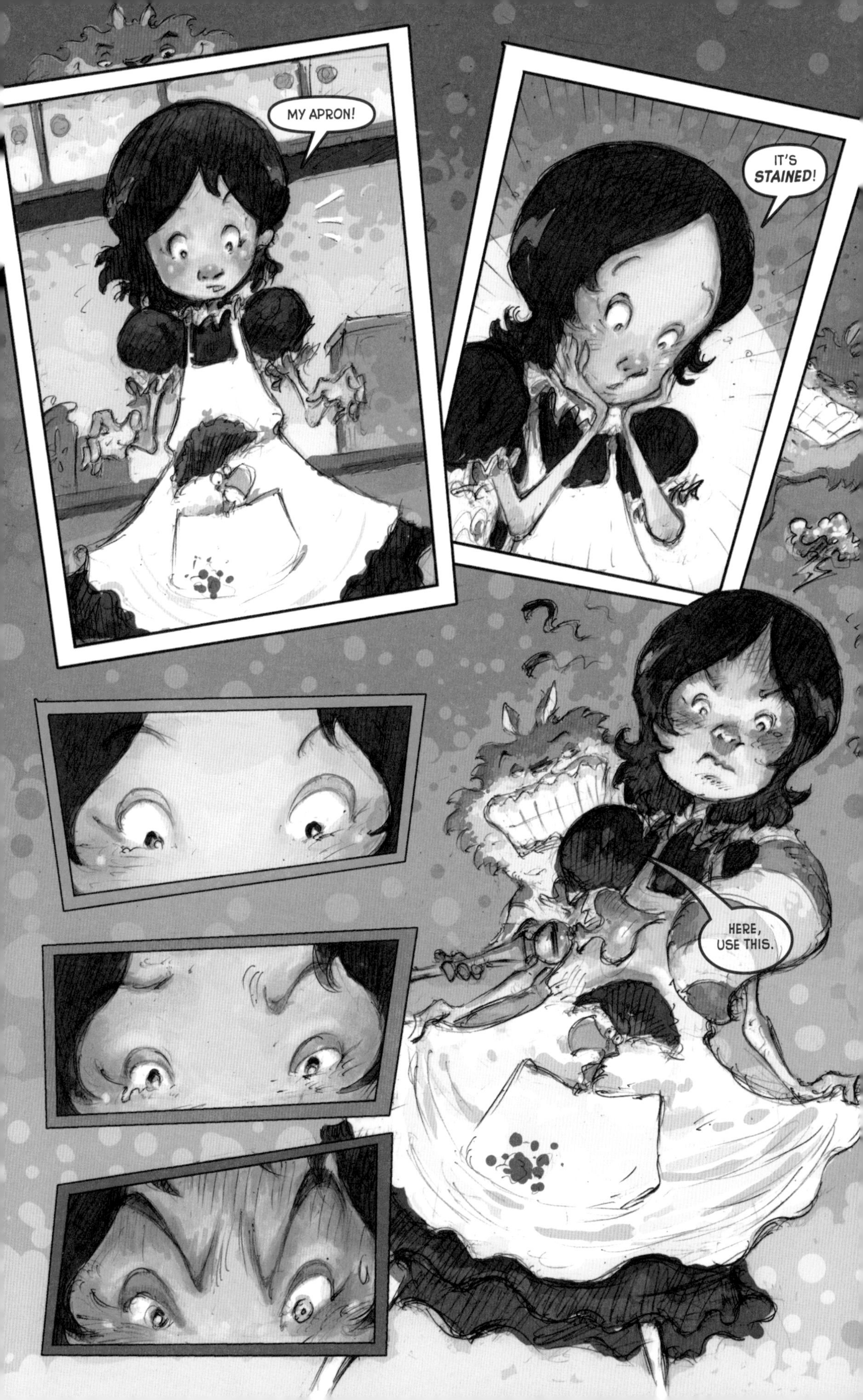
MY APRON!
IT'S STAINED!
HERE, USE THIS.

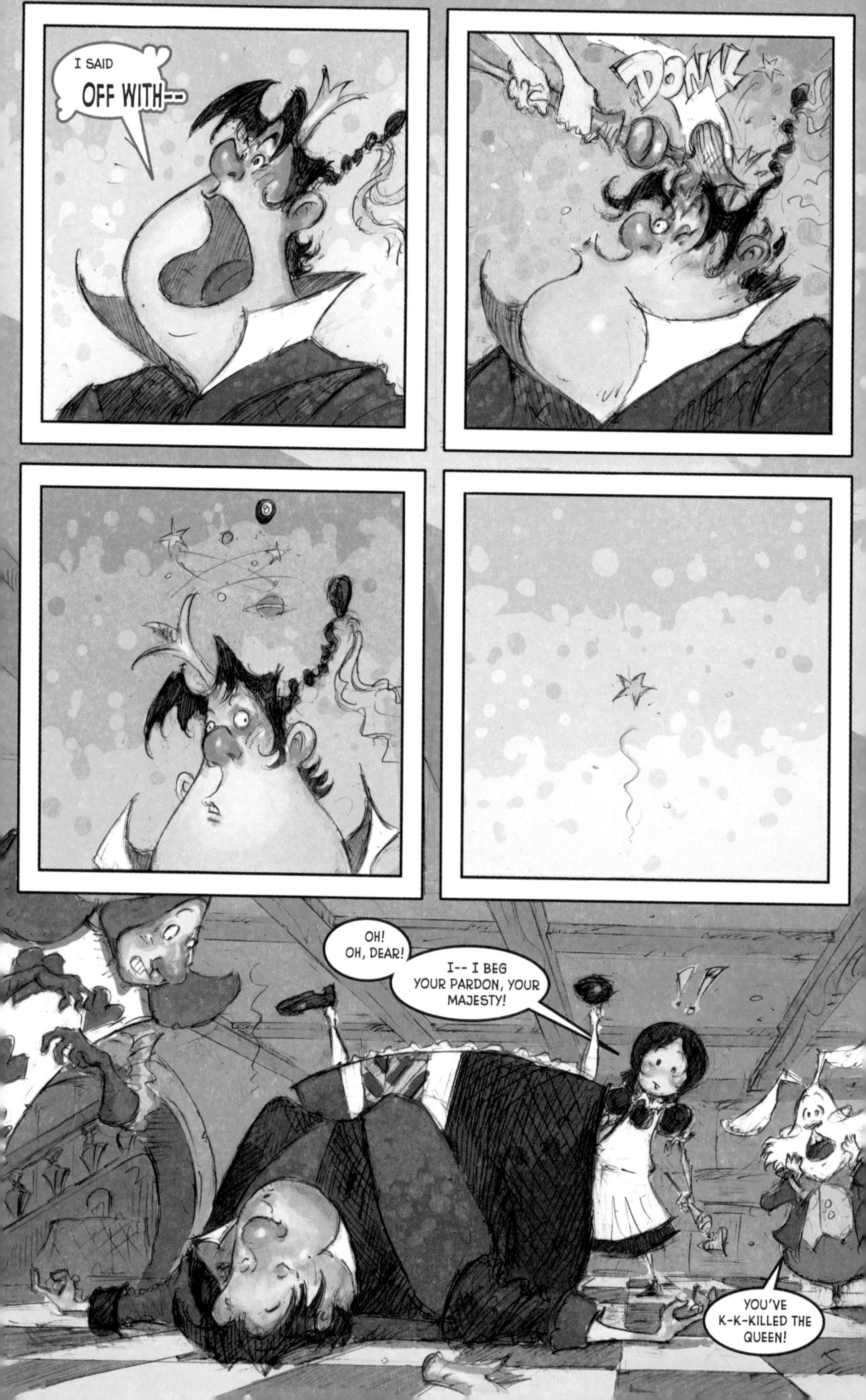
I SAID
OFF WITH--
DONK
OH! OH, DEAR!
I-- I BEG YOUR PARDON, YOUR MAJESTY!
YOU'VE K-K-KILLED THE QUEEN!

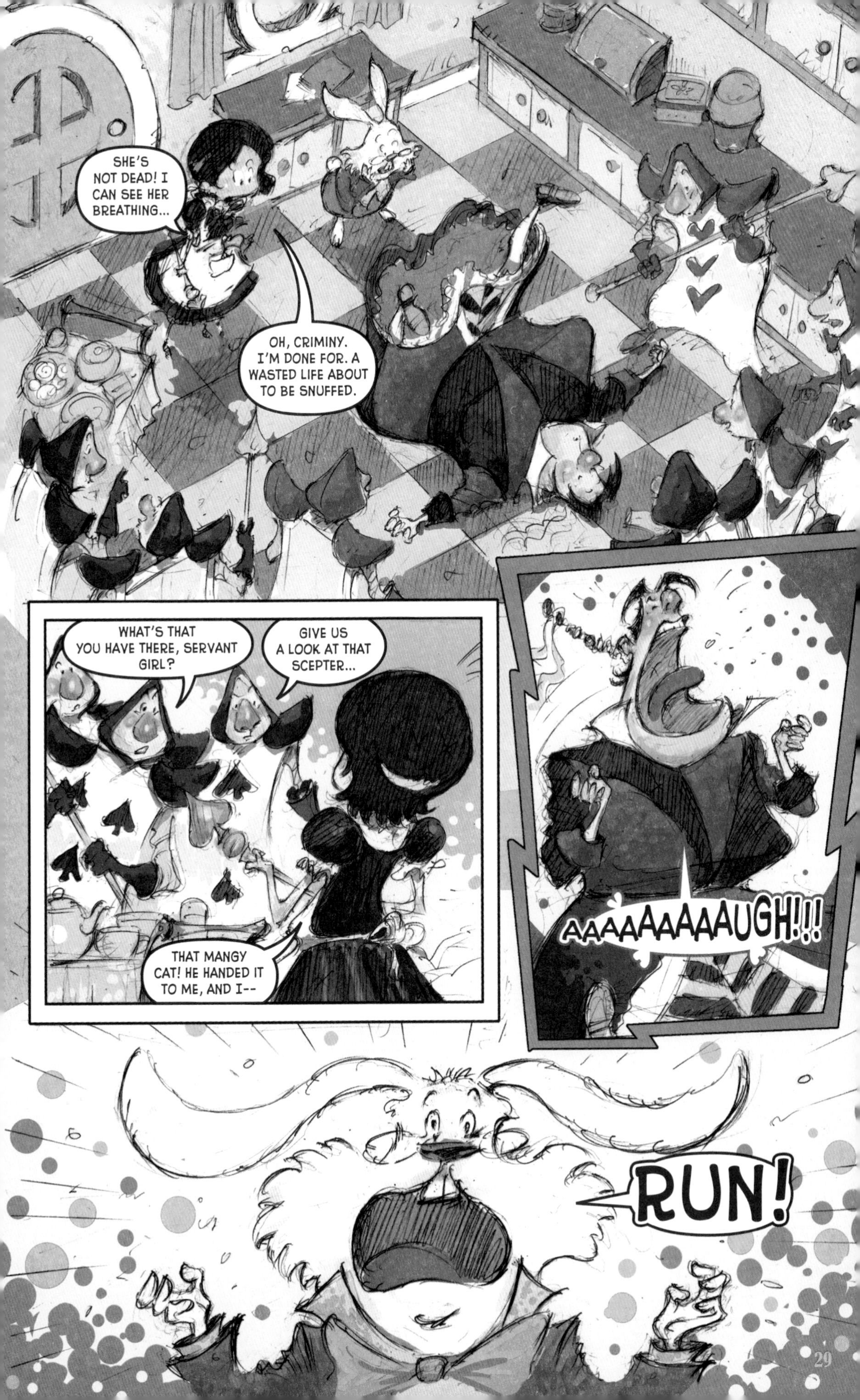

SHE'S NOT DEAD! I CAN SEE HER BREATHING...
OH, CRIMINY. I'M DONE FOR. A WASTED LIFE ABOUT TO BE SNUFFED.
WHAT'S THAT YOU HAVE THERE, SERVANT GIRL?
GIVE US A LOOK AT THAT SCEPTER...
THAT MANGY CAT! HE HANDED IT TO ME, AND I--
AAAAAAAAAUGH!!!
RUN!

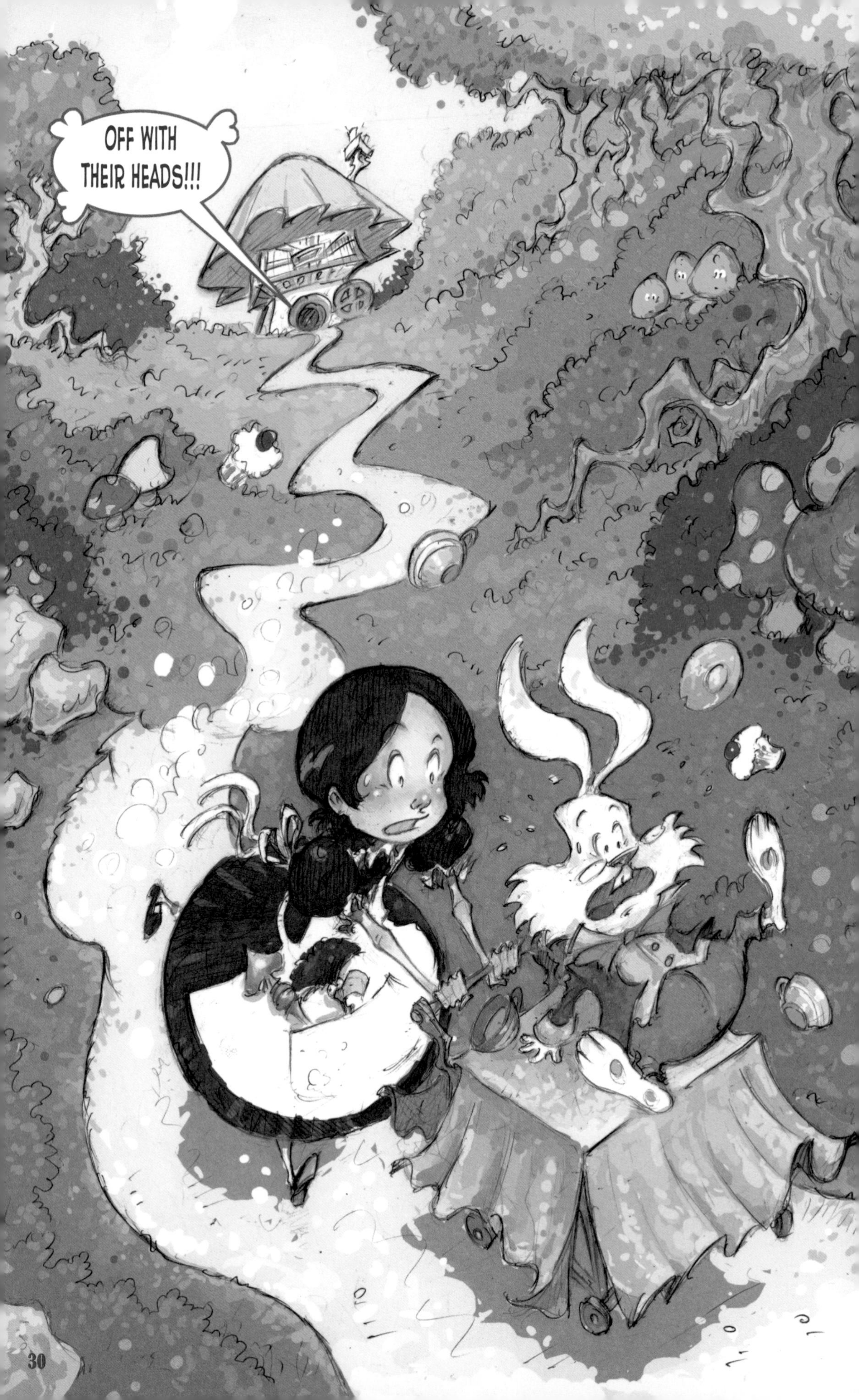
OFF WITH THEIR HEADS!!!

Chapter Two

The Tulgey Wood & the Treacle Well

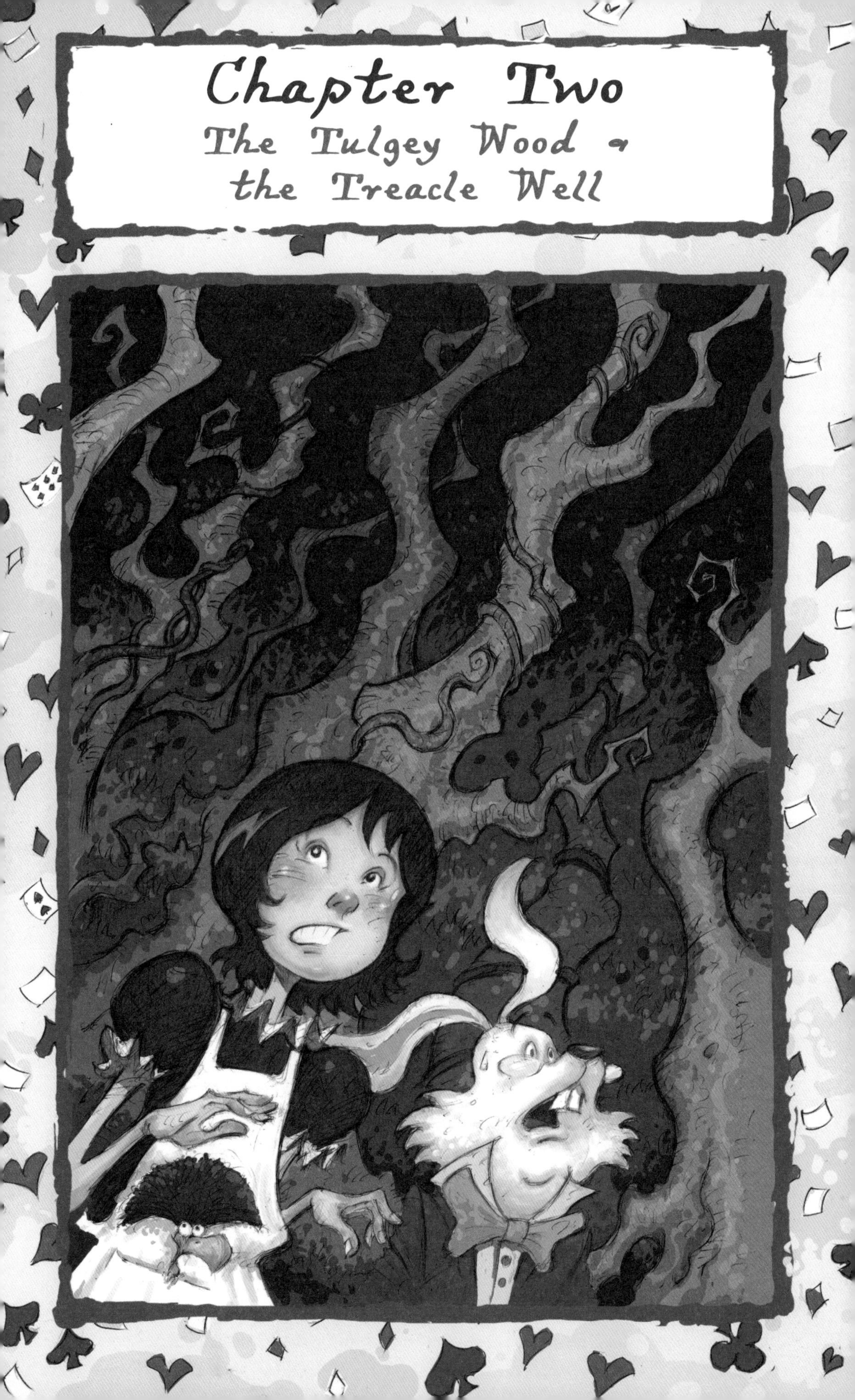

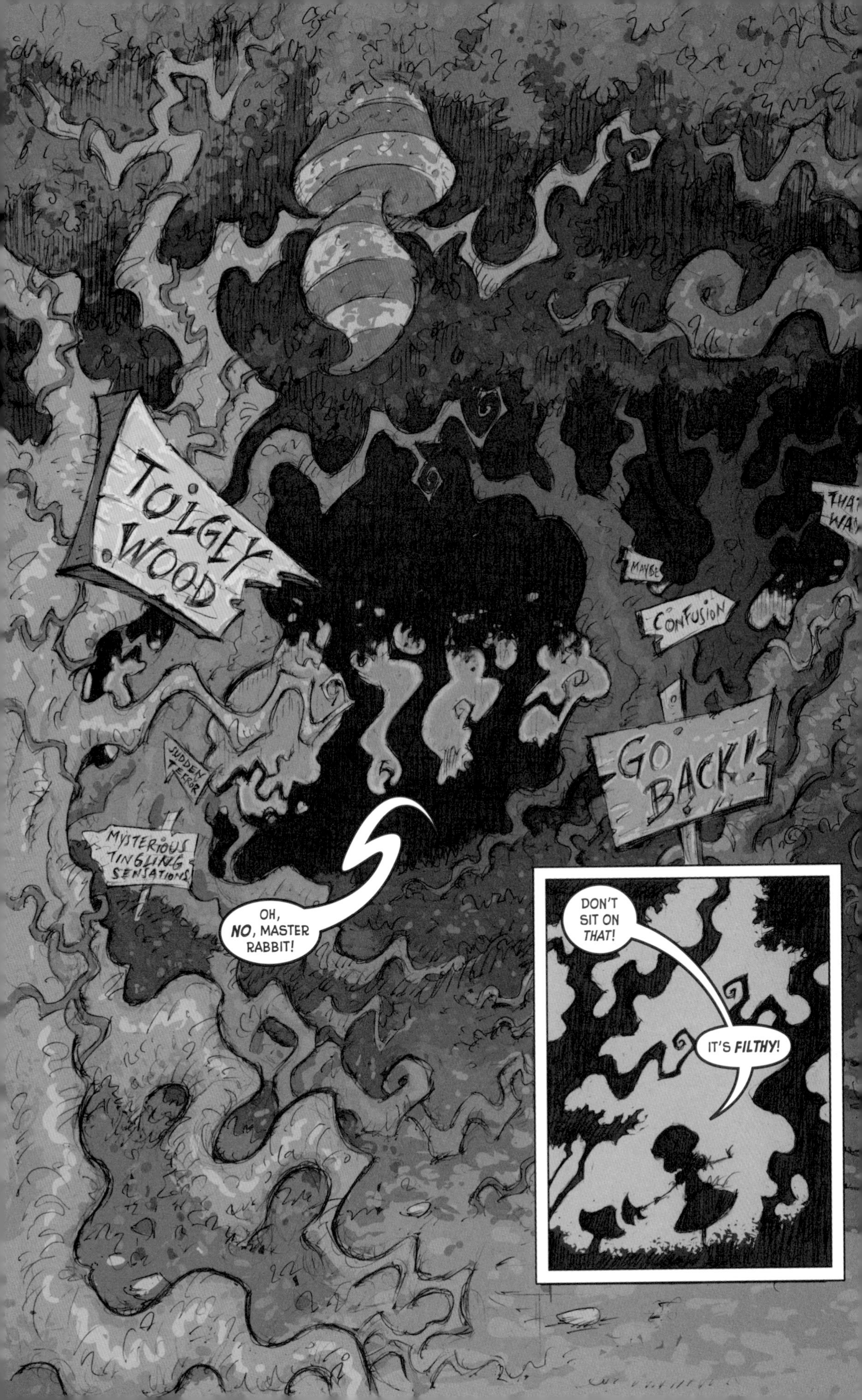

TULGEY WOOD
MAYBE
CONFUSION
SUDDEN TERROR
MYSTERIOUS TINGLING SENSATIONS
GO BACK!
OH, *NO*, MASTER RABBIT!
DON'T SIT ON *THAT*!
IT'S *FILTHY*!

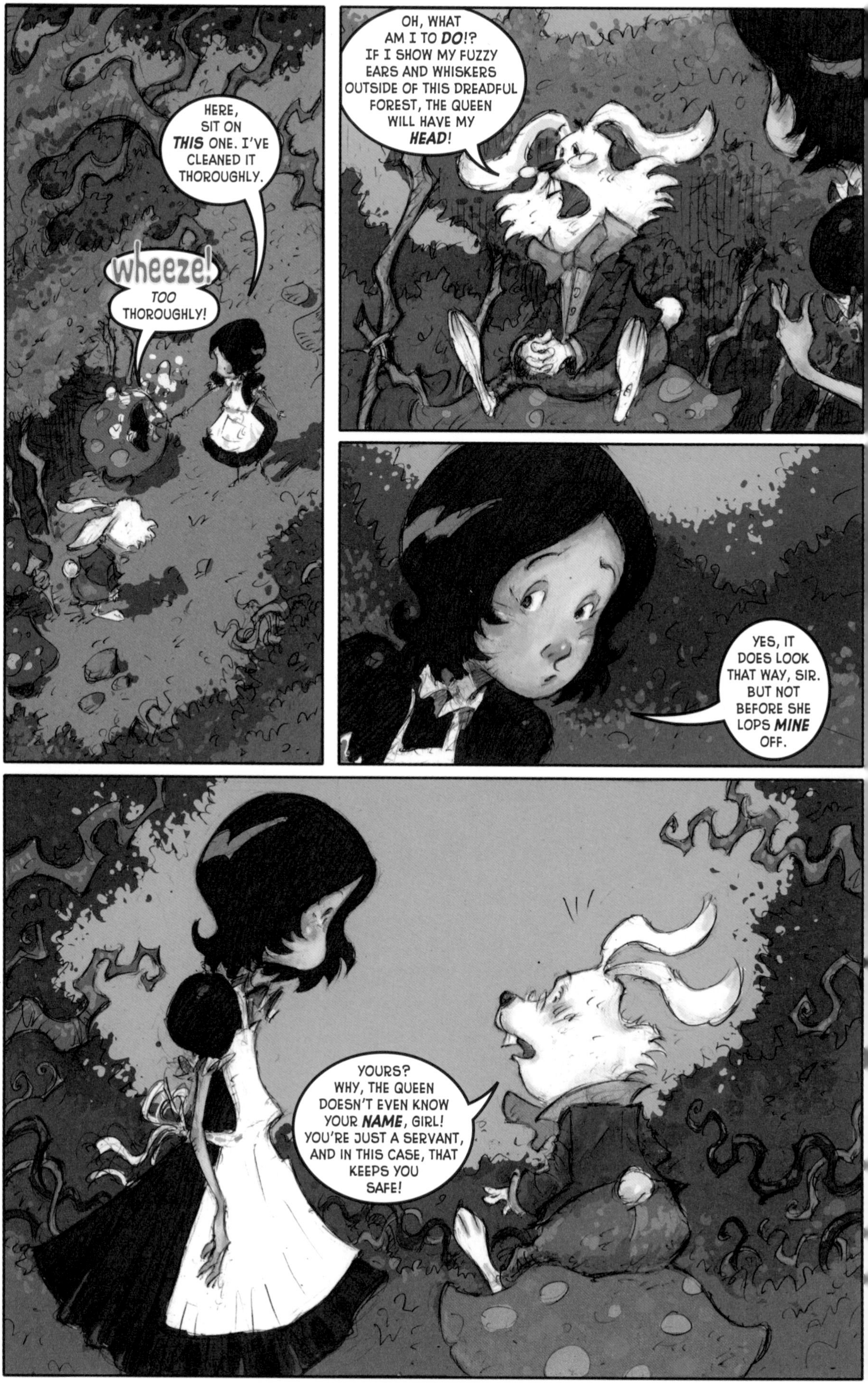
HERE, SIT ON THIS ONE. I'VE CLEANED IT THOROUGHLY.
wheeze!
TOO THOROUGHLY!
OH, WHAT AM I TO DO!? IF I SHOW MY FUZZY EARS AND WHISKERS OUTSIDE OF THIS DREADFUL FOREST, THE QUEEN WILL HAVE MY HEAD!
YES, IT DOES LOOK THAT WAY, SIR. BUT NOT BEFORE SHE LOPS MINE OFF.
YOURS? WHY, THE QUEEN DOESN'T EVEN KNOW YOUR NAME, GIRL! YOU'RE JUST A SERVANT, AND IN THIS CASE, THAT KEEPS YOU SAFE!

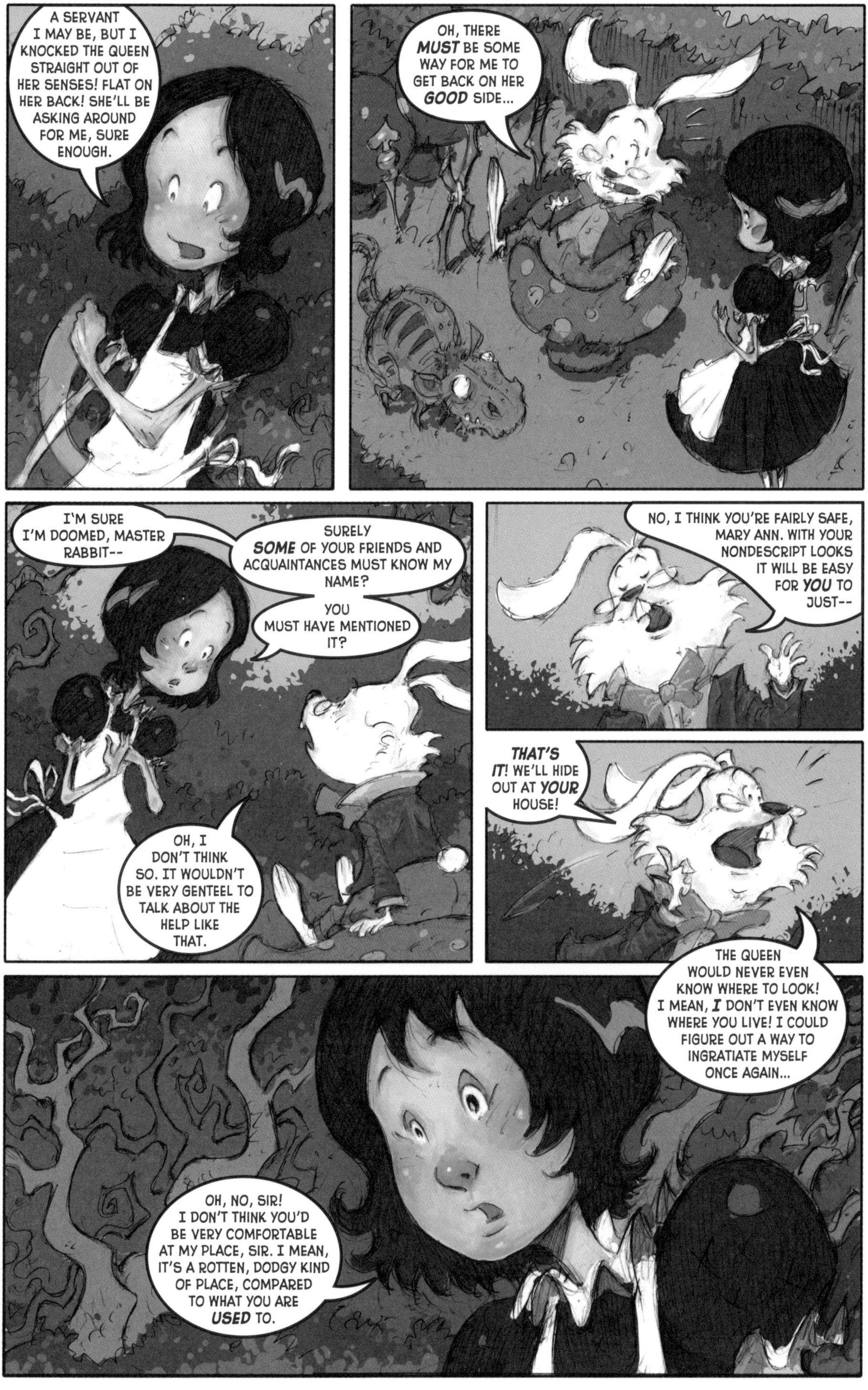
A SERVANT I MAY BE, BUT I KNOCKED THE QUEEN STRAIGHT OUT OF HER SENSES! FLAT ON HER BACK! SHE'LL BE ASKING AROUND FOR ME, SURE ENOUGH.
OH, THERE MUST BE SOME WAY FOR ME TO GET BACK ON HER GOOD SIDE...
I'M SURE I'M DOOMED, MASTER RABBIT--
SURELY SOME OF YOUR FRIENDS AND ACQUAINTANCES MUST KNOW MY NAME?
YOU MUST HAVE MENTIONED IT?
OH, I DON'T THINK SO. IT WOULDN'T BE VERY GENTEEL TO TALK ABOUT THE HELP LIKE THAT.
NO, I THINK YOU'RE FAIRLY SAFE, MARY ANN. WITH YOUR NONDESCRIPT LOOKS IT WILL BE EASY FOR YOU TO JUST--
THAT'S IT! WE'LL HIDE OUT AT YOUR HOUSE!
THE QUEEN WOULD NEVER EVEN KNOW WHERE TO LOOK! I MEAN, I DON'T EVEN KNOW WHERE YOU LIVE! I COULD FIGURE OUT A WAY TO INGRATIATE MYSELF ONCE AGAIN...
OH, NO, SIR! I DON'T THINK YOU'D BE VERY COMFORTABLE AT MY PLACE, SIR. I MEAN, IT'S A ROTTEN, DODGY KIND OF PLACE, COMPARED TO WHAT YOU ARE USED TO.

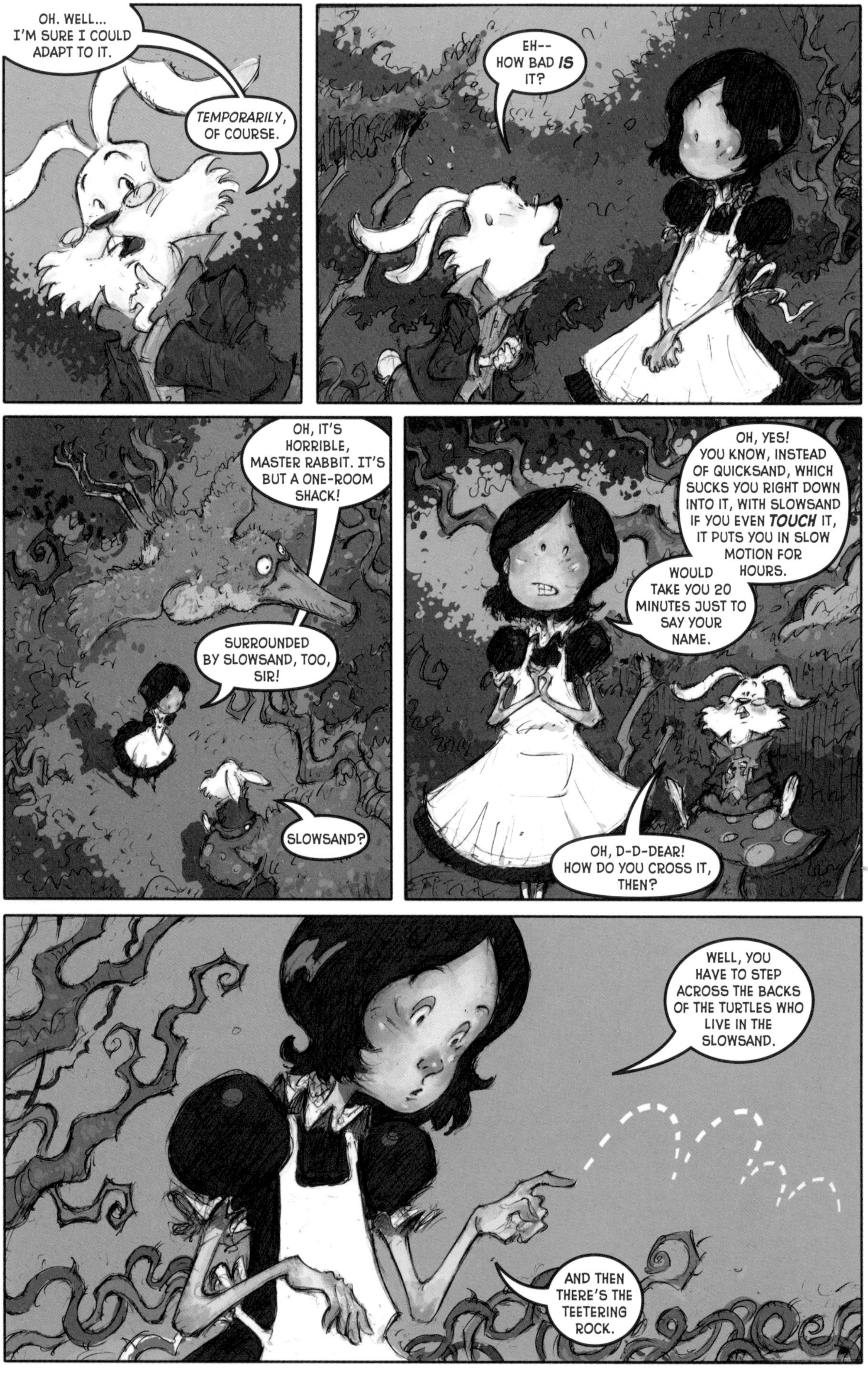
OH. WELL... I'M SURE I COULD ADAPT TO IT.
TEMPORARILY, OF COURSE.
EH-- HOW BAD ***IS*** IT?
OH, IT'S HORRIBLE, MASTER RABBIT. IT'S BUT A ONE-ROOM SHACK!
SURROUNDED BY SLOWSAND, TOO, SIR!
SLOWSAND?
OH, YES! YOU KNOW, INSTEAD OF QUICKSAND, WHICH SUCKS YOU RIGHT DOWN INTO IT, WITH SLOWSAND IF YOU EVEN ***TOUCH*** IT, IT PUTS YOU IN SLOW MOTION FOR HOURS.
WOULD TAKE YOU 20 MINUTES JUST TO SAY YOUR NAME.
OH, D-D-DEAR! HOW DO YOU CROSS IT, THEN?
WELL, YOU HAVE TO STEP ACROSS THE BACKS OF THE TURTLES WHO LIVE IN THE SLOWSAND.
AND THEN THERE'S THE TEETERING ROCK.

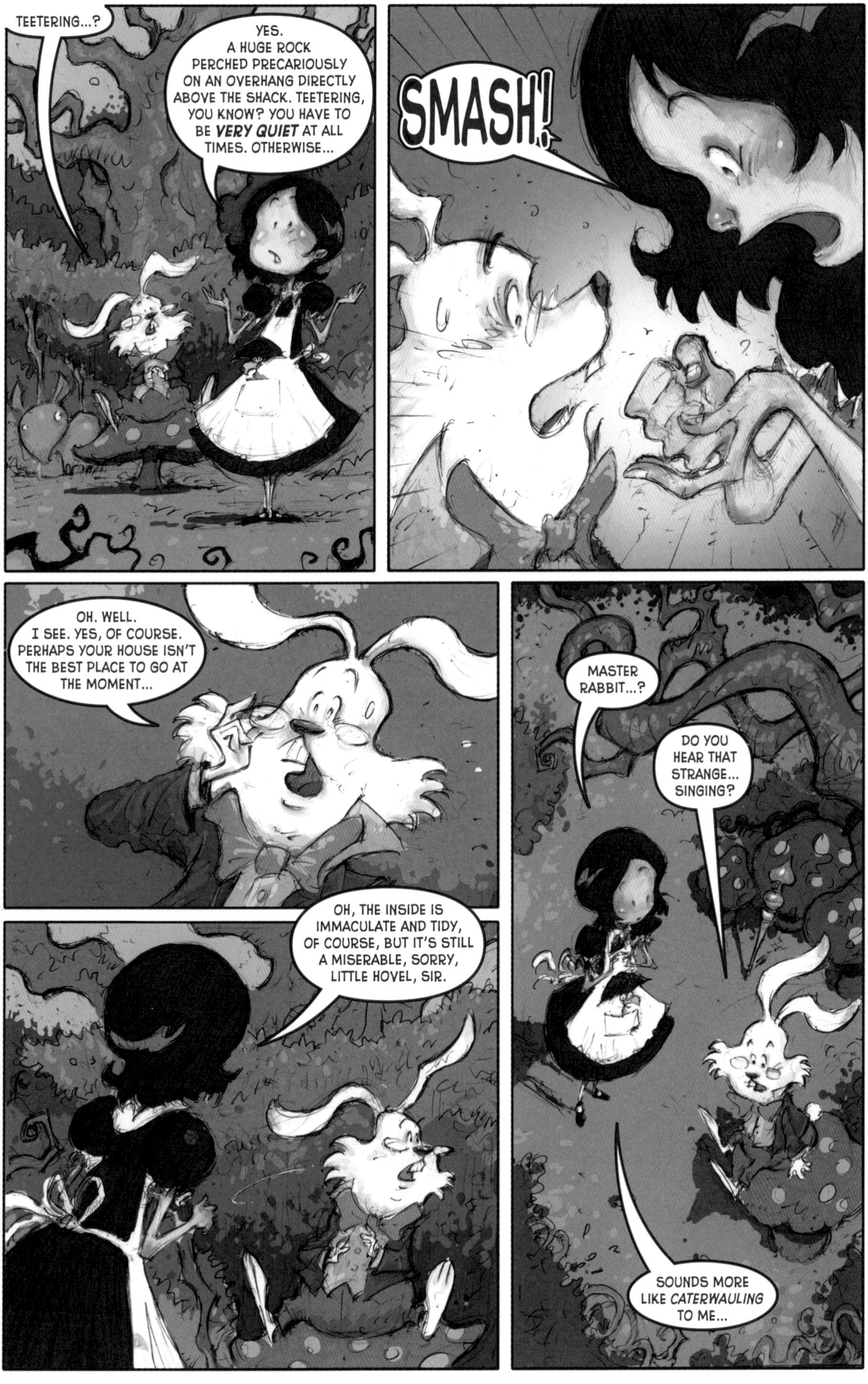
TEETERING...?
YES. A HUGE ROCK PERCHED PRECARIOUSLY ON AN OVERHANG DIRECTLY ABOVE THE SHACK. TEETERING, YOU KNOW? YOU HAVE TO BE *VERY QUIET* AT ALL TIMES. OTHERWISE...
SMASH!
OH. WELL. I SEE. YES, OF COURSE. PERHAPS YOUR HOUSE ISN'T THE BEST PLACE TO GO AT THE MOMENT...
OH, THE INSIDE IS IMMACULATE AND TIDY, OF COURSE, BUT IT'S STILL A MISERABLE, SORRY, LITTLE HOVEL, SIR.
MASTER RABBIT...?
DO YOU HEAR THAT STRANGE... SINGING?
SOUNDS MORE LIKE *CATERWAULING* TO ME...

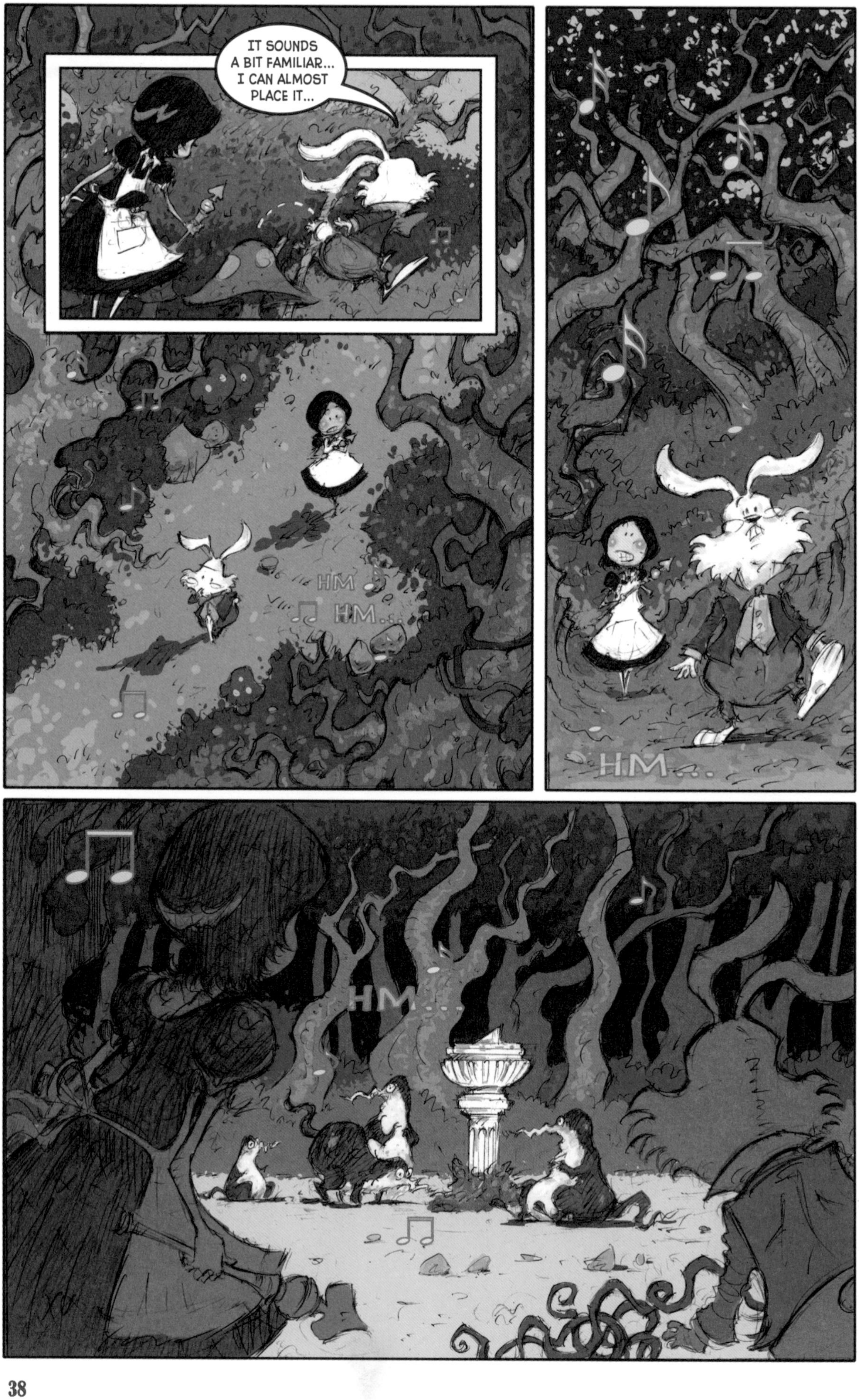
IT SOUNDS A BIT FAMILIAR... I CAN ALMOST PLACE IT...
HM HM...
HM...
HM...

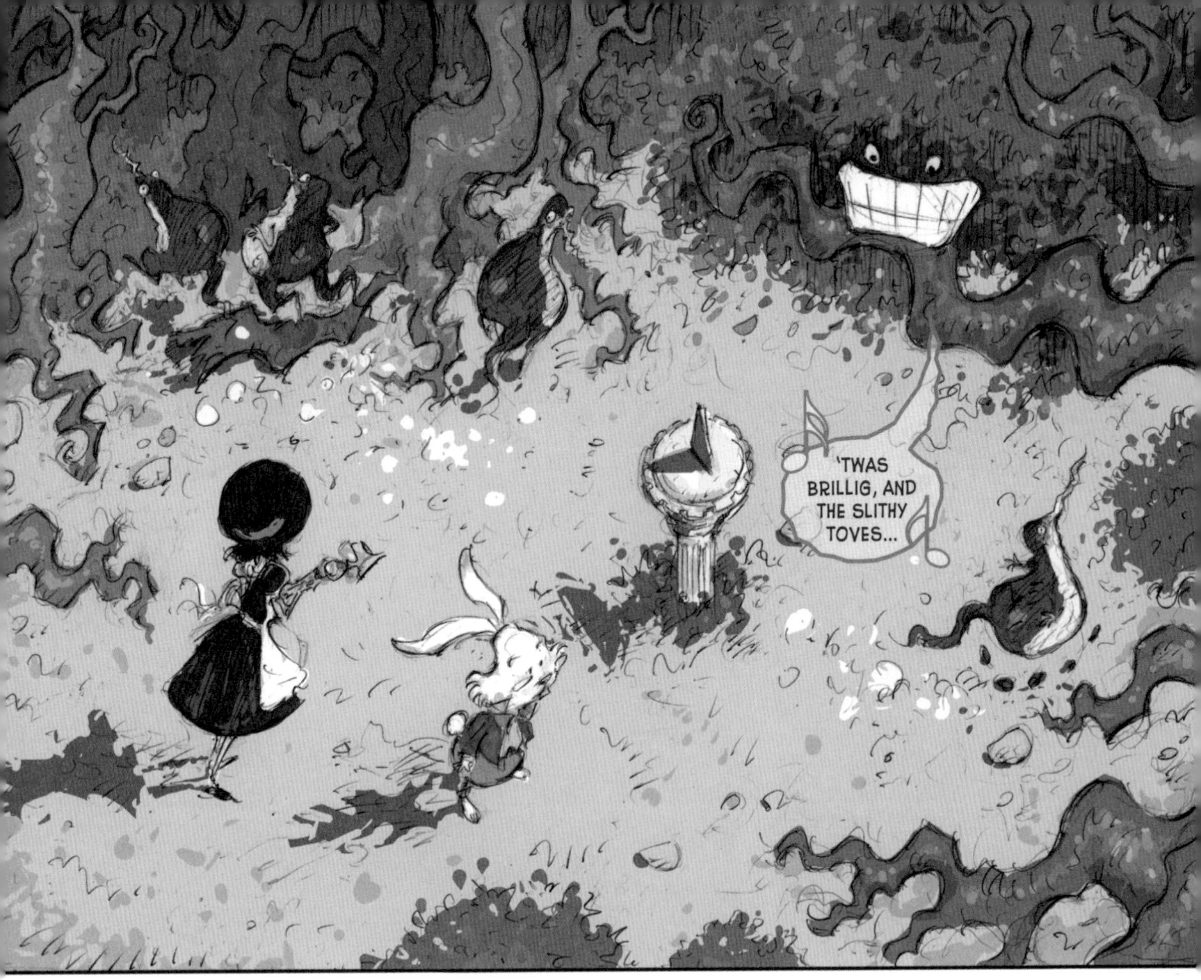
'TWAS BRILLIG, AND THE SLITHY TOVES...

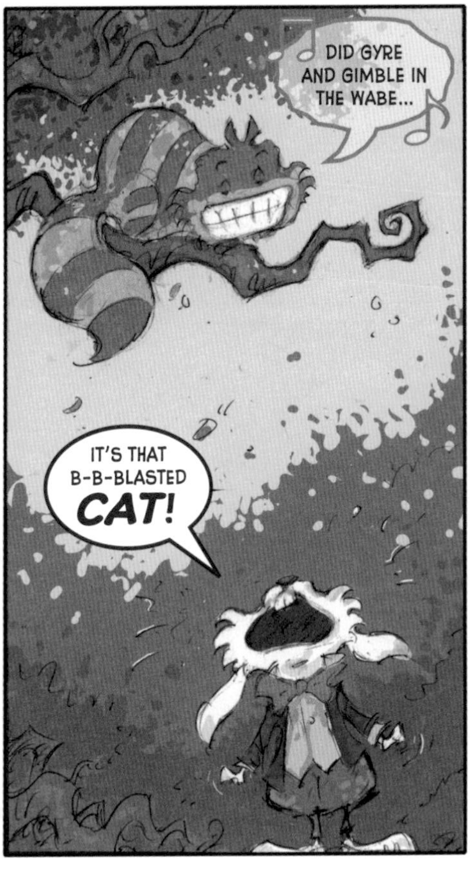
DID GYRE AND GIMBLE IN THE WABE...
IT'S THAT B-B-BLASTED CAT!

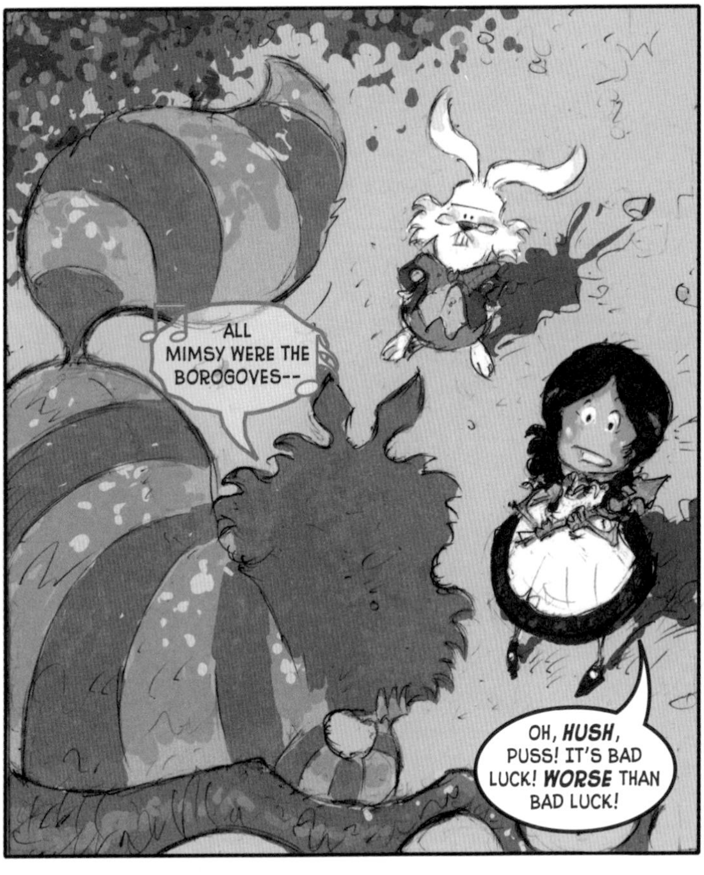
ALL MIMSY WERE THE BOROGOVES--
OH, HUSH, PUSS! IT'S BAD LUCK! WORSE THAN BAD LUCK!

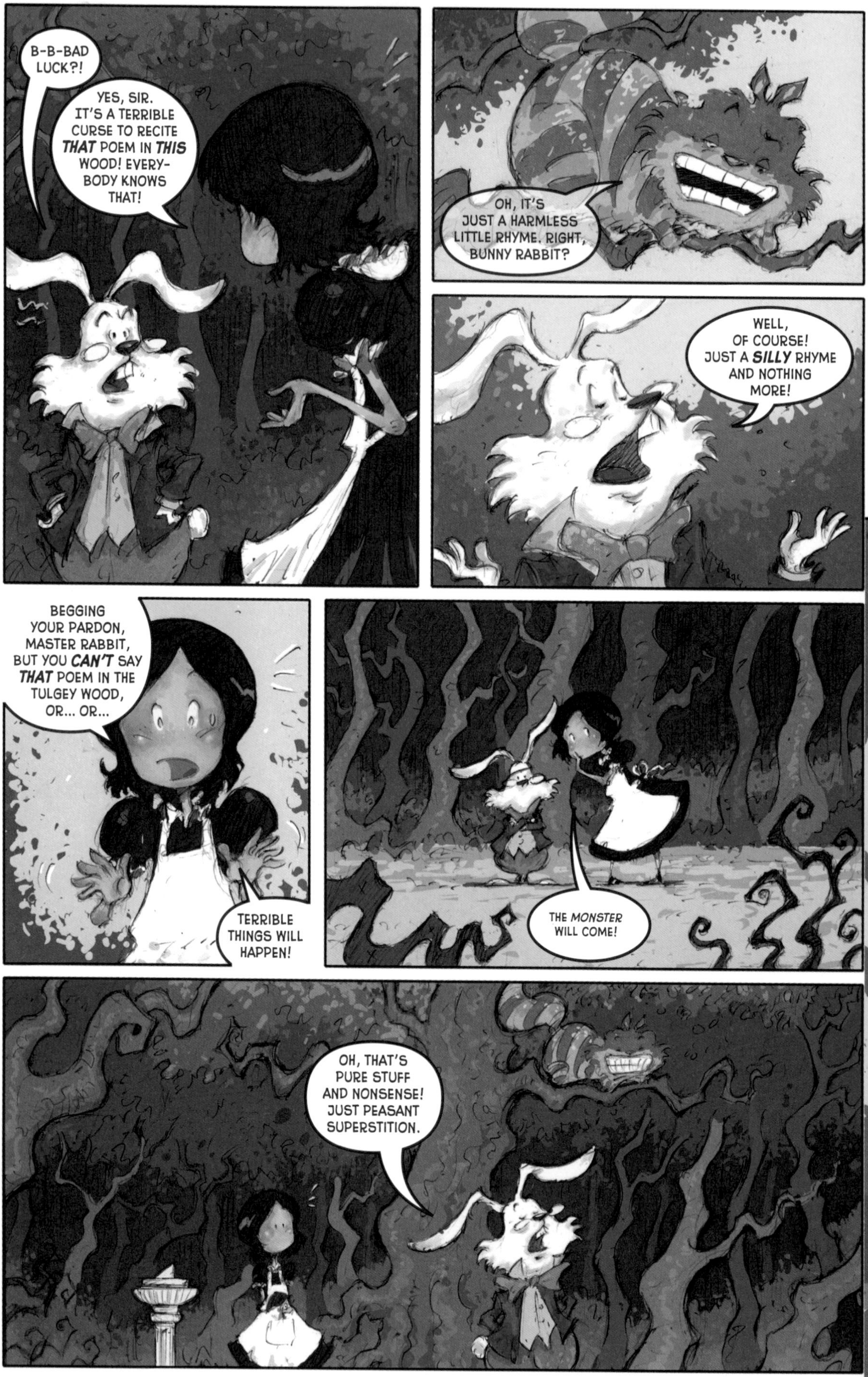
B-B-BAD LUCK?!
YES, SIR. IT'S A TERRIBLE CURSE TO RECITE THAT POEM IN THIS WOOD! EVERY-BODY KNOWS THAT!
OH, IT'S JUST A HARMLESS LITTLE RHYME. RIGHT, BUNNY RABBIT?
WELL, OF COURSE! JUST A SILLY RHYME AND NOTHING MORE!
BEGGING YOUR PARDON, MASTER RABBIT, BUT YOU CAN'T SAY THAT POEM IN THE TULGEY WOOD, OR... OR...
TERRIBLE THINGS WILL HAPPEN!
THE MONSTER WILL COME!
OH, THAT'S PURE STUFF AND NONSENSE! JUST PEASANT SUPERSTITION.

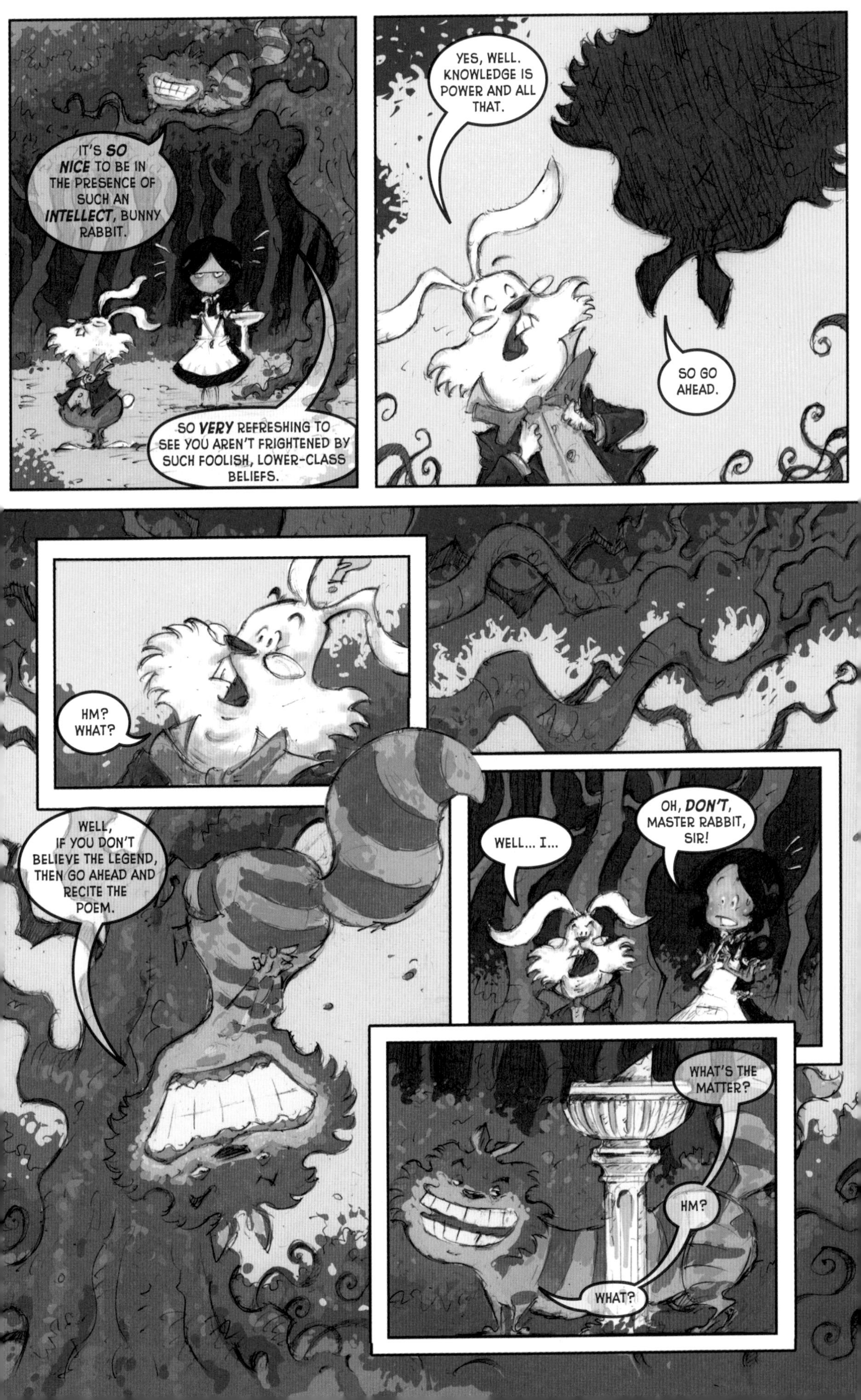

IT'S **SO NICE** TO BE IN THE PRESENCE OF SUCH AN ***INTELLECT***, BUNNY RABBIT.
SO ***VERY*** REFRESHING TO SEE YOU AREN'T FRIGHTENED BY SUCH FOOLISH, LOWER-CLASS BELIEFS.
YES, WELL. KNOWLEDGE IS POWER AND ALL THAT.
SO GO AHEAD.
HM? WHAT?
WELL, IF YOU DON'T BELIEVE THE LEGEND, THEN GO AHEAD AND RECITE THE POEM.
WELL... I...
OH, ***DON'T***, MASTER RABBIT, SIR!
WHAT'S THE MATTER?
HM?
WHAT?

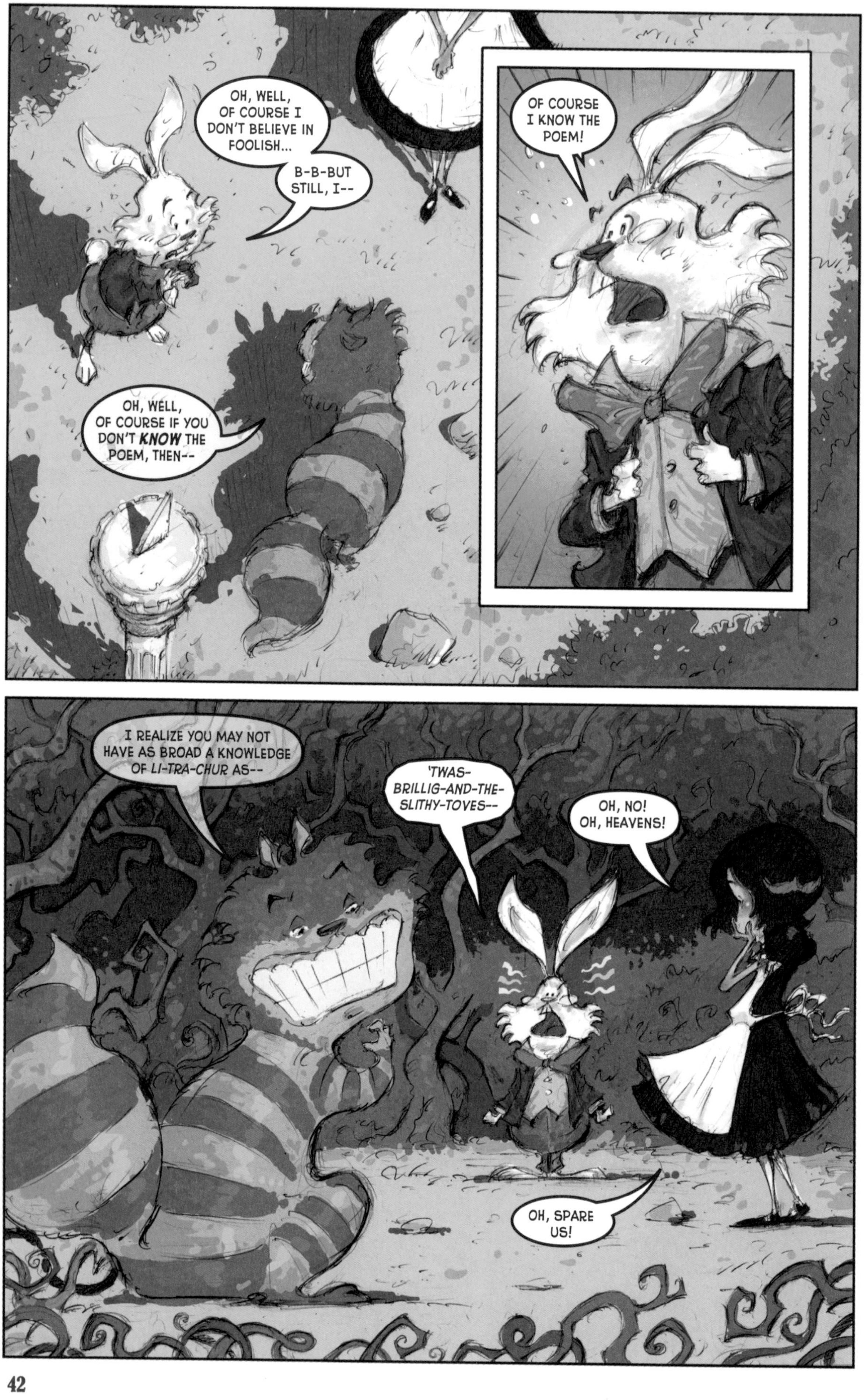
OH, WELL, OF COURSE I DON'T BELIEVE IN FOOLISH...
B-B-BUT STILL, I--
OH, WELL, OF COURSE IF YOU DON'T *KNOW* THE POEM, THEN--
OF COURSE I KNOW THE POEM!
I REALIZE YOU MAY NOT HAVE AS BROAD A KNOWLEDGE OF *LI-TRA-CHUR* AS--
'TWAS-BRILLIG-AND-THE-SLITHY-TOVES--
OH, NO! OH, HEAVENS!
OH, SPARE US!

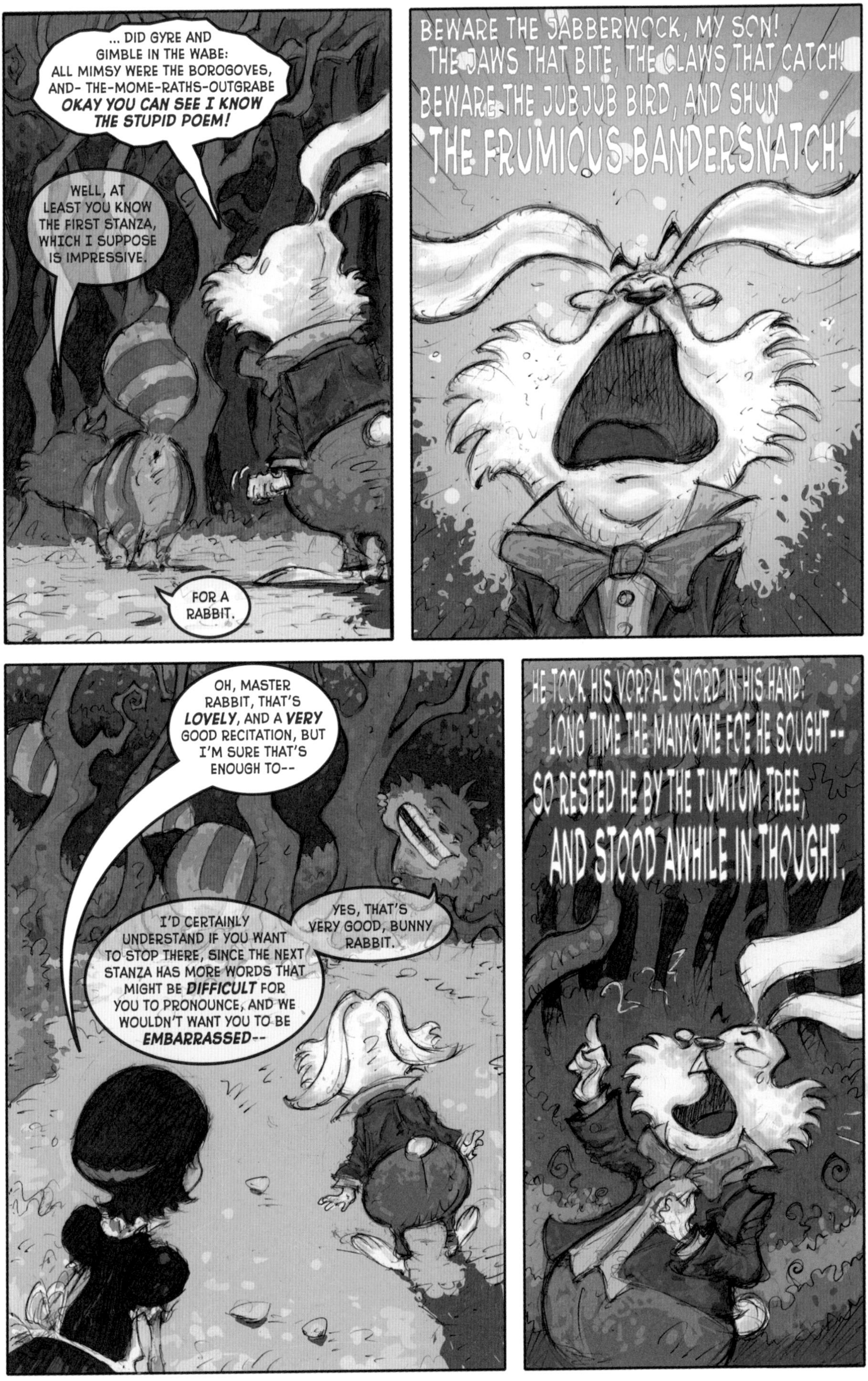
... DID GYRE AND GIMBLE IN THE WABE: ALL MIMSY WERE THE BOROGOVES, AND- THE-MOME-RATHS-OUTGRABE ***OKAY YOU CAN SEE I KNOW THE STUPID POEM!***
WELL, AT LEAST YOU KNOW THE FIRST STANZA, WHICH I SUPPOSE IS IMPRESSIVE.
FOR A RABBIT.
BEWARE THE JABBERWOCK, MY SON!
THE JAWS THAT BITE, THE CLAWS THAT CATCH!
BEWARE THE JUBJUB BIRD, AND SHUN
THE FRUMIOUS BANDERSNATCH!
OH, MASTER RABBIT, THAT'S ***LOVELY***, AND A ***VERY*** GOOD RECITATION, BUT I'M SURE THAT'S ENOUGH TO--
YES, THAT'S VERY GOOD, BUNNY RABBIT.
I'D CERTAINLY UNDERSTAND IF YOU WANT TO STOP THERE, SINCE THE NEXT STANZA HAS MORE WORDS THAT MIGHT BE ***DIFFICULT*** FOR YOU TO PRONOUNCE, AND WE WOULDN'T WANT YOU TO BE ***EMBARRASSED***--
HE TOOK HIS VORPAL SWORD IN HIS HAND:
LONG TIME THE MANXOME FOE HE SOUGHT--
SO RESTED HE BY THE TUMTUM TREE,
AND STOOD AWHILE IN THOUGHT.

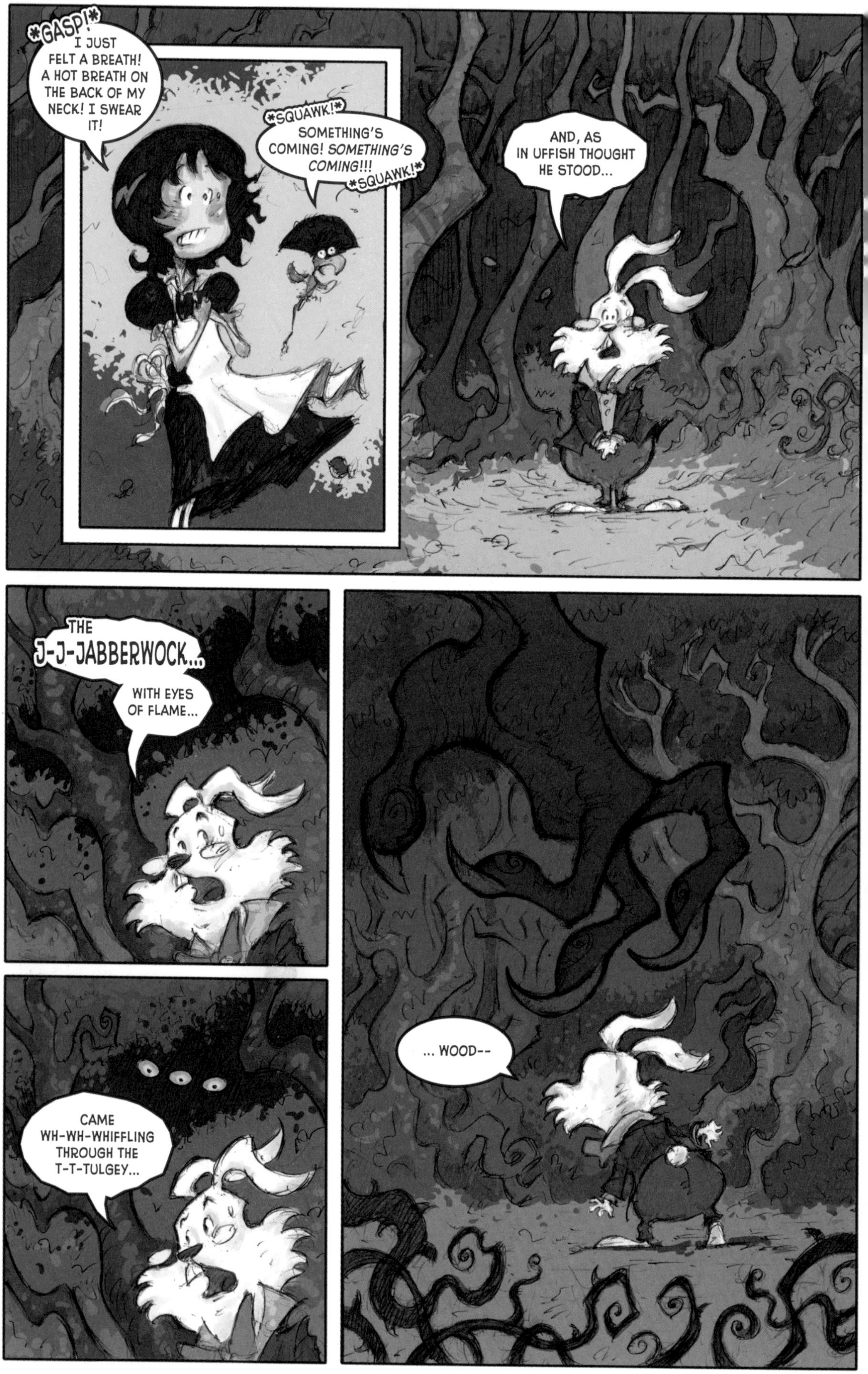
GASP!
I JUST FELT A BREATH! A HOT BREATH ON THE BACK OF MY NECK! I SWEAR IT!
SQUAWK!
SOMETHING'S COMING! *SOMETHING'S COMING!!!*
SQUAWK!
AND, AS IN UFFISH THOUGHT HE STOOD...
THE J-J-JABBERWOCK...
WITH EYES OF FLAME...
CAME WH-WH-WHIFFLING THROUGH THE T-T-TULGEY...
... WOOD--

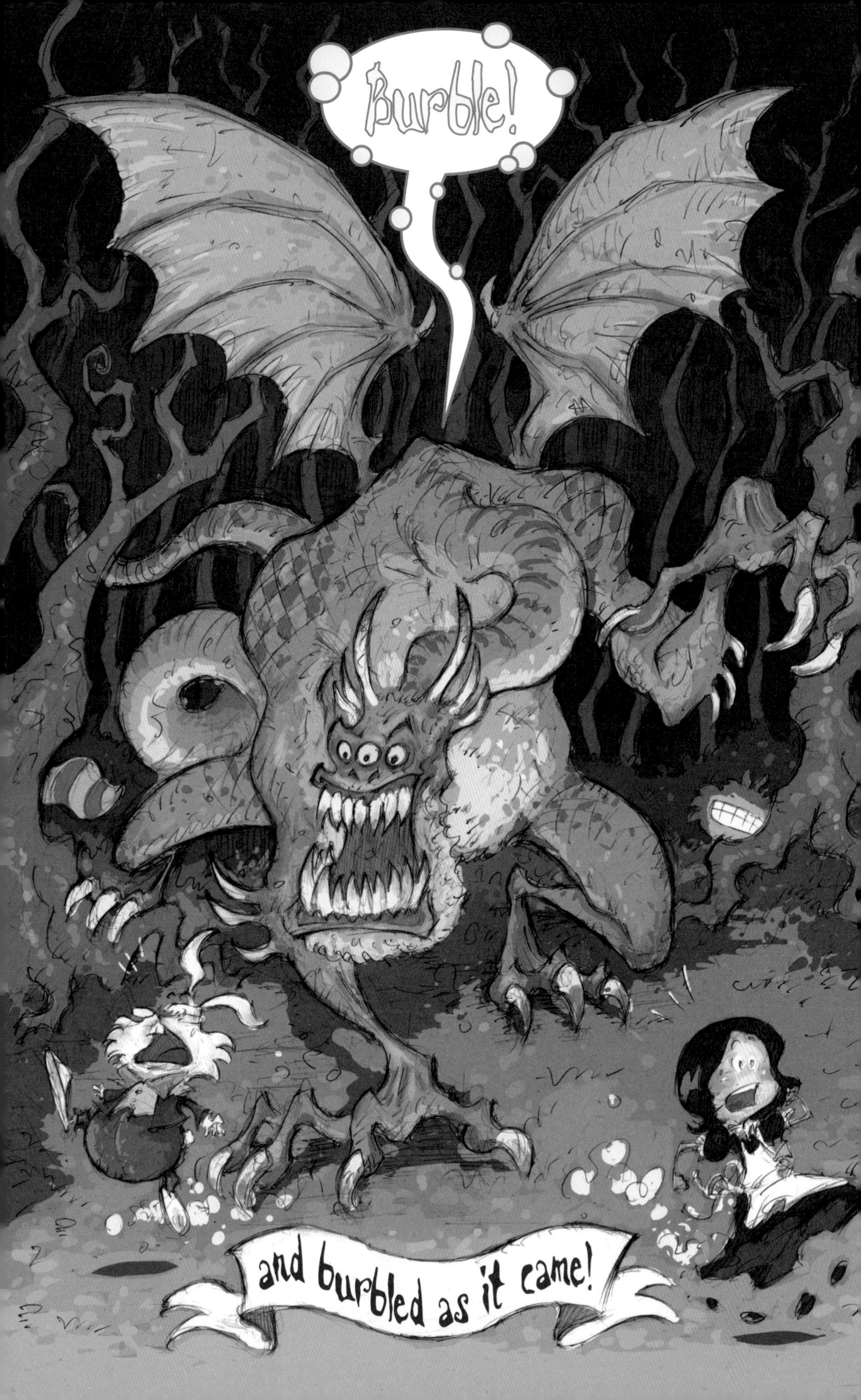
Burble!
and burbled as it came!

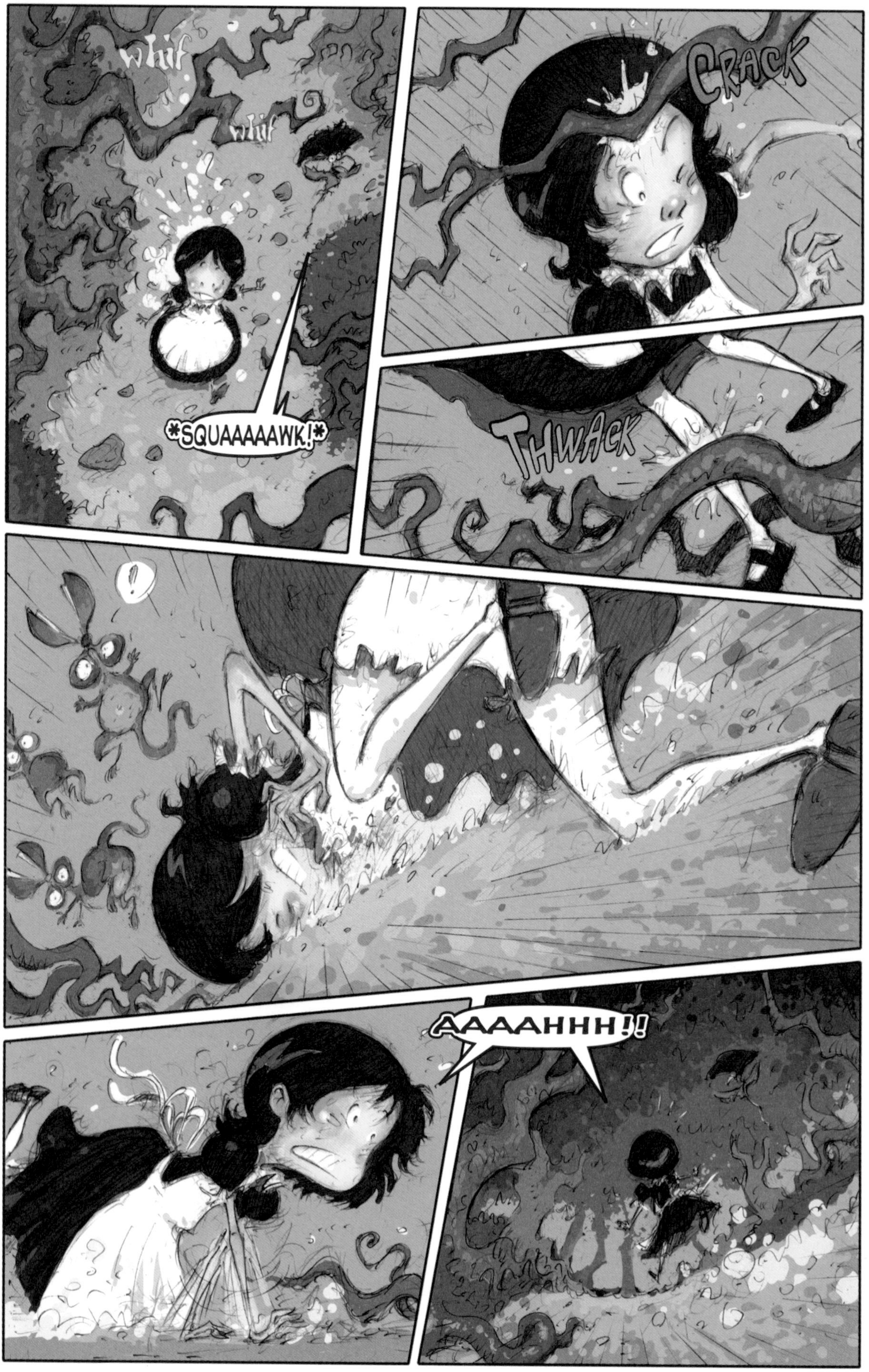
whif
whif
SQUAAAAAWK!
CRACK
THWACK
!
AAAAHHH!!

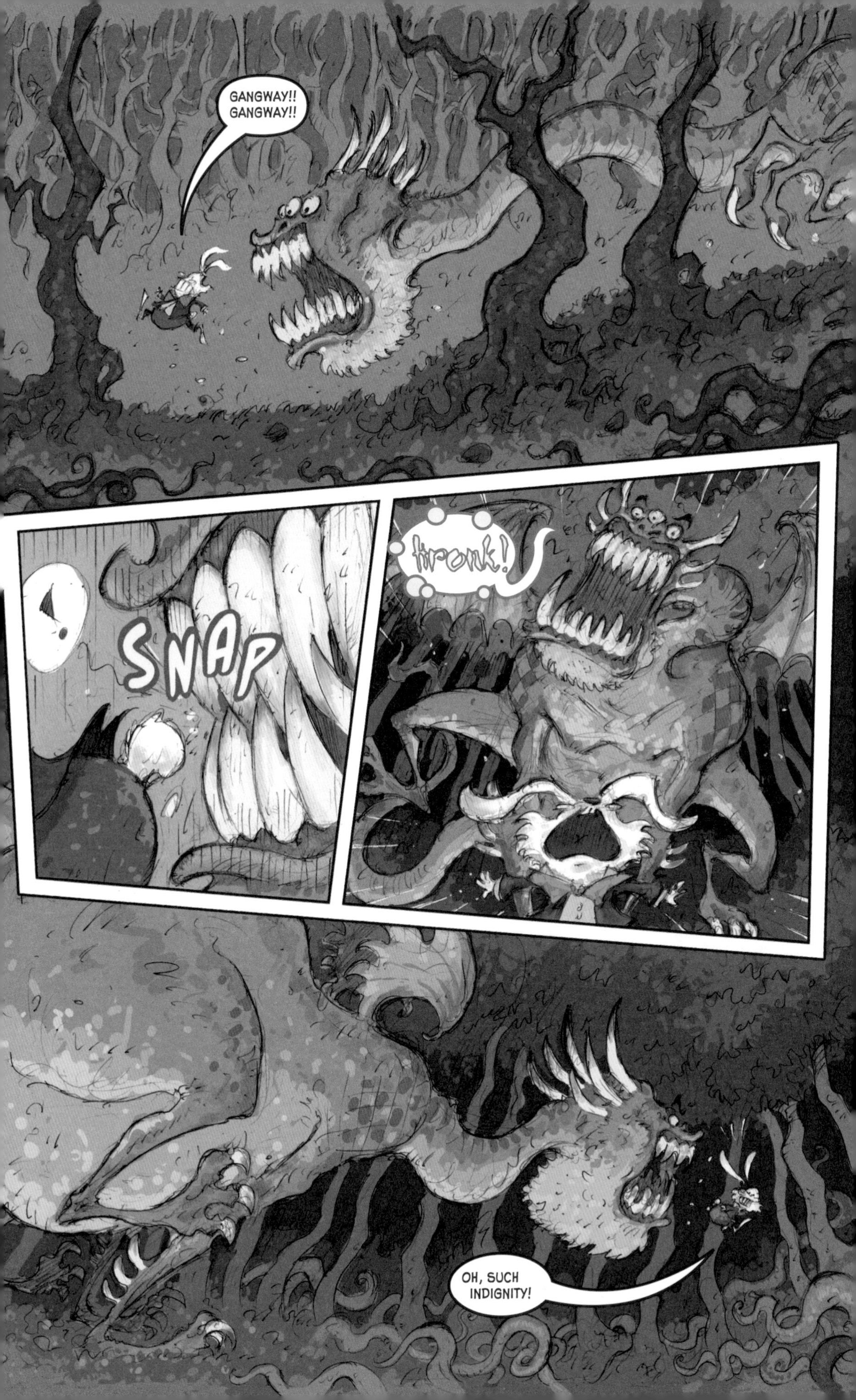
GANGWAY!!
GANGWAY!!
!
SNAP
FRONK!
OH, SUCH
INDIGNITY!

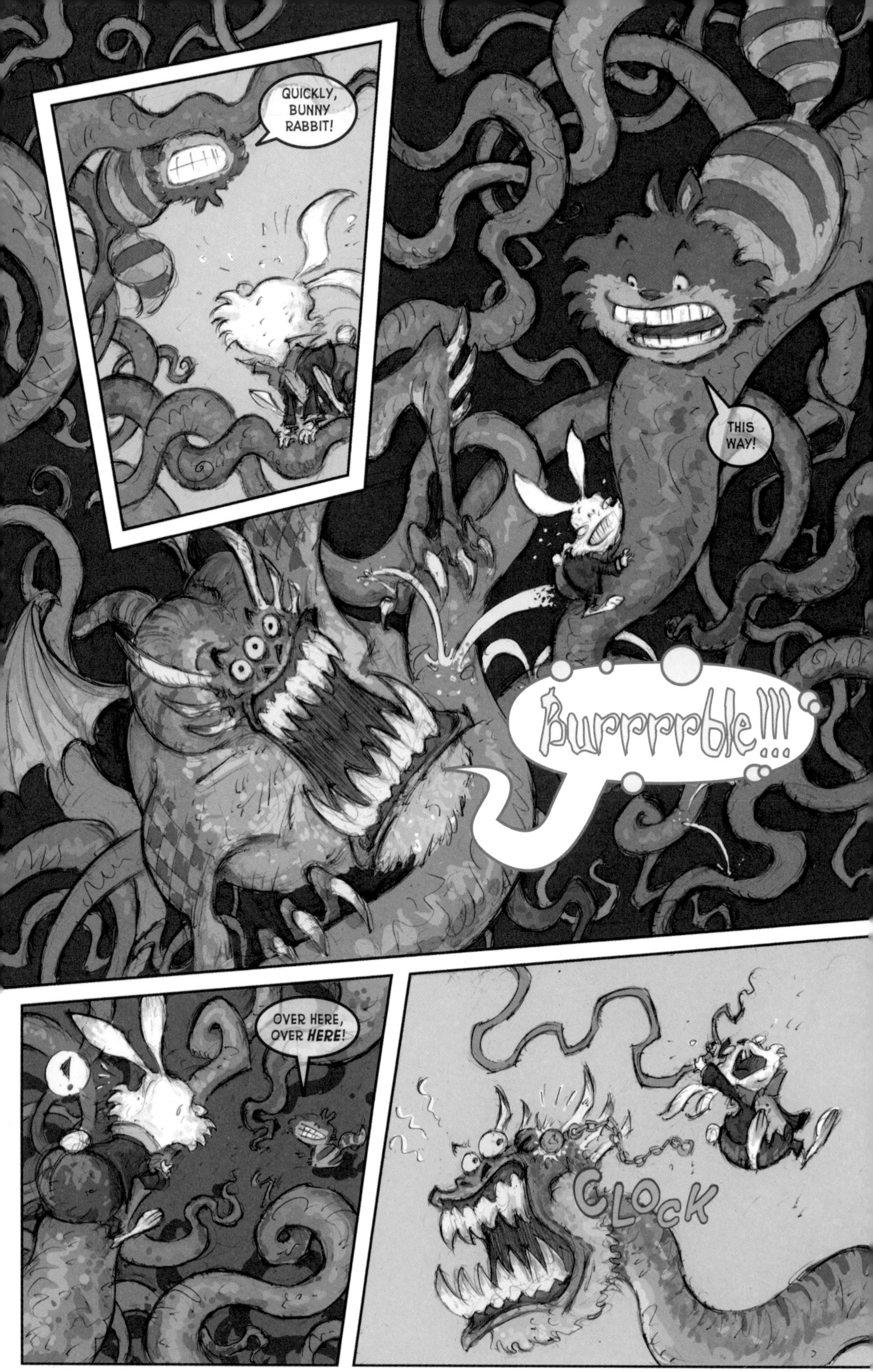
QUICKLY, BUNNY RABBIT!
THIS WAY!
Burrrrble!!!...
!
OVER HERE, OVER HERE!
CLOCK

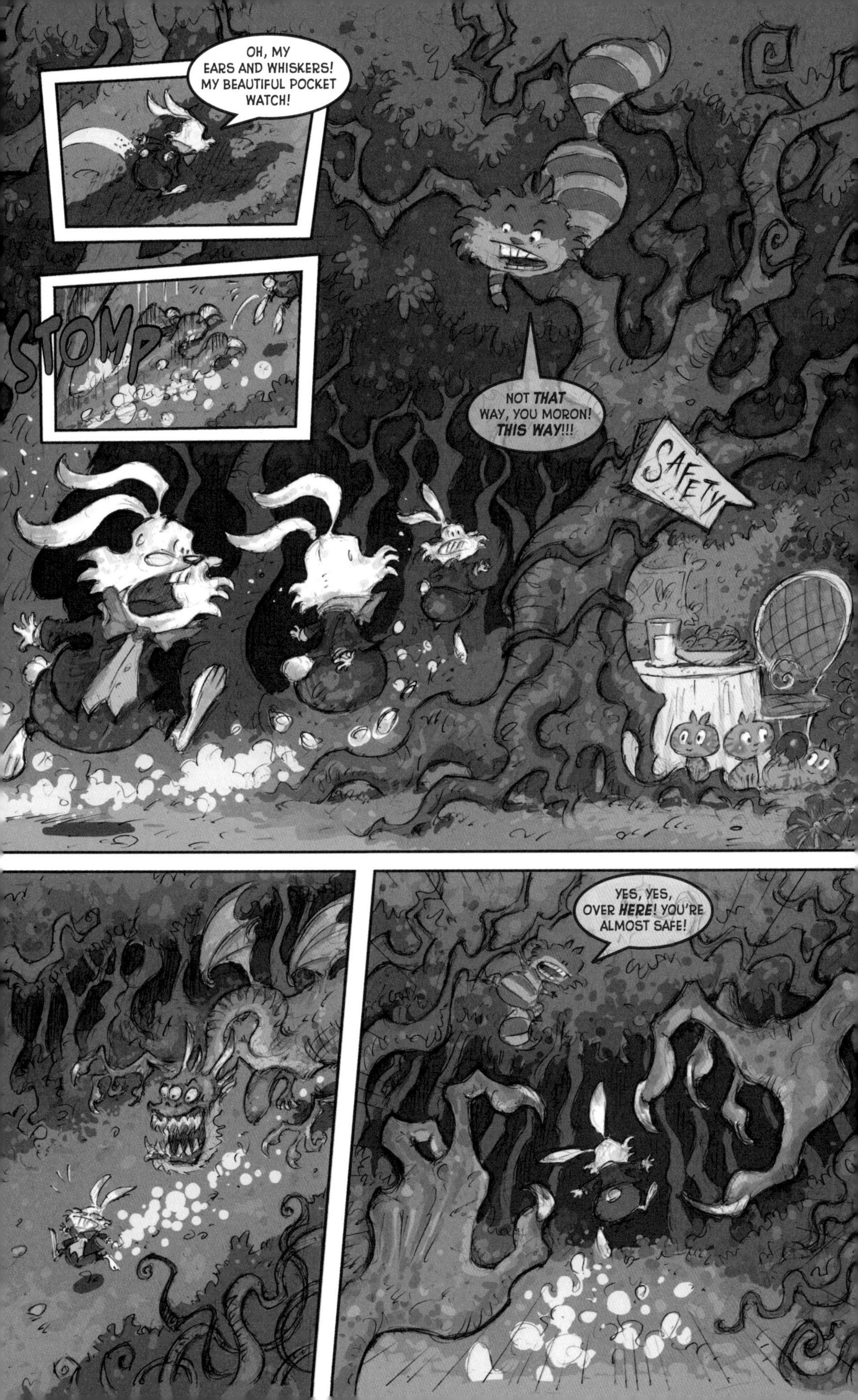
OH, MY EARS AND WHISKERS! MY BEAUTIFUL POCKET WATCH!
STOMP
NOT THAT WAY, YOU MORON! THIS WAY!!!
SAFETY
YES, YES, OVER HERE! YOU'RE ALMOST SAFE!

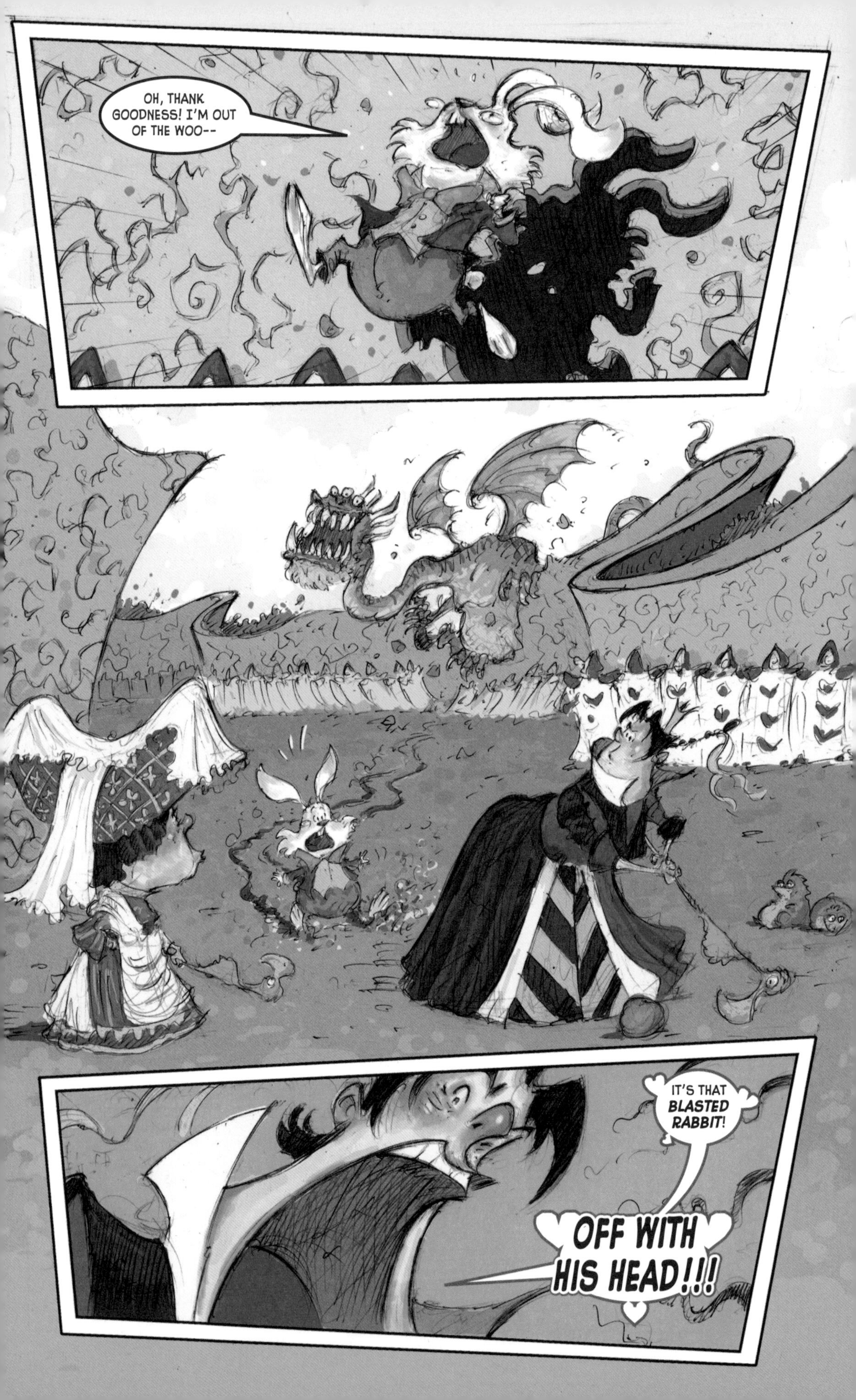

OH, THANK GOODNESS! I'M OUT OF THE WOO--
IT'S THAT *BLASTED RABBIT!*
OFF WITH HIS HEAD!!!

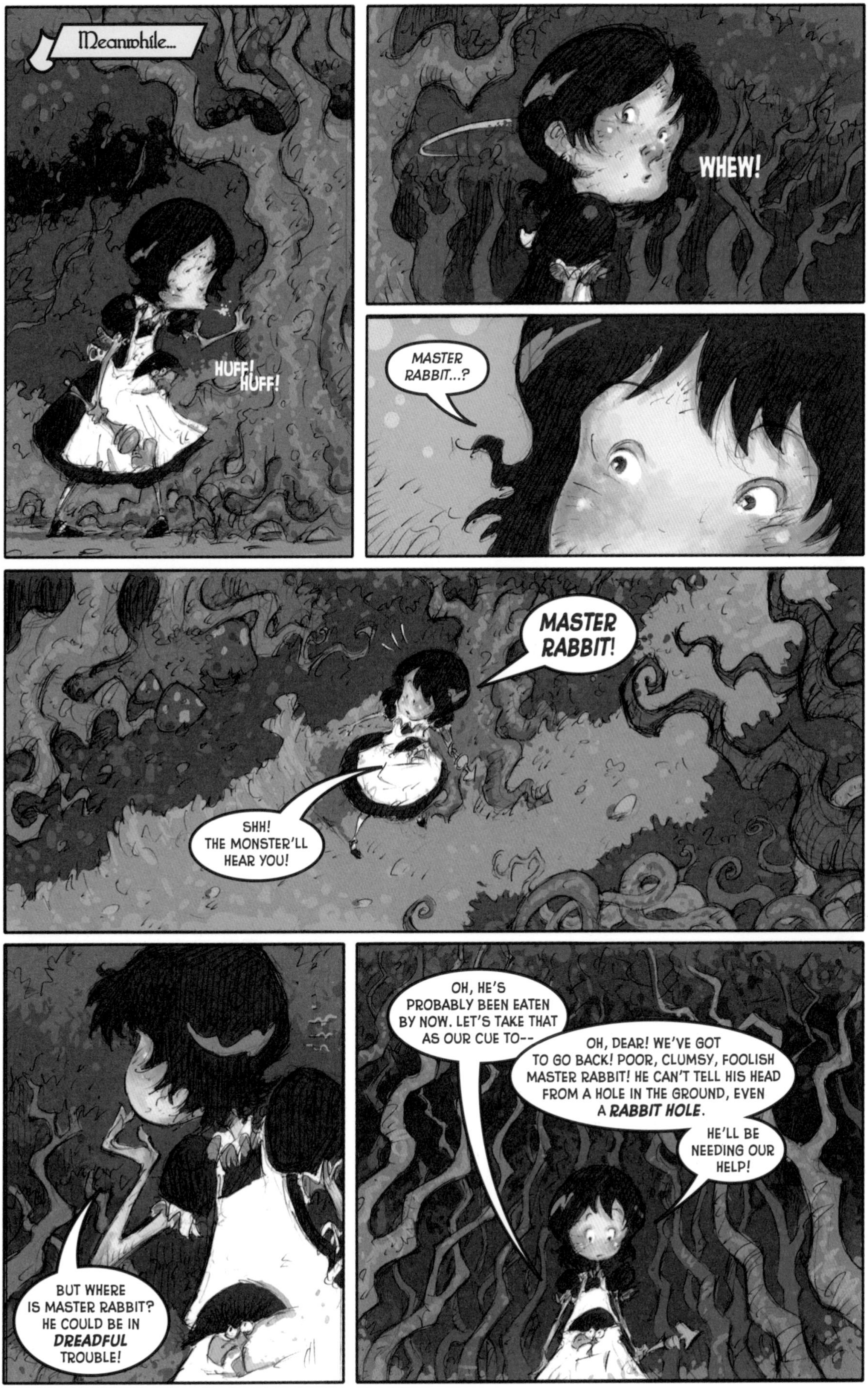
Meanwhile...
HUFF! HUFF!
WHEW!
MASTER RABBIT...?
MASTER RABBIT!
SHH! THE MONSTER'LL HEAR YOU!
BUT WHERE IS MASTER RABBIT? HE COULD BE IN DREADFUL TROUBLE!
OH, HE'S PROBABLY BEEN EATEN BY NOW. LET'S TAKE THAT AS OUR CUE TO--
OH, DEAR! WE'VE GOT TO GO BACK! POOR, CLUMSY, FOOLISH MASTER RABBIT! HE CAN'T TELL HIS HEAD FROM A HOLE IN THE GROUND, EVEN A RABBIT HOLE.
HE'LL BE NEEDING OUR HELP!

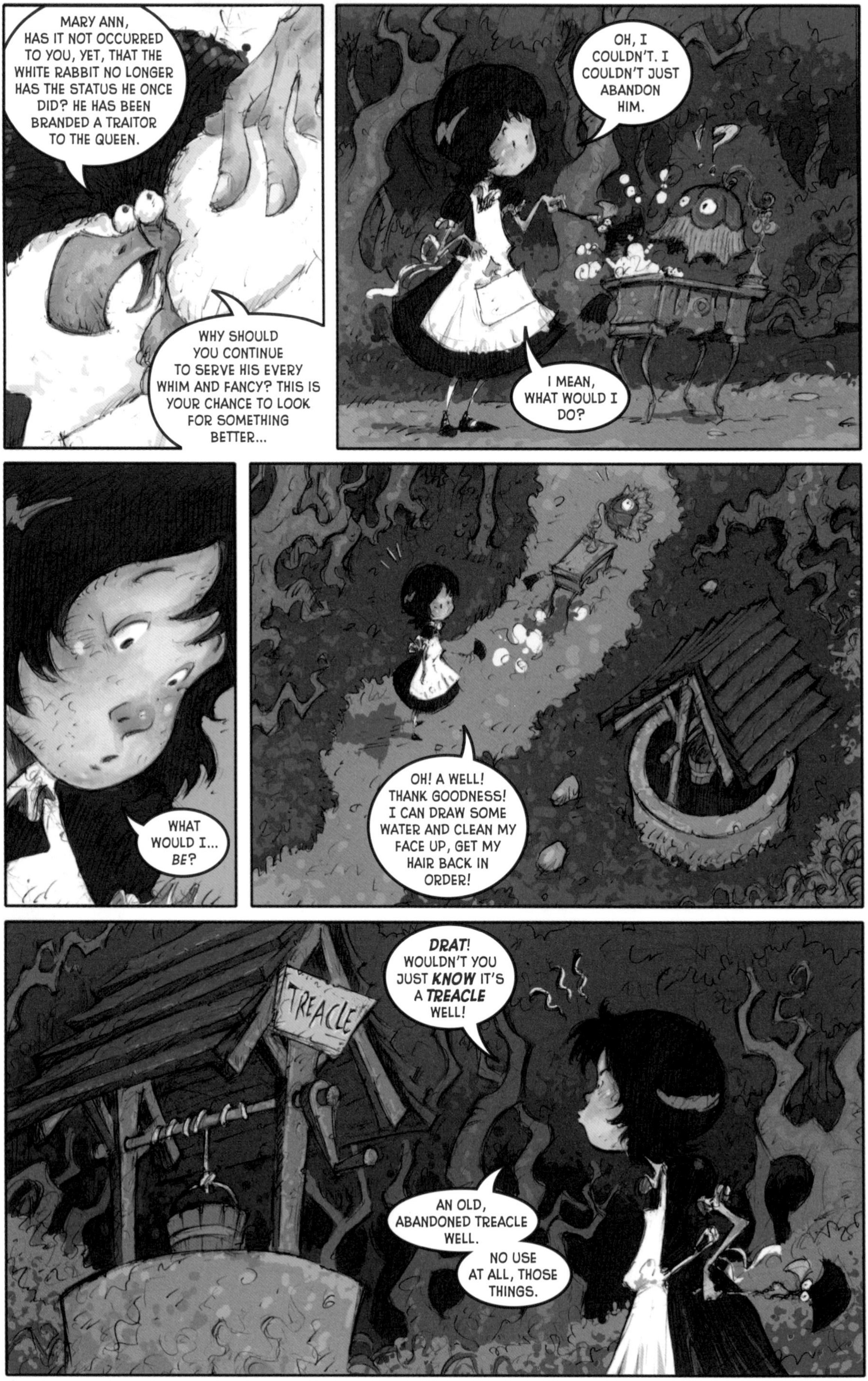
MARY ANN, HAS IT NOT OCCURRED TO YOU, YET, THAT THE WHITE RABBIT NO LONGER HAS THE STATUS HE ONCE DID? HE HAS BEEN BRANDED A TRAITOR TO THE QUEEN.
WHY SHOULD YOU CONTINUE TO SERVE HIS EVERY WHIM AND FANCY? THIS IS YOUR CHANCE TO LOOK FOR SOMETHING BETTER...
OH, I COULDN'T. I COULDN'T JUST ABANDON HIM.
I MEAN, WHAT WOULD I DO?
WHAT WOULD I... *BE*?
OH! A WELL! THANK GOODNESS! I CAN DRAW SOME WATER AND CLEAN MY FACE UP, GET MY HAIR BACK IN ORDER!
TREACLE
DRAT! WOULDN'T YOU JUST ***KNOW*** IT'S A ***TREACLE*** WELL!
AN OLD, ABANDONED TREACLE WELL.
NO USE AT ALL, THOSE THINGS.

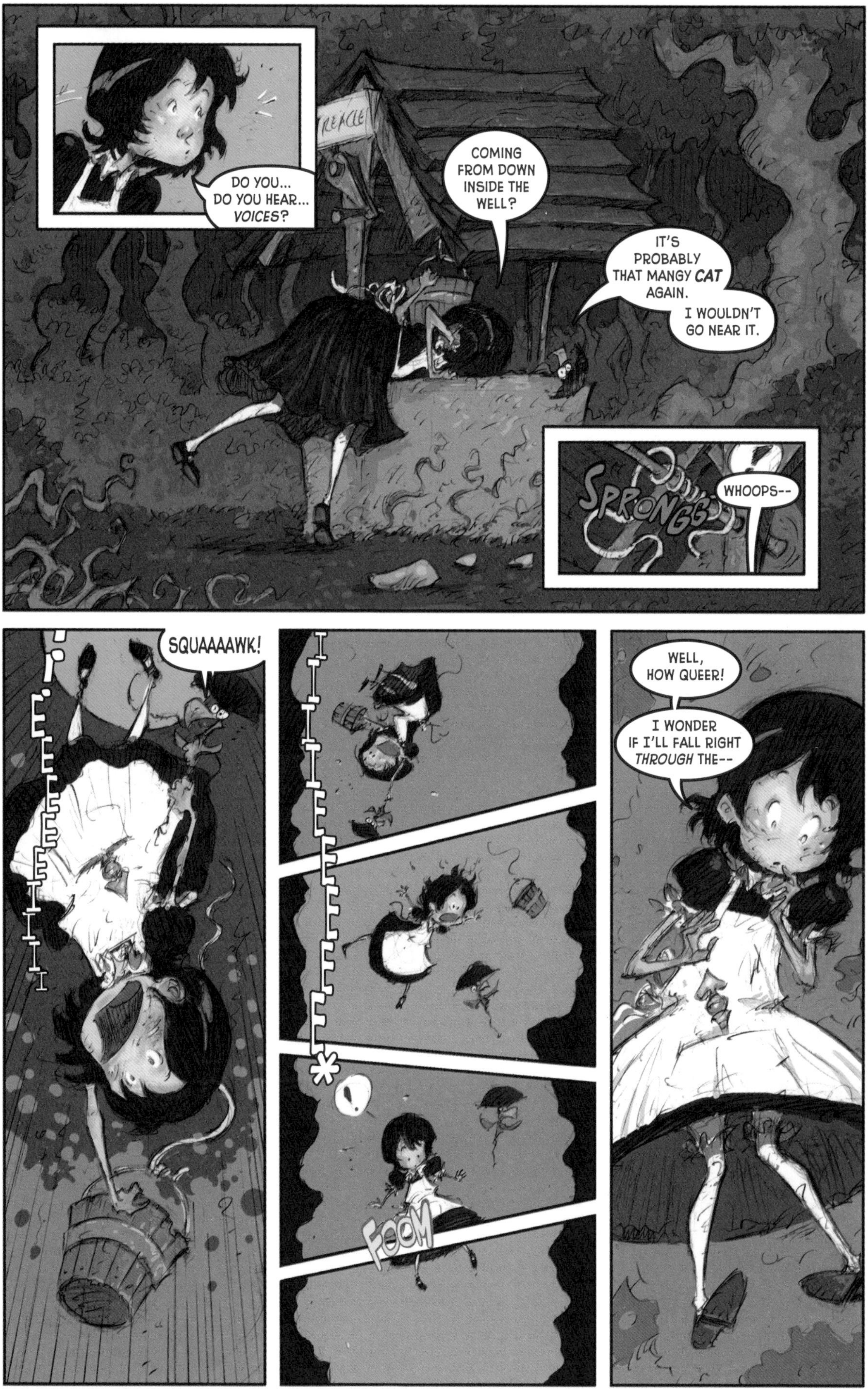
TREACLE
DO YOU...
DO YOU HEAR...
VOICES?
COMING FROM DOWN INSIDE THE WELL?
IT'S PROBABLY THAT MANGY **CAT** AGAIN.
I WOULDN'T GO NEAR IT.
SPRONGG
WHOOPS--
SQUAAAAWK!
FOOM
WELL, HOW QUEER!
I WONDER IF I'LL FALL RIGHT *THROUGH* THE--

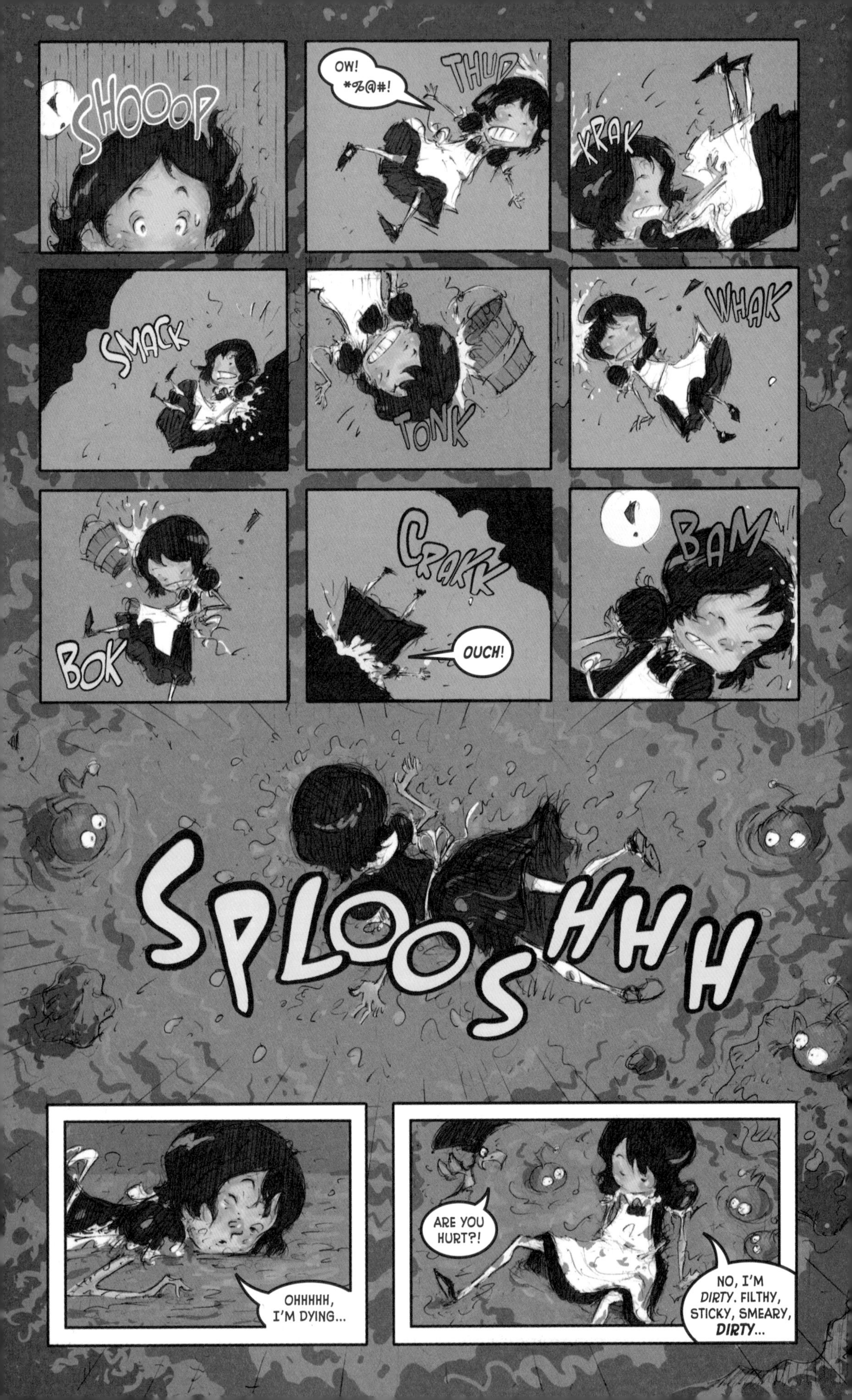
SHOOOP
OW! *%@#!
THUD
KRAK
SMACK
TONK
WHAK
BOK
CRAKK
OUCH!
!
BAM
SPLOOSHHH
OHHHHH, I'M DYING...
ARE YOU HURT?!
NO, I'M *DIRTY*. FILTHY, STICKY, SMEARY, ***DIRTY***...

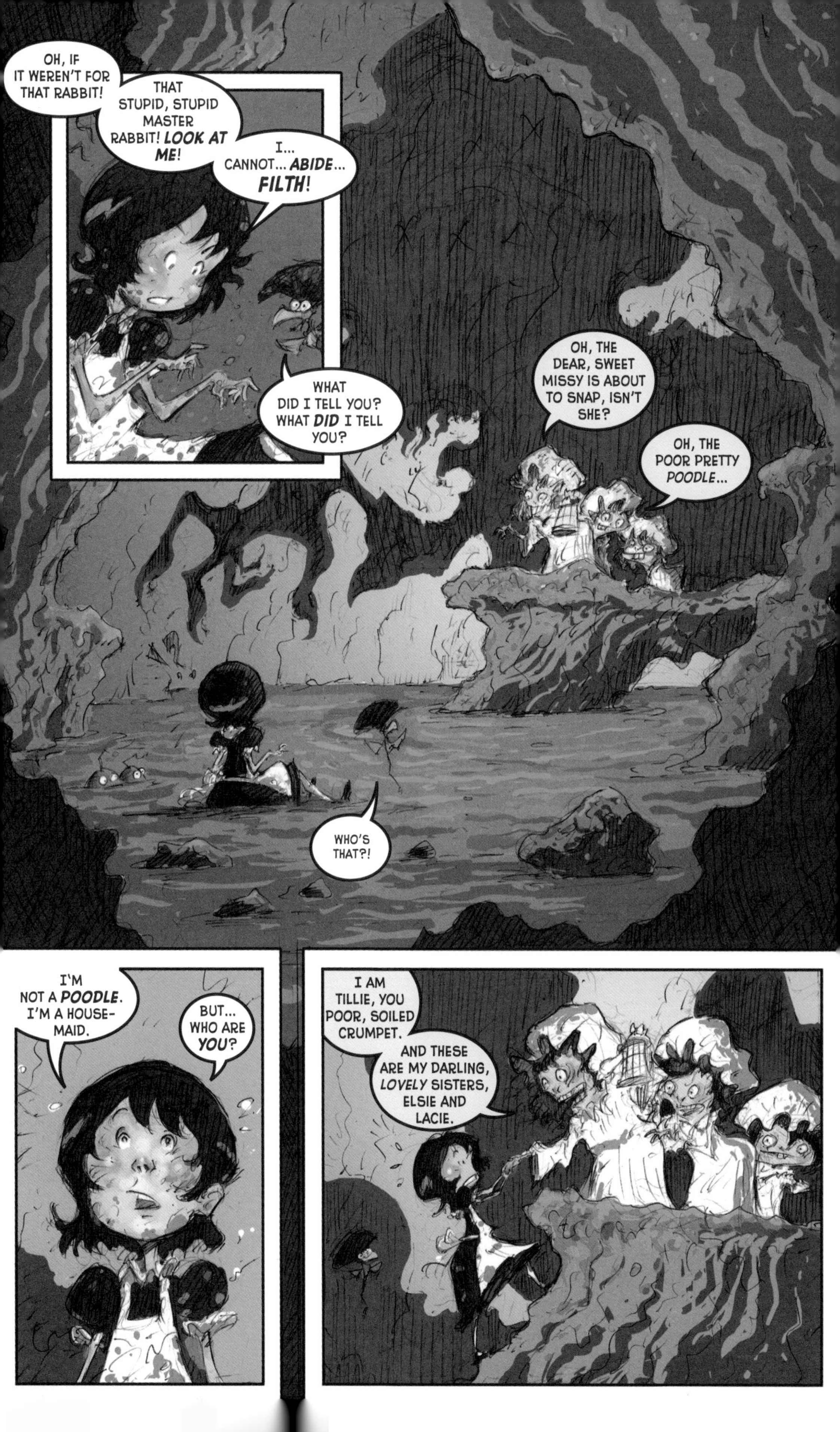
OH, IF IT WEREN'T FOR THAT RABBIT!
THAT STUPID, STUPID MASTER RABBIT! **LOOK AT ME**!
I... CANNOT... **ABIDE**... **FILTH**!
WHAT DID I TELL YOU? WHAT ***DID*** I TELL YOU?
OH, THE DEAR, SWEET MISSY IS ABOUT TO SNAP, ISN'T SHE?
OH, THE POOR PRETTY *POODLE*...
WHO'S THAT?!
I'M NOT A ***POODLE***. I'M A HOUSE-MAID.
BUT... WHO ARE ***YOU***?
I AM TILLIE, YOU POOR, SOILED CRUMPET.
AND THESE ARE MY DARLING, *LOVELY* SISTERS, ELSIE AND LACIE.

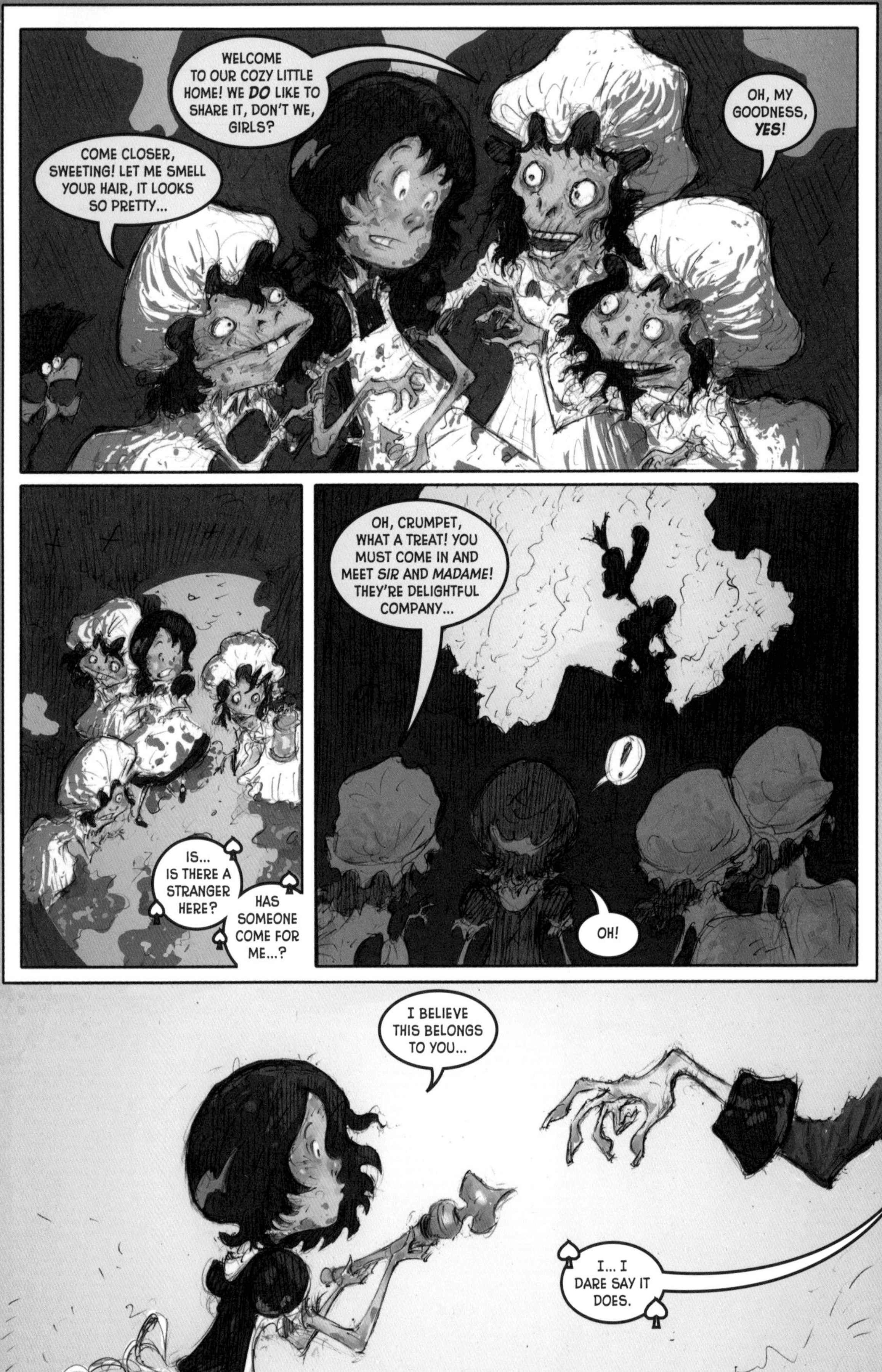
COME CLOSER, SWEETING! LET ME SMELL YOUR HAIR, IT LOOKS SO PRETTY...
WELCOME TO OUR COZY LITTLE HOME! WE DO LIKE TO SHARE IT, DON'T WE, GIRLS?
OH, MY GOODNESS, YES!
IS... IS THERE A STRANGER HERE?
HAS SOMEONE COME FOR ME...?
OH, CRUMPET, WHAT A TREAT! YOU MUST COME IN AND MEET SIR AND MADAME! THEY'RE DELIGHTFUL COMPANY...
!
OH!
I BELIEVE THIS BELONGS TO YOU...
I... I DARE SAY IT DOES.

Chapter Three

You're *My* Maid Now!

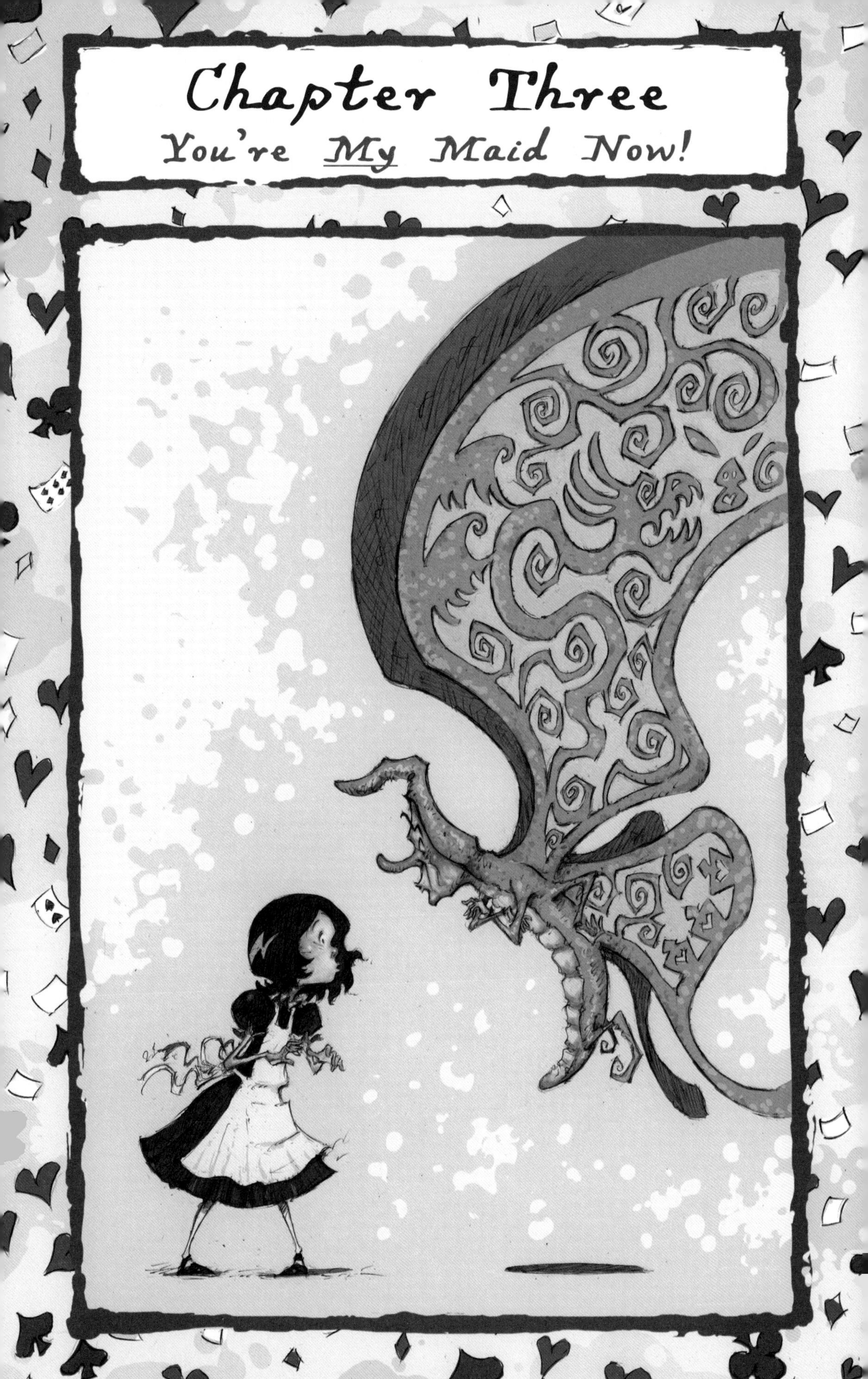

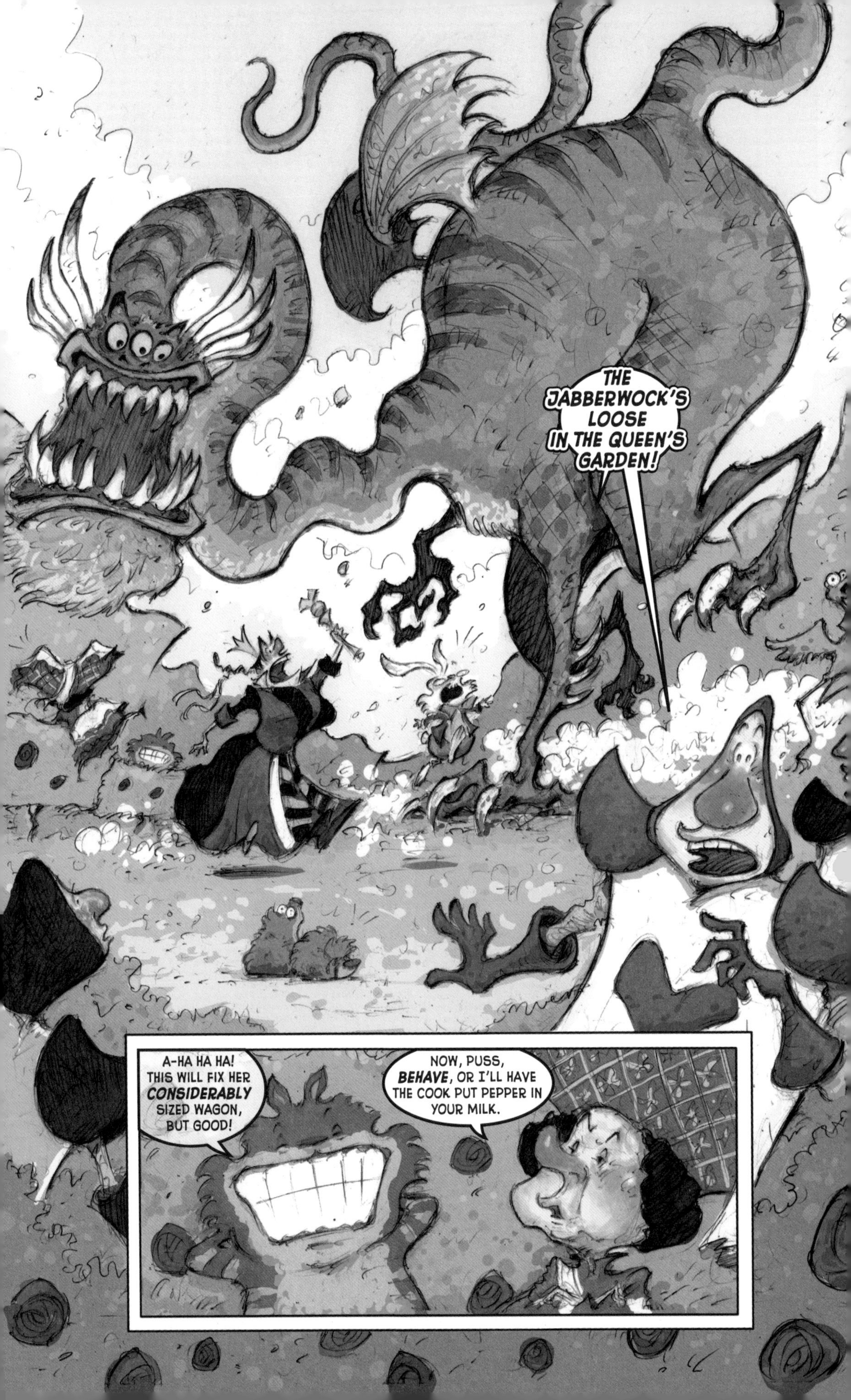
THE JABBERWOCK'S LOOSE IN THE QUEEN'S GARDEN!
A-HA HA HA! THIS WILL FIX HER **CONSIDERABLY** SIZED WAGON, BUT GOOD!
NOW, PUSS, **BEHAVE**, OR I'LL HAVE THE COOK PUT PEPPER IN YOUR MILK.

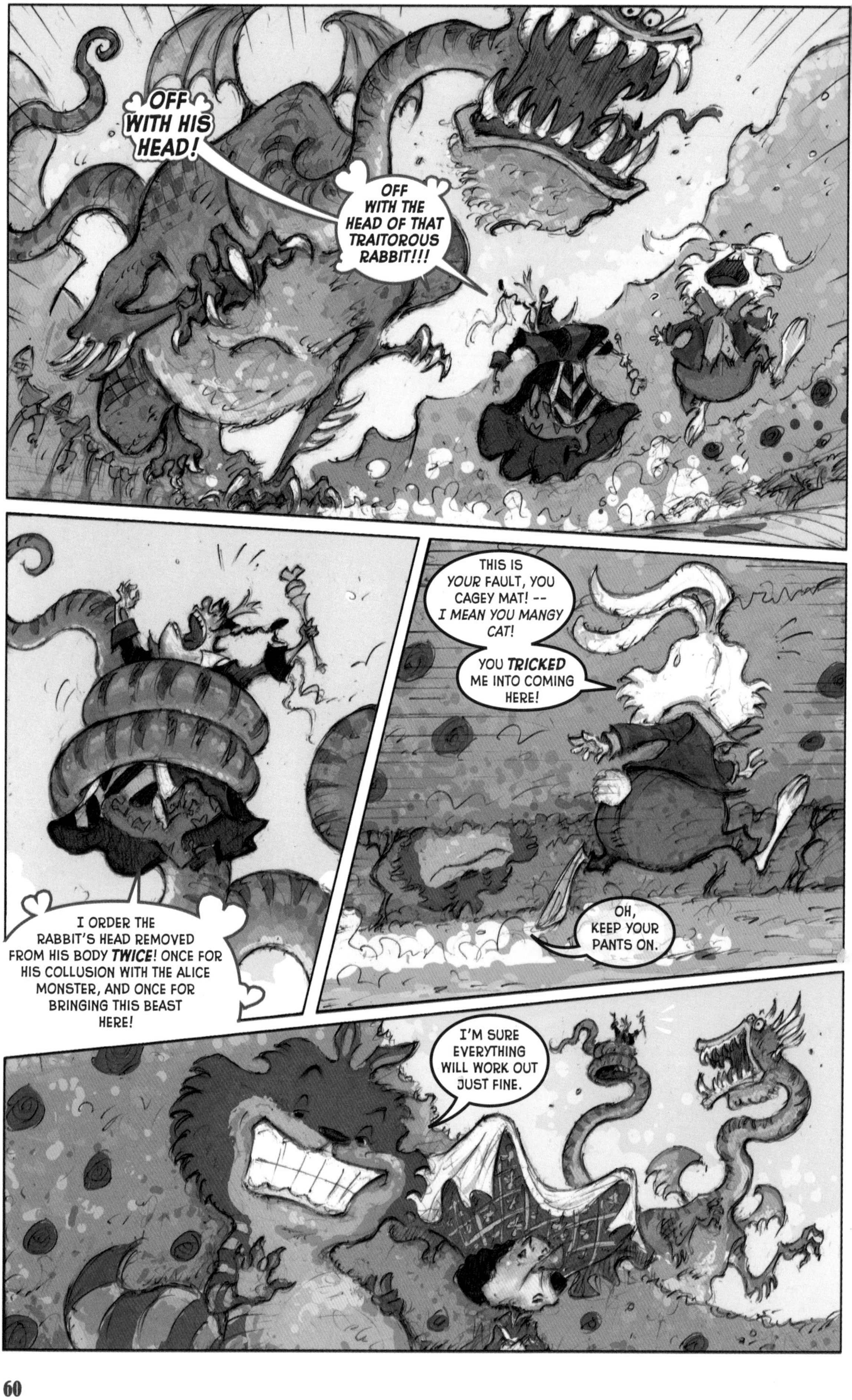
OFF WITH HIS HEAD!
OFF WITH THE HEAD OF THAT TRAITOROUS RABBIT!!!
I ORDER THE RABBIT'S HEAD REMOVED FROM HIS BODY TWICE! ONCE FOR HIS COLLUSION WITH THE ALICE MONSTER, AND ONCE FOR BRINGING THIS BEAST HERE!
THIS IS YOUR FAULT, YOU CAGEY MAT! -- I MEAN YOU MANGY CAT!
YOU TRICKED ME INTO COMING HERE!
OH, KEEP YOUR PANTS ON.
I'M SURE EVERYTHING WILL WORK OUT JUST FINE.

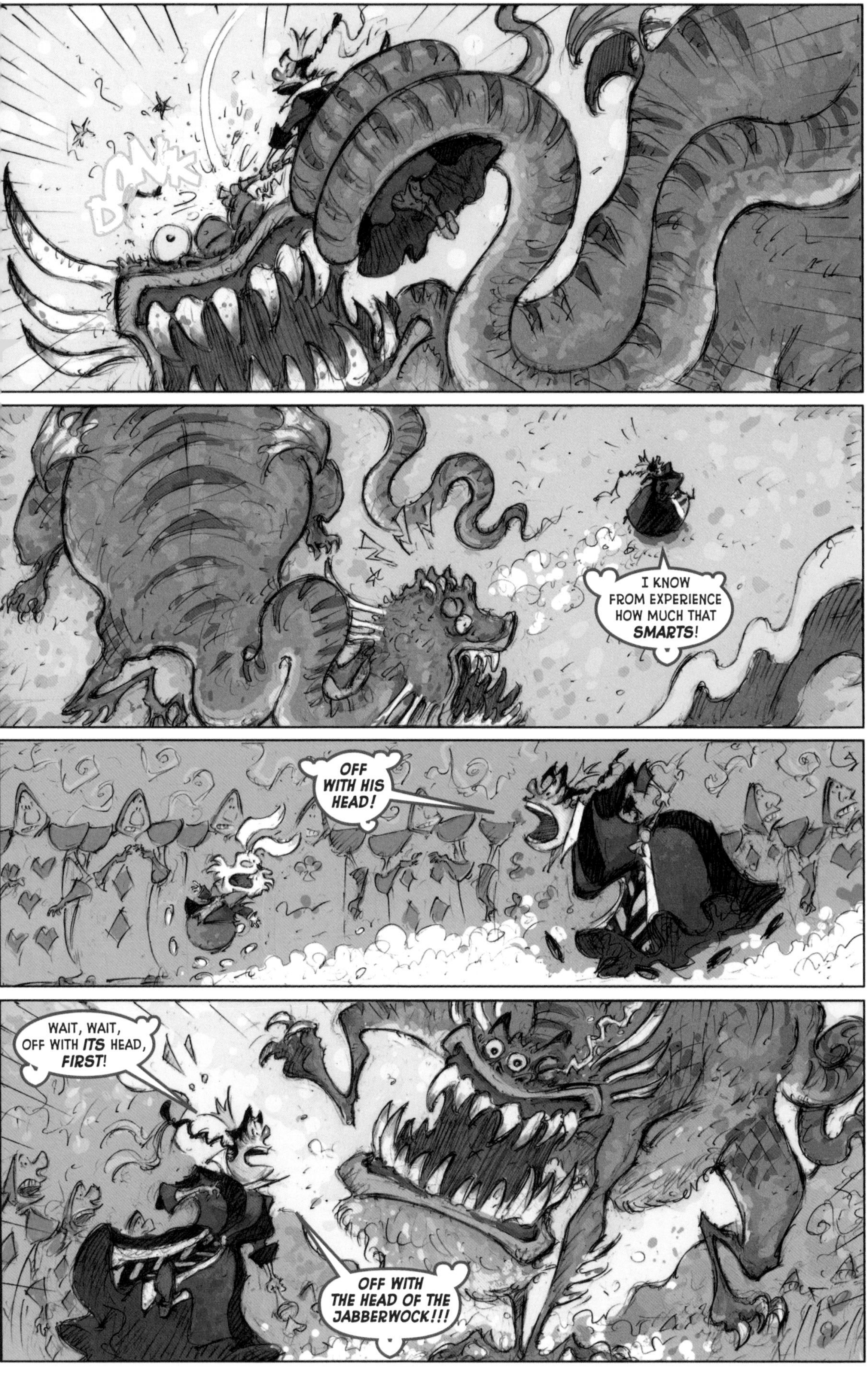
I KNOW FROM EXPERIENCE HOW MUCH THAT SMARTS!
OFF WITH HIS HEAD!
WAIT, WAIT, OFF WITH ITS HEAD, FIRST!
OFF WITH THE HEAD OF THE JABBERWOCK!!!

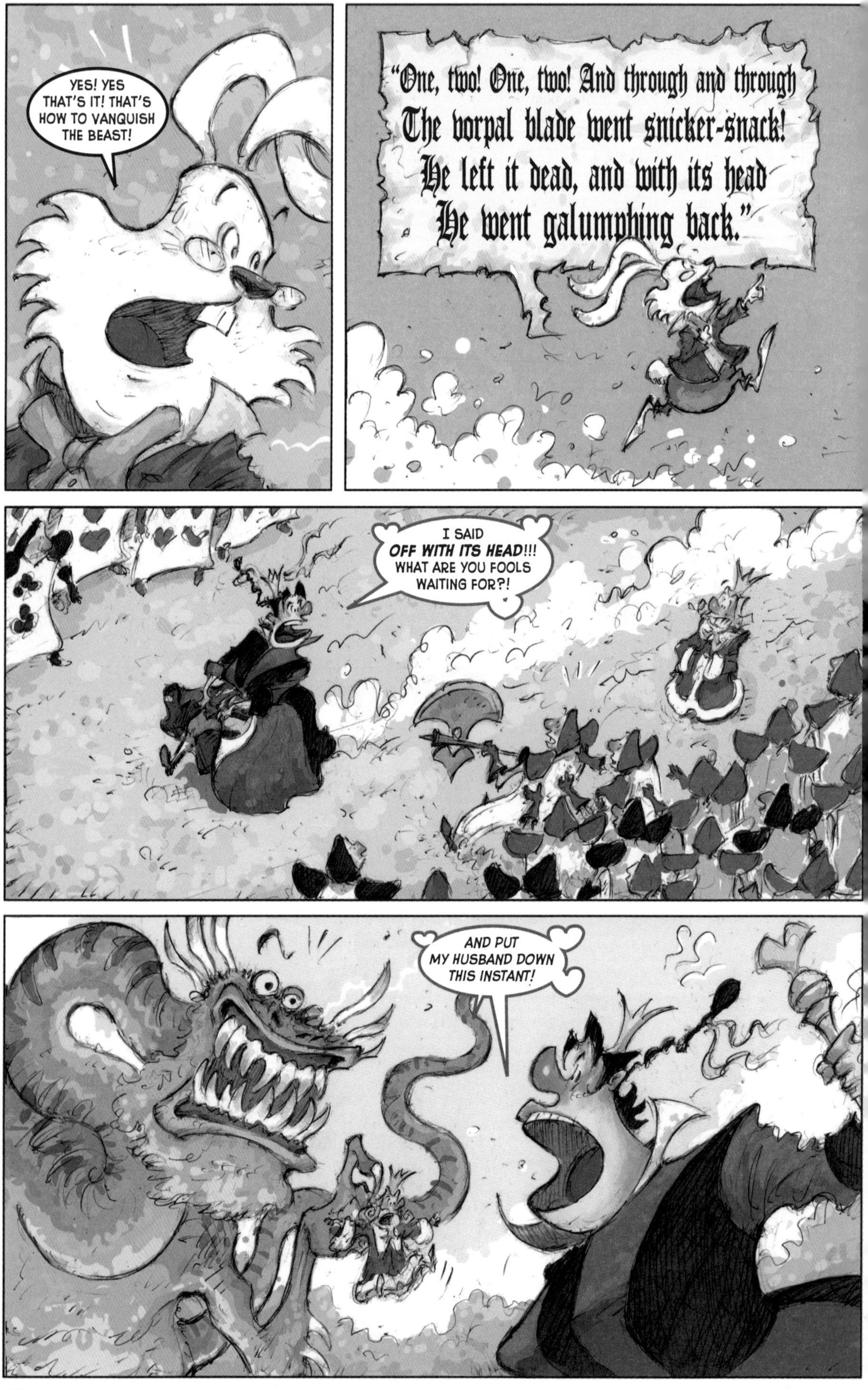
YES! YES THAT'S IT! THAT'S HOW TO VANQUISH THE BEAST!
"One, two! One, two! And through and through
The vorpal blade went snicker-snack!
He left it dead, and with its head
He went galumphing back."
I SAID *OFF WITH ITS HEAD*!!! WHAT ARE YOU FOOLS WAITING FOR?!
AND PUT MY HUSBAND DOWN THIS INSTANT!

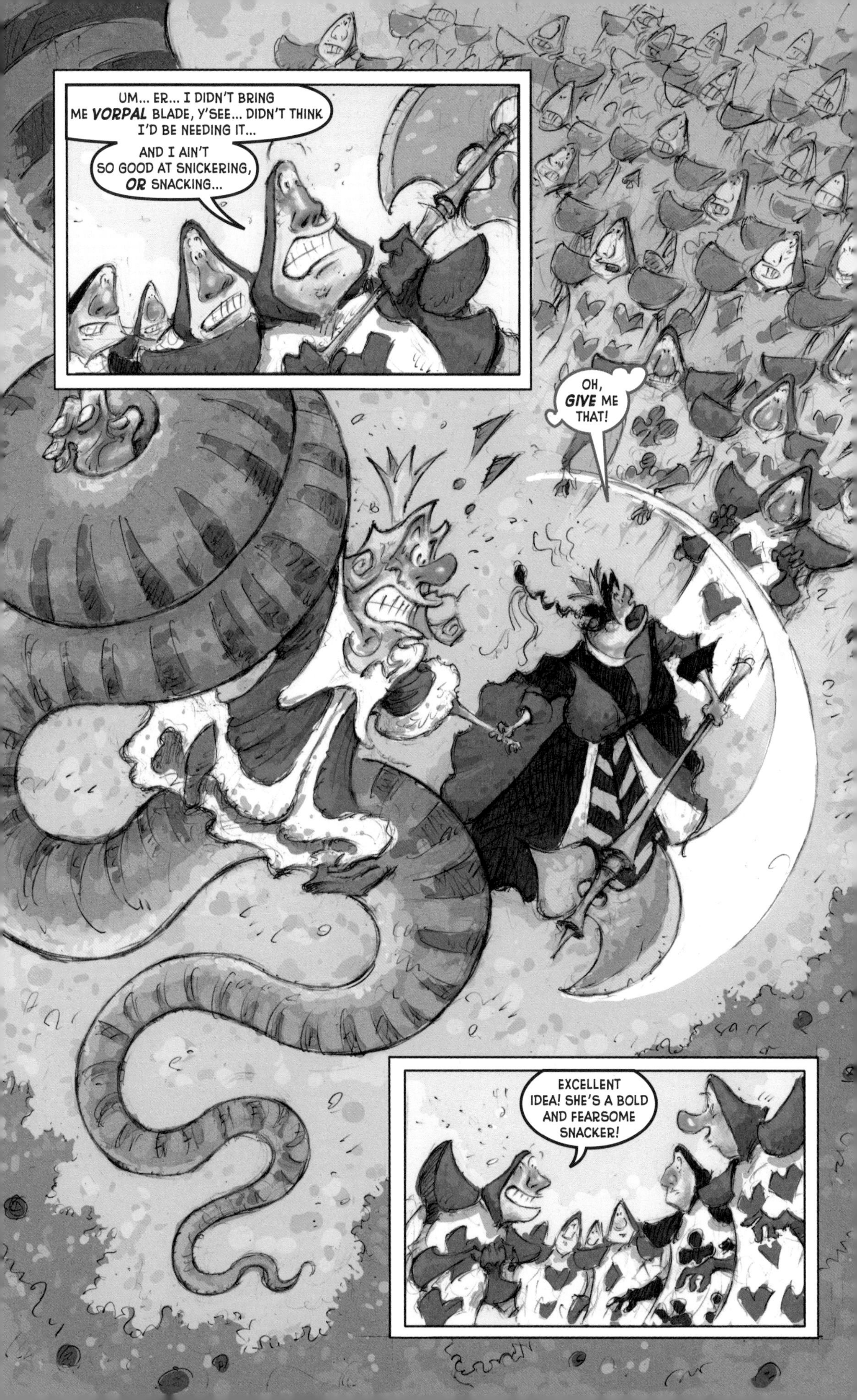
UM... ER... I DIDN'T BRING ME VORPAL BLADE, Y'SEE... DIDN'T THINK I'D BE NEEDING IT...
AND I AIN'T SO GOOD AT SNICKERING, OR SNACKING...
OH, GIVE ME THAT!
EXCELLENT IDEA! SHE'S A BOLD AND FEARSOME SNACKER!

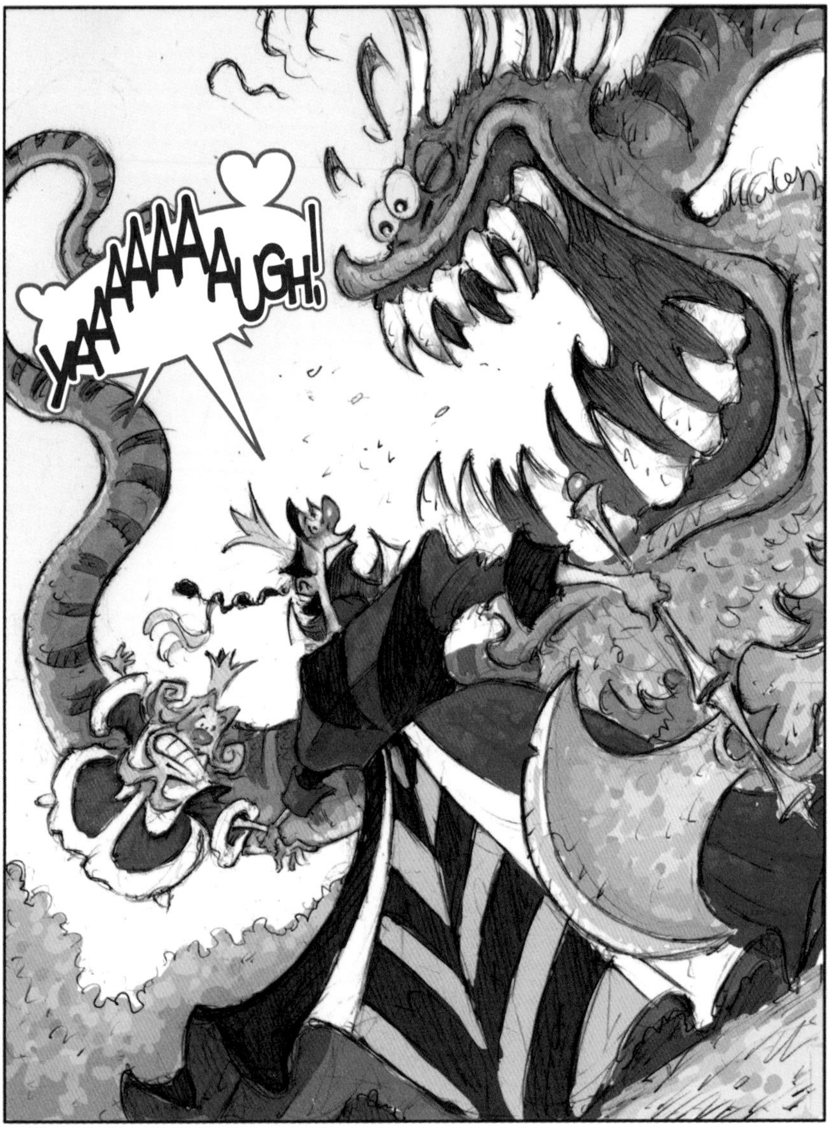
YAAAAAAAAUGH!

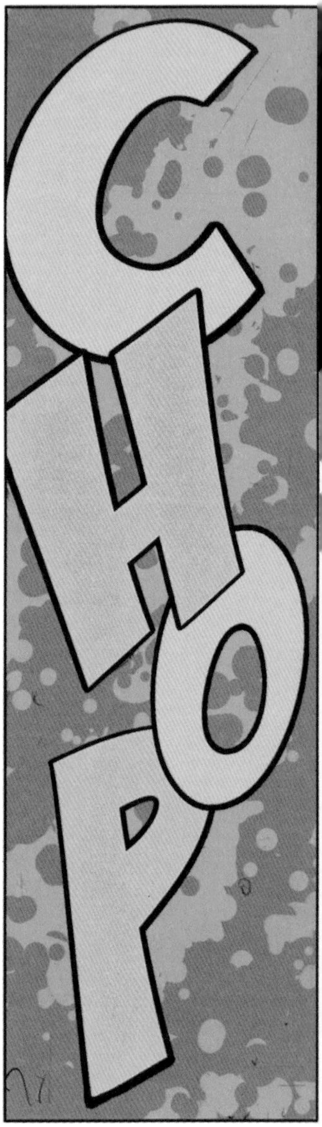
CHOP

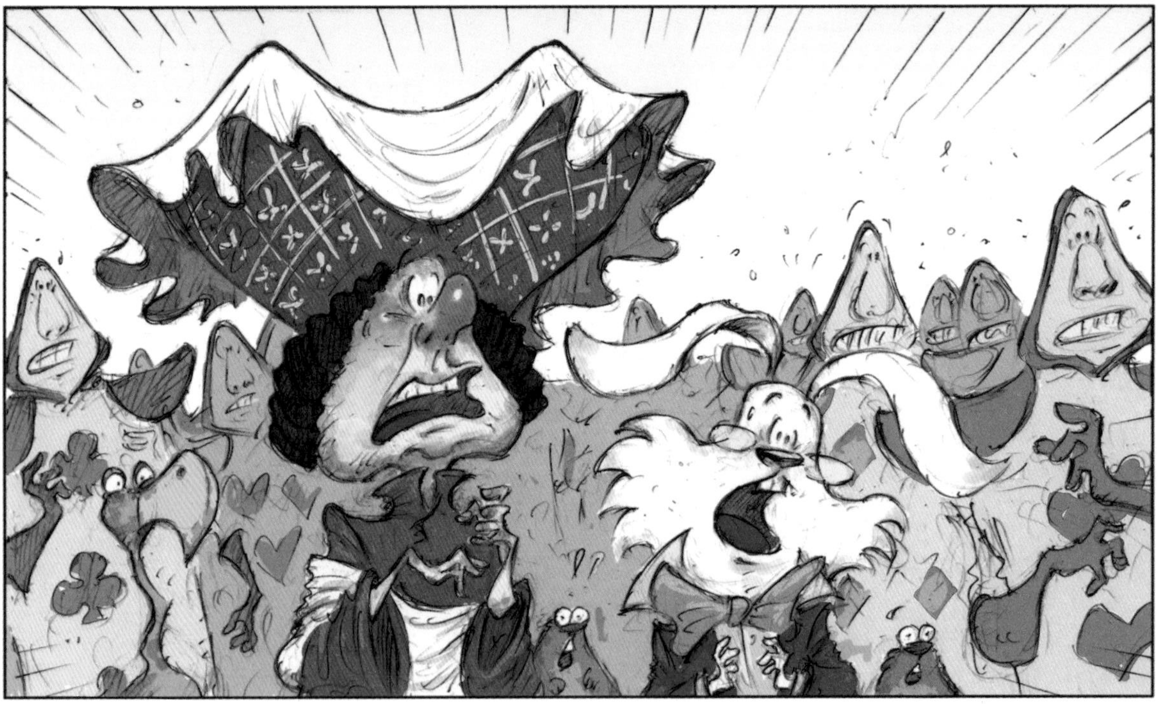

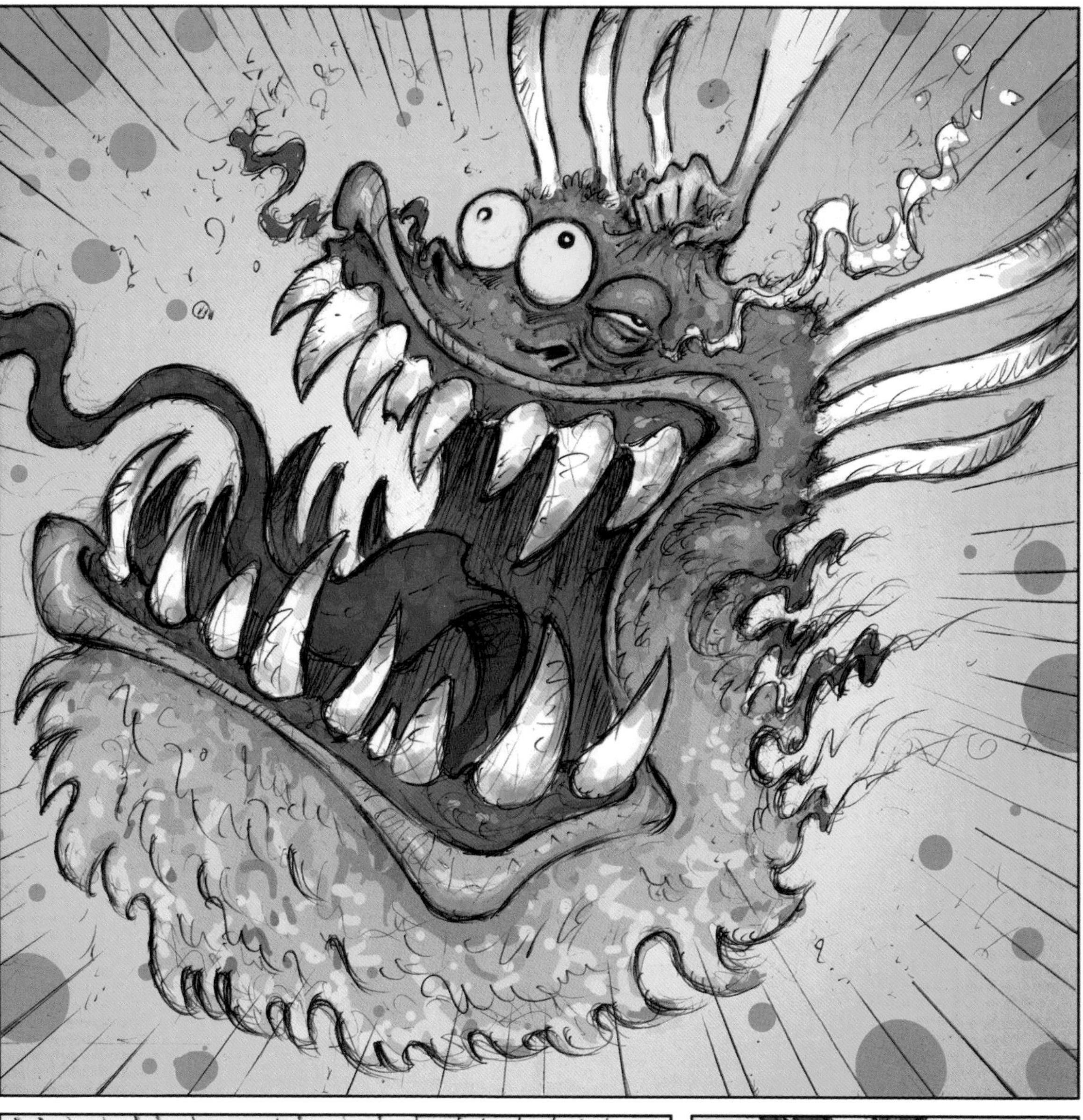

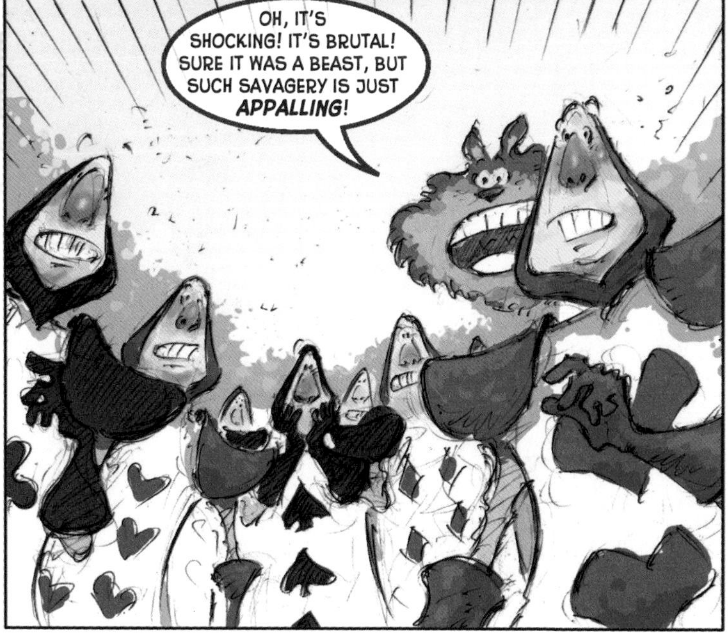
OH, IT'S SHOCKING! IT'S BRUTAL! SURE IT WAS A BEAST, BUT SUCH SAVAGERY IS JUST **APPALLING**!

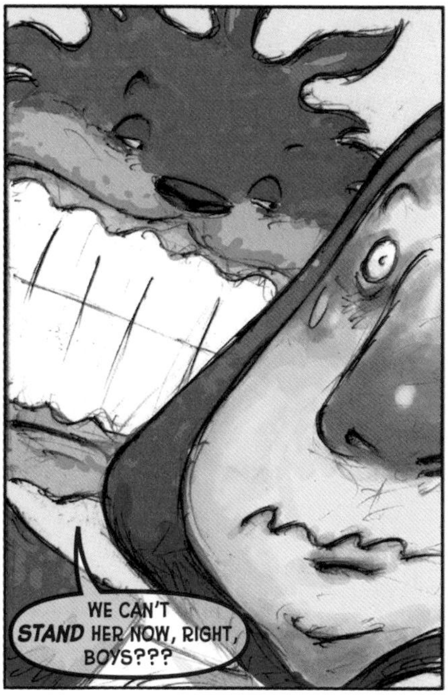
WE CAN'T **STAND** HER NOW, RIGHT, BOYS???

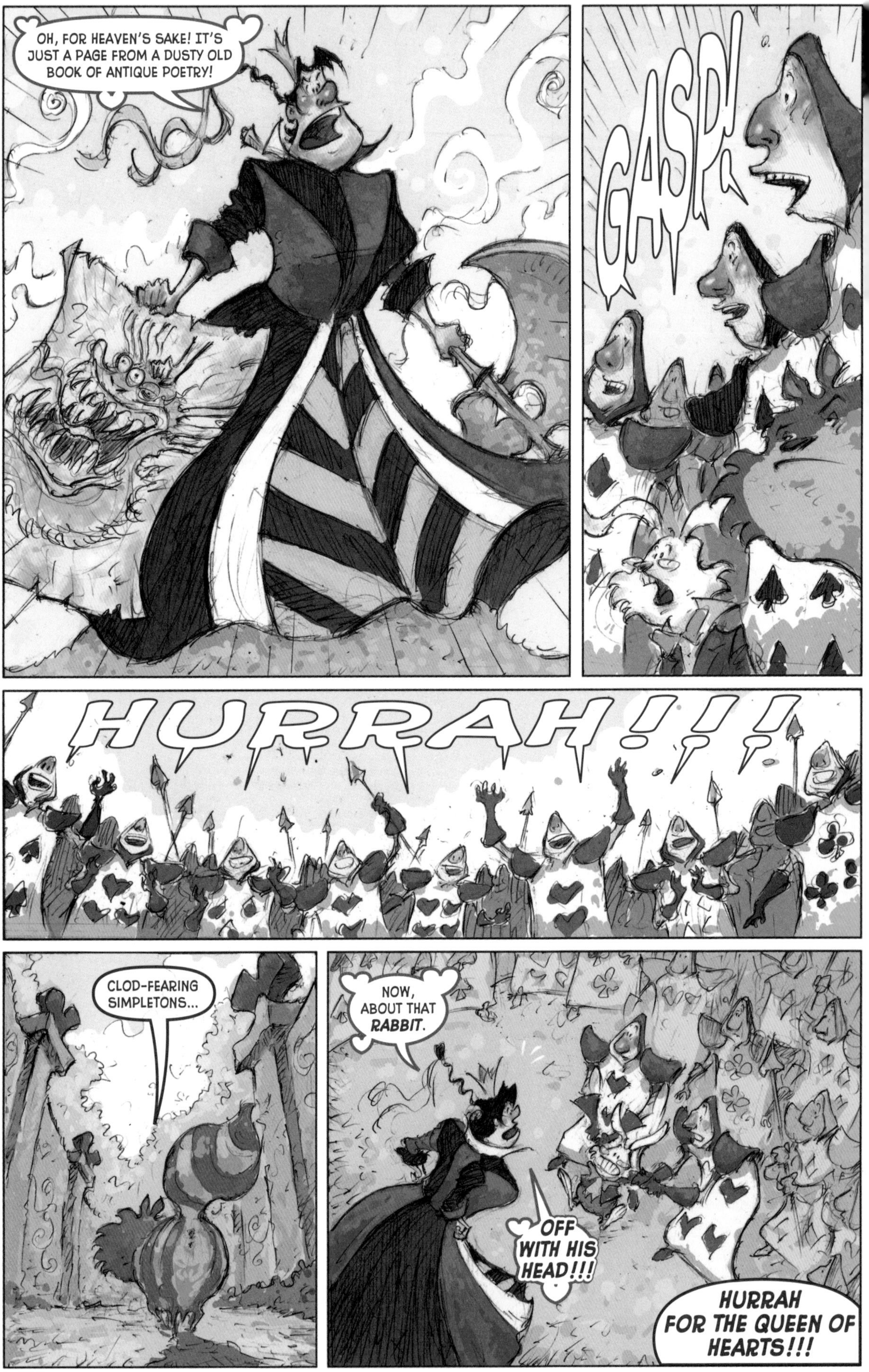
OH, FOR HEAVEN'S SAKE! IT'S JUST A PAGE FROM A DUSTY OLD BOOK OF ANTIQUE POETRY!
GASP!
HURRAH!!!
CLOD-FEARING SIMPLETONS...
NOW, ABOUT THAT *RABBIT*.
OFF WITH HIS HEAD!!!
HURRAH FOR THE QUEEN OF HEARTS!!!

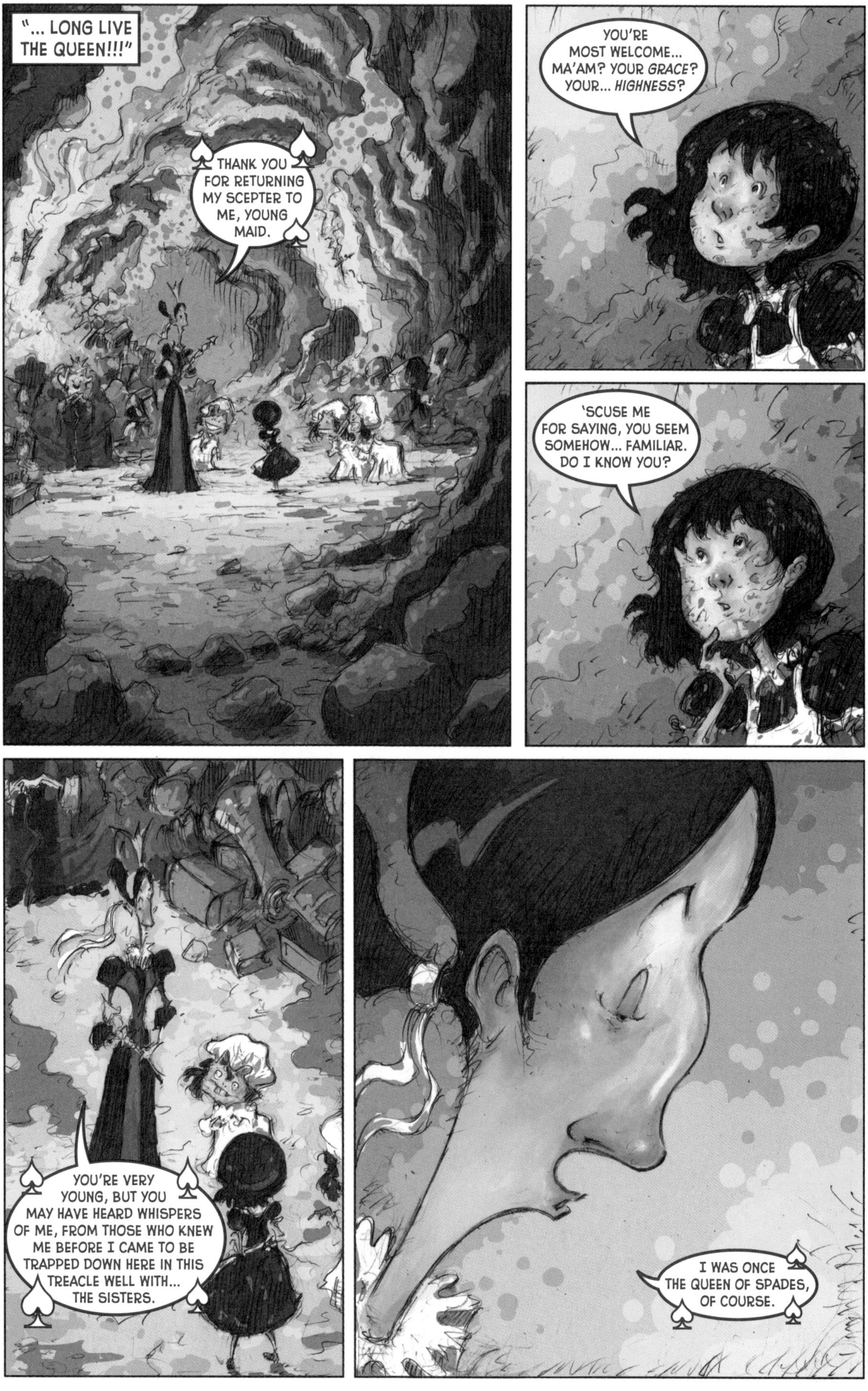
"... LONG LIVE THE QUEEN!!!"
THANK YOU FOR RETURNING MY SCEPTER TO ME, YOUNG MAID.
YOU'RE MOST WELCOME... MA'AM? YOUR *GRACE*? YOUR... *HIGHNESS*?
'SCUSE ME FOR SAYING, YOU SEEM SOMEHOW... FAMILIAR. DO I KNOW YOU?
YOU'RE VERY YOUNG, BUT YOU MAY HAVE HEARD WHISPERS OF ME, FROM THOSE WHO KNEW ME BEFORE I CAME TO BE TRAPPED DOWN HERE IN THIS TREACLE WELL WITH... THE SISTERS.
I WAS ONCE THE QUEEN OF SPADES, OF COURSE.

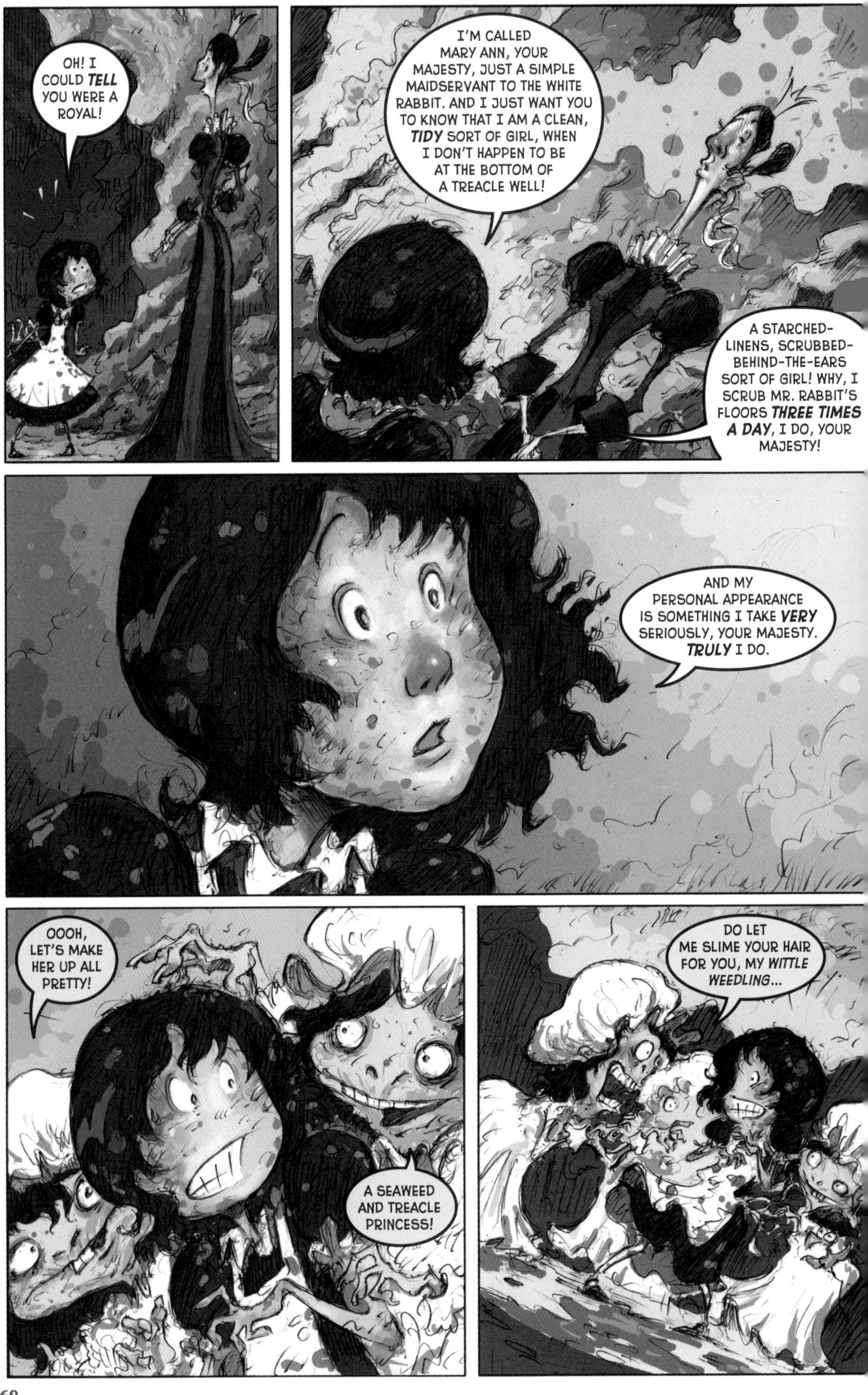
OH! I COULD **TELL** YOU WERE A ROYAL!
I'M CALLED MARY ANN, YOUR MAJESTY, JUST A SIMPLE MAIDSERVANT TO THE WHITE RABBIT. AND I JUST WANT YOU TO KNOW THAT I AM A CLEAN, **TIDY** SORT OF GIRL, WHEN I DON'T HAPPEN TO BE AT THE BOTTOM OF A TREACLE WELL!
A STARCHED-LINENS, SCRUBBED-BEHIND-THE-EARS SORT OF GIRL! WHY, I SCRUB MR. RABBIT'S FLOORS **THREE TIMES A DAY**, I DO, YOUR MAJESTY!
AND MY PERSONAL APPEARANCE IS SOMETHING I TAKE **VERY** SERIOUSLY, YOUR MAJESTY. **TRULY** I DO.
OOOH, LET'S MAKE HER UP ALL PRETTY!
A SEAWEED AND TREACLE PRINCESS!
DO LET ME SLIME YOUR HAIR FOR YOU, MY *WITTLE WEEDLING*...

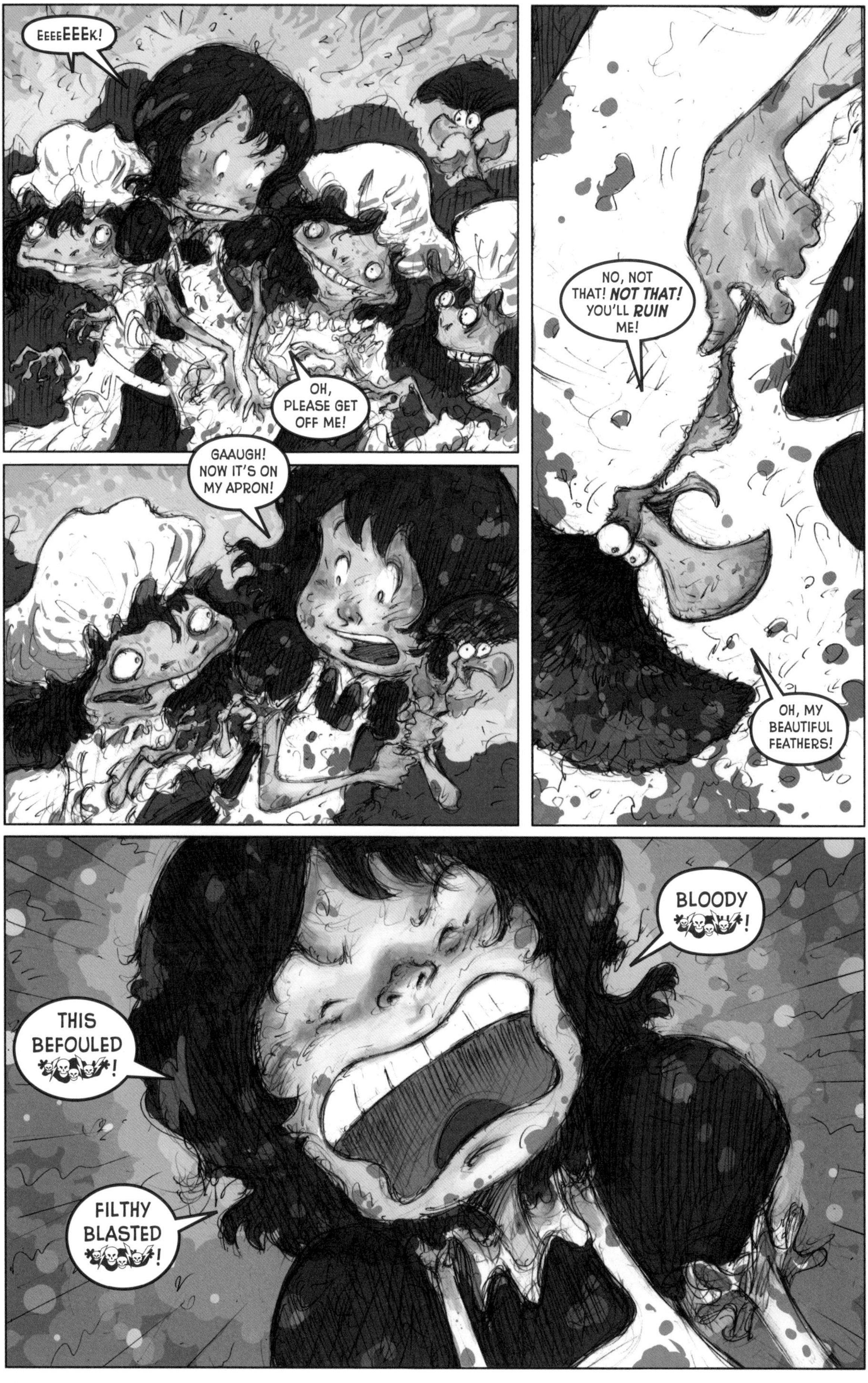
EEEEEEEK!
OH, PLEASE GET OFF ME!
NO, NOT THAT! NOT THAT! YOU'LL RUIN ME!
OH, MY BEAUTIFUL FEATHERS!
GAAUGH! NOW IT'S ON MY APRON!
BLOODY !
THIS BEFOULED !
FILTHY BLASTED !

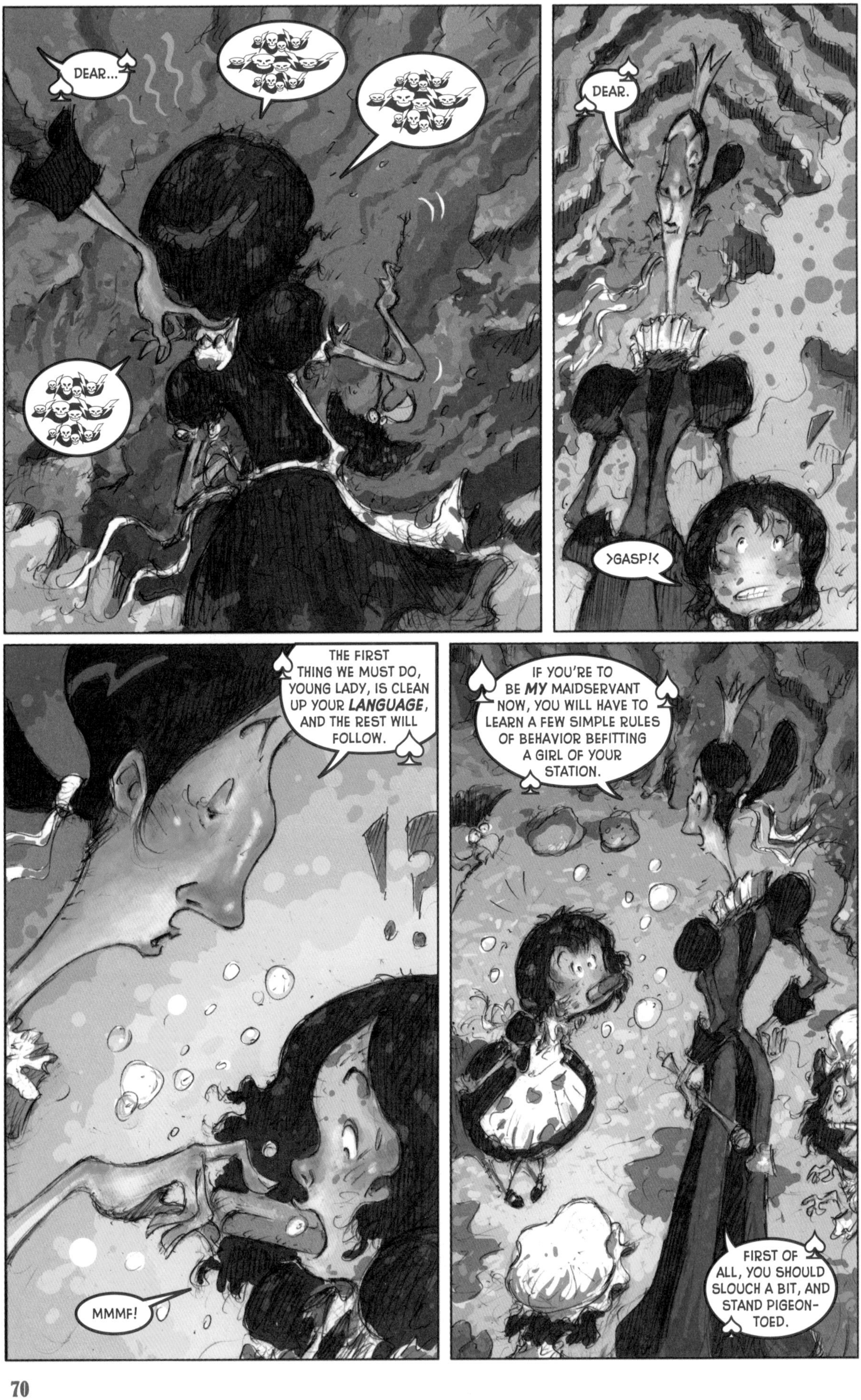
DEAR...
DEAR.
>GASP!<
THE FIRST THING WE MUST DO, YOUNG LADY, IS CLEAN UP YOUR *LANGUAGE*, AND THE REST WILL FOLLOW.
MMMF!
IF YOU'RE TO BE *MY* MAIDSERVANT NOW, YOU WILL HAVE TO LEARN A FEW SIMPLE RULES OF BEHAVIOR BEFITTING A GIRL OF YOUR STATION.
FIRST OF ALL, YOU SHOULD SLOUCH A BIT, AND STAND PIGEON-TOED.

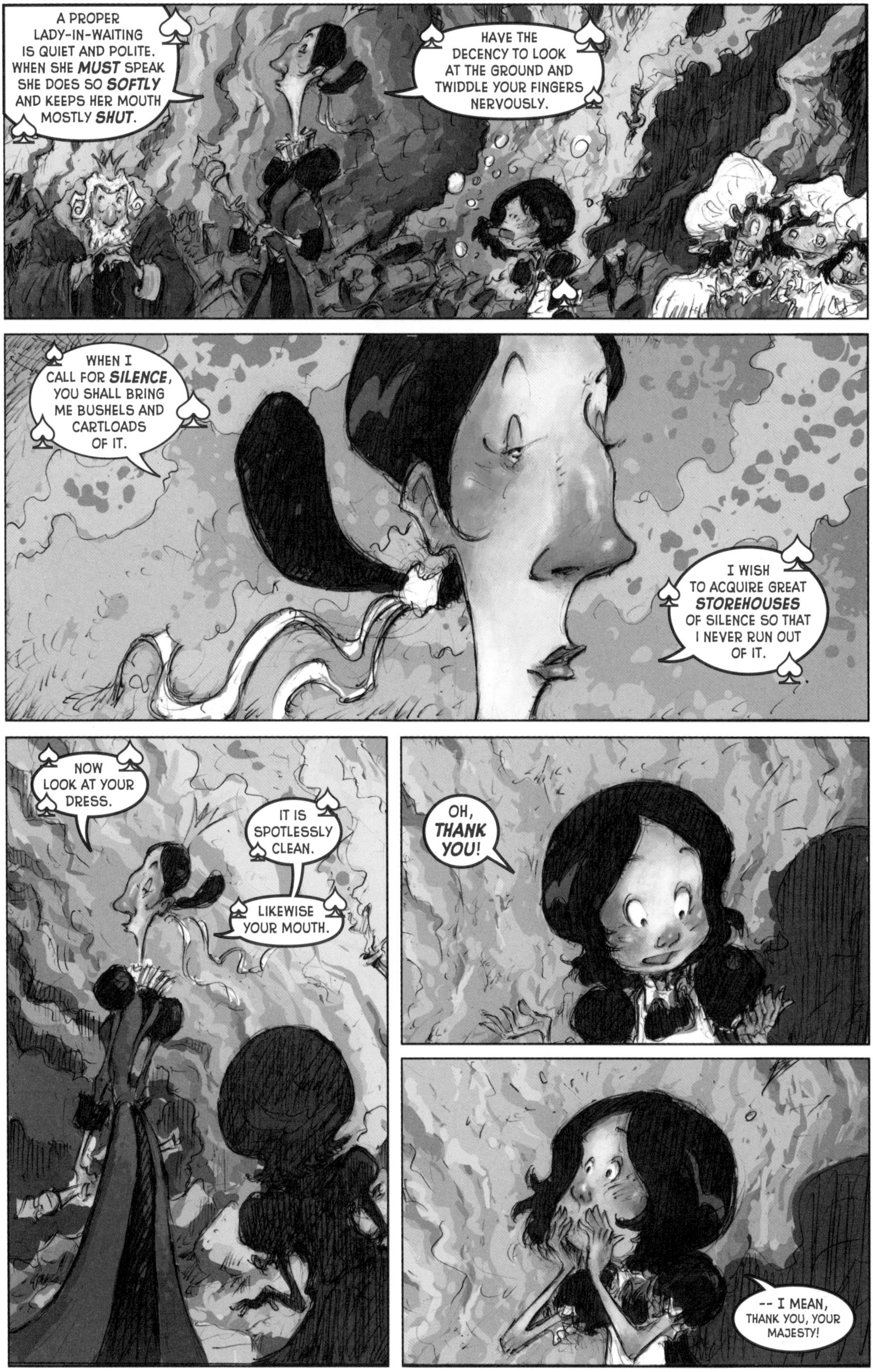

A PROPER LADY-IN-WAITING IS QUIET AND POLITE. WHEN SHE **MUST** SPEAK SHE DOES SO **SOFTLY** AND KEEPS HER MOUTH MOSTLY **SHUT**.
HAVE THE DECENCY TO LOOK AT THE GROUND AND TWIDDLE YOUR FINGERS NERVOUSLY.
WHEN I CALL FOR **SILENCE**, YOU SHALL BRING ME BUSHELS AND CARTLOADS OF IT.
I WISH TO ACQUIRE GREAT **STOREHOUSES** OF SILENCE SO THAT I NEVER RUN OUT OF IT.
NOW LOOK AT YOUR DRESS.
IT IS SPOTLESSLY CLEAN.
LIKEWISE YOUR MOUTH.
OH, **THANK YOU**!
-- I MEAN, THANK YOU, YOUR MAJESTY!

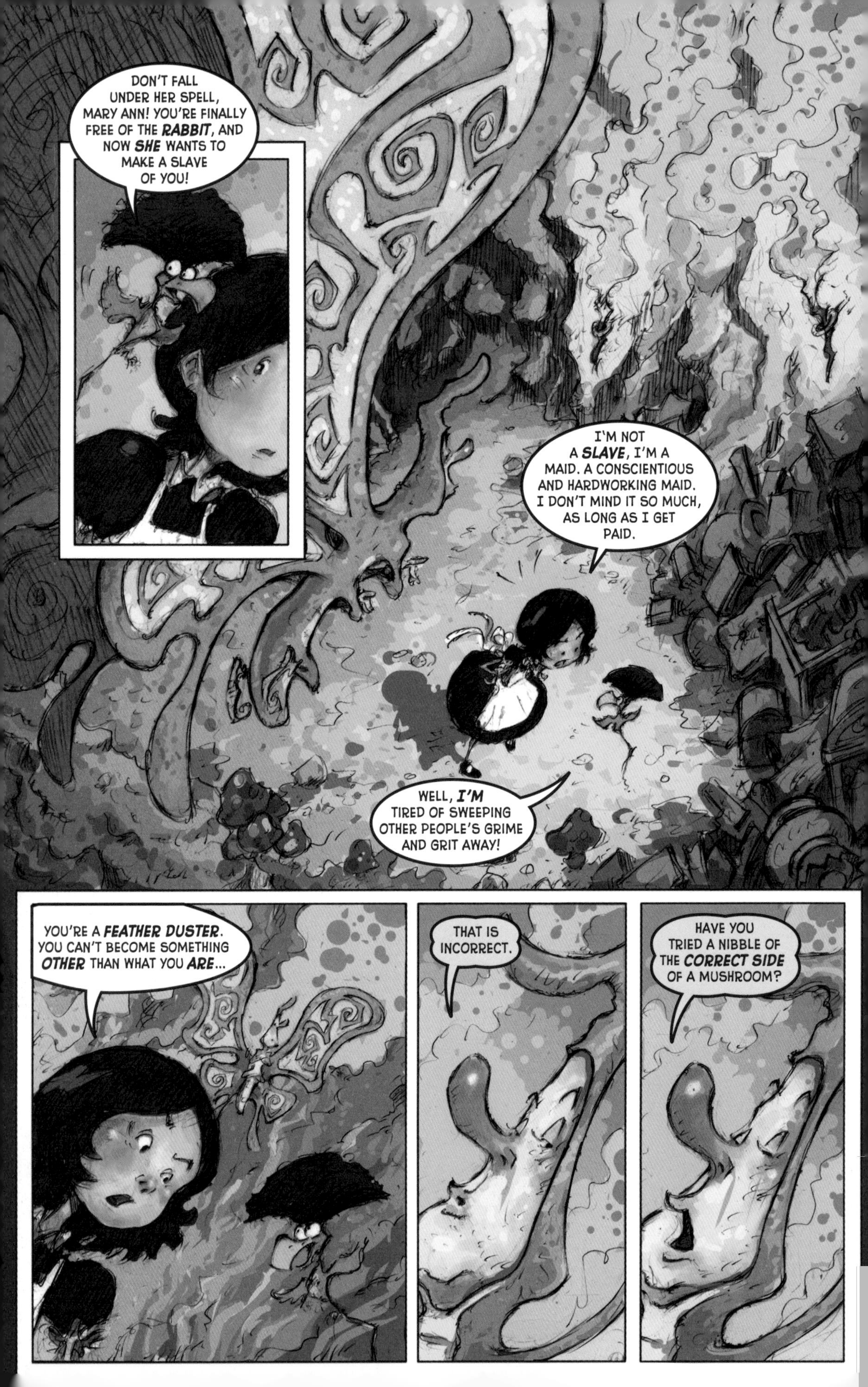
DON'T FALL UNDER HER SPELL, MARY ANN! YOU'RE FINALLY FREE OF THE RABBIT, AND NOW SHE WANTS TO MAKE A SLAVE OF YOU!
I'M NOT A SLAVE, I'M A MAID. A CONSCIENTIOUS AND HARDWORKING MAID. I DON'T MIND IT SO MUCH, AS LONG AS I GET PAID.
WELL, I'M TIRED OF SWEEPING OTHER PEOPLE'S GRIME AND GRIT AWAY!
YOU'RE A FEATHER DUSTER. YOU CAN'T BECOME SOMETHING OTHER THAN WHAT YOU ARE...
THAT IS INCORRECT.
HAVE YOU TRIED A NIBBLE OF THE CORRECT SIDE OF A MUSHROOM?

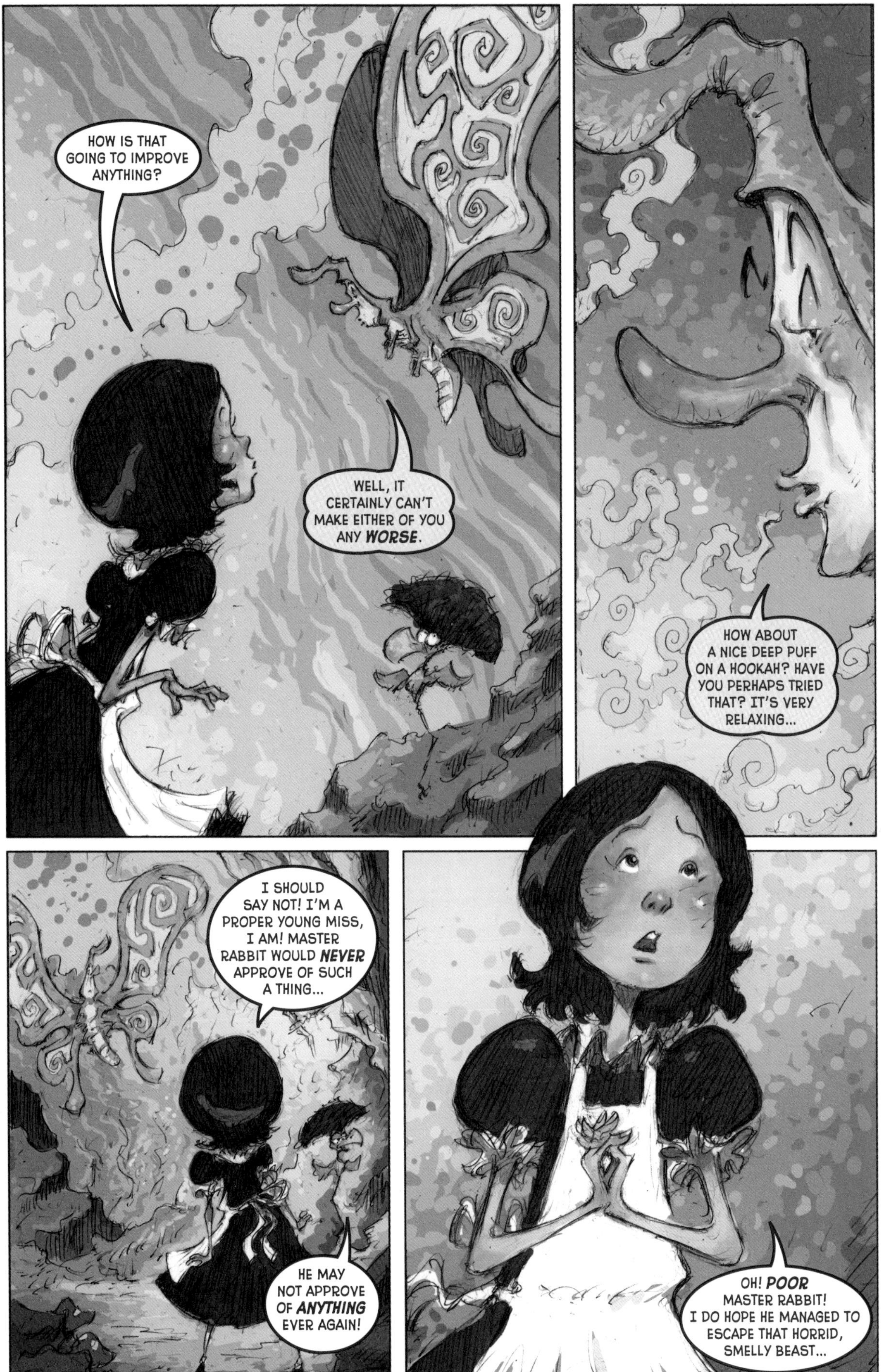
HOW IS THAT GOING TO IMPROVE ANYTHING?
WELL, IT CERTAINLY CAN'T MAKE EITHER OF YOU ANY **WORSE**.
HOW ABOUT A NICE DEEP PUFF ON A HOOKAH? HAVE YOU PERHAPS TRIED THAT? IT'S VERY RELAXING...
I SHOULD SAY NOT! I'M A PROPER YOUNG MISS, I AM! MASTER RABBIT WOULD **NEVER** APPROVE OF SUCH A THING...
HE MAY NOT APPROVE OF **ANYTHING** EVER AGAIN!
OH! **POOR** MASTER RABBIT! I DO HOPE HE MANAGED TO ESCAPE THAT HORRID, SMELLY BEAST...

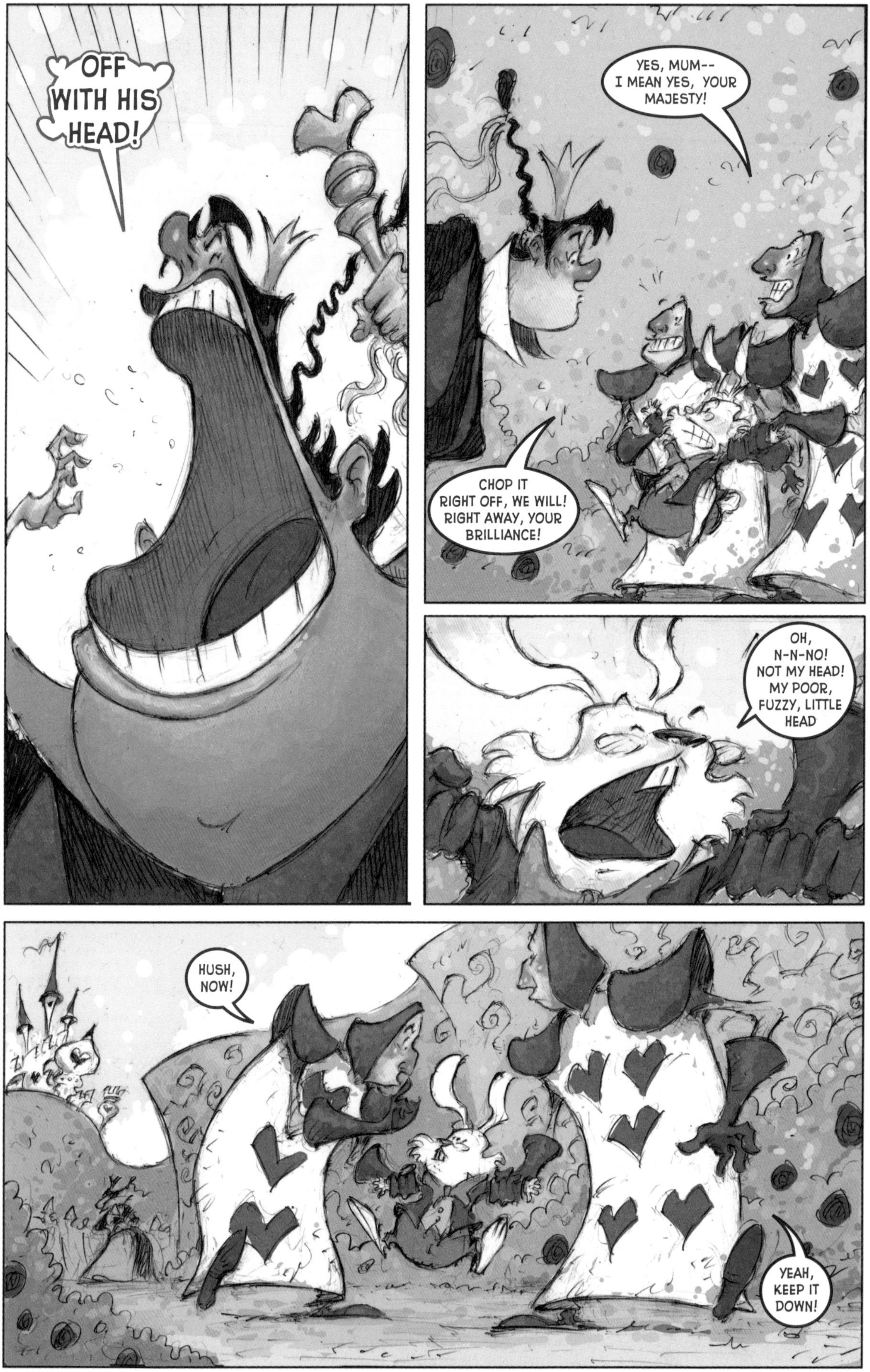
OFF WITH HIS HEAD!
YES, MUM-- I MEAN YES, YOUR MAJESTY!
CHOP IT RIGHT OFF, WE WILL! RIGHT AWAY, YOUR BRILLIANCE!
OH, N-N-NO! NOT MY HEAD! MY POOR, FUZZY, LITTLE HEAD
HUSH, NOW!
YEAH, KEEP IT DOWN!

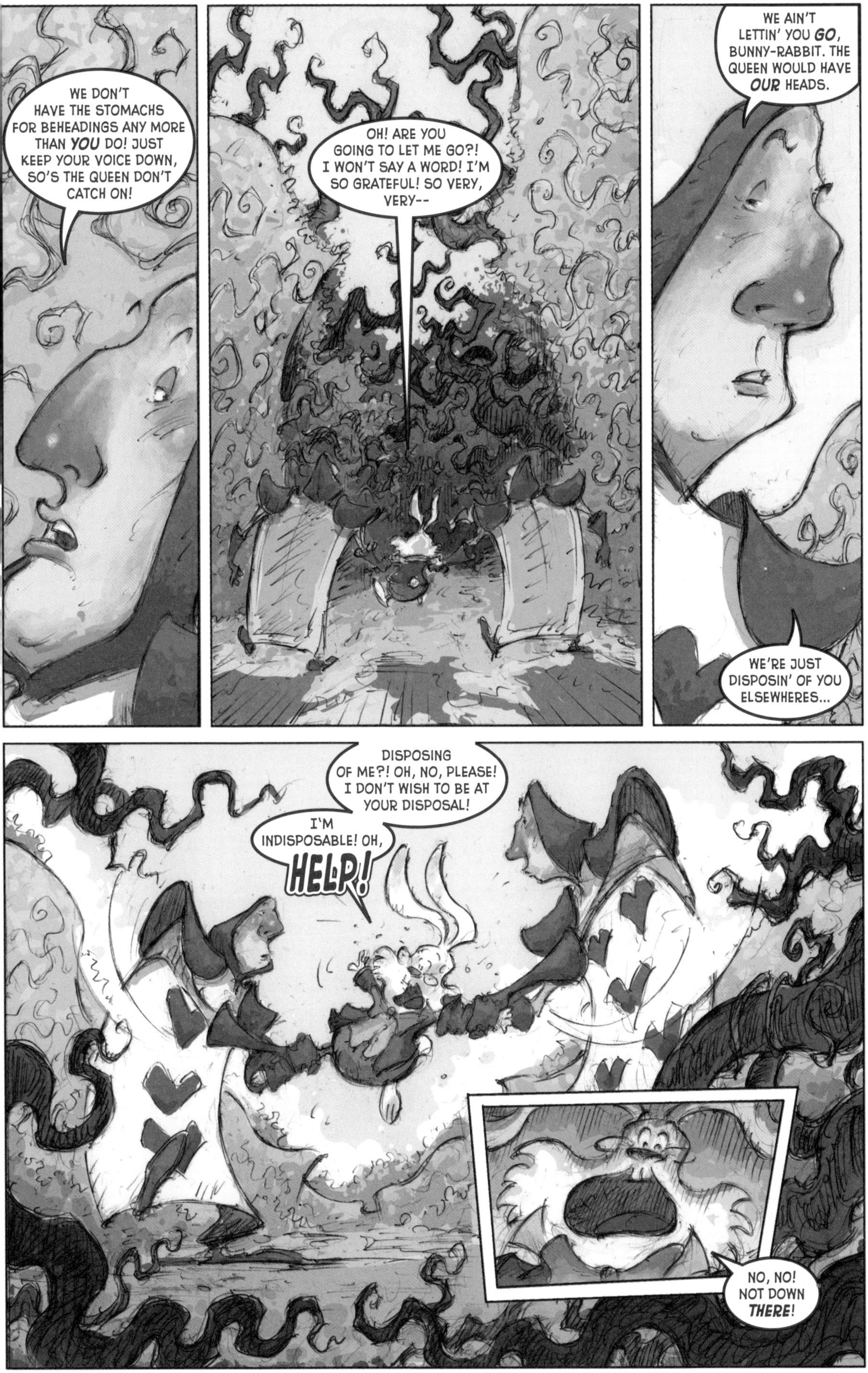
WE DON'T HAVE THE STOMACHS FOR BEHEADINGS ANY MORE THAN YOU DO! JUST KEEP YOUR VOICE DOWN, SO'S THE QUEEN DON'T CATCH ON!
OH! ARE YOU GOING TO LET ME GO?! I WON'T SAY A WORD! I'M SO GRATEFUL! SO VERY, VERY--
WE AIN'T LETTIN' YOU GO, BUNNY-RABBIT. THE QUEEN WOULD HAVE OUR HEADS.
WE'RE JUST DISPOSIN' OF YOU ELSEWHERES...
DISPOSING OF ME?! OH, NO, PLEASE! I DON'T WISH TO BE AT YOUR DISPOSAL!
I'M INDISPOSABLE! OH, HELP!
NO, NO! NOT DOWN THERE!

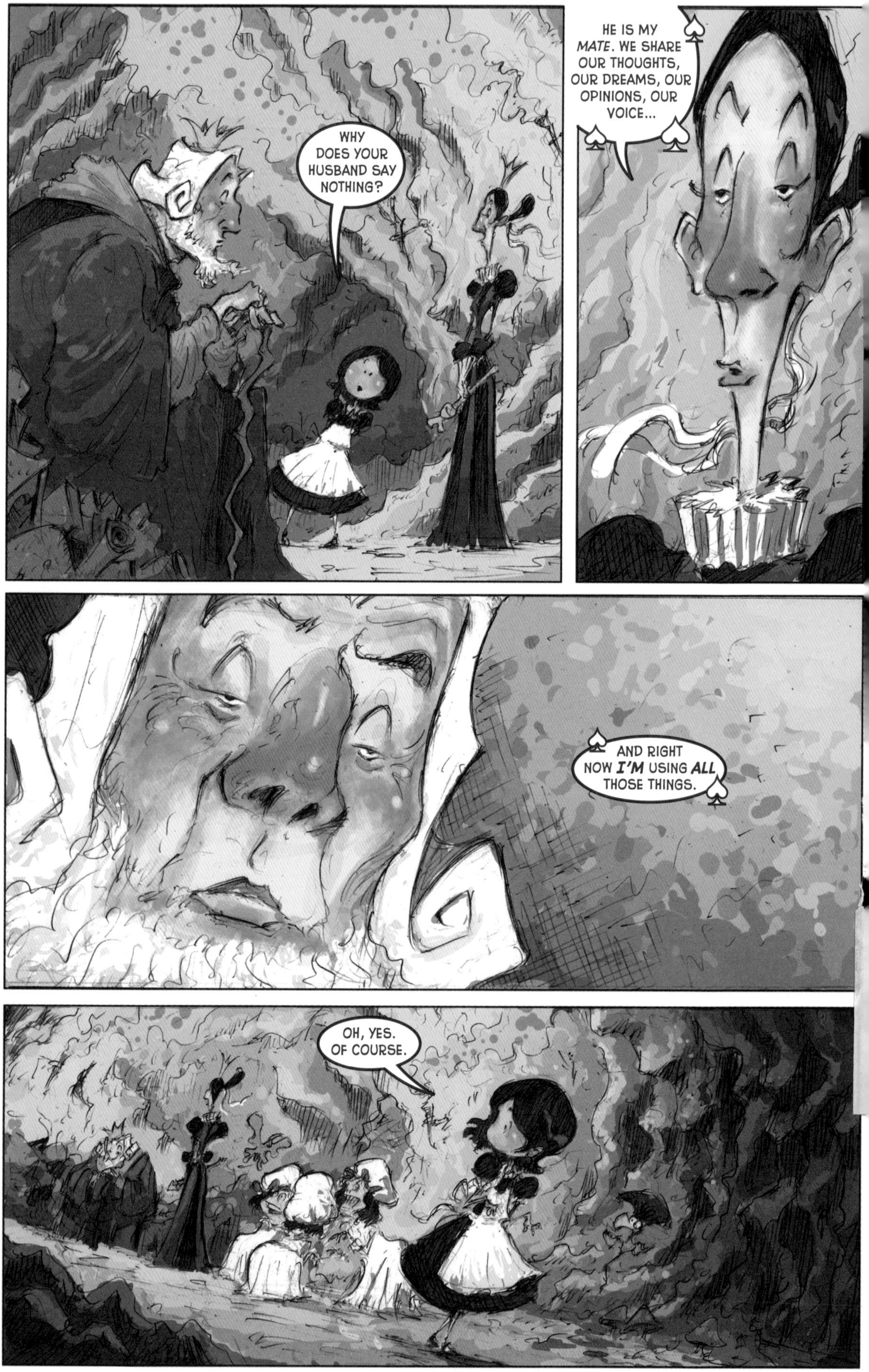
WHY DOES YOUR HUSBAND SAY NOTHING?
HE IS MY MATE. WE SHARE OUR THOUGHTS, OUR DREAMS, OUR OPINIONS, OUR VOICE...
AND RIGHT NOW I'M USING ALL THOSE THINGS.
OH, YES. OF COURSE.

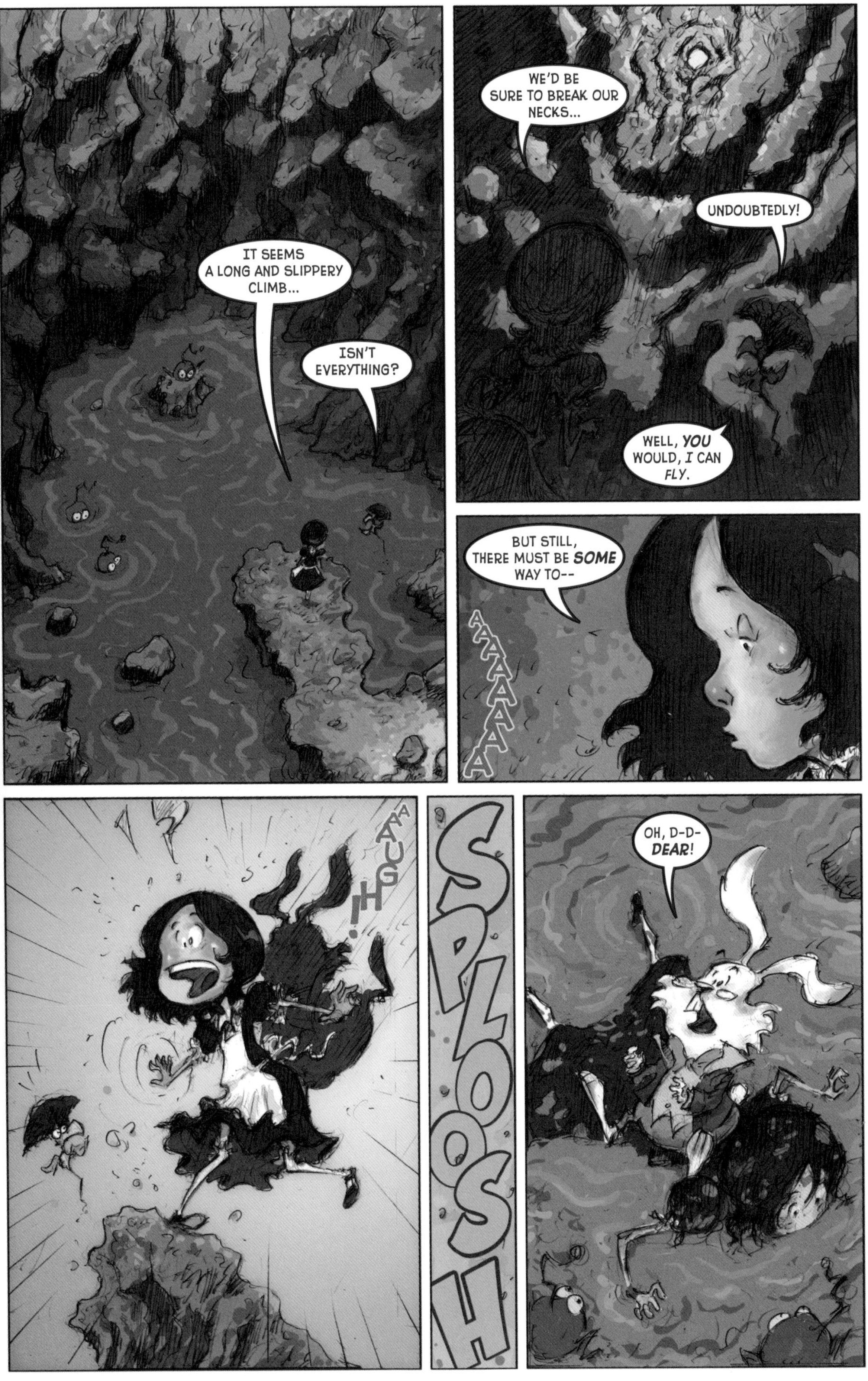
IT SEEMS A LONG AND SLIPPERY CLIMB...
ISN'T EVERYTHING?
WE'D BE SURE TO BREAK OUR NECKS...
UNDOUBTEDLY!
WELL, YOU WOULD, I CAN FLY.
BUT STILL, THERE MUST BE SOME WAY TO--
AAAAAAAA
AAAUGH!
SPLOOSH
OH, D-D-DEAR!

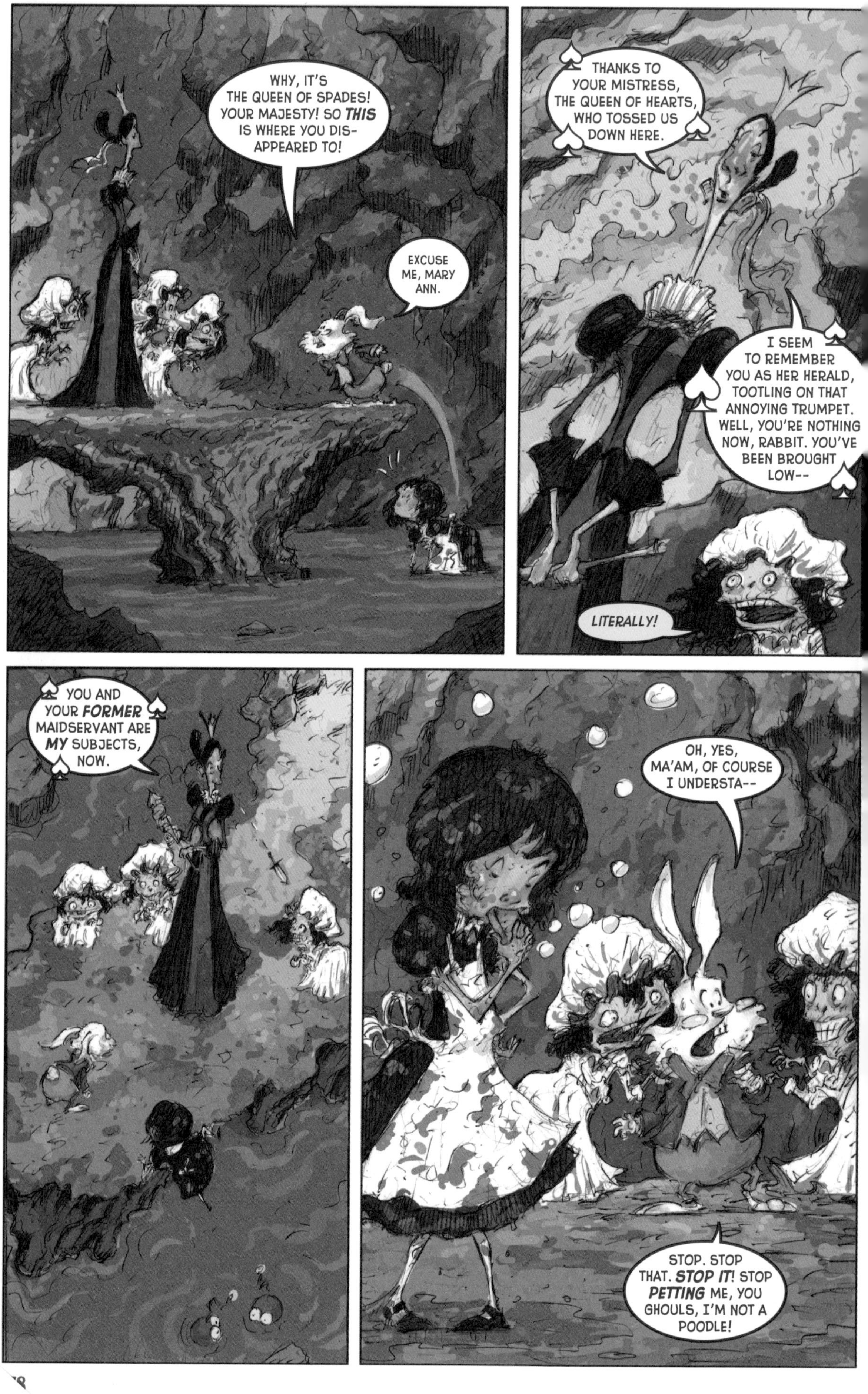
WHY, IT'S THE QUEEN OF SPADES! YOUR MAJESTY! SO THIS IS WHERE YOU DIS-APPEARED TO!
EXCUSE ME, MARY ANN.
THANKS TO YOUR MISTRESS, THE QUEEN OF HEARTS, WHO TOSSED US DOWN HERE.
I SEEM TO REMEMBER YOU AS HER HERALD, TOOTLING ON THAT ANNOYING TRUMPET. WELL, YOU'RE NOTHING NOW, RABBIT. YOU'VE BEEN BROUGHT LOW--
LITERALLY!
YOU AND YOUR FORMER MAIDSERVANT ARE MY SUBJECTS, NOW.
OH, YES, MA'AM, OF COURSE I UNDERSTA--
STOP. STOP THAT. STOP IT! STOP PETTING ME, YOU GHOULS, I'M NOT A POODLE!

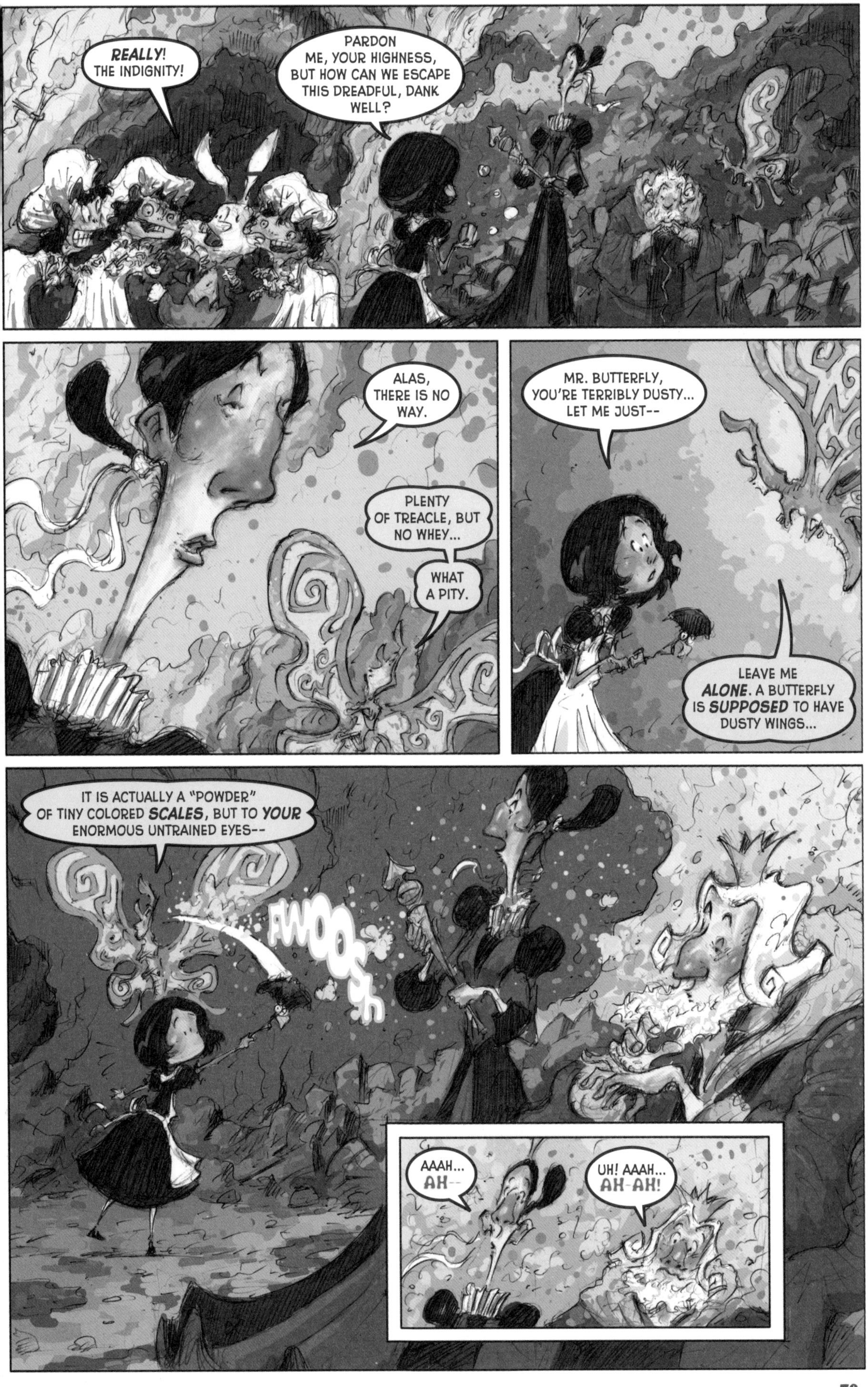
REALLY! THE INDIGNITY!
PARDON ME, YOUR HIGHNESS, BUT HOW CAN WE ESCAPE THIS DREADFUL, DANK WELL?
ALAS, THERE IS NO WAY.
PLENTY OF TREACLE, BUT NO WHEY...
WHAT A PITY.
MR. BUTTERFLY, YOU'RE TERRIBLY DUSTY... LET ME JUST--
LEAVE ME ALONE. A BUTTERFLY IS SUPPOSED TO HAVE DUSTY WINGS...
IT IS ACTUALLY A "POWDER" OF TINY COLORED SCALES, BUT TO YOUR ENORMOUS UNTRAINED EYES--
FWOOSh
AAAH... AH--
UH! AAAH... AH-AH!

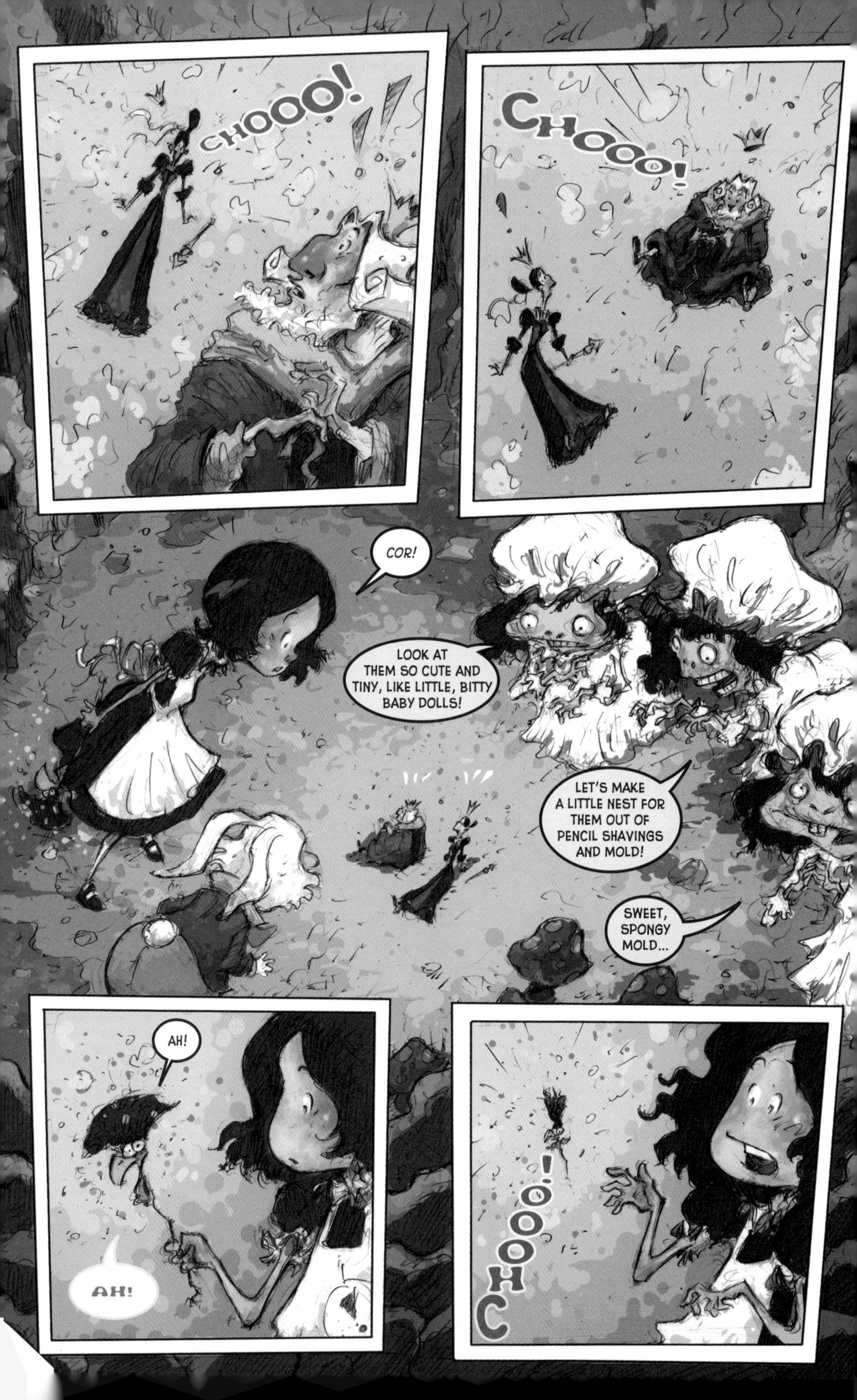
CHOOO!
CHOOOO!
COR!
LOOK AT THEM SO CUTE AND TINY, LIKE LITTLE, BITTY BABY DOLLS!
LET'S MAKE A LITTLE NEST FOR THEM OUT OF PENCIL SHAVINGS AND MOLD!
SWEET, SPONGY MOLD...
AH!
AH!
CHOOOO!

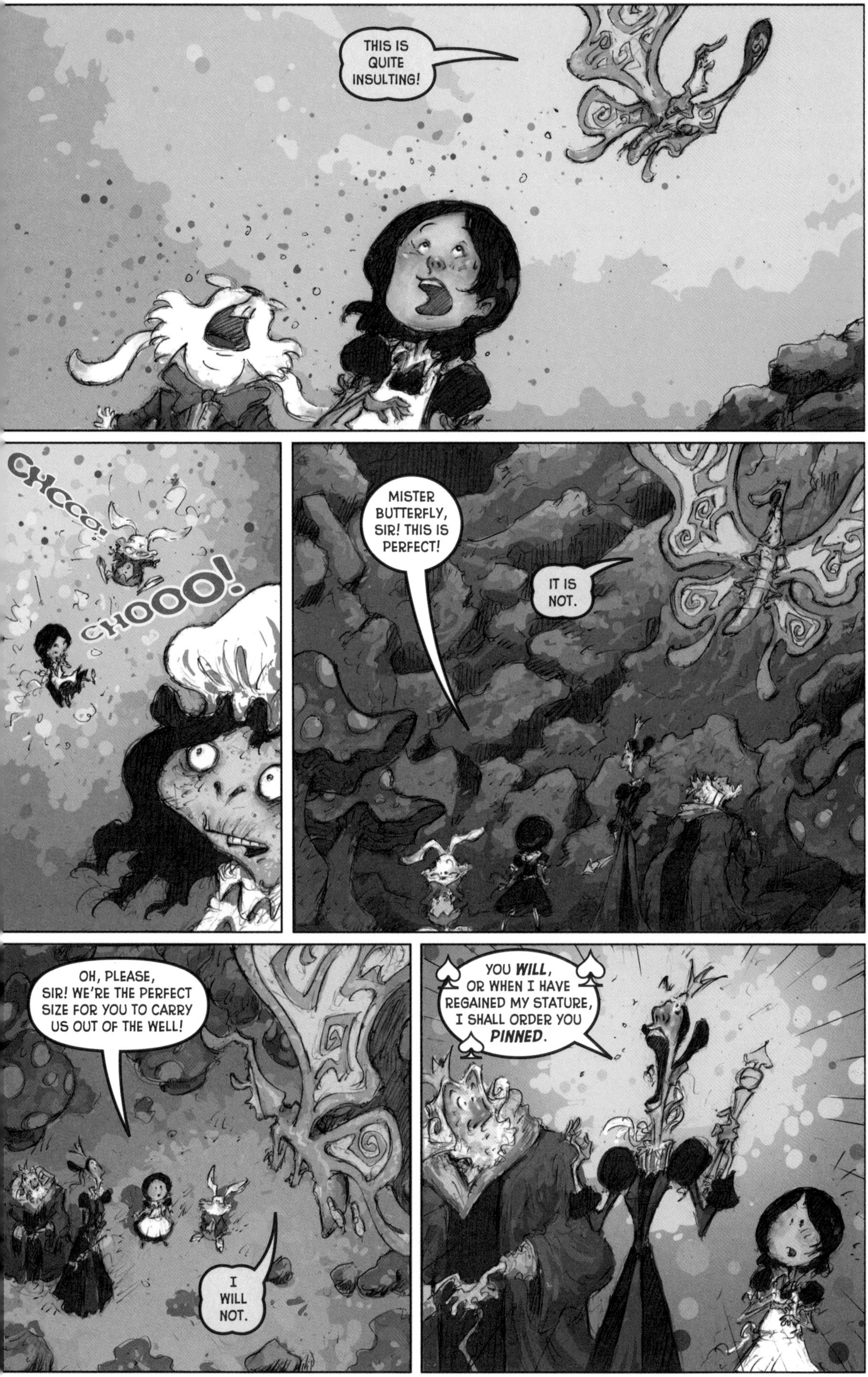
THIS IS QUITE INSULTING!
CHOOO!
CHOOOO!
MISTER BUTTERFLY, SIR! THIS IS PERFECT!
IT IS NOT.
OH, PLEASE, SIR! WE'RE THE PERFECT SIZE FOR YOU TO CARRY US OUT OF THE WELL!
I WILL NOT.
YOU **WILL**, OR WHEN I HAVE REGAINED MY STATURE, I SHALL ORDER YOU **PINNED**.

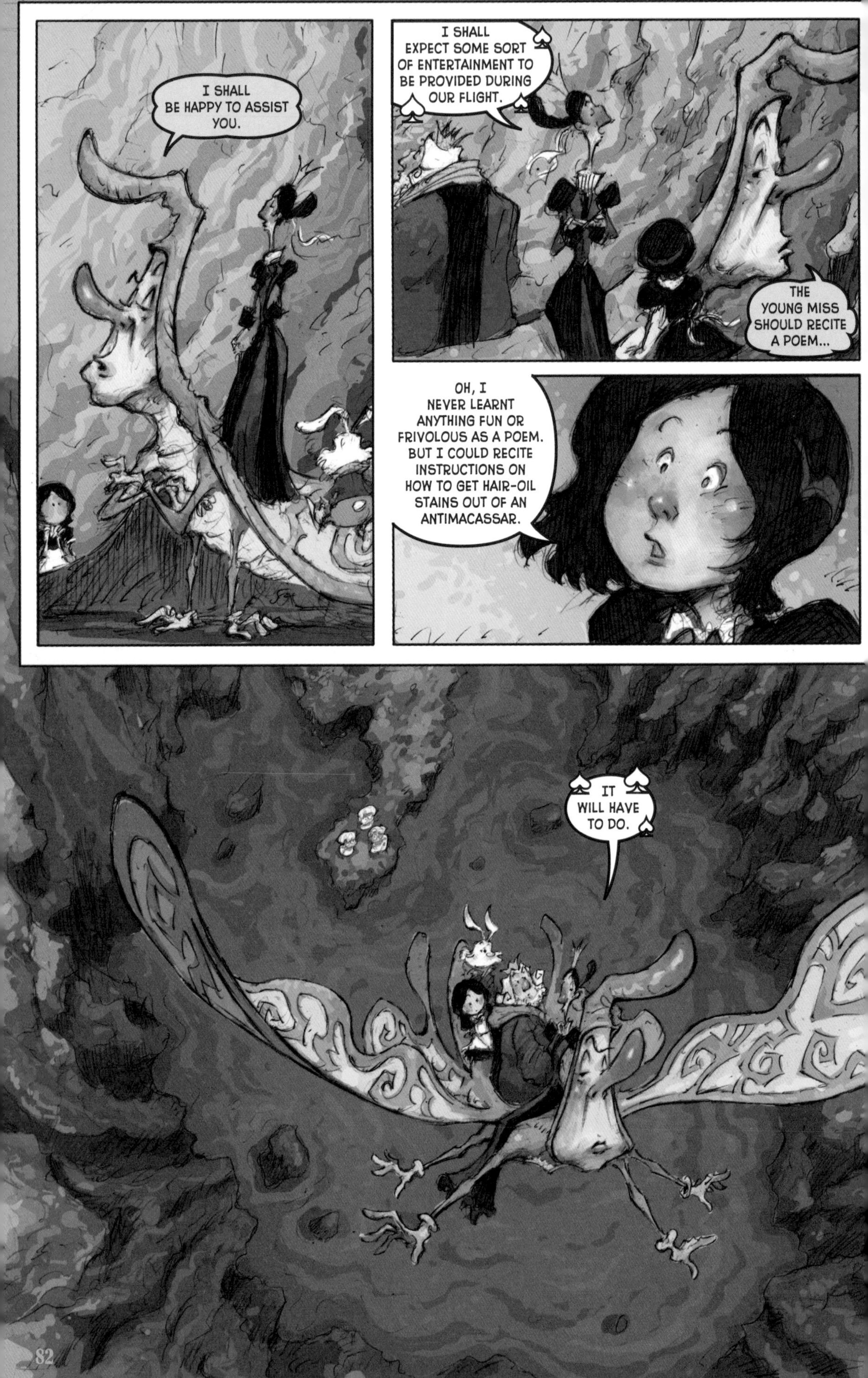
I SHALL BE HAPPY TO ASSIST YOU.
I SHALL EXPECT SOME SORT OF ENTERTAINMENT TO BE PROVIDED DURING OUR FLIGHT.
THE YOUNG MISS SHOULD RECITE A POEM...
OH, I NEVER LEARNT ANYTHING FUN OR FRIVOLOUS AS A POEM. BUT I COULD RECITE INSTRUCTIONS ON HOW TO GET HAIR-OIL STAINS OUT OF AN ANTIMACASSAR.
IT WILL HAVE TO DO.

Chapter Four
The Curious

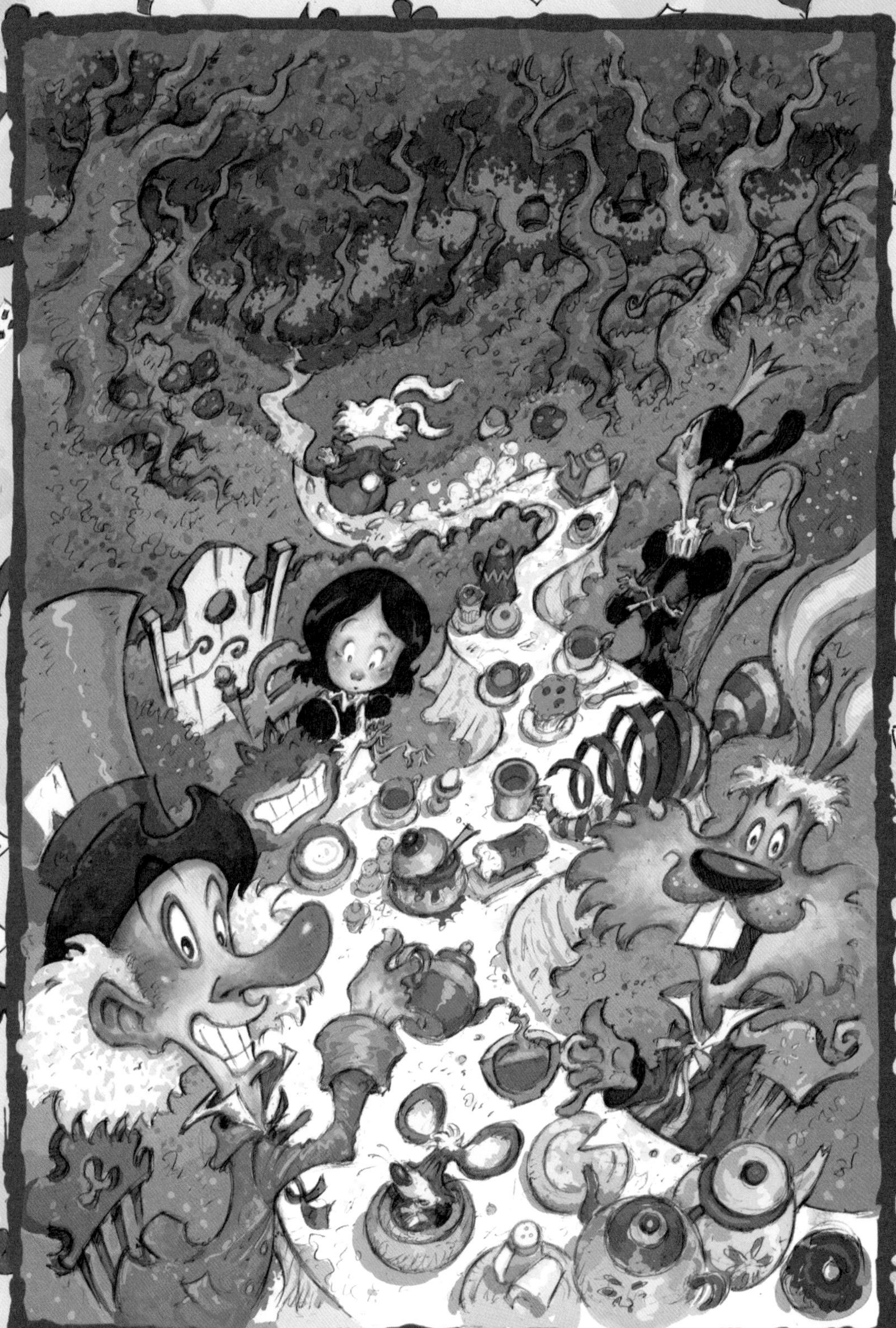

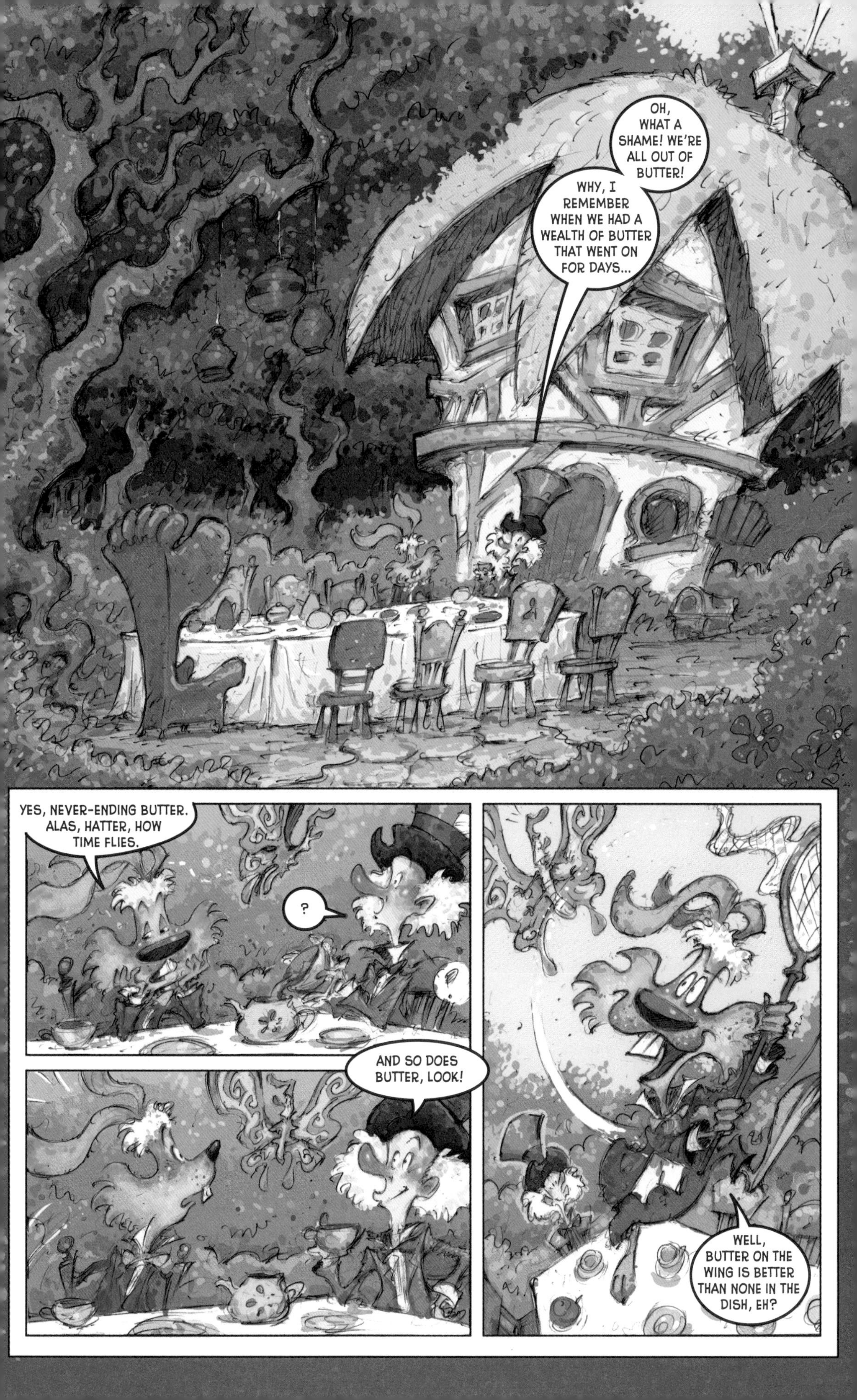
OH, WHAT A SHAME! WE'RE ALL OUT OF BUTTER!
WHY, I REMEMBER WHEN WE HAD A WEALTH OF BUTTER THAT WENT ON FOR DAYS...
YES, NEVER-ENDING BUTTER. ALAS, HATTER, HOW TIME FLIES.
?
AND SO DOES BUTTER, LOOK!
WELL, BUTTER ON THE WING IS BETTER THAN NONE IN THE DISH, EH?

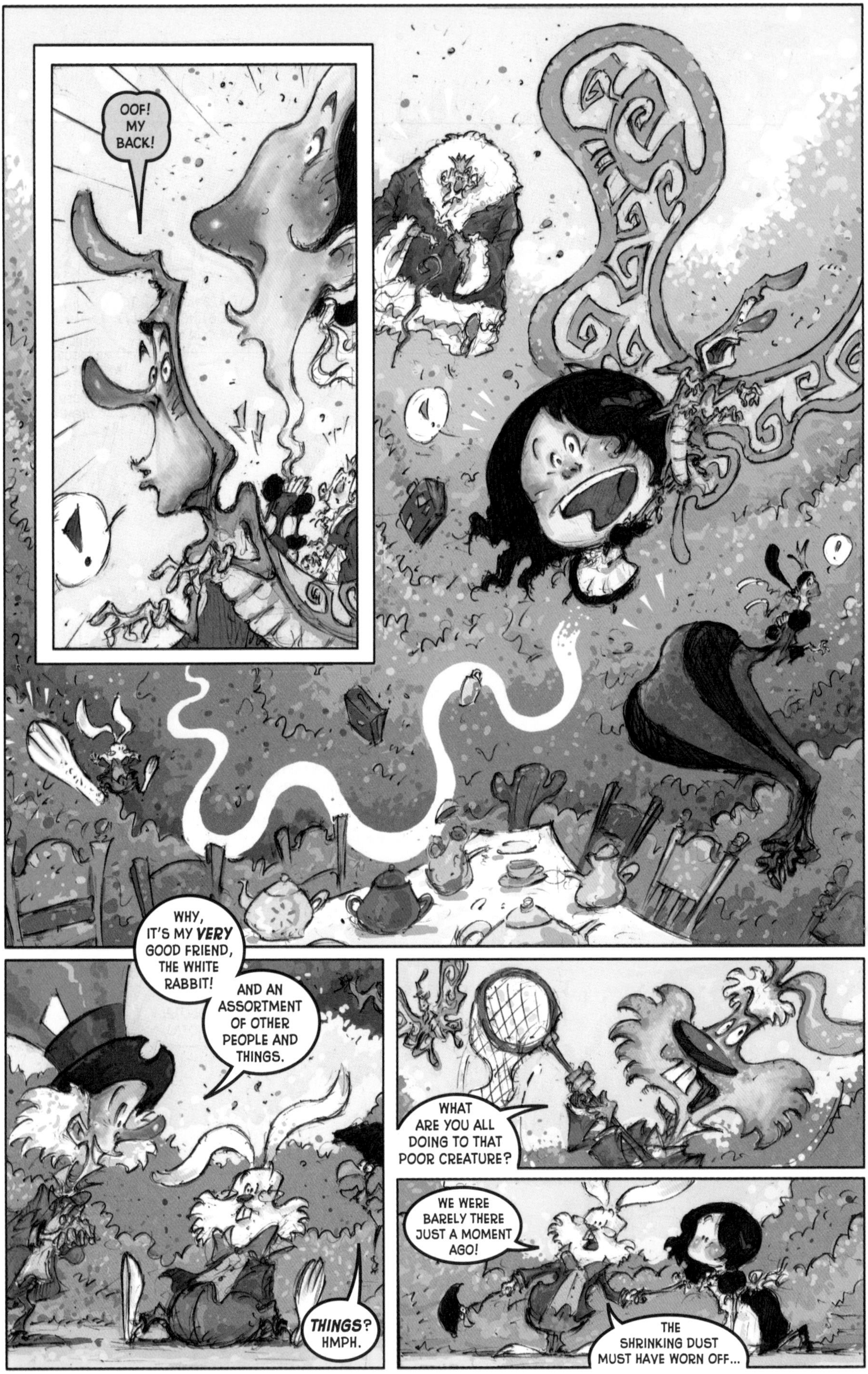
OOF! MY BACK!
WHY, IT'S MY ***VERY*** GOOD FRIEND, THE WHITE RABBIT!
AND AN ASSORTMENT OF OTHER PEOPLE AND THINGS.
THINGS? HMPH.
WHAT ARE YOU ALL DOING TO THAT POOR CREATURE?
WE WERE BARELY THERE JUST A MOMENT AGO!
THE SHRINKING DUST MUST HAVE WORN OFF...

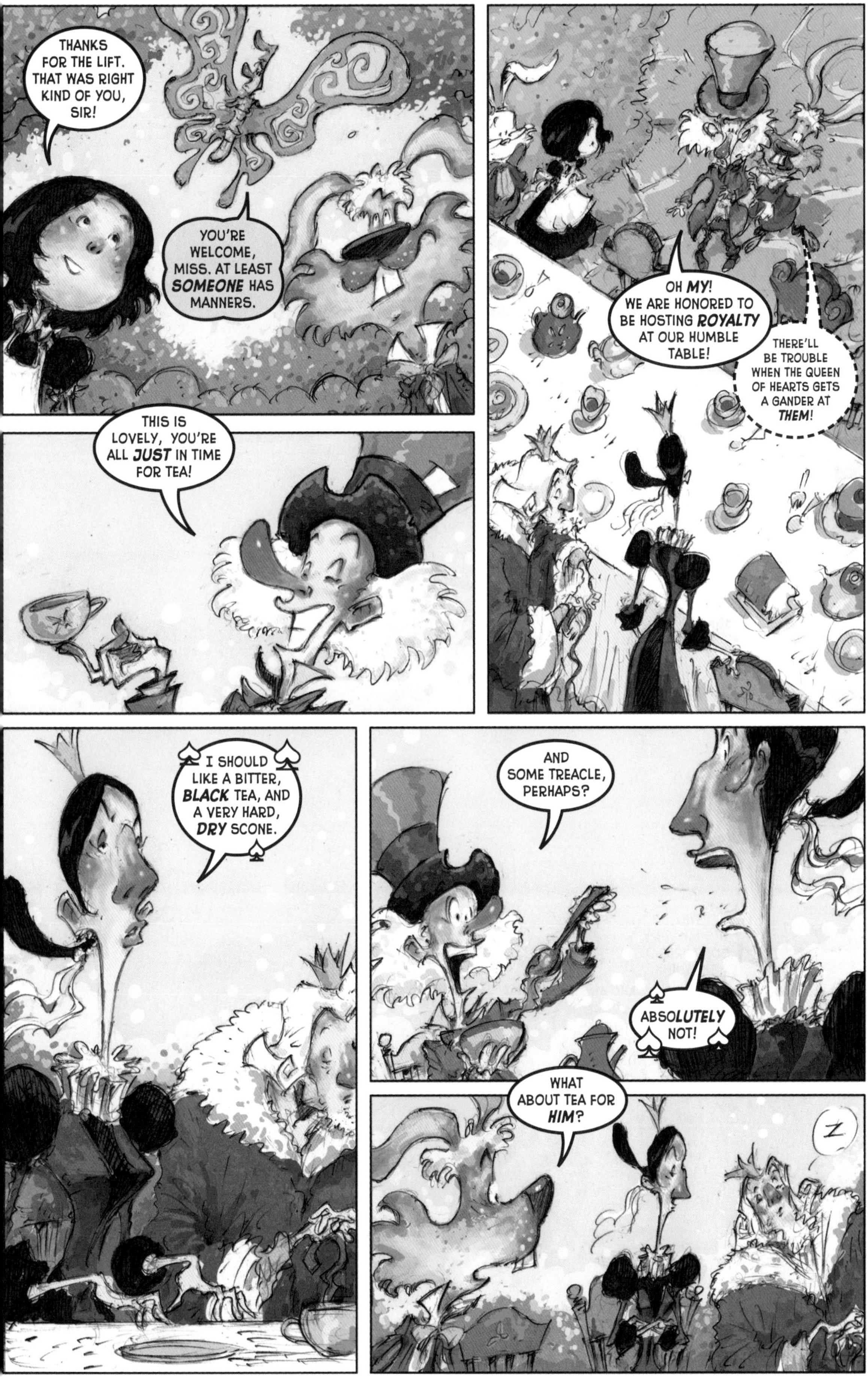
THANKS FOR THE LIFT. THAT WAS RIGHT KIND OF YOU, SIR!
YOU'RE WELCOME, MISS. AT LEAST SOMEONE HAS MANNERS.
OH MY! WE ARE HONORED TO BE HOSTING ROYALTY AT OUR HUMBLE TABLE!
THERE'LL BE TROUBLE WHEN THE QUEEN OF HEARTS GETS A GANDER AT THEM!
THIS IS LOVELY, YOU'RE ALL JUST IN TIME FOR TEA!
I SHOULD LIKE A BITTER, BLACK TEA, AND A VERY HARD, DRY SCONE.
AND SOME TREACLE, PERHAPS?
ABSOLUTELY NOT!
WHAT ABOUT TEA FOR HIM?
Z

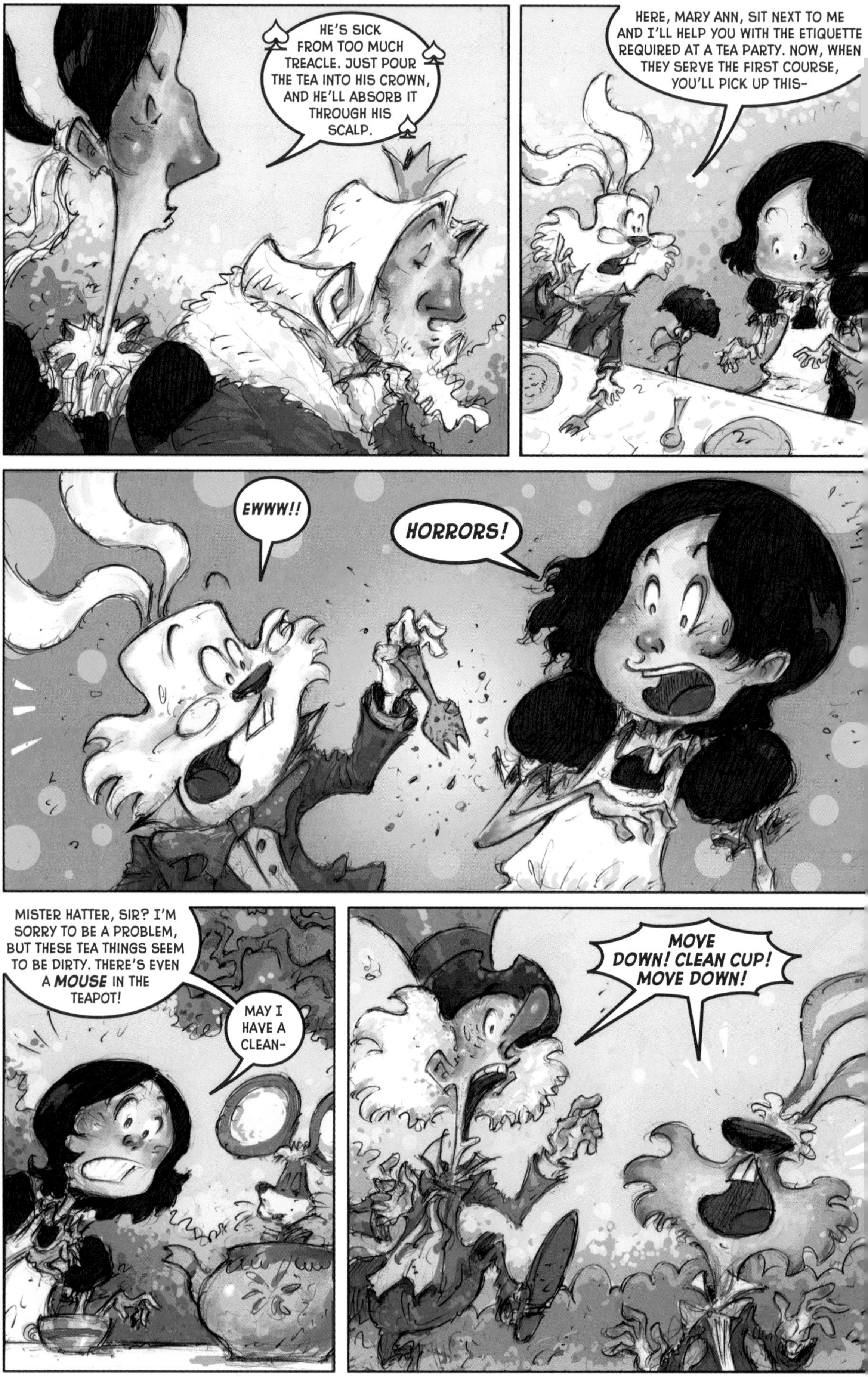
HE'S SICK FROM TOO MUCH TREACLE. JUST POUR THE TEA INTO HIS CROWN, AND HE'LL ABSORB IT THROUGH HIS SCALP.
HERE, MARY ANN, SIT NEXT TO ME AND I'LL HELP YOU WITH THE ETIQUETTE REQUIRED AT A TEA PARTY. NOW, WHEN THEY SERVE THE FIRST COURSE, YOU'LL PICK UP THIS-
EWWW!!
HORRORS!
MISTER HATTER, SIR? I'M SORRY TO BE A PROBLEM, BUT THESE TEA THINGS SEEM TO BE DIRTY. THERE'S EVEN A MOUSE IN THE TEAPOT!
MAY I HAVE A CLEAN-
MOVE DOWN! CLEAN CUP! MOVE DOWN!

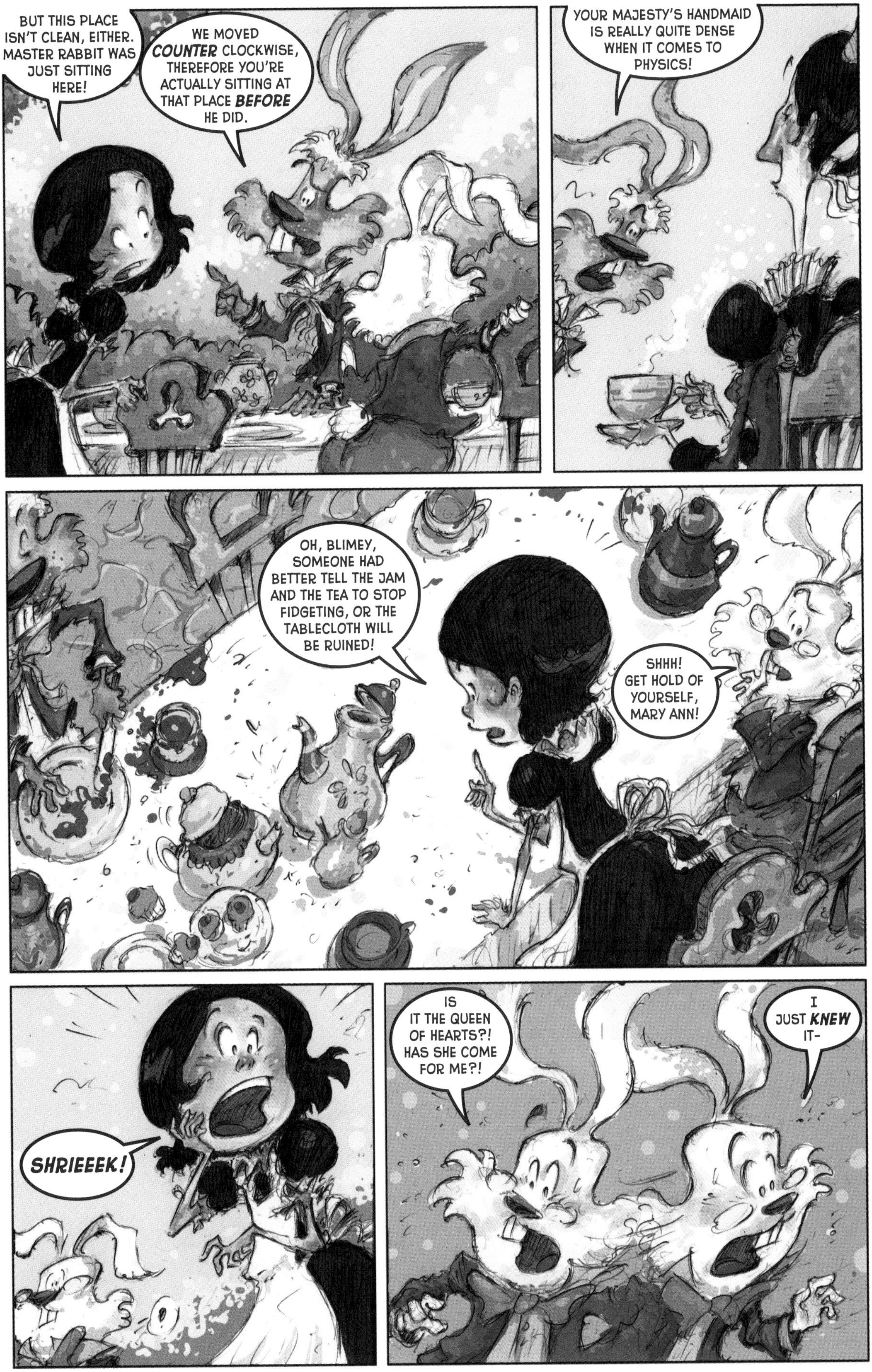
BUT THIS PLACE ISN'T CLEAN, EITHER. MASTER RABBIT WAS JUST SITTING HERE!
WE MOVED COUNTER CLOCKWISE, THEREFORE YOU'RE ACTUALLY SITTING AT THAT PLACE BEFORE HE DID.
YOUR MAJESTY'S HANDMAID IS REALLY QUITE DENSE WHEN IT COMES TO PHYSICS!
OH, BLIMEY, SOMEONE HAD BETTER TELL THE JAM AND THE TEA TO STOP FIDGETING, OR THE TABLECLOTH WILL BE RUINED!
SHHH! GET HOLD OF YOURSELF, MARY ANN!
SHRIEEEK!
IS IT THE QUEEN OF HEARTS?! HAS SHE COME FOR ME?!
I JUST KNEW IT-

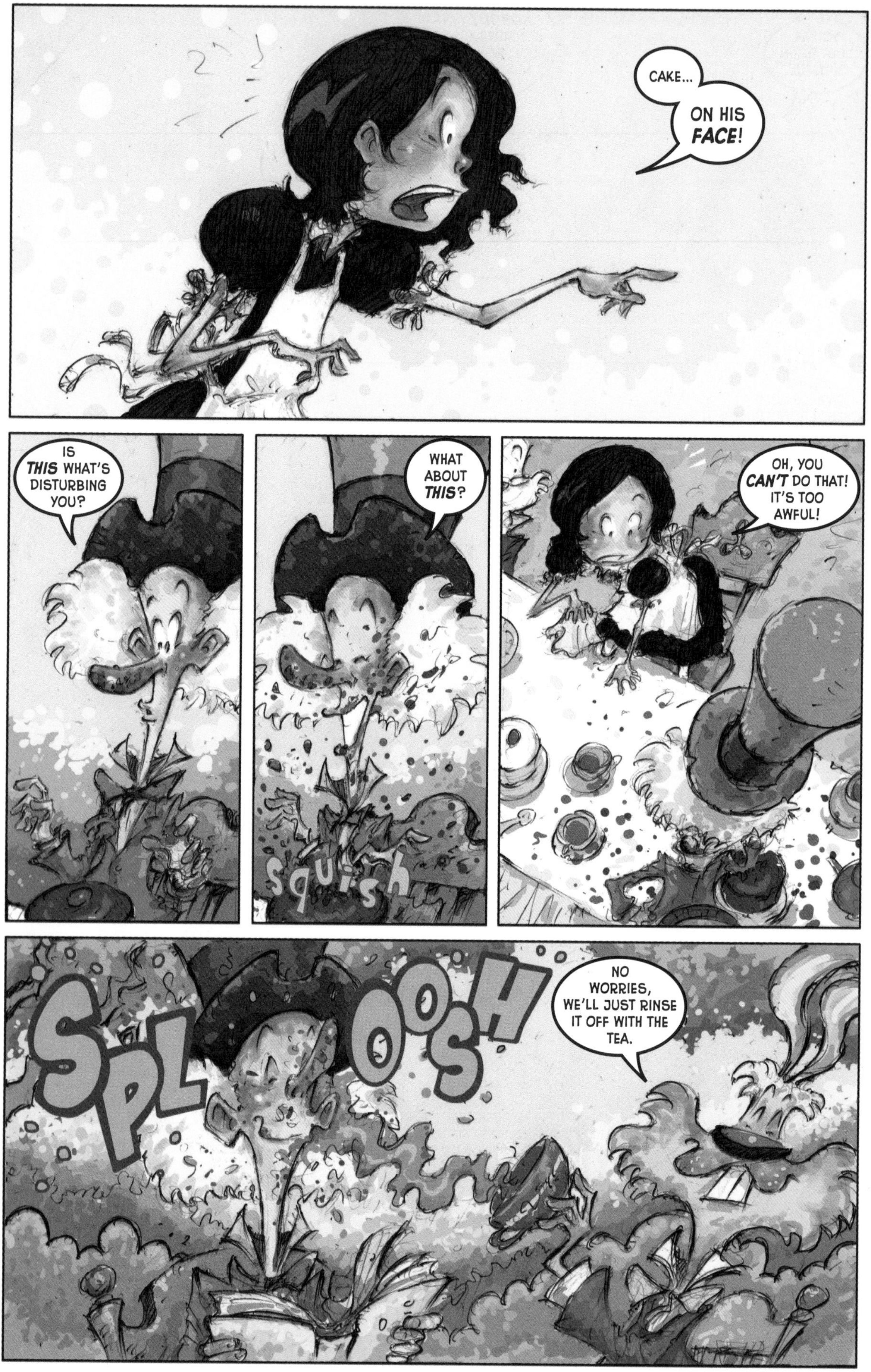
CAKE...
ON HIS FACE!
IS THIS WHAT'S DISTURBING YOU?
WHAT ABOUT THIS?
squish
OH, YOU CAN'T DO THAT! IT'S TOO AWFUL!
SPLOOSH
NO WORRIES, WE'LL JUST RINSE IT OFF WITH THE TEA.

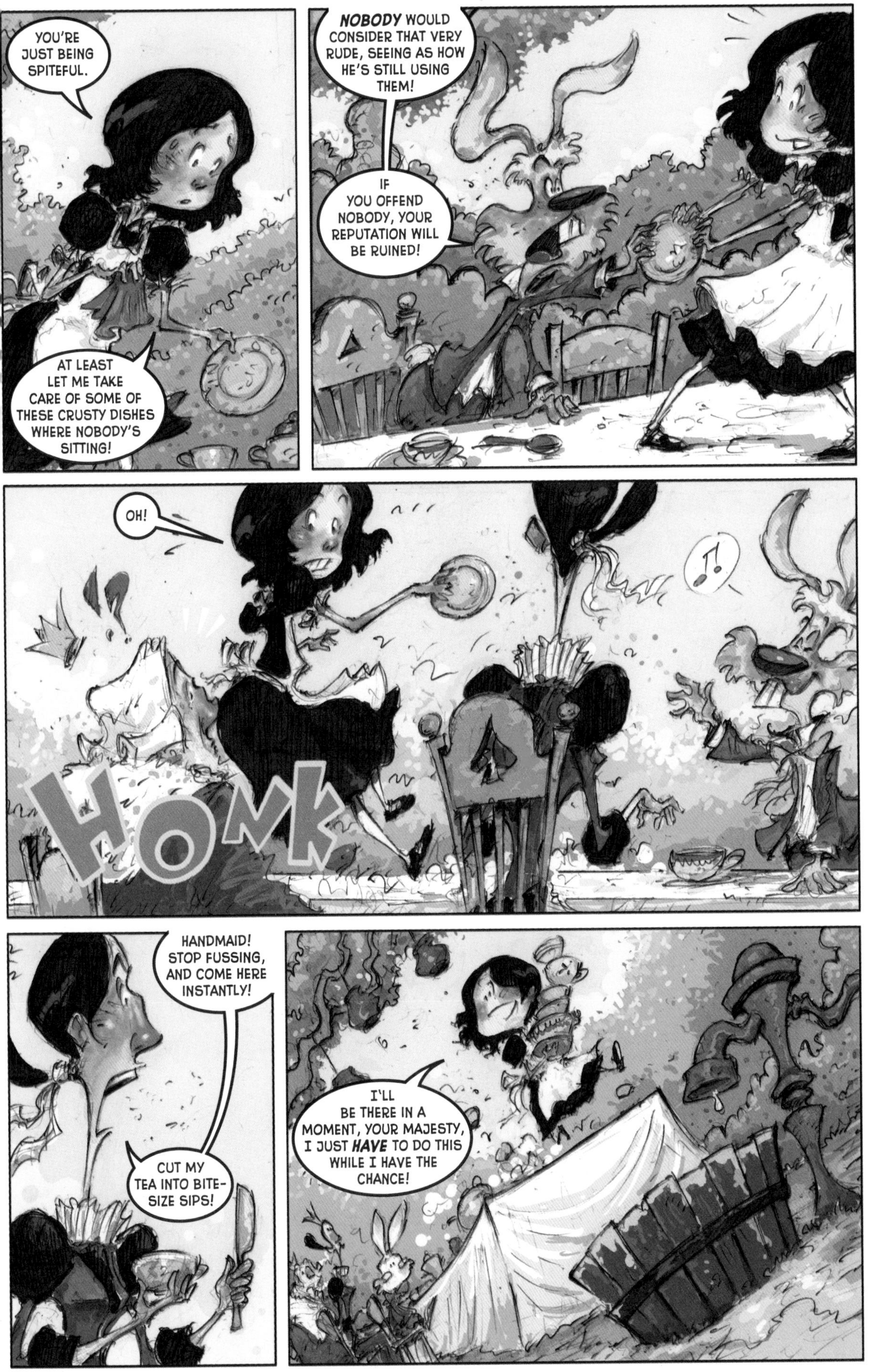
YOU'RE JUST BEING SPITEFUL.
AT LEAST LET ME TAKE CARE OF SOME OF THESE CRUSTY DISHES WHERE NOBODY'S SITTING!
NOBODY WOULD CONSIDER THAT VERY RUDE, SEEING AS HOW HE'S STILL USING THEM!
IF YOU OFFEND NOBODY, YOUR REPUTATION WILL BE RUINED!
OH!
HONK
HANDMAID! STOP FUSSING, AND COME HERE INSTANTLY!
CUT MY TEA INTO BITE-SIZE SIPS!
I'LL BE THERE IN A MOMENT, YOUR MAJESTY, I JUST HAVE TO DO THIS WHILE I HAVE THE CHANCE!

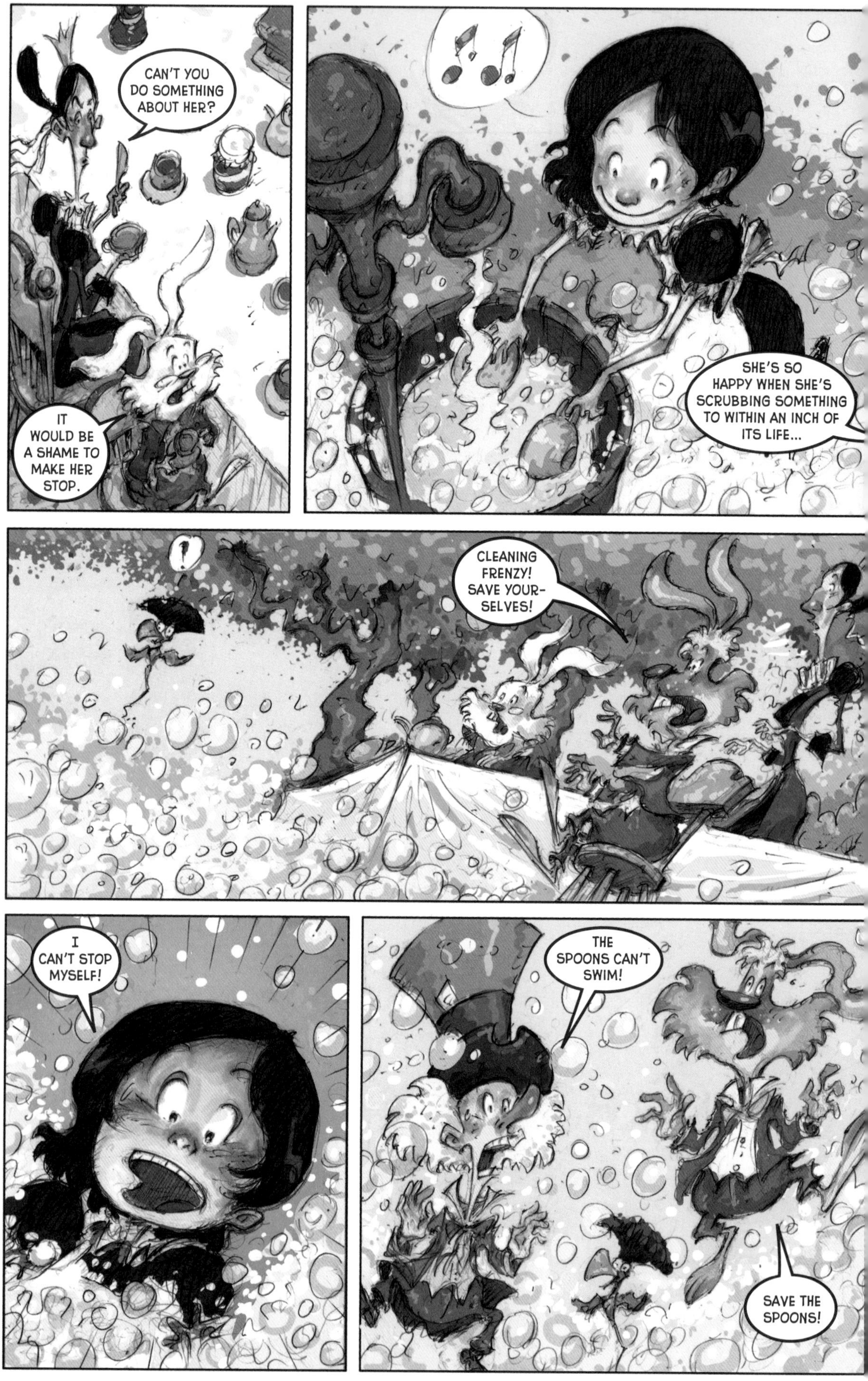
CAN'T YOU DO SOMETHING ABOUT HER?
IT WOULD BE A SHAME TO MAKE HER STOP.
SHE'S SO HAPPY WHEN SHE'S SCRUBBING SOMETHING TO WITHIN AN INCH OF ITS LIFE...
!
CLEANING FRENZY! SAVE YOUR-SELVES!
I CAN'T STOP MYSELF!
THE SPOONS CAN'T SWIM!
SAVE THE SPOONS!

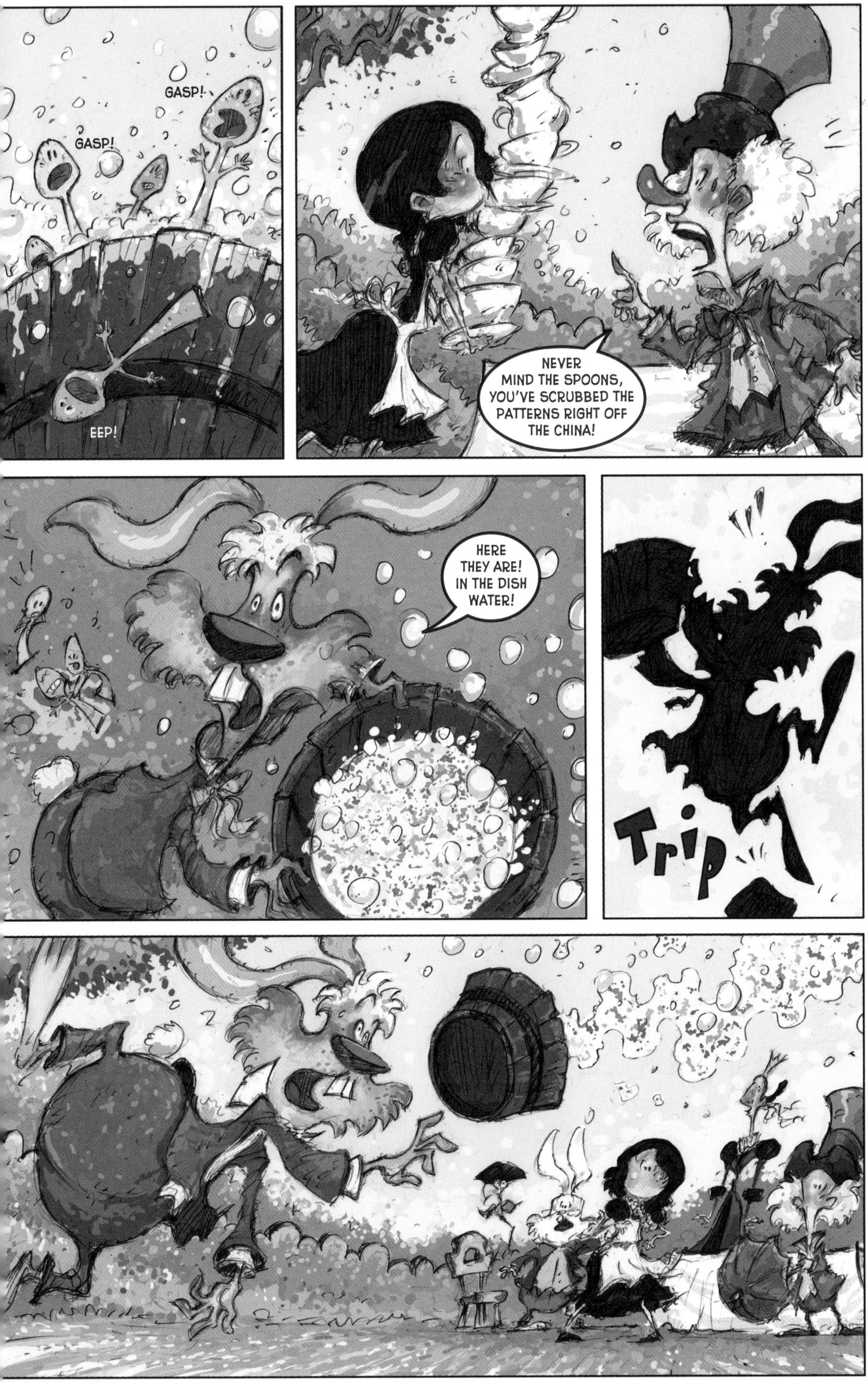
GASP!
GASP!
EEP!
NEVER MIND THE SPOONS, YOU'VE SCRUBBED THE PATTERNS RIGHT OFF THE CHINA!
HERE THEY ARE! IN THE DISH WATER!
Trip

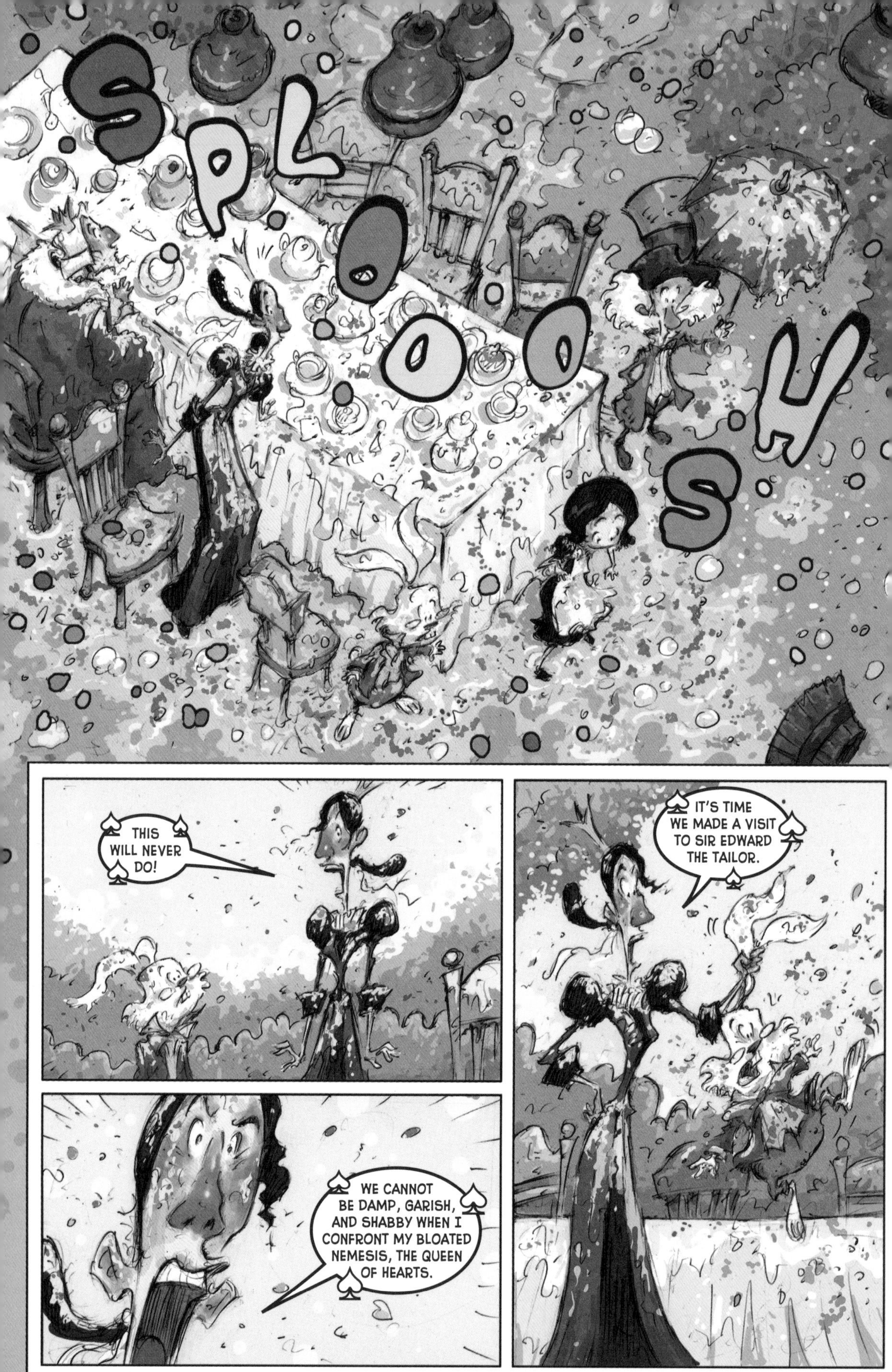
SPLOOOOSH
THIS WILL NEVER DO!
WE CANNOT BE DAMP, GARISH, AND SHABBY WHEN I CONFRONT MY BLOATED NEMESIS, THE QUEEN OF HEARTS.
IT'S TIME WE MADE A VISIT TO SIR EDWARD THE TAILOR.

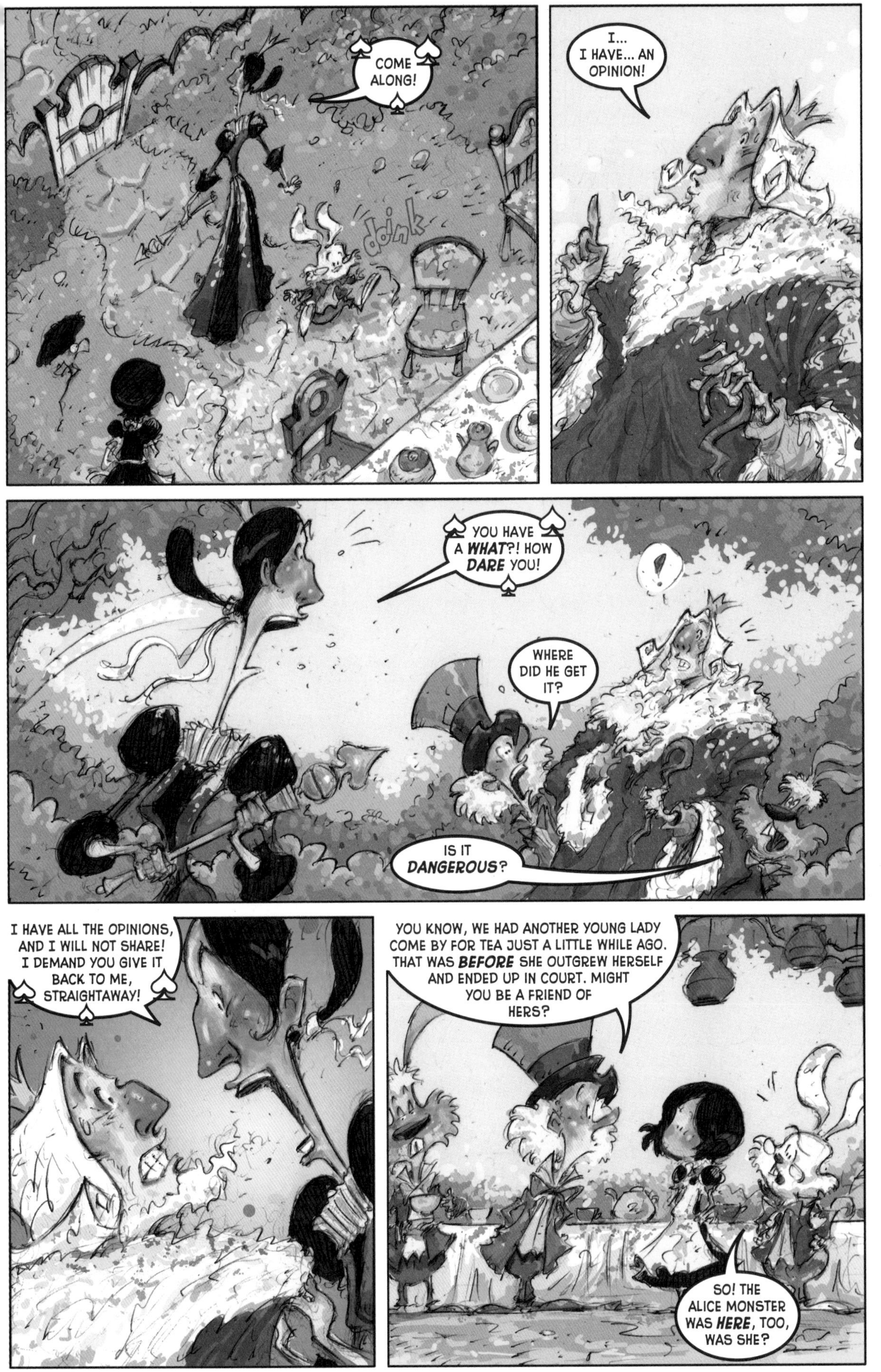
COME ALONG!
doink
I... I HAVE... AN OPINION!
YOU HAVE A **WHAT**?! HOW **DARE** YOU!
!
WHERE DID HE GET IT?
IS IT **DANGEROUS**?
I HAVE ALL THE OPINIONS, AND I WILL NOT SHARE! I DEMAND YOU GIVE IT BACK TO ME, STRAIGHTAWAY!
YOU KNOW, WE HAD ANOTHER YOUNG LADY COME BY FOR TEA JUST A LITTLE WHILE AGO. THAT WAS **BEFORE** SHE OUTGREW HERSELF AND ENDED UP IN COURT. MIGHT YOU BE A FRIEND OF HERS?
SO! THE ALICE MONSTER WAS **HERE**, TOO, WAS SHE?

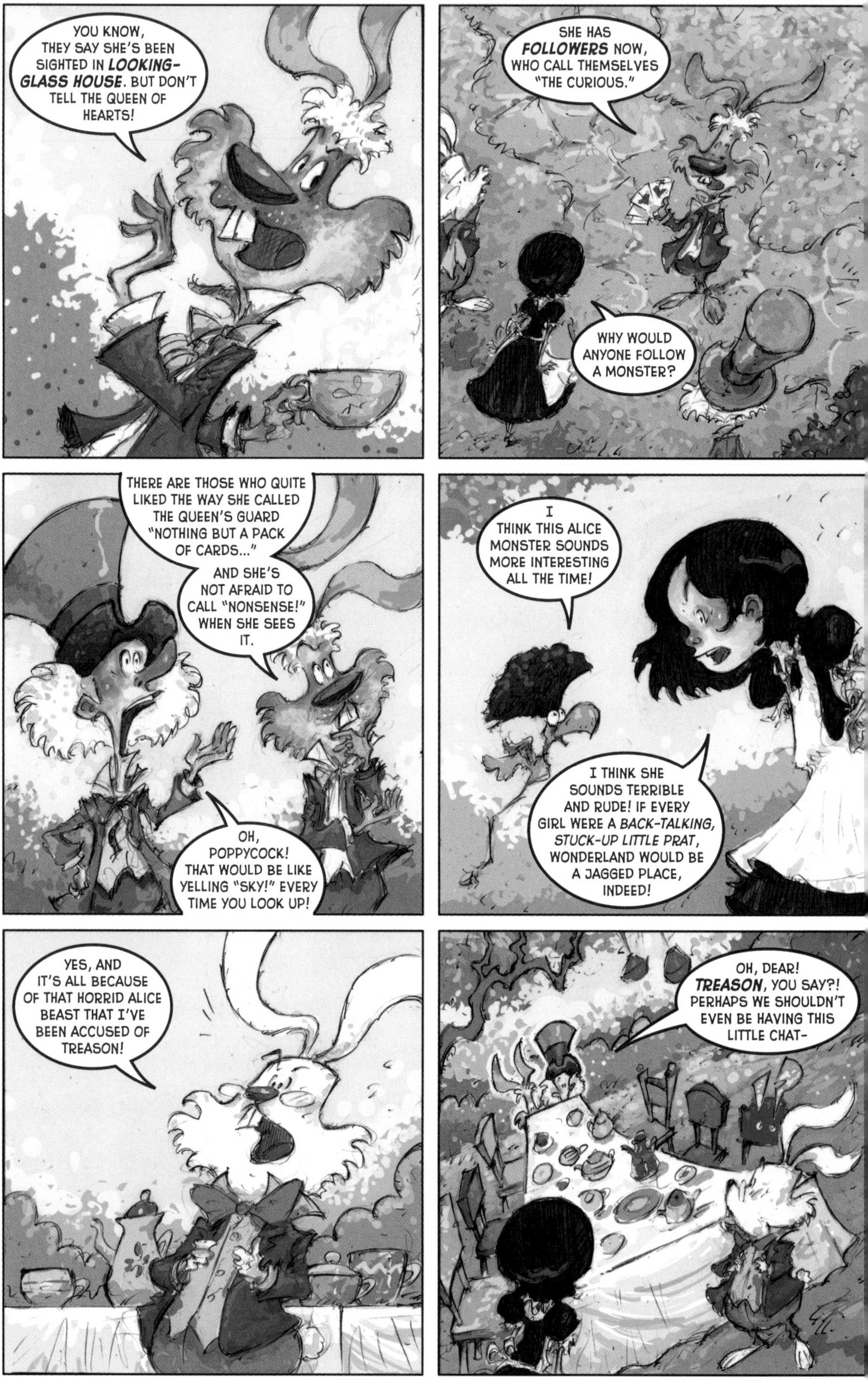
YOU KNOW, THEY SAY SHE'S BEEN SIGHTED IN LOOKING-GLASS HOUSE. BUT DON'T TELL THE QUEEN OF HEARTS!
SHE HAS FOLLOWERS NOW, WHO CALL THEMSELVES "THE CURIOUS."
WHY WOULD ANYONE FOLLOW A MONSTER?
THERE ARE THOSE WHO QUITE LIKED THE WAY SHE CALLED THE QUEEN'S GUARD "NOTHING BUT A PACK OF CARDS..."
AND SHE'S NOT AFRAID TO CALL "NONSENSE!" WHEN SHE SEES IT.
OH, POPPYCOCK! THAT WOULD BE LIKE YELLING "SKY!" EVERY TIME YOU LOOK UP!
I THINK THIS ALICE MONSTER SOUNDS MORE INTERESTING ALL THE TIME!
I THINK SHE SOUNDS TERRIBLE AND RUDE! IF EVERY GIRL WERE A BACK-TALKING, STUCK-UP LITTLE PRAT, WONDERLAND WOULD BE A JAGGED PLACE, INDEED!
YES, AND IT'S ALL BECAUSE OF THAT HORRID ALICE BEAST THAT I'VE BEEN ACCUSED OF TREASON!
OH, DEAR! TREASON, YOU SAY?! PERHAPS WE SHOULDN'T EVEN BE HAVING THIS LITTLE CHAT-

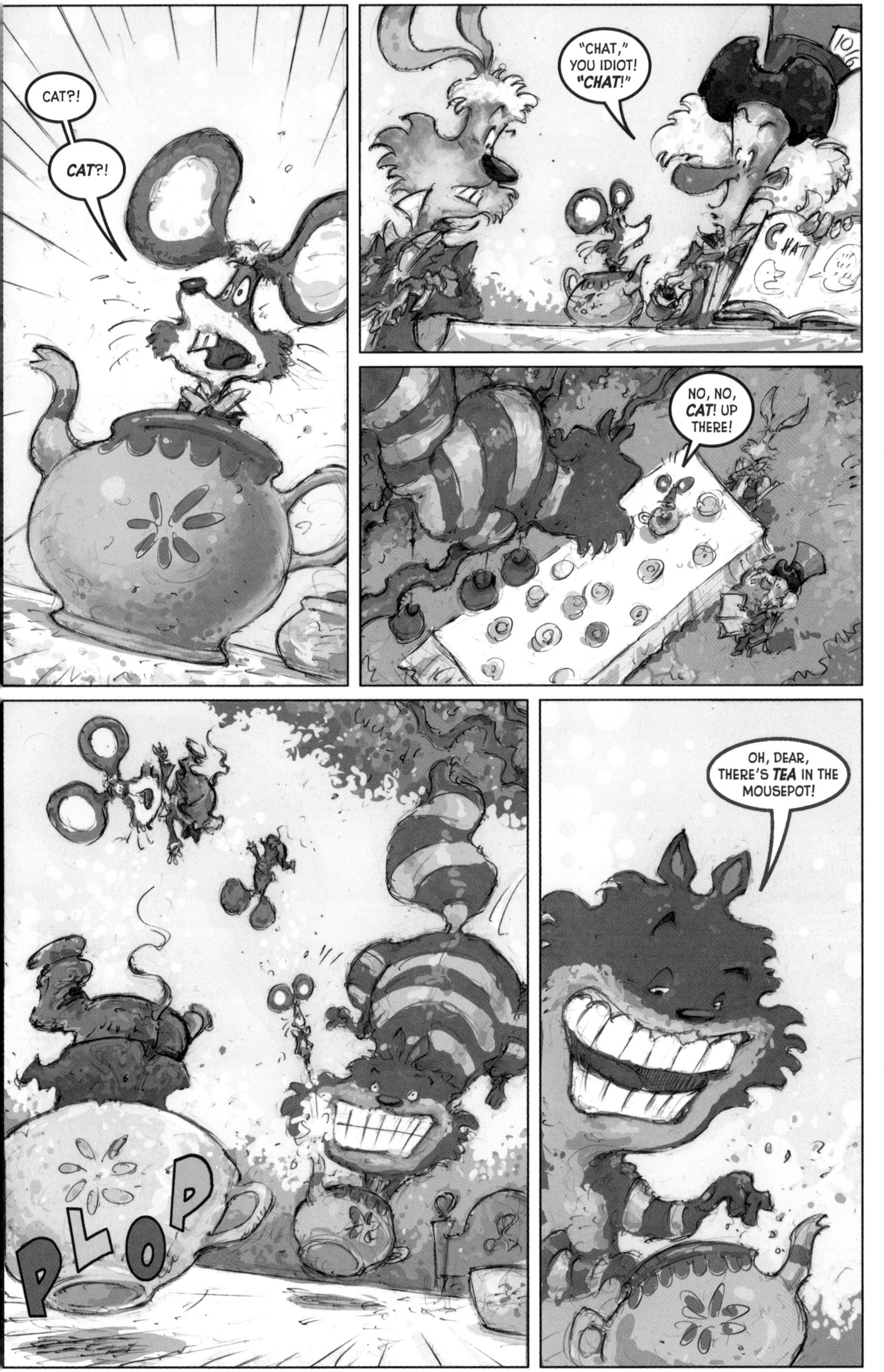
CAT?!
CAT?!
"CHAT," YOU IDIOT! **"CHAT!"**
NO, NO, *CAT*! UP THERE!
PLOP
OH, DEAR, THERE'S *TEA* IN THE MOUSEPOT!

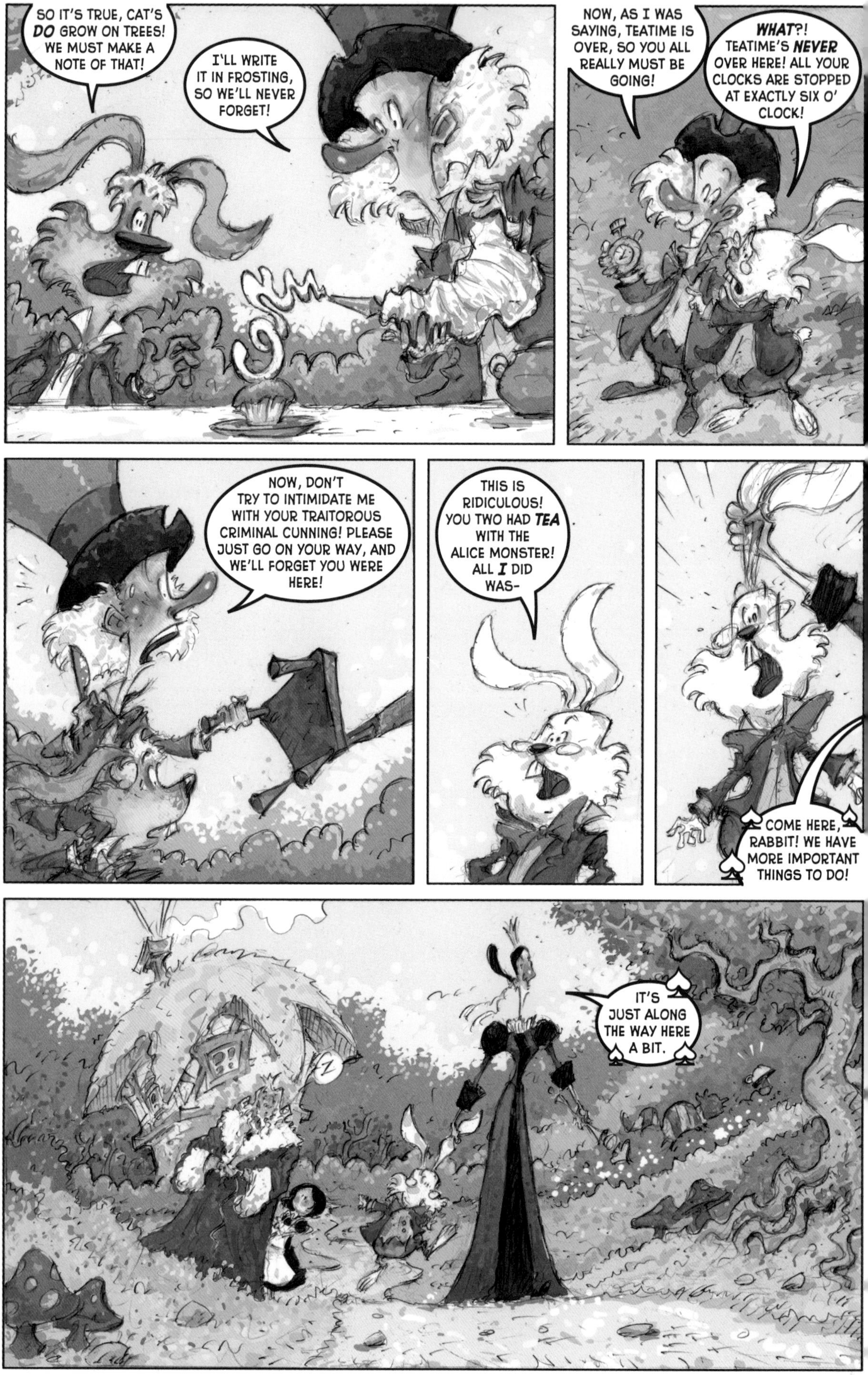
SO IT'S TRUE, CAT'S DO GROW ON TREES! WE MUST MAKE A NOTE OF THAT!
I'LL WRITE IT IN FROSTING, SO WE'LL NEVER FORGET!
NOW, AS I WAS SAYING, TEATIME IS OVER, SO YOU ALL REALLY MUST BE GOING!
WHAT?! TEATIME'S NEVER OVER HERE! ALL YOUR CLOCKS ARE STOPPED AT EXACTLY SIX O' CLOCK!
NOW, DON'T TRY TO INTIMIDATE ME WITH YOUR TRAITOROUS CRIMINAL CUNNING! PLEASE JUST GO ON YOUR WAY, AND WE'LL FORGET YOU WERE HERE!
THIS IS RIDICULOUS! YOU TWO HAD TEA WITH THE ALICE MONSTER! ALL I DID WAS-
COME HERE, RABBIT! WE HAVE MORE IMPORTANT THINGS TO DO!
IT'S JUST ALONG THE WAY HERE A BIT.

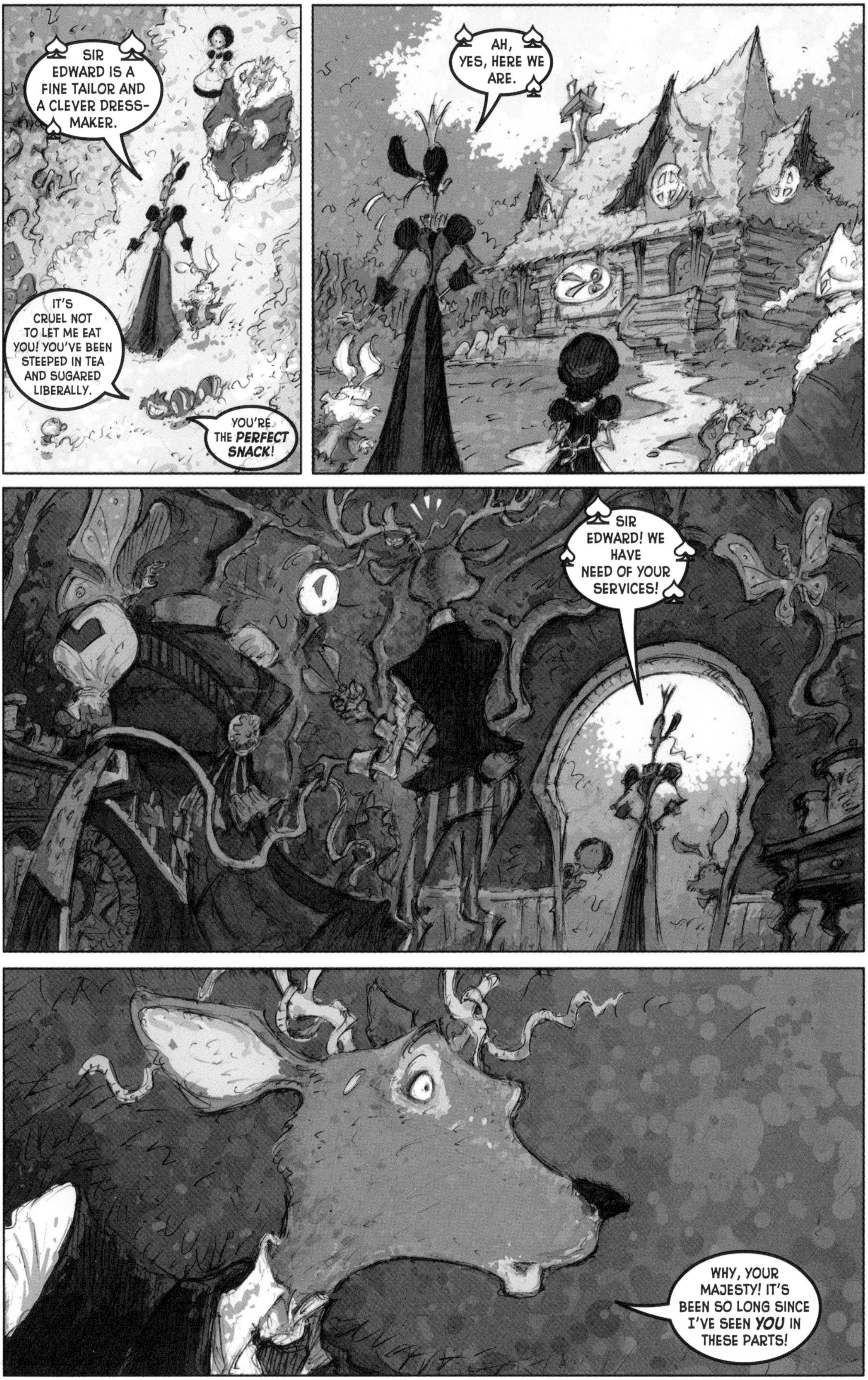
SIR EDWARD IS A FINE TAILOR AND A CLEVER DRESS-MAKER.
IT'S CRUEL NOT TO LET ME EAT YOU! YOU'VE BEEN STEEPED IN TEA AND SUGARED LIBERALLY.
YOU'RE THE *PERFECT SNACK*!
AH, YES, HERE WE ARE.
SIR EDWARD! WE HAVE NEED OF YOUR SERVICES!
WHY, YOUR MAJESTY! IT'S BEEN SO LONG SINCE I'VE SEEN *YOU* IN THESE PARTS!

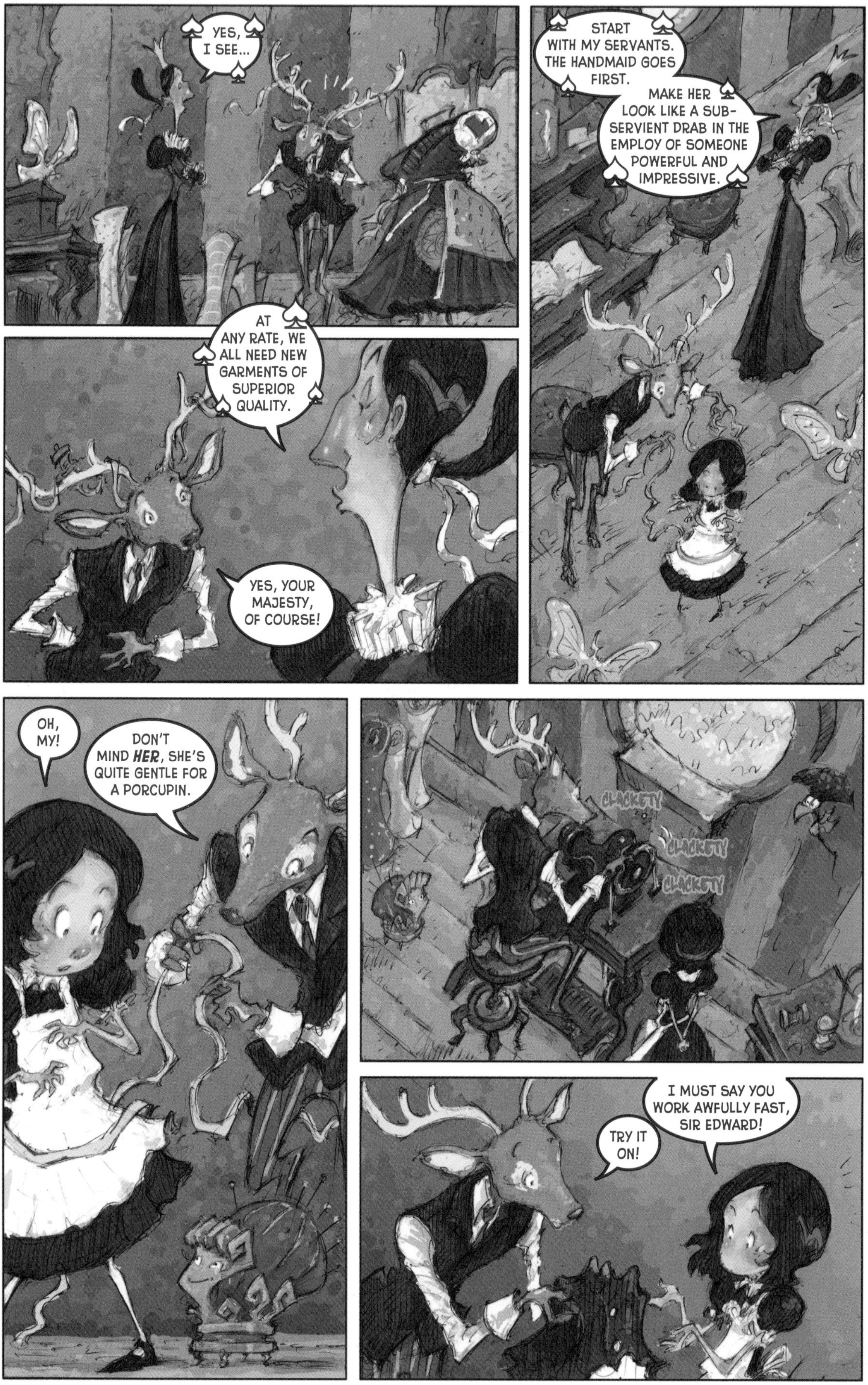
YES, I SEE...
START WITH MY SERVANTS. THE HANDMAID GOES FIRST.
MAKE HER LOOK LIKE A SUB-SERVIENT DRAB IN THE EMPLOY OF SOMEONE POWERFUL AND IMPRESSIVE.
AT ANY RATE, WE ALL NEED NEW GARMENTS OF SUPERIOR QUALITY.
YES, YOUR MAJESTY, OF COURSE!
OH, MY!
DON'T MIND ***HER***, SHE'S QUITE GENTLE FOR A PORCUPIN.
CLACKETY
CLACKETY
CLACKETY
I MUST SAY YOU WORK AWFULLY FAST, SIR EDWARD!
TRY IT ON!

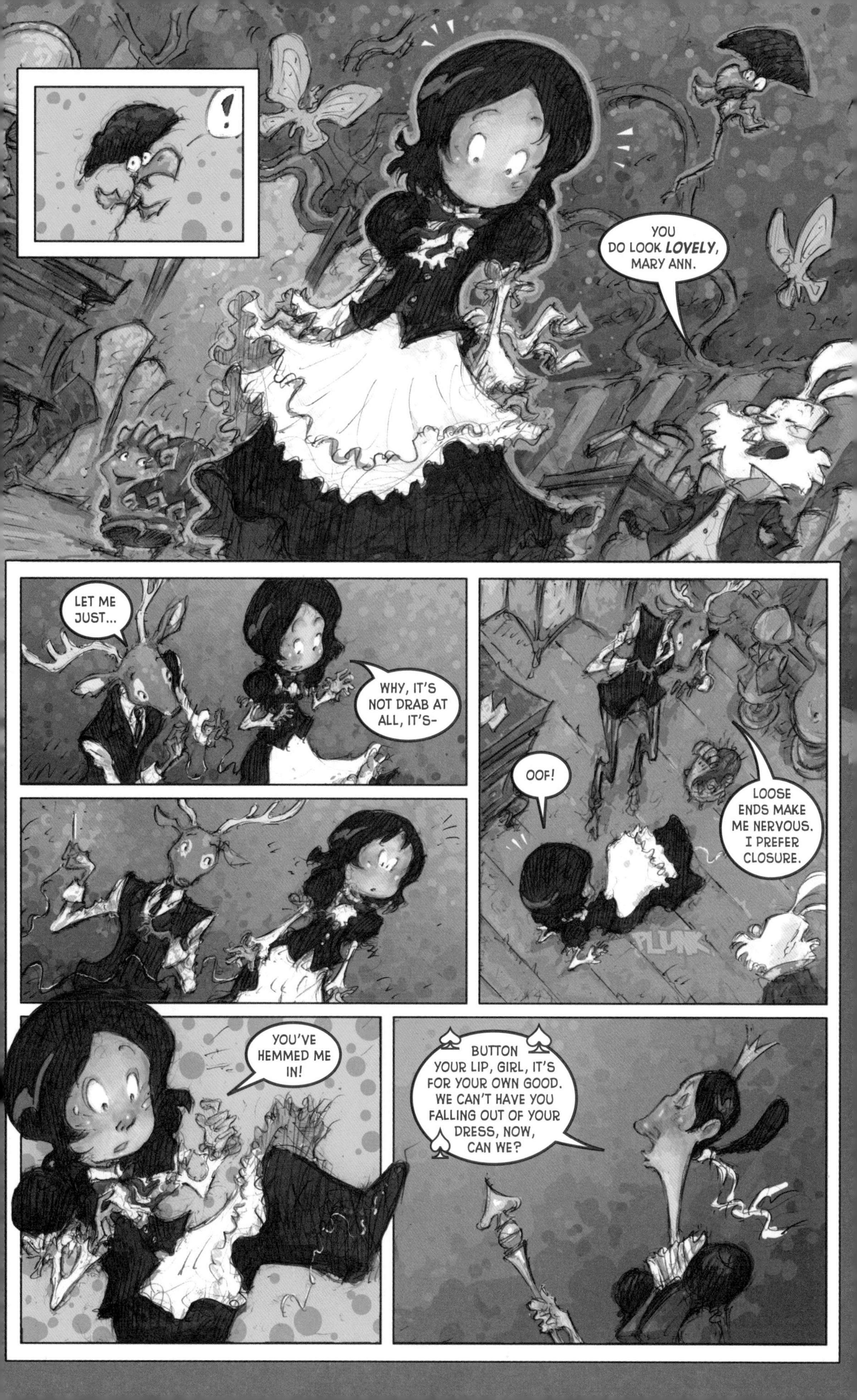
!
YOU DO LOOK LOVELY, MARY ANN.
LET ME JUST...
WHY, IT'S NOT DRAB AT ALL, IT'S-
OOF!
LOOSE ENDS MAKE ME NERVOUS. I PREFER CLOSURE.
FLUNK
YOU'VE HEMMED ME IN!
BUTTON YOUR LIP, GIRL, IT'S FOR YOUR OWN GOOD. WE CAN'T HAVE YOU FALLING OUT OF YOUR DRESS, NOW, CAN WE?

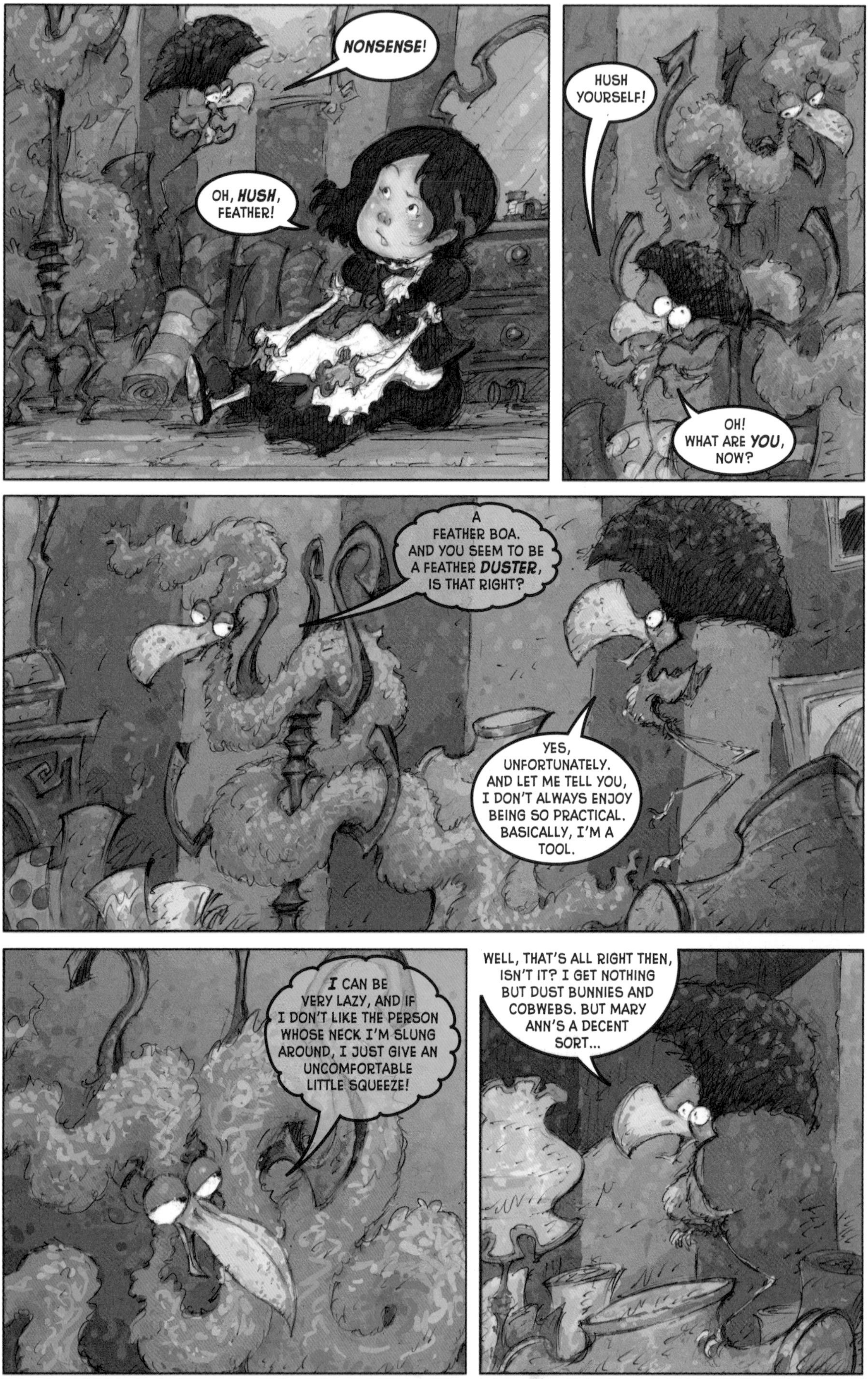
NONSENSE!
OH, HUSH, FEATHER!
HUSH YOURSELF!
OH! WHAT ARE YOU, NOW?
A FEATHER BOA. AND YOU SEEM TO BE A FEATHER DUSTER, IS THAT RIGHT?
YES, UNFORTUNATELY. AND LET ME TELL YOU, I DON'T ALWAYS ENJOY BEING SO PRACTICAL. BASICALLY, I'M A TOOL.
I CAN BE VERY LAZY, AND IF I DON'T LIKE THE PERSON WHOSE NECK I'M SLUNG AROUND, I JUST GIVE AN UNCOMFORTABLE LITTLE SQUEEZE!
WELL, THAT'S ALL RIGHT THEN, ISN'T IT? I GET NOTHING BUT DUST BUNNIES AND COBWEBS. BUT MARY ANN'S A DECENT SORT...

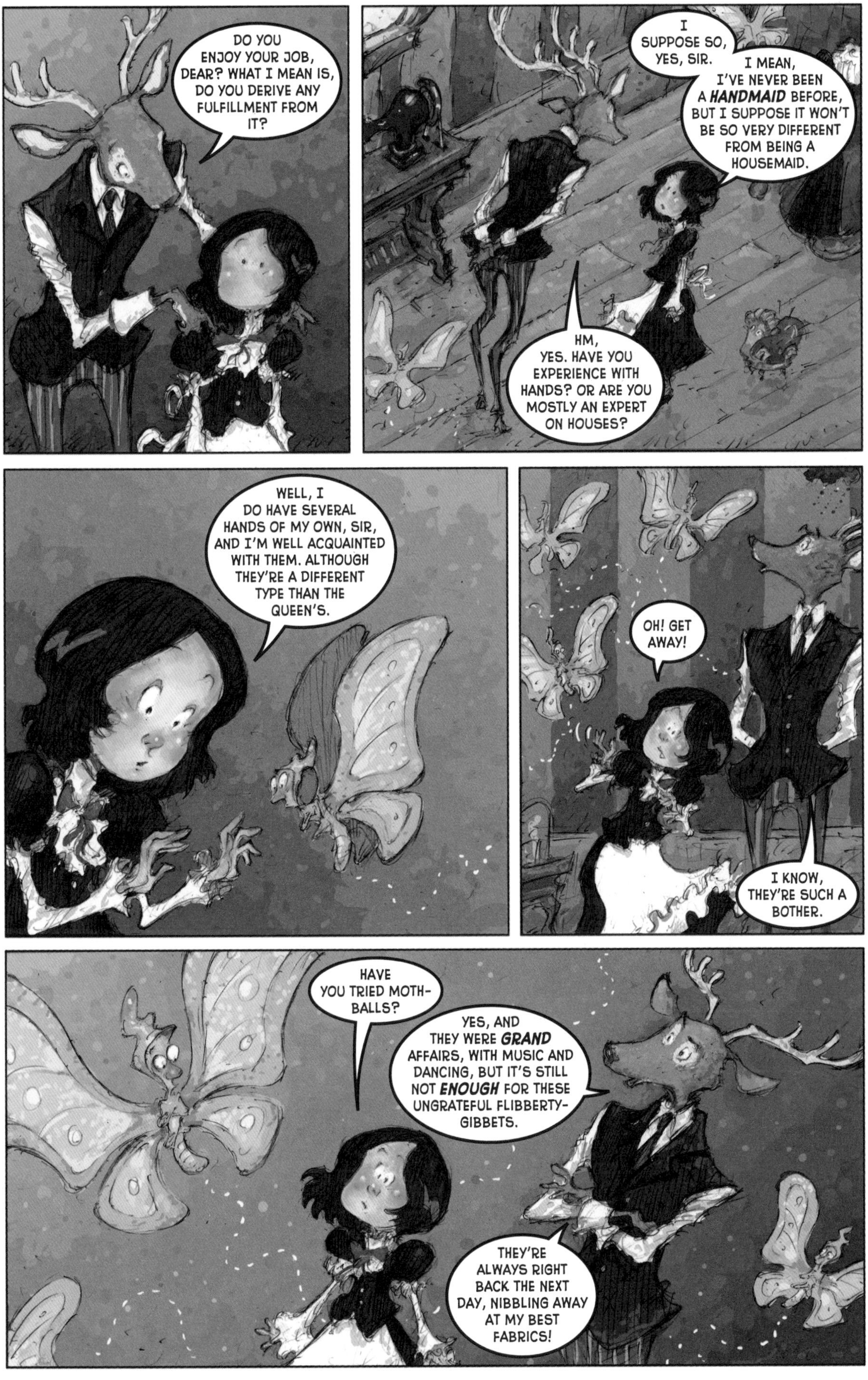
DO YOU ENJOY YOUR JOB, DEAR? WHAT I MEAN IS, DO YOU DERIVE ANY FULFILLMENT FROM IT?
I SUPPOSE SO, YES, SIR.
I MEAN, I'VE NEVER BEEN A **HANDMAID** BEFORE, BUT I SUPPOSE IT WON'T BE SO VERY DIFFERENT FROM BEING A HOUSEMAID.
HM, YES. HAVE YOU EXPERIENCE WITH HANDS? OR ARE YOU MOSTLY AN EXPERT ON HOUSES?
WELL, I DO HAVE SEVERAL HANDS OF MY OWN, SIR, AND I'M WELL ACQUAINTED WITH THEM. ALTHOUGH THEY'RE A DIFFERENT TYPE THAN THE QUEEN'S.
OH! GET AWAY!
I KNOW, THEY'RE SUCH A BOTHER.
HAVE YOU TRIED MOTH-BALLS?
YES, AND THEY WERE **GRAND** AFFAIRS, WITH MUSIC AND DANCING, BUT IT'S STILL NOT **ENOUGH** FOR THESE UNGRATEFUL FLIBBERTY-GIBBETS.
THEY'RE ALWAYS RIGHT BACK THE NEXT DAY, NIBBLING AWAY AT MY BEST FABRICS!

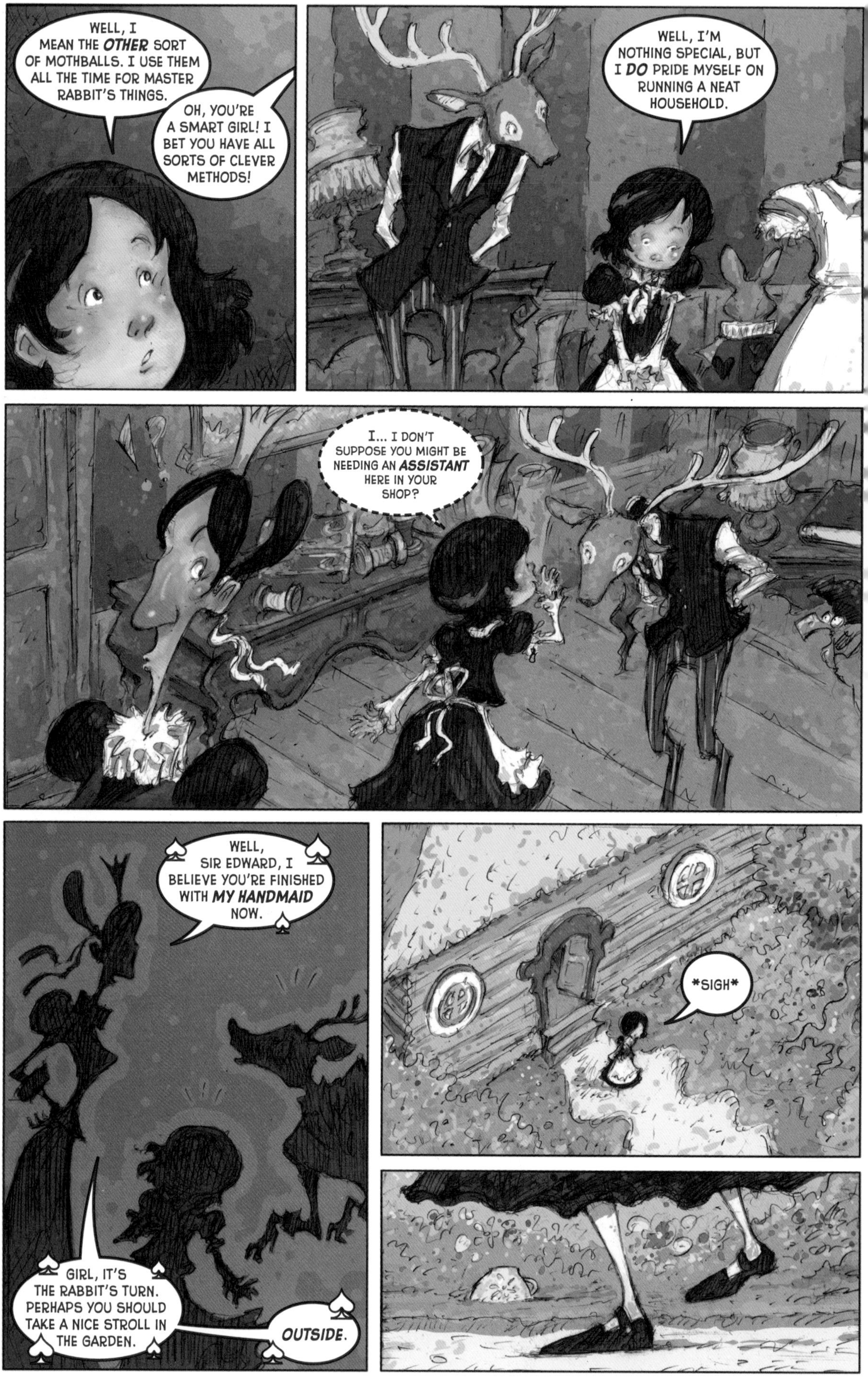
WELL, I MEAN THE OTHER SORT OF MOTHBALLS. I USE THEM ALL THE TIME FOR MASTER RABBIT'S THINGS.
OH, YOU'RE A SMART GIRL! I BET YOU HAVE ALL SORTS OF CLEVER METHODS!
WELL, I'M NOTHING SPECIAL, BUT I DO PRIDE MYSELF ON RUNNING A NEAT HOUSEHOLD.
I... I DON'T SUPPOSE YOU MIGHT BE NEEDING AN ASSISTANT HERE IN YOUR SHOP?
WELL, SIR EDWARD, I BELIEVE YOU'RE FINISHED WITH MY HANDMAID NOW.
GIRL, IT'S THE RABBIT'S TURN. PERHAPS YOU SHOULD TAKE A NICE STROLL IN THE GARDEN.
OUTSIDE.
SIGH

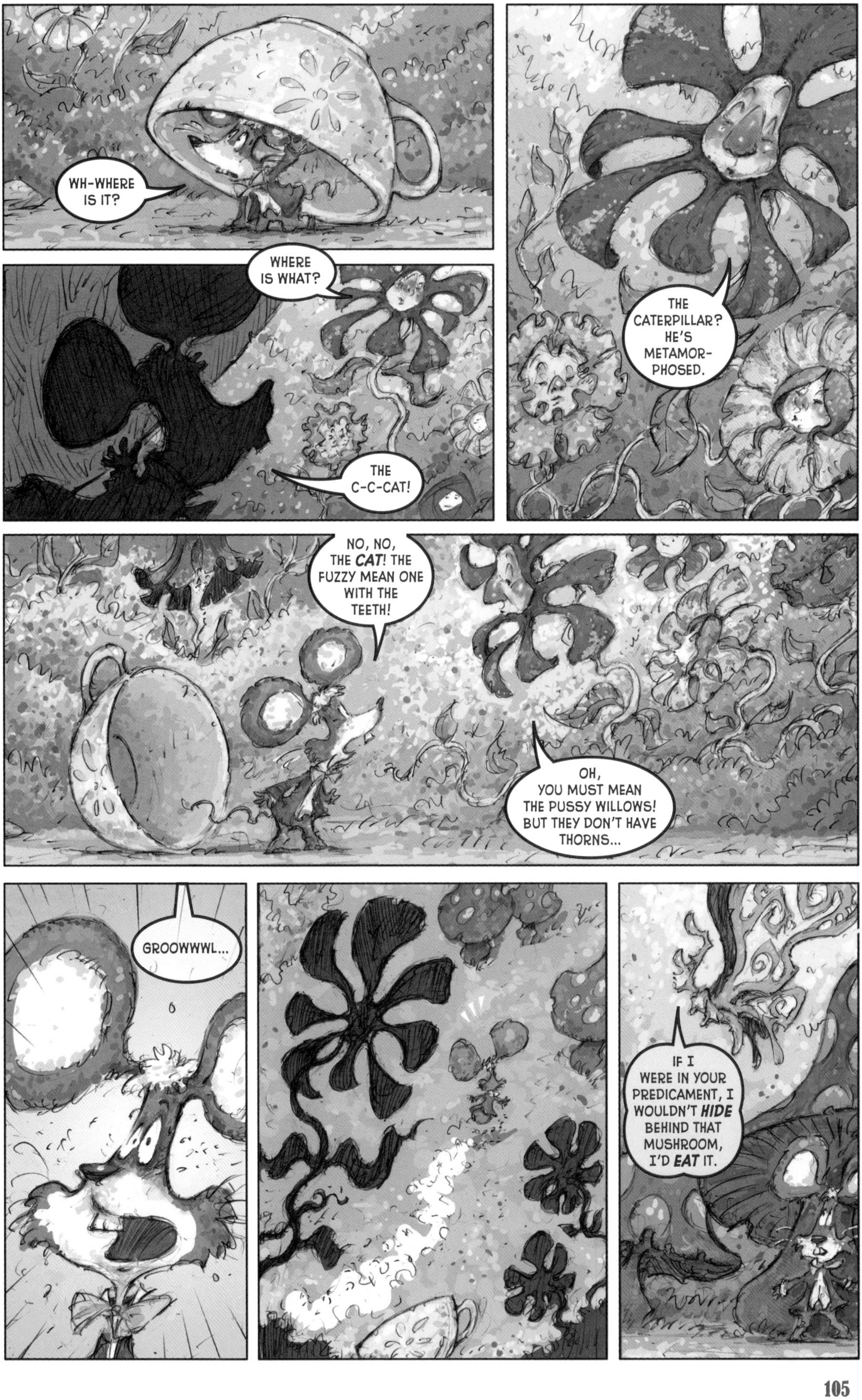
WH-WHERE IS IT?
WHERE IS WHAT?
THE C-C-CAT!
THE CATERPILLAR? HE'S METAMOR-PHOSED.
NO, NO, THE **CAT**! THE FUZZY MEAN ONE WITH THE TEETH!
OH, YOU MUST MEAN THE PUSSY WILLOWS! BUT THEY DON'T HAVE THORNS...
GROOWWWL...
IF I WERE IN YOUR PREDICAMENT, I WOULDN'T **HIDE** BEHIND THAT MUSHROOM, I'D **EAT** IT.

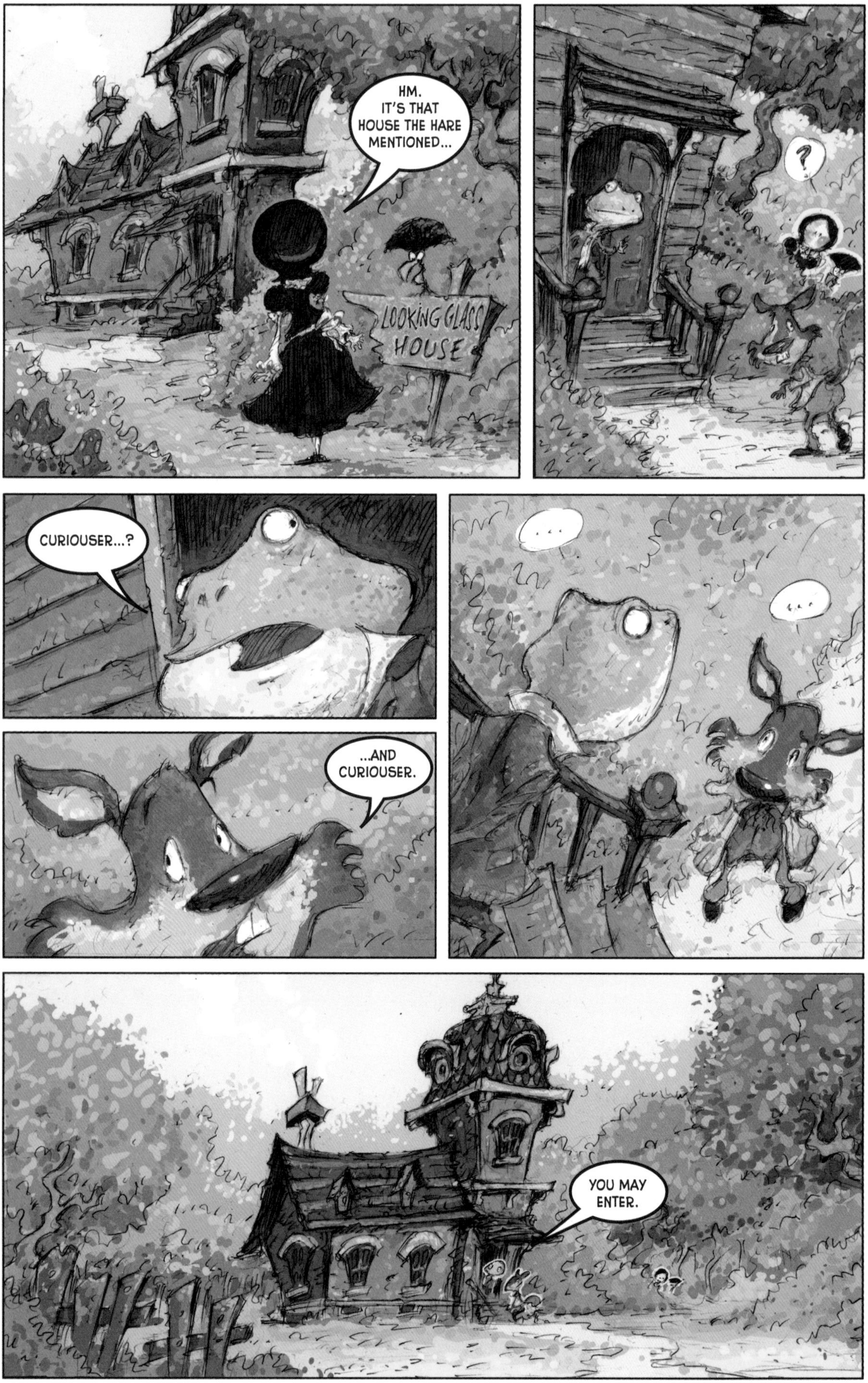
HM.
IT'S THAT
HOUSE THE HARE
MENTIONED...
LOOKING GLASS
HOUSE
?
CURIOUSER...?
...
...
...AND
CURIOUSER.
YOU MAY
ENTER.

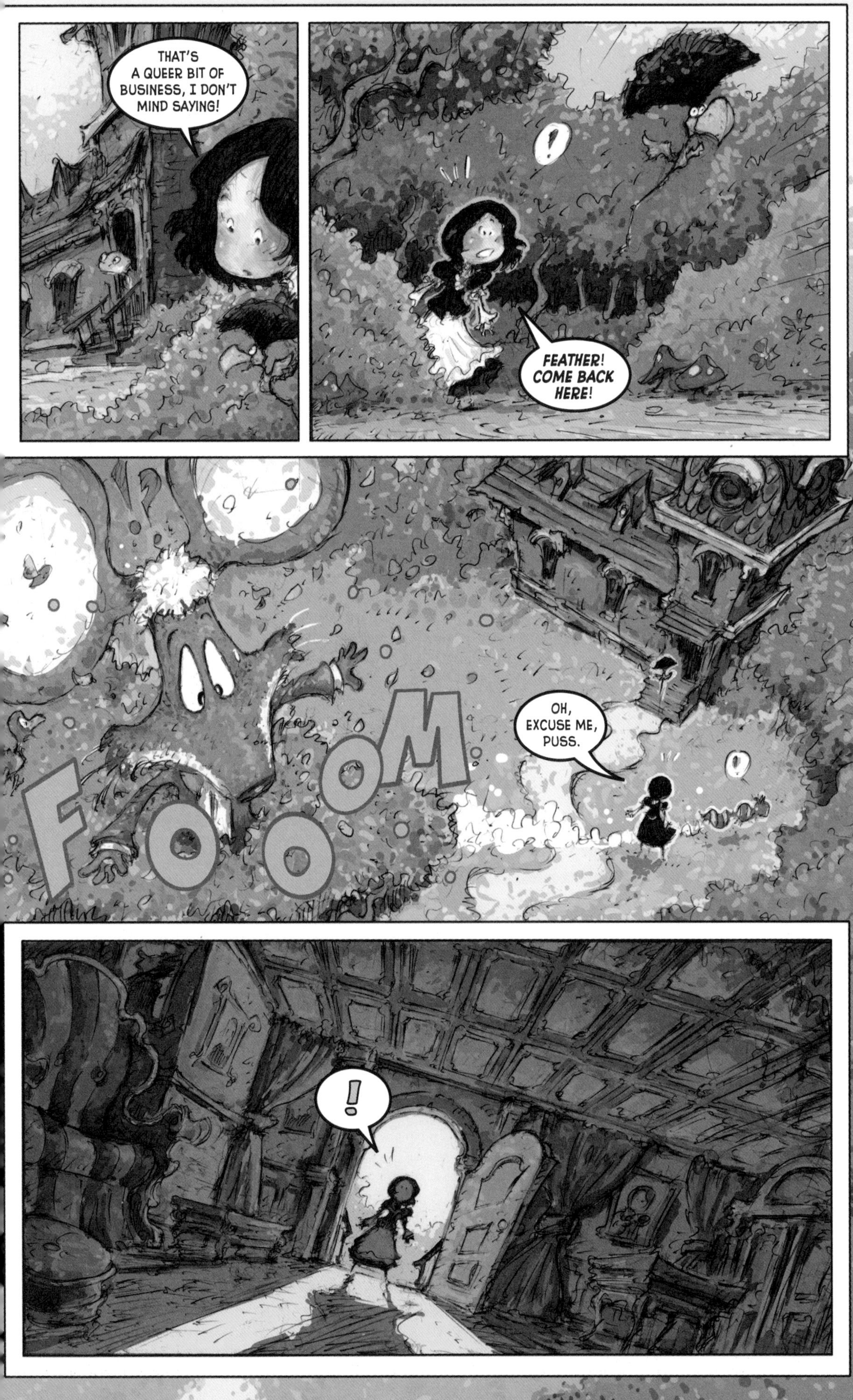
THAT'S A QUEER BIT OF BUSINESS, I DON'T MIND SAYING!
!
FEATHER! COME BACK HERE!
FOOOM
OH, EXCUSE ME, PUSS.
!
!

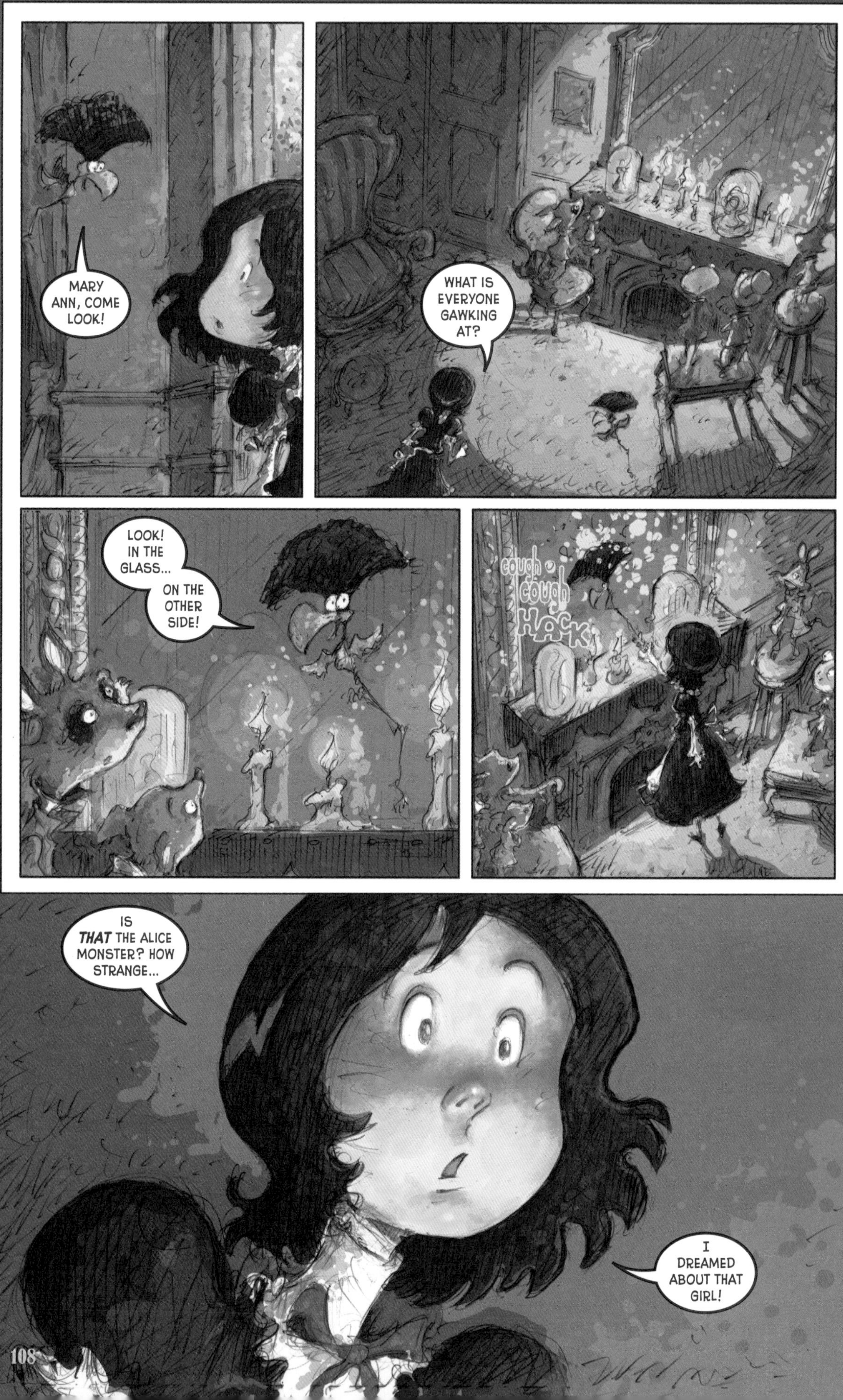
MARY ANN, COME LOOK!
WHAT IS EVERYONE GAWKING AT?
LOOK! IN THE GLASS...
ON THE OTHER SIDE!
cough cough HACK
IS *THAT* THE ALICE MONSTER? HOW STRANGE...
I DREAMED ABOUT THAT GIRL!

Chapter Five
The Dusty Dunes

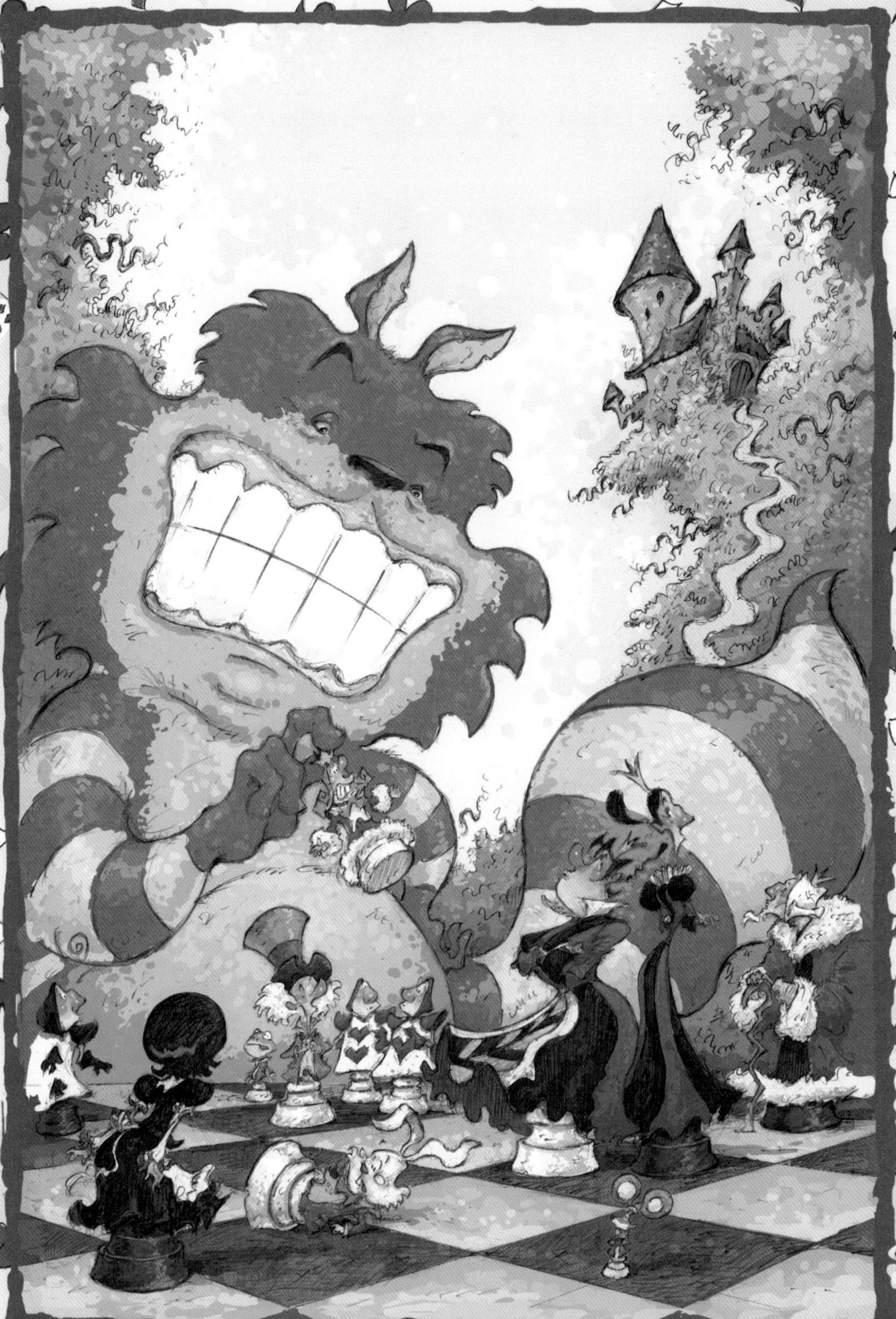

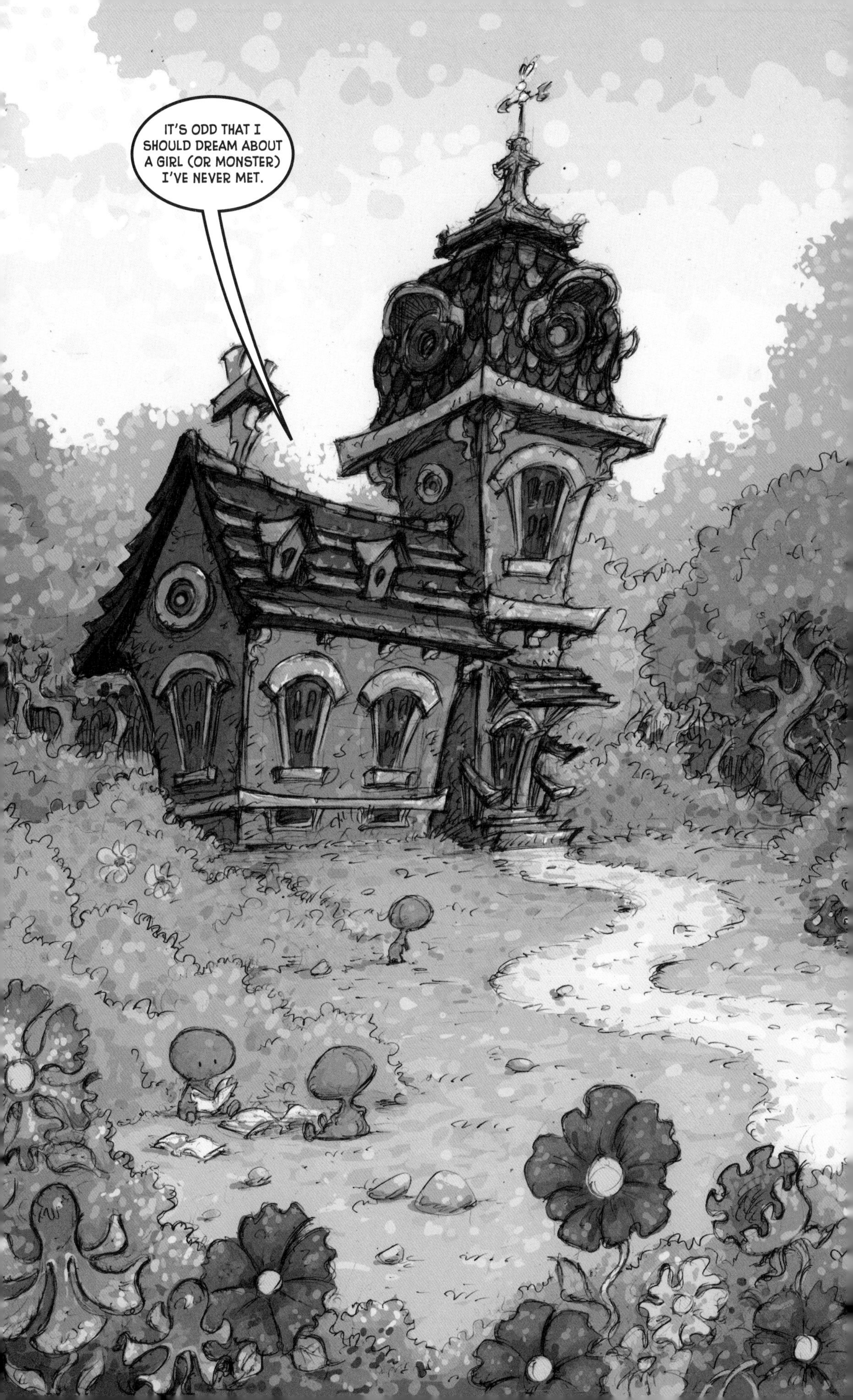
IT'S ODD THAT I SHOULD DREAM ABOUT A GIRL (OR MONSTER) I'VE NEVER MET.

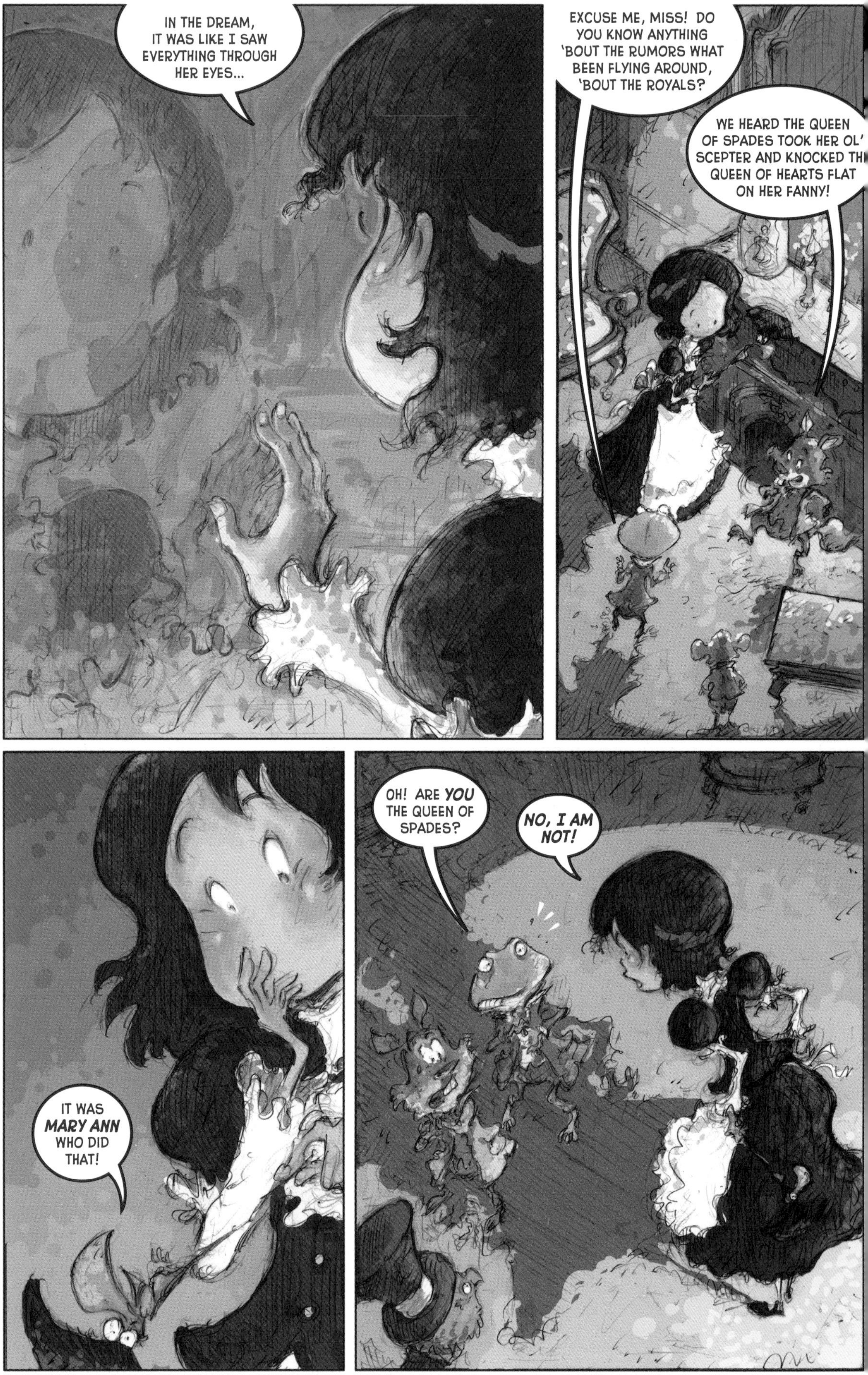
IN THE DREAM, IT WAS LIKE I SAW EVERYTHING THROUGH HER EYES...
EXCUSE ME, MISS! DO YOU KNOW ANYTHING 'BOUT THE RUMORS WHAT BEEN FLYING AROUND, 'BOUT THE ROYALS?
WE HEARD THE QUEEN OF SPADES TOOK HER OL' SCEPTER AND KNOCKED THE QUEEN OF HEARTS FLAT ON HER FANNY!
IT WAS ***MARY ANN*** WHO DID THAT!
OH! ARE ***YOU*** THE QUEEN OF SPADES?
NO, I AM NOT!

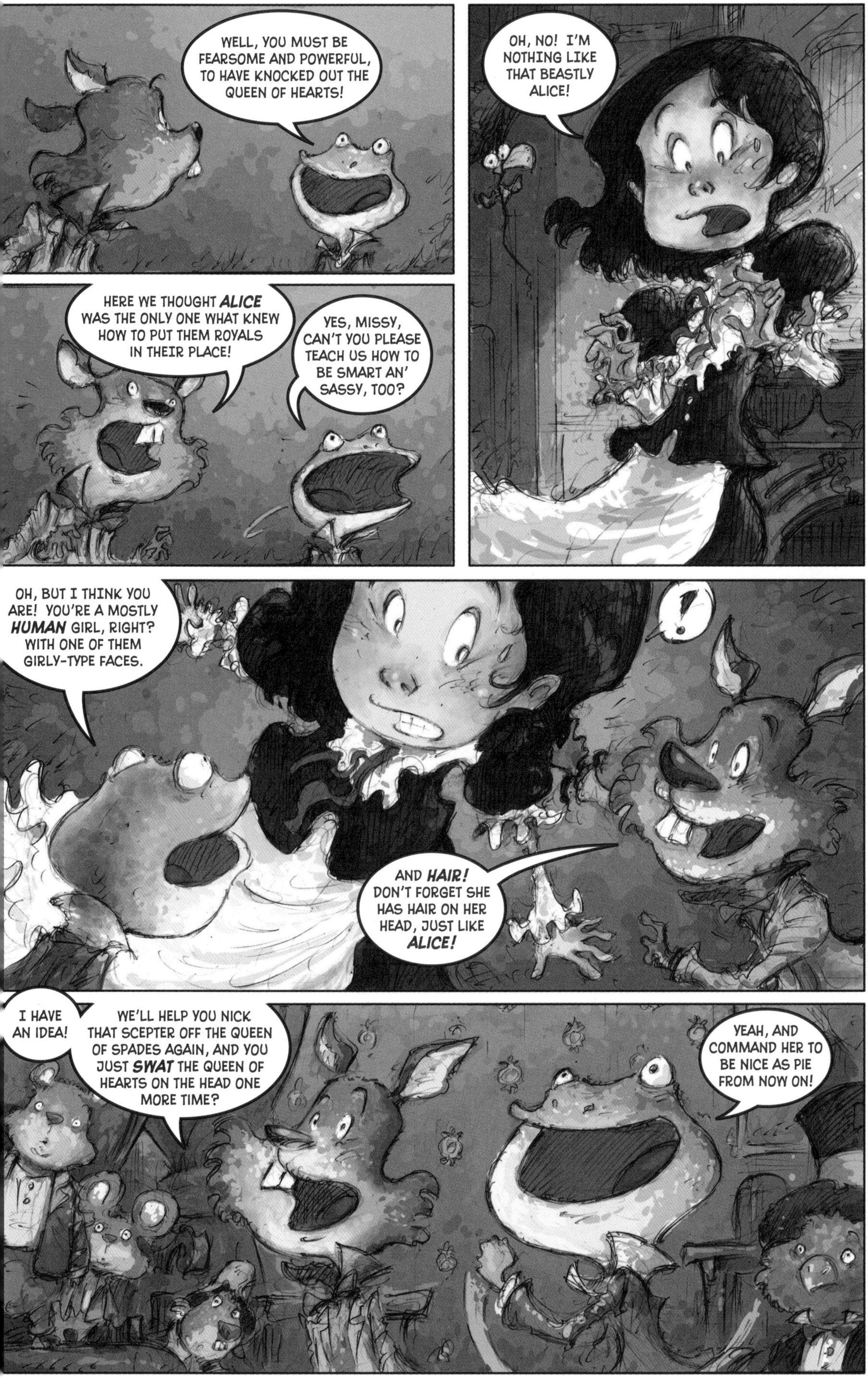
WELL, YOU MUST BE FEARSOME AND POWERFUL, TO HAVE KNOCKED OUT THE QUEEN OF HEARTS!
HERE WE THOUGHT ALICE WAS THE ONLY ONE WHAT KNEW HOW TO PUT THEM ROYALS IN THEIR PLACE!
YES, MISSY, CAN'T YOU PLEASE TEACH US HOW TO BE SMART AN' SASSY, TOO?
OH, NO! I'M NOTHING LIKE THAT BEASTLY ALICE!
OH, BUT I THINK YOU ARE! YOU'RE A MOSTLY HUMAN GIRL, RIGHT? WITH ONE OF THEM GIRLY-TYPE FACES.
!
AND HAIR! DON'T FORGET SHE HAS HAIR ON HER HEAD, JUST LIKE ALICE!
I HAVE AN IDEA!
WE'LL HELP YOU NICK THAT SCEPTER OFF THE QUEEN OF SPADES AGAIN, AND YOU JUST SWAT THE QUEEN OF HEARTS ON THE HEAD ONE MORE TIME?
YEAH, AND COMMAND HER TO BE NICE AS PIE FROM NOW ON!

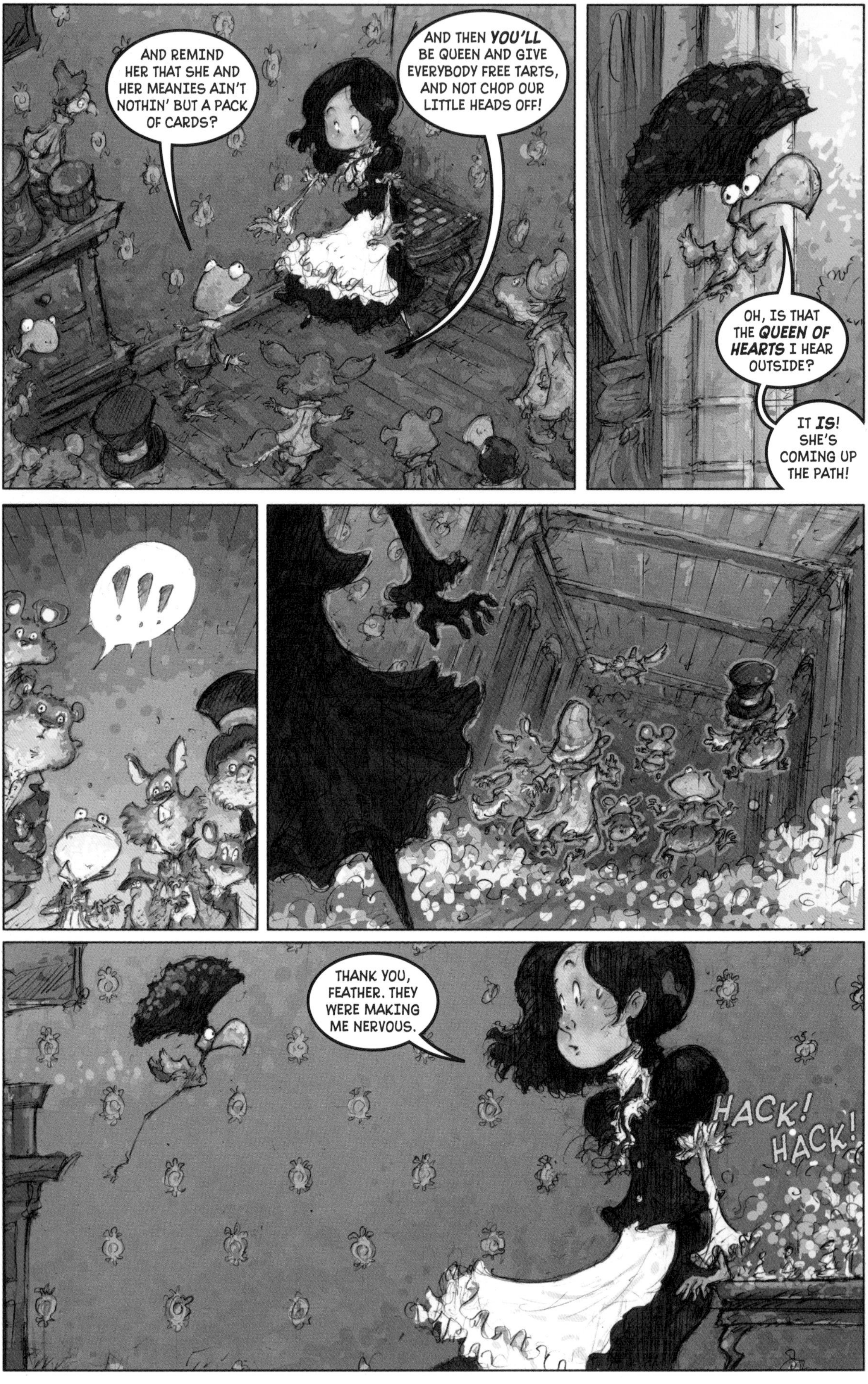
AND REMIND HER THAT SHE AND HER MEANIES AIN'T NOTHIN' BUT A PACK OF CARDS?
AND THEN ***YOU'LL*** BE QUEEN AND GIVE EVERYBODY FREE TARTS, AND NOT CHOP OUR LITTLE HEADS OFF!
OH, IS THAT THE ***QUEEN OF HEARTS*** I HEAR OUTSIDE?
IT ***IS***! SHE'S COMING UP THE PATH!
!!!
THANK YOU, FEATHER. THEY WERE MAKING ME NERVOUS.
HACK! HACK!

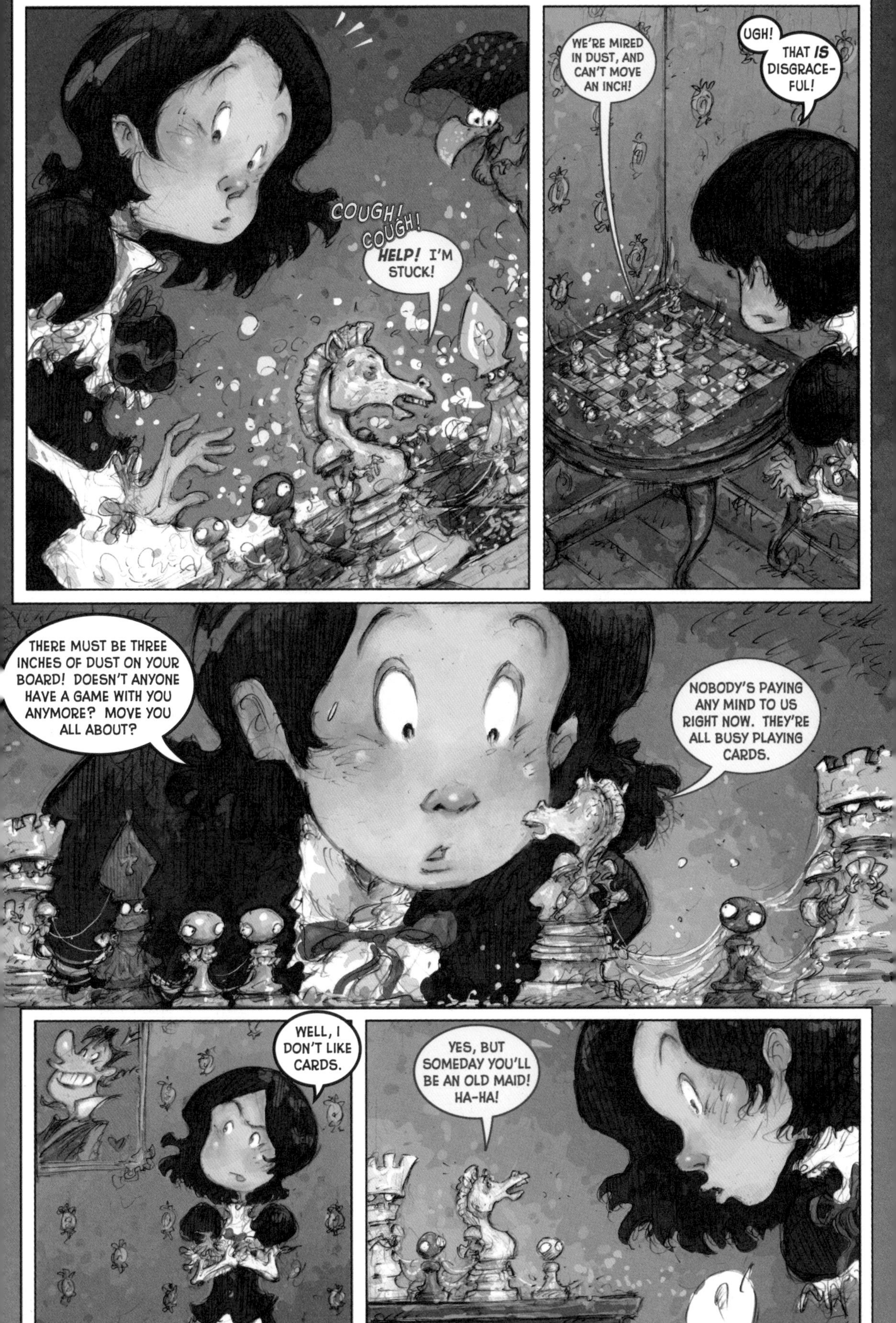
COUGH! COUGH!
HELP! I'M STUCK!
WE'RE MIRED IN DUST, AND CAN'T MOVE AN INCH!
UGH!
THAT IS DISGRACE-FUL!
THERE MUST BE THREE INCHES OF DUST ON YOUR BOARD! DOESN'T ANYONE HAVE A GAME WITH YOU ANYMORE? MOVE YOU ALL ABOUT?
NOBODY'S PAYING ANY MIND TO US RIGHT NOW. THEY'RE ALL BUSY PLAYING CARDS.
WELL, I DON'T LIKE CARDS.
YES, BUT SOMEDAY YOU'LL BE AN OLD MAID! HA-HA!

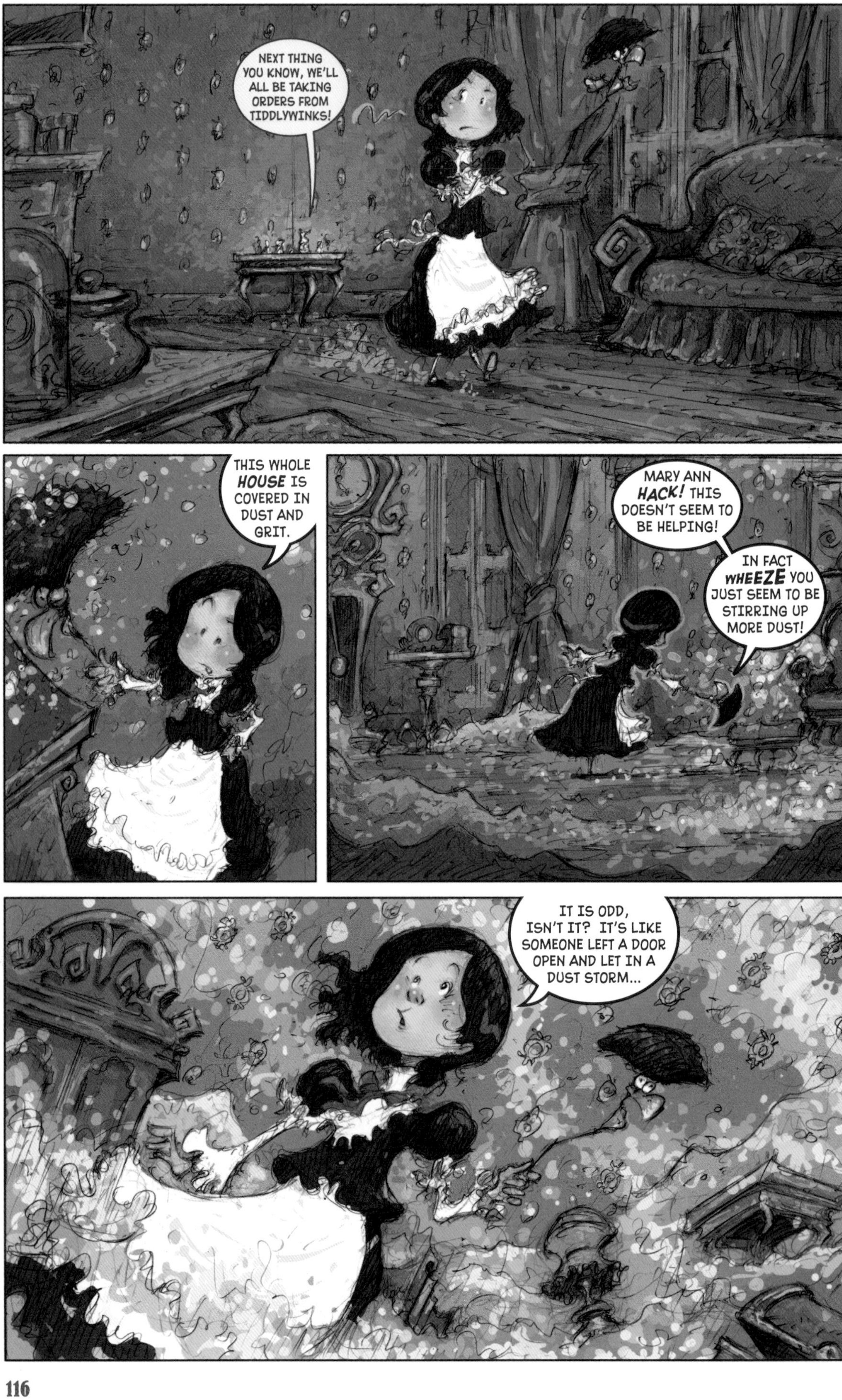
NEXT THING YOU KNOW, WE'LL ALL BE TAKING ORDERS FROM TIDDLYWINKS!
THIS WHOLE HOUSE IS COVERED IN DUST AND GRIT.
MARY ANN HACK! THIS DOESN'T SEEM TO BE HELPING!
IN FACT WHEEZE YOU JUST SEEM TO BE STIRRING UP MORE DUST!
IT IS ODD, ISN'T IT? IT'S LIKE SOMEONE LEFT A DOOR OPEN AND LET IN A DUST STORM...

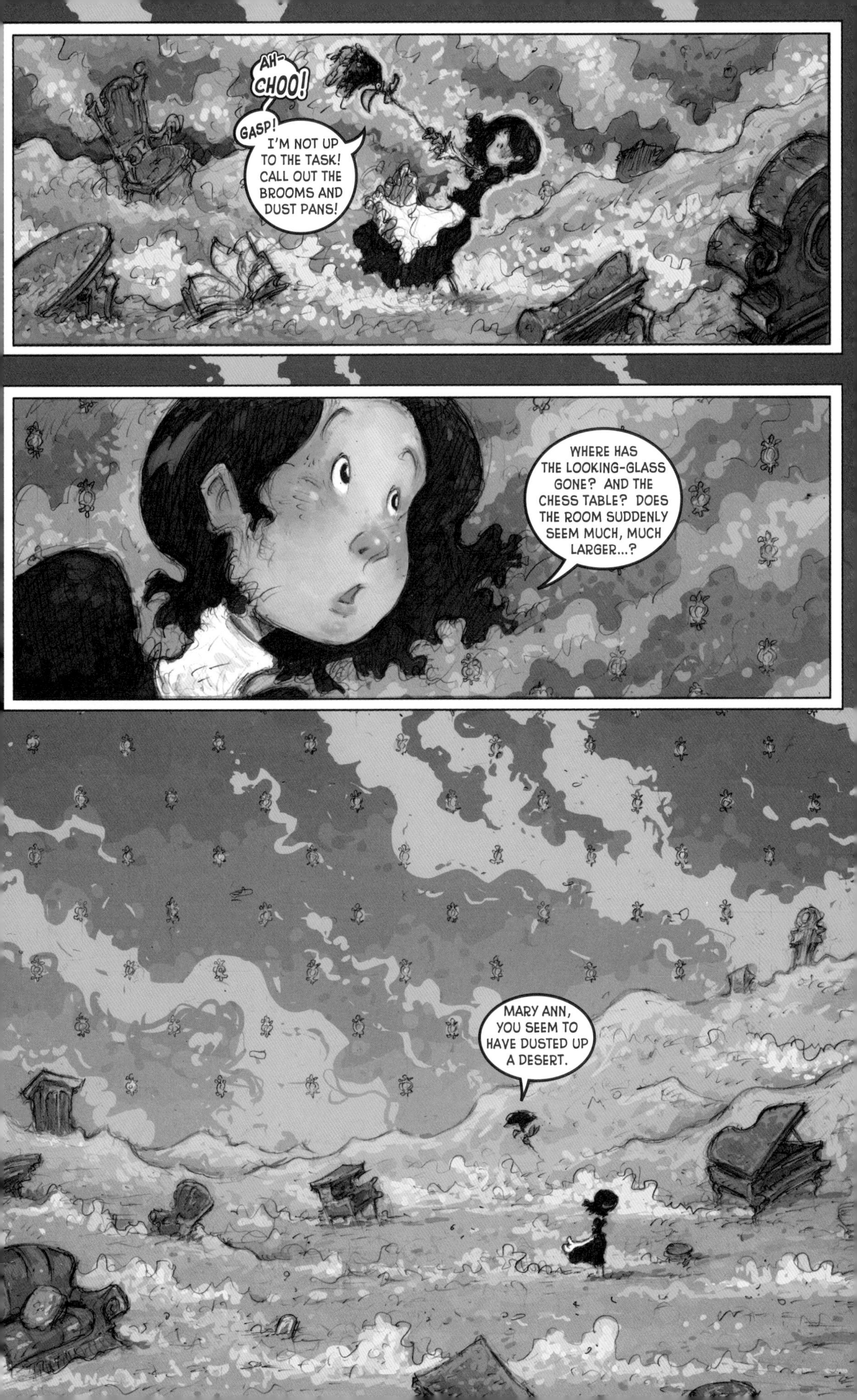
AH-CHOO!
GASP! I'M NOT UP TO THE TASK! CALL OUT THE BROOMS AND DUST PANS!
WHERE HAS THE LOOKING-GLASS GONE? AND THE CHESS TABLE? DOES THE ROOM SUDDENLY SEEM MUCH, MUCH LARGER...?
MARY ANN, YOU SEEM TO HAVE DUSTED UP A DESERT.

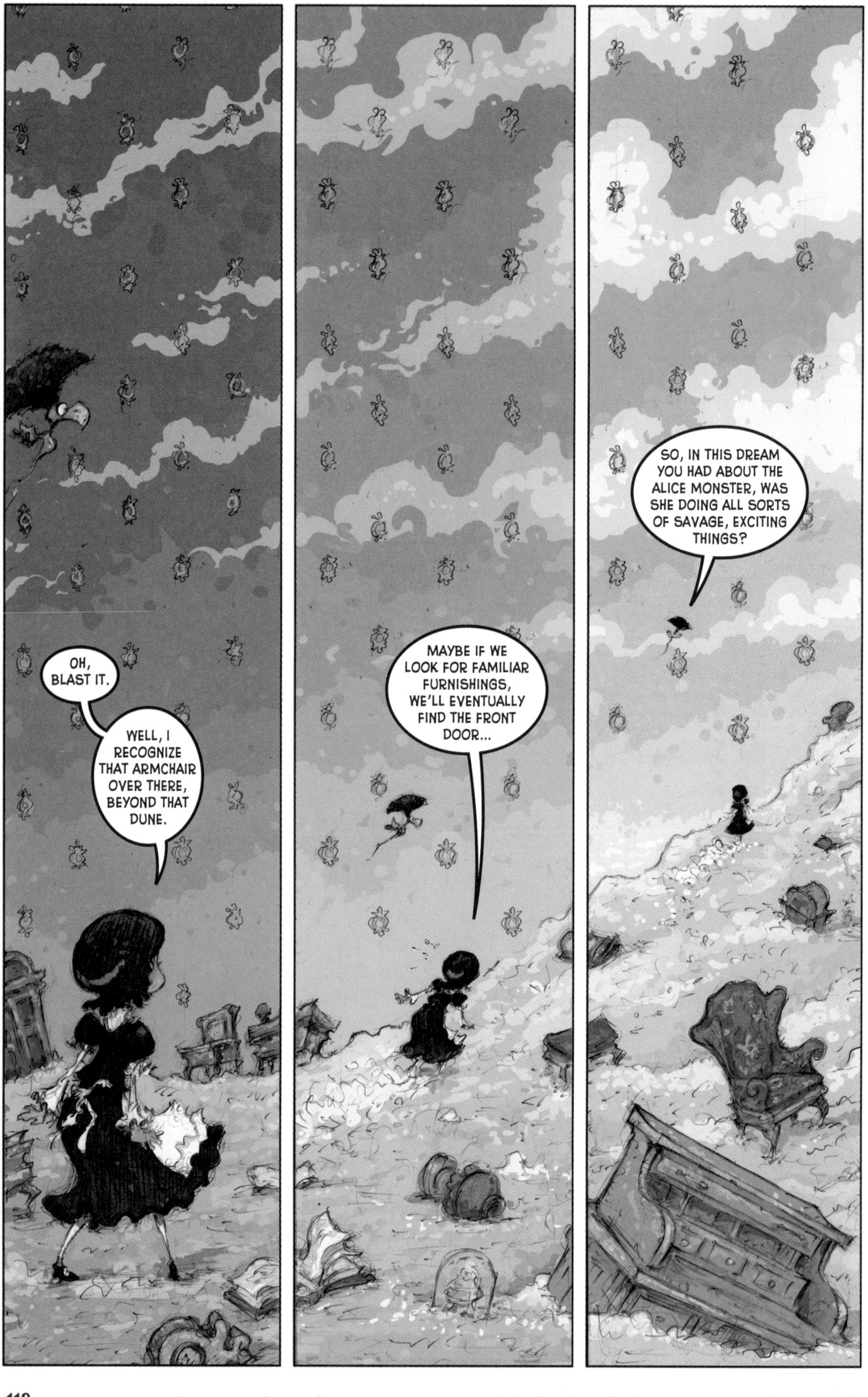
OH, BLAST IT.
WELL, I RECOGNIZE THAT ARMCHAIR OVER THERE, BEYOND THAT DUNE.
MAYBE IF WE LOOK FOR FAMILIAR FURNISHINGS, WE'LL EVENTUALLY FIND THE FRONT DOOR...
SO, IN THIS DREAM YOU HAD ABOUT THE ALICE MONSTER, WAS SHE DOING ALL SORTS OF SAVAGE, EXCITING THINGS?

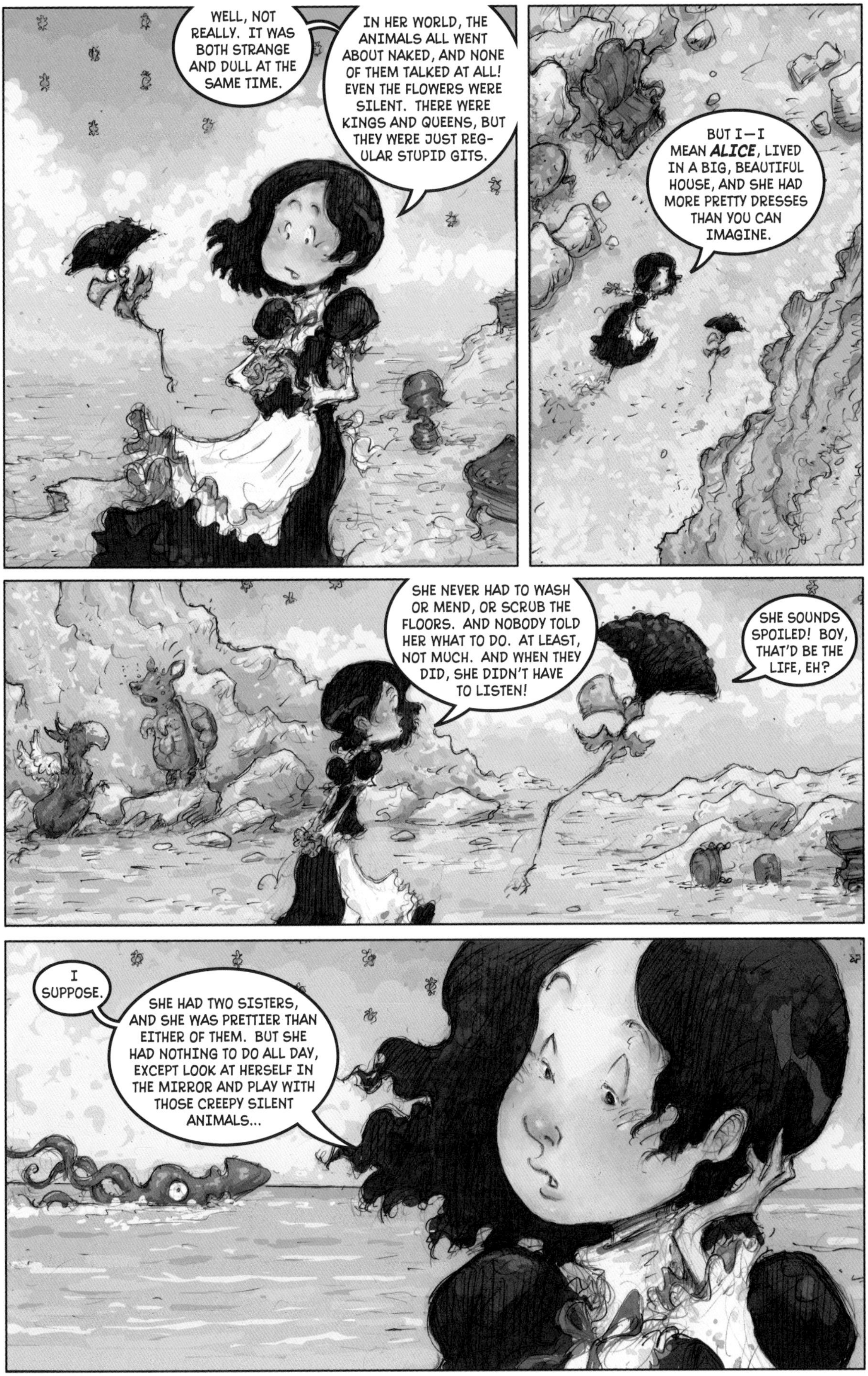
WELL, NOT REALLY. IT WAS BOTH STRANGE AND DULL AT THE SAME TIME.
IN HER WORLD, THE ANIMALS ALL WENT ABOUT NAKED, AND NONE OF THEM TALKED AT ALL! EVEN THE FLOWERS WERE SILENT. THERE WERE KINGS AND QUEENS, BUT THEY WERE JUST REGULAR STUPID GITS.
BUT I—I MEAN ***ALICE***, LIVED IN A BIG, BEAUTIFUL HOUSE, AND SHE HAD MORE PRETTY DRESSES THAN YOU CAN IMAGINE.
SHE NEVER HAD TO WASH OR MEND, OR SCRUB THE FLOORS. AND NOBODY TOLD HER WHAT TO DO. AT LEAST, NOT MUCH. AND WHEN THEY DID, SHE DIDN'T HAVE TO LISTEN!
SHE SOUNDS SPOILED! BOY, THAT'D BE THE LIFE, EH?
I SUPPOSE.
SHE HAD TWO SISTERS, AND SHE WAS PRETTIER THAN EITHER OF THEM. BUT SHE HAD NOTHING TO DO ALL DAY, EXCEPT LOOK AT HERSELF IN THE MIRROR AND PLAY WITH THOSE CREEPY SILENT ANIMALS...

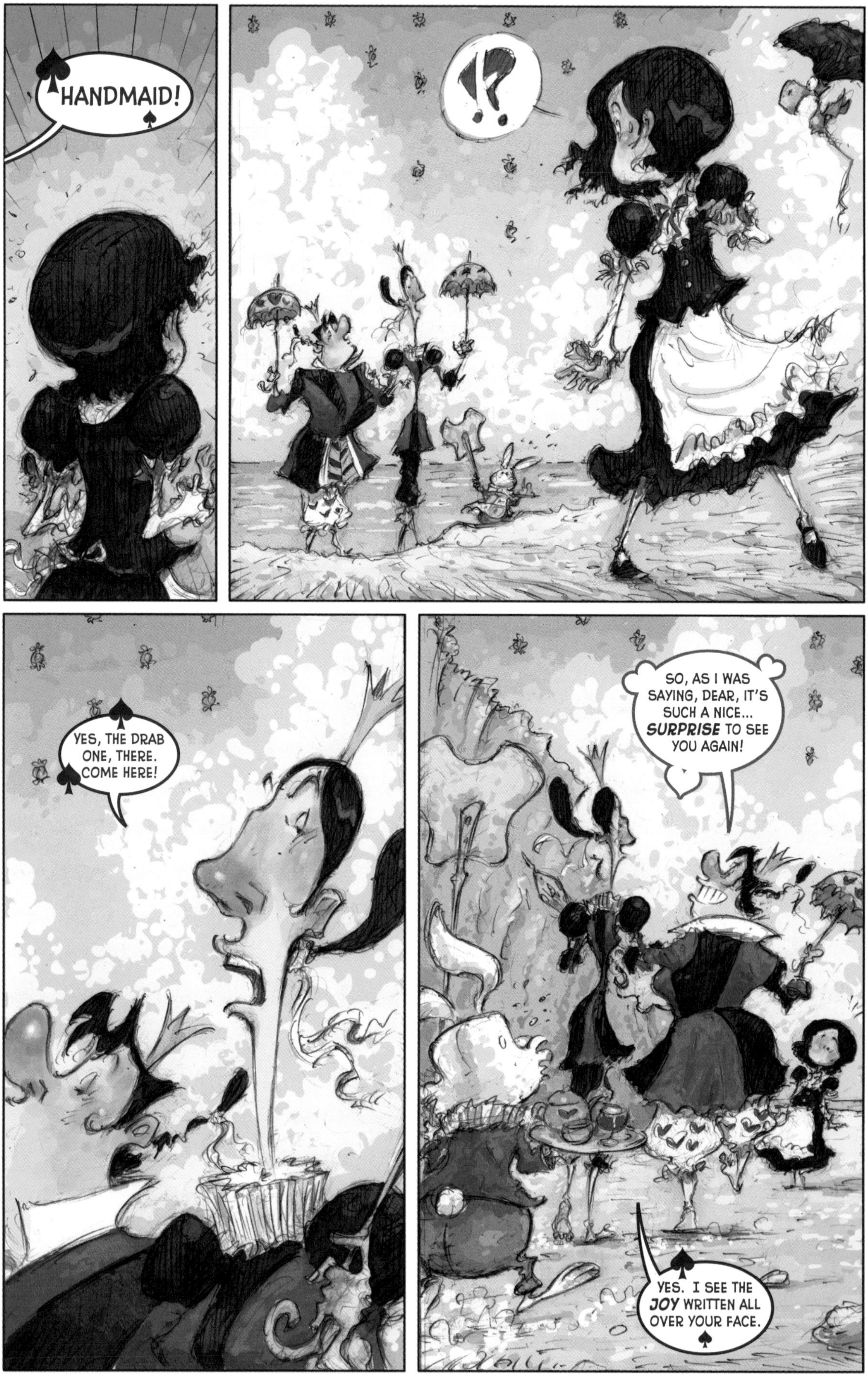
HANDMAID!
!?
YES, THE DRAB ONE, THERE. COME HERE!
SO, AS I WAS SAYING, DEAR, IT'S SUCH A NICE... **SURPRISE** TO SEE YOU AGAIN!
YES. I SEE THE **JOY** WRITTEN ALL OVER YOUR FACE.

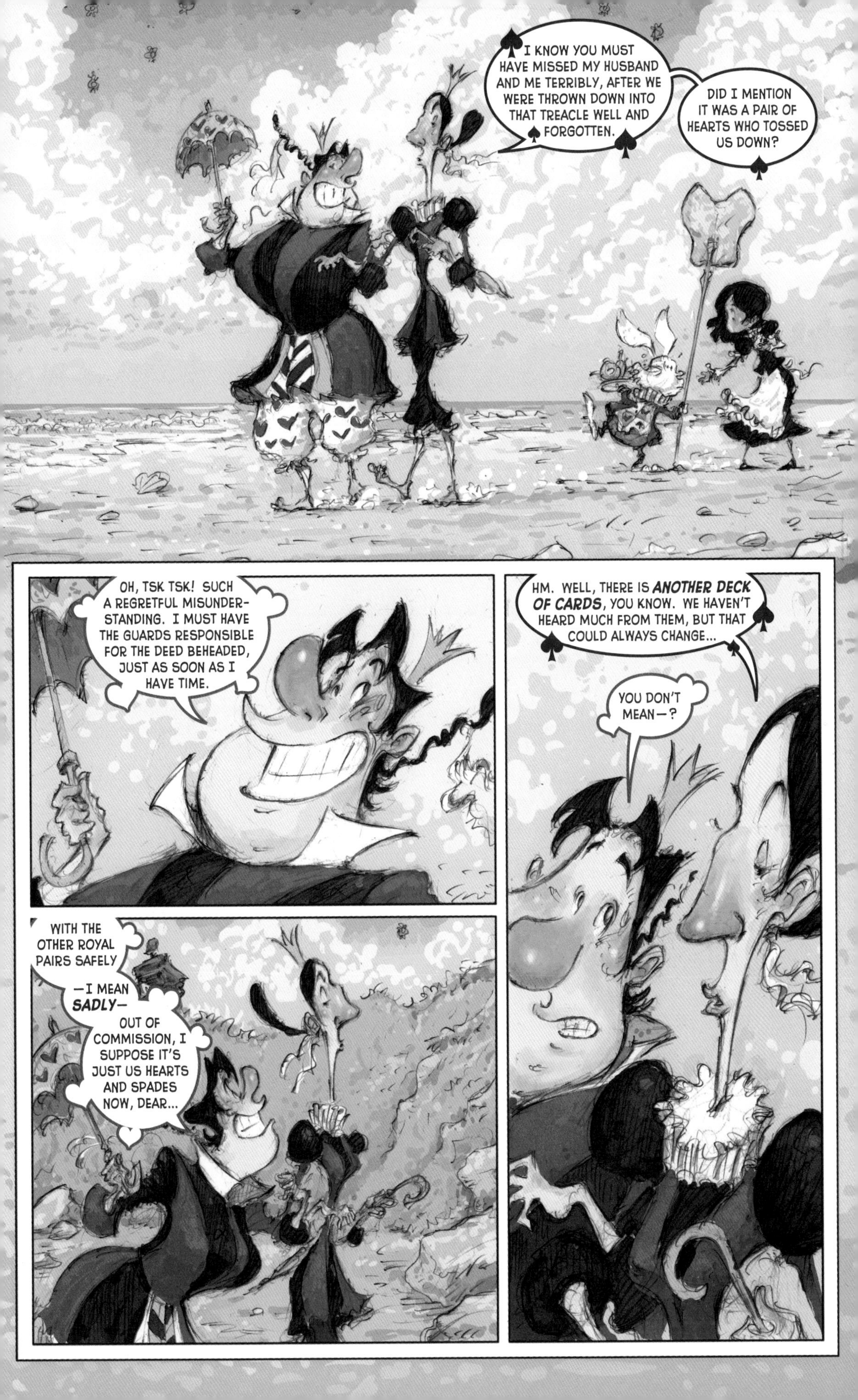
I KNOW YOU MUST HAVE MISSED MY HUSBAND AND ME TERRIBLY, AFTER WE WERE THROWN DOWN INTO THAT TREACLE WELL AND FORGOTTEN.
DID I MENTION IT WAS A PAIR OF HEARTS WHO TOSSED US DOWN?
OH, TSK TSK! SUCH A REGRETFUL MISUNDER-STANDING. I MUST HAVE THE GUARDS RESPONSIBLE FOR THE DEED BEHEADED, JUST AS SOON AS I HAVE TIME.
WITH THE OTHER ROYAL PAIRS SAFELY
—I MEAN SADLY—
OUT OF COMMISSION, I SUPPOSE IT'S JUST US HEARTS AND SPADES NOW, DEAR...
HM. WELL, THERE IS ANOTHER DECK OF CARDS, YOU KNOW. WE HAVEN'T HEARD MUCH FROM THEM, BUT THAT COULD ALWAYS CHANGE...
YOU DON'T MEAN—?

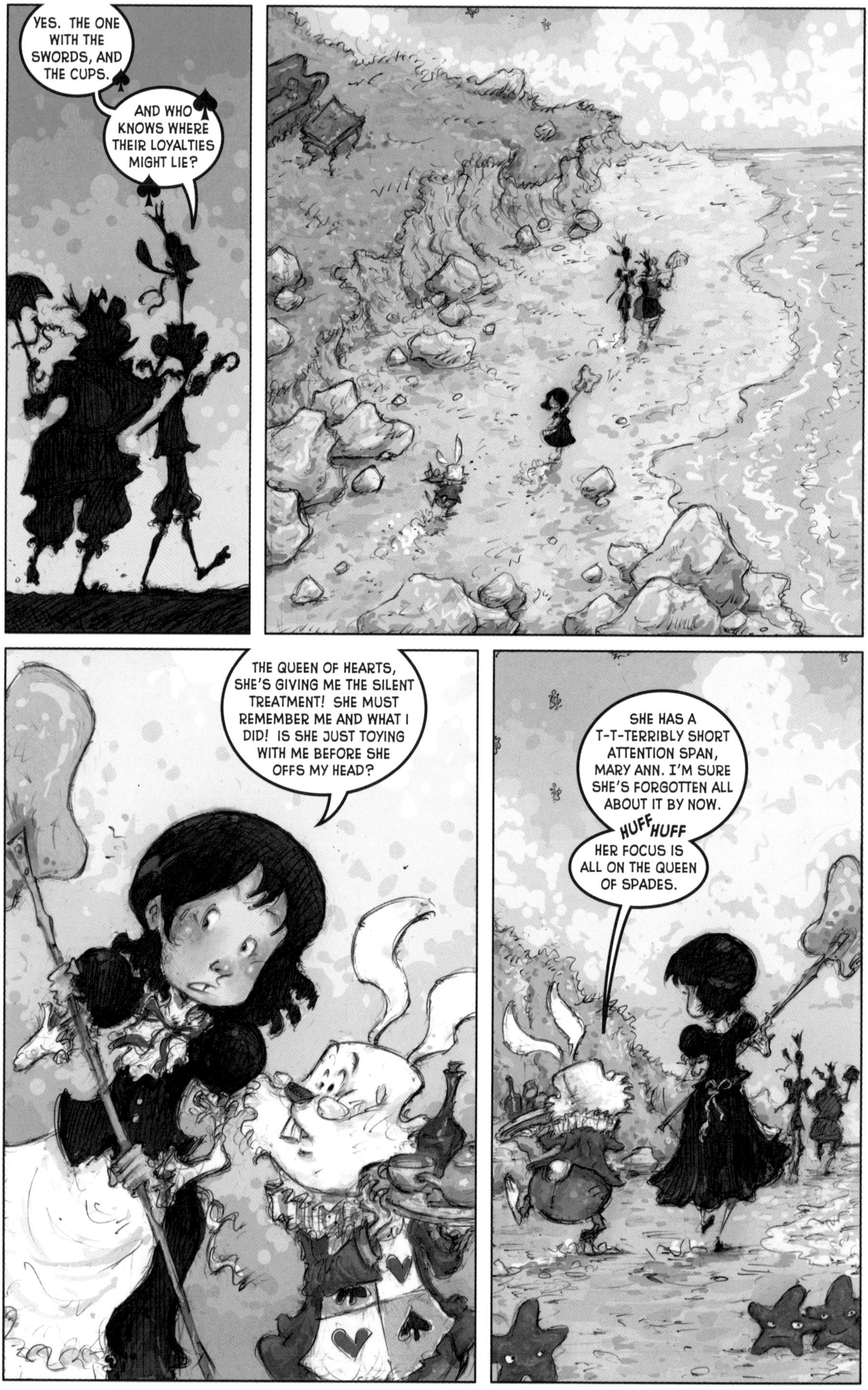
YES. THE ONE WITH THE SWORDS, AND THE CUPS.
AND WHO KNOWS WHERE THEIR LOYALTIES MIGHT LIE?
THE QUEEN OF HEARTS, SHE'S GIVING ME THE SILENT TREATMENT! SHE MUST REMEMBER ME AND WHAT I DID! IS SHE JUST TOYING WITH ME BEFORE SHE OFFS MY HEAD?
SHE HAS A T-T-TERRIBLY SHORT ATTENTION SPAN, MARY ANN. I'M SURE SHE'S FORGOTTEN ALL ABOUT IT BY NOW.
HUFF HUFF
HER FOCUS IS ALL ON THE QUEEN OF SPADES.

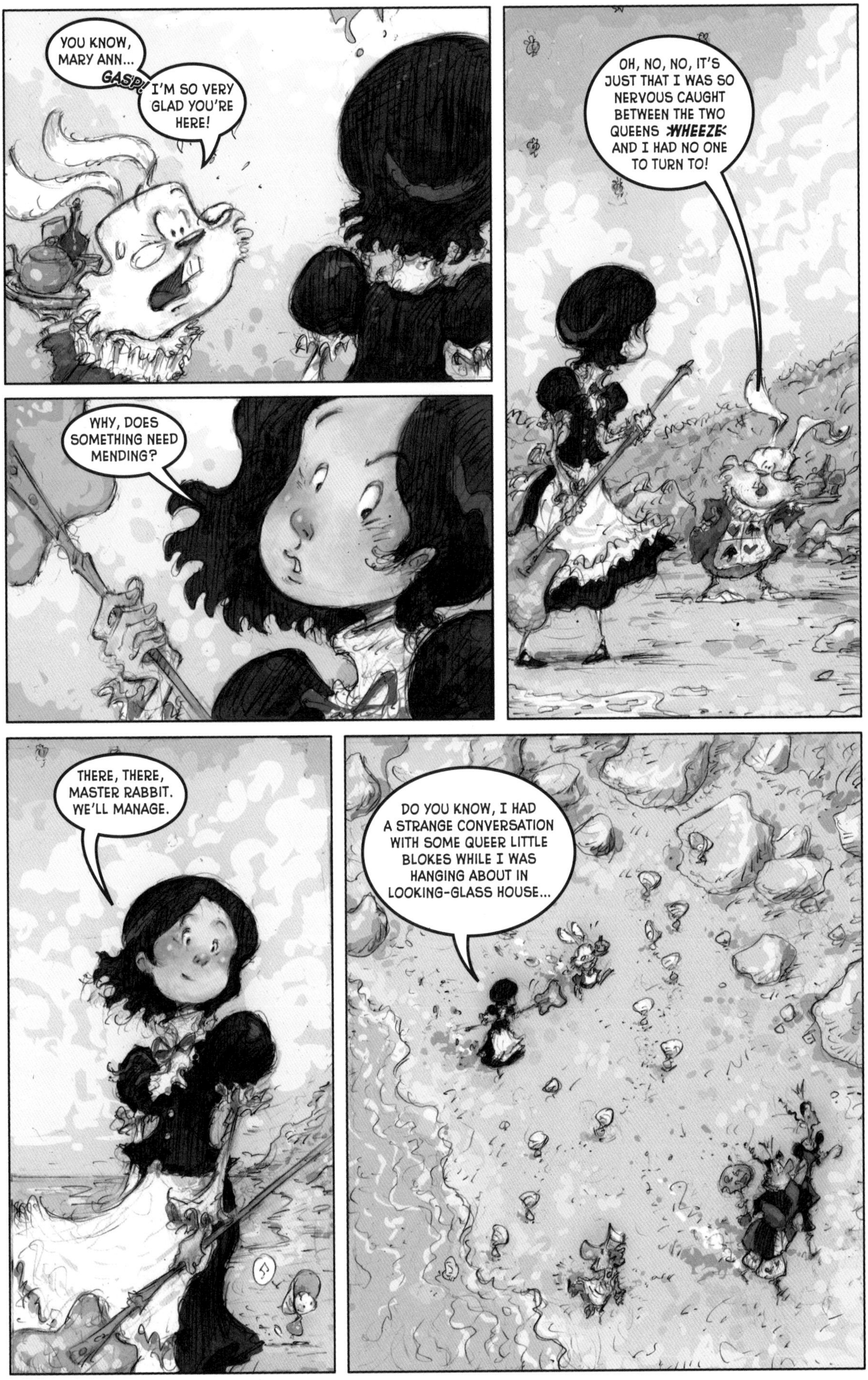
YOU KNOW, MARY ANN...
GASP!
I'M SO VERY GLAD YOU'RE HERE!
WHY, DOES SOMETHING NEED MENDING?
OH, NO, NO, IT'S JUST THAT I WAS SO NERVOUS CAUGHT BETWEEN THE TWO QUEENS *WHEEZE* AND I HAD NO ONE TO TURN TO!
THERE, THERE, MASTER RABBIT. WE'LL MANAGE.
DO YOU KNOW, I HAD A STRANGE CONVERSATION WITH SOME QUEER LITTLE BLOKES WHILE I WAS HANGING ABOUT IN LOOKING-GLASS HOUSE...

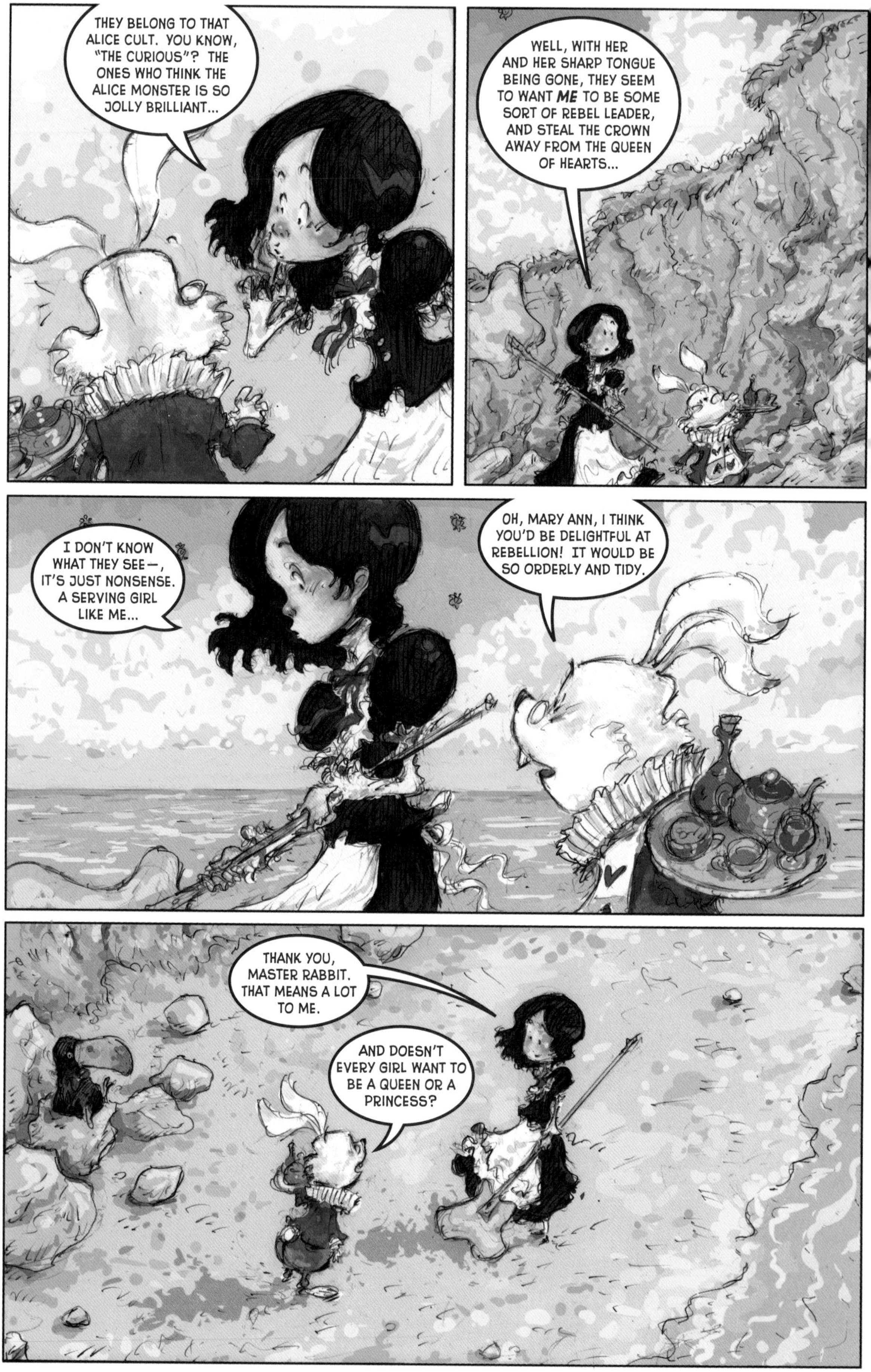
THEY BELONG TO THAT ALICE CULT. YOU KNOW, "THE CURIOUS"? THE ONES WHO THINK THE ALICE MONSTER IS SO JOLLY BRILLIANT...
WELL, WITH HER AND HER SHARP TONGUE BEING GONE, THEY SEEM TO WANT *ME* TO BE SOME SORT OF REBEL LEADER, AND STEAL THE CROWN AWAY FROM THE QUEEN OF HEARTS...
I DON'T KNOW WHAT THEY SEE—, IT'S JUST NONSENSE. A SERVING GIRL LIKE ME...
OH, MARY ANN, I THINK YOU'D BE DELIGHTFUL AT REBELLION! IT WOULD BE SO ORDERLY AND TIDY.
THANK YOU, MASTER RABBIT. THAT MEANS A LOT TO ME.
AND DOESN'T EVERY GIRL WANT TO BE A QUEEN OR A PRINCESS?

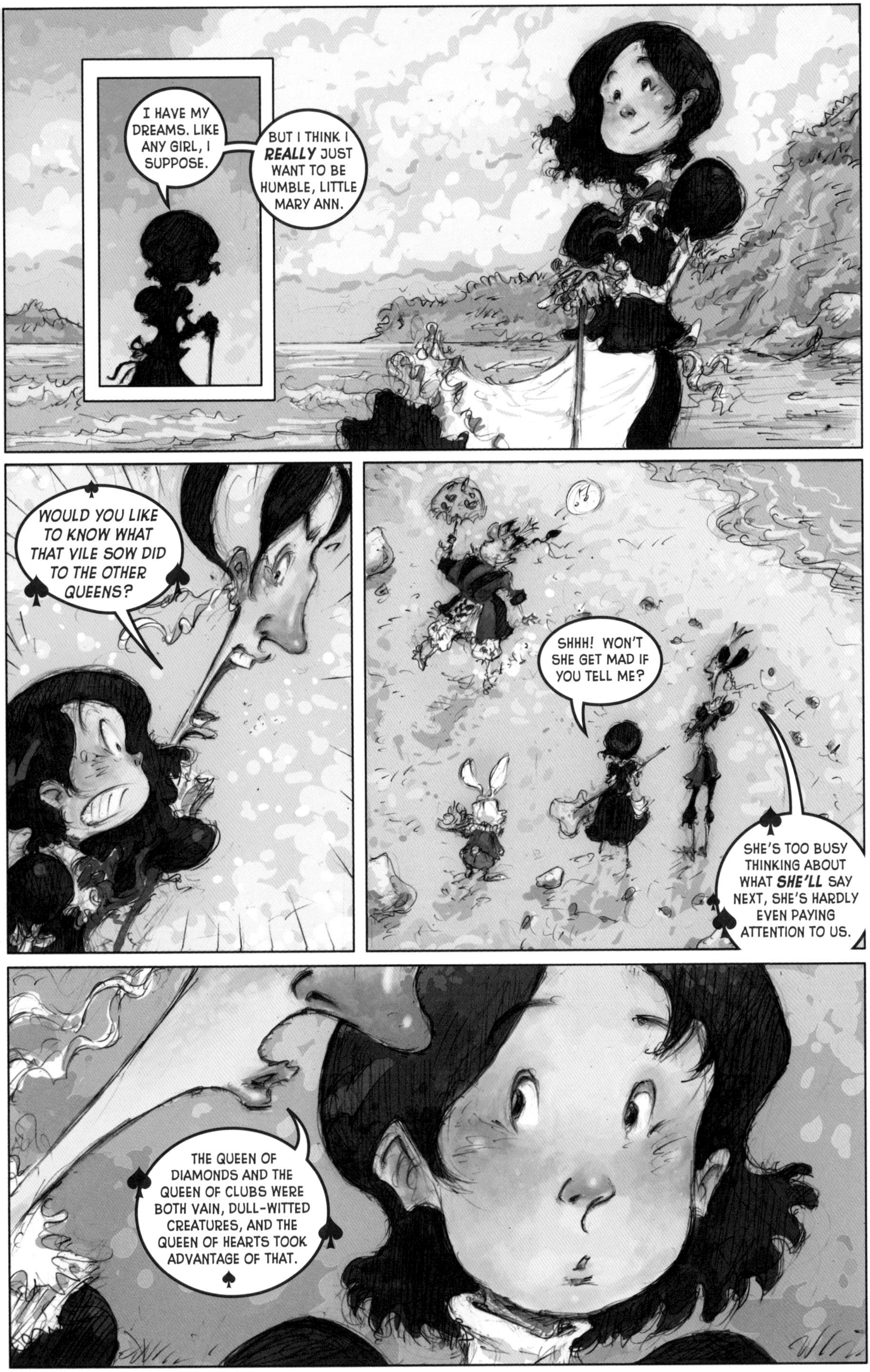
I HAVE MY DREAMS. LIKE ANY GIRL, I SUPPOSE.
BUT I THINK I **REALLY** JUST WANT TO BE HUMBLE, LITTLE MARY ANN.
WOULD YOU LIKE TO KNOW WHAT THAT VILE SOW DID TO THE OTHER QUEENS?
SHHH! WON'T SHE GET MAD IF YOU TELL ME?
SHE'S TOO BUSY THINKING ABOUT WHAT ***SHE'LL*** SAY NEXT, SHE'S HARDLY EVEN PAYING ATTENTION TO US.
THE QUEEN OF DIAMONDS AND THE QUEEN OF CLUBS WERE BOTH VAIN, DULL-WITTED CREATURES, AND THE QUEEN OF HEARTS TOOK ADVANTAGE OF THAT.

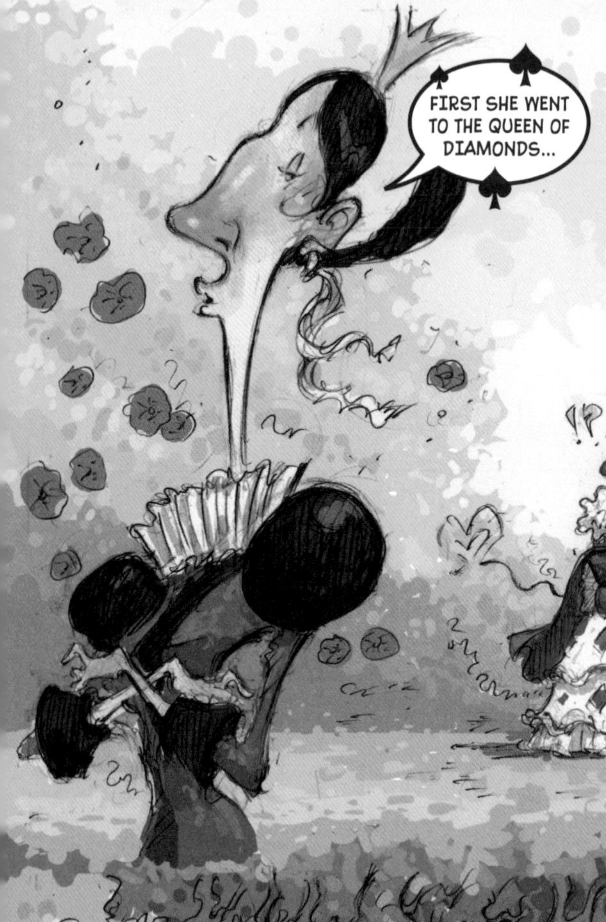
FIRST SHE WENT TO THE QUEEN OF DIAMONDS...

Our queenly friend,
My ear does bend
To claim your rings are fake!

She snorts and laughs
And says "they're glass."
The Queen of Clubs — that snake!

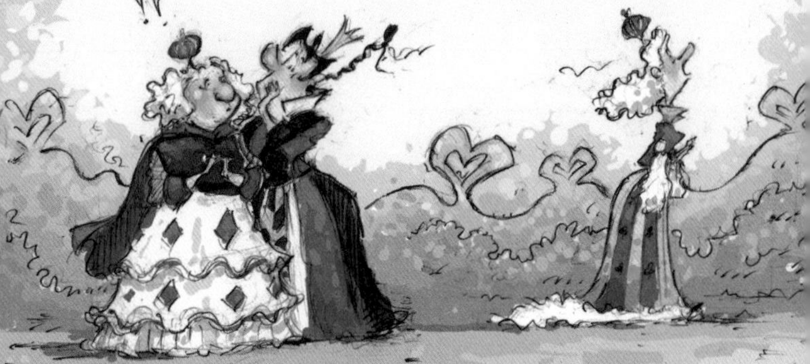

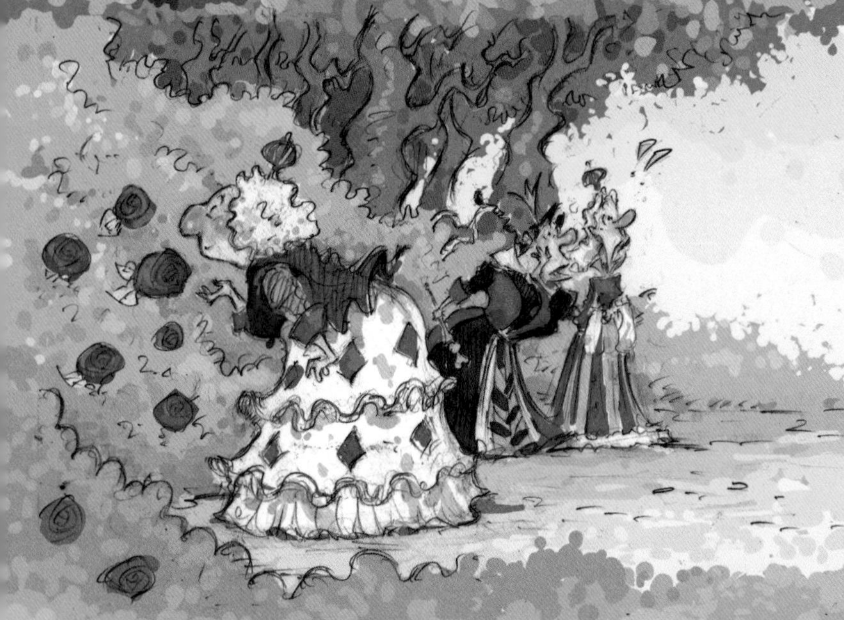

Then to the
Queen of clubs...

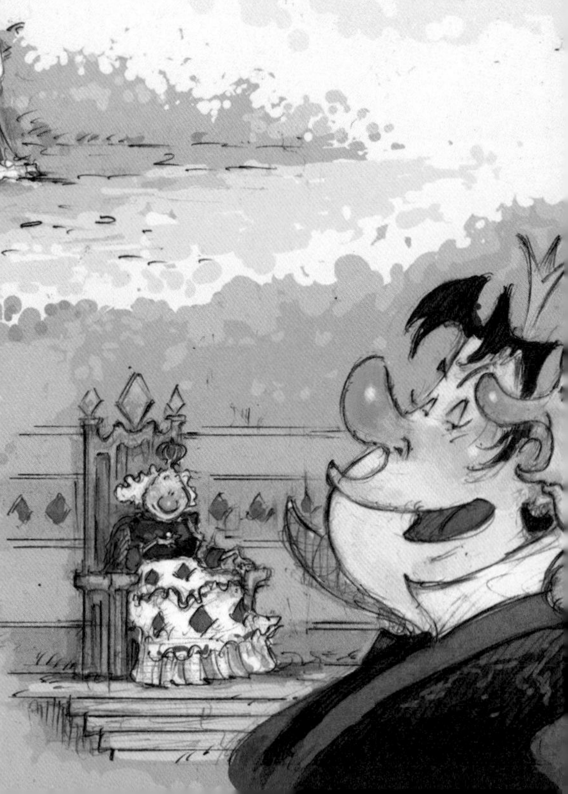

The diamond queen,
She sure is mean.
You ought to hear her talk.

She says your foot
Is clubbed, and that
Explains the way you walk!

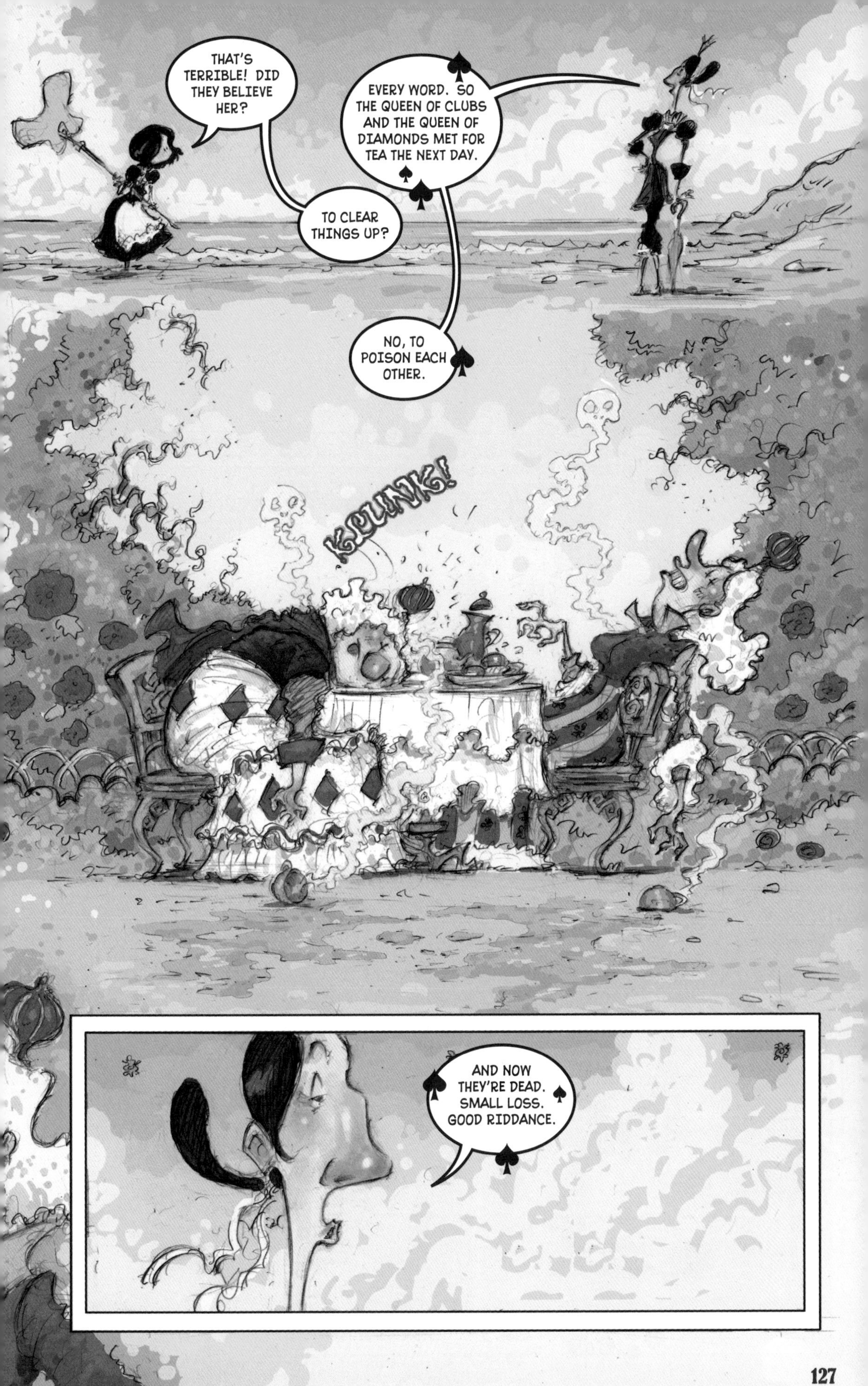
THAT'S TERRIBLE! DID THEY BELIEVE HER?
EVERY WORD. SO THE QUEEN OF CLUBS AND THE QUEEN OF DIAMONDS MET FOR TEA THE NEXT DAY.
TO CLEAR THINGS UP?
NO, TO POISON EACH OTHER.
KLUNK!
AND NOW THEY'RE DEAD. SMALL LOSS. GOOD RIDDANCE.

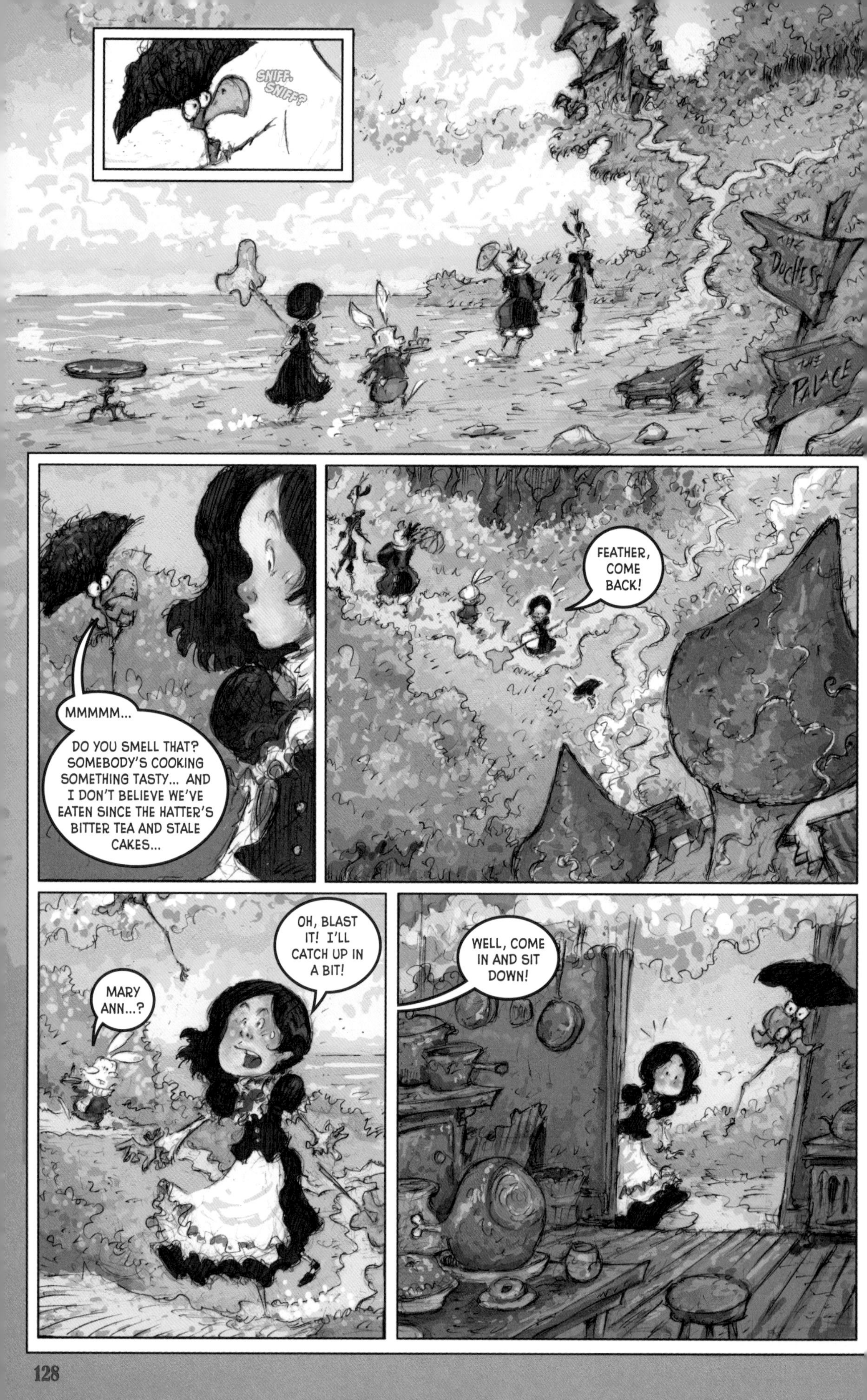
SNIFF.
SNIFF?
THE DUCHESS
THE PALACE
MMMMM...
DO YOU SMELL THAT? SOMEBODY'S COOKING SOMETHING TASTY... AND I DON'T BELIEVE WE'VE EATEN SINCE THE HATTER'S BITTER TEA AND STALE CAKES...
FEATHER, COME BACK!
MARY ANN...?
OH, BLAST IT! I'LL CATCH UP IN A BIT!
WELL, COME IN AND SIT DOWN!

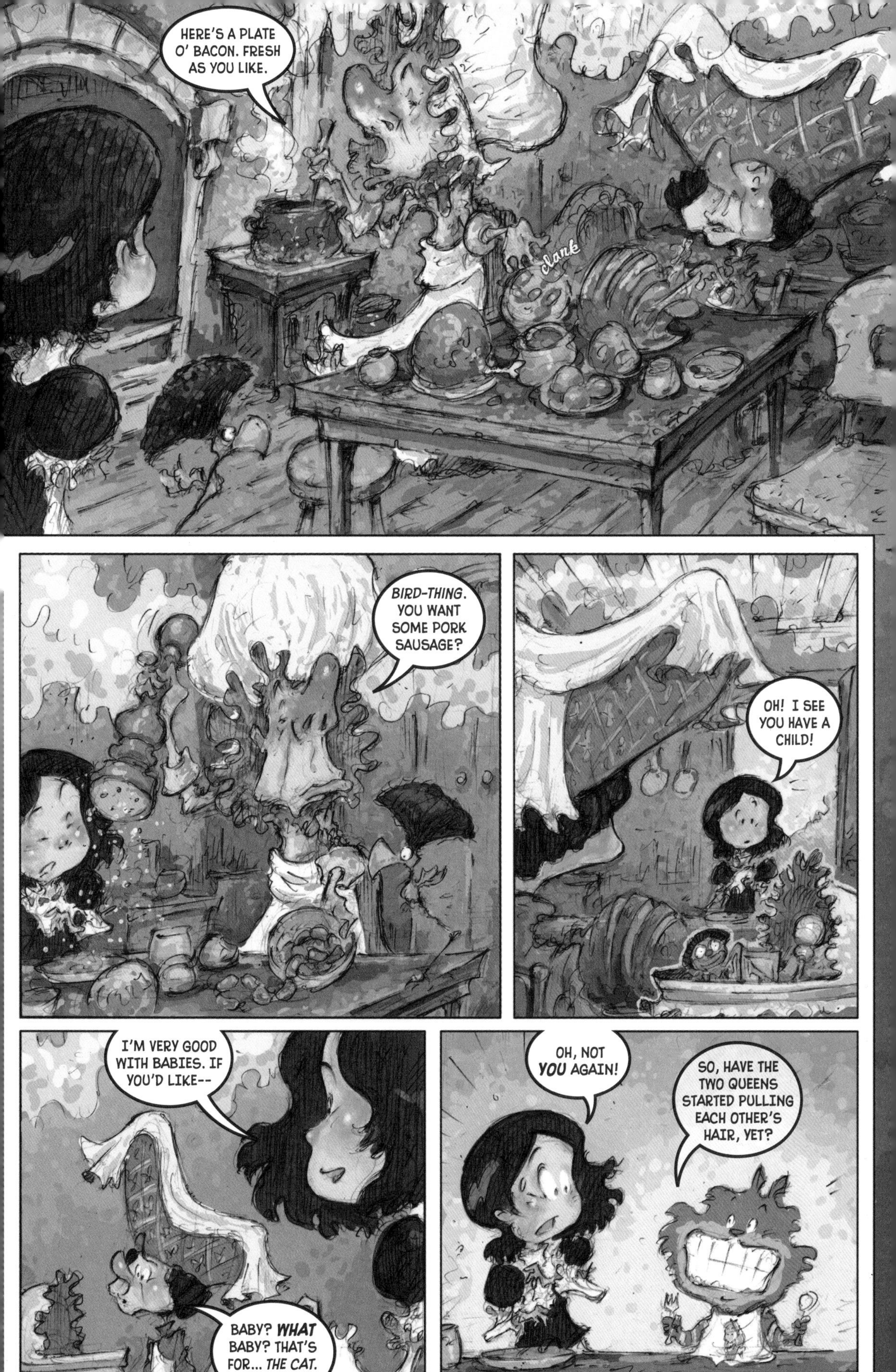
HERE'S A PLATE O' BACON. FRESH AS YOU LIKE.
clank
BIRD-THING. YOU WANT SOME PORK SAUSAGE?
OH! I SEE YOU HAVE A CHILD!
I'M VERY GOOD WITH BABIES. IF YOU'D LIKE--
BABY? WHAT BABY? THAT'S FOR... THE CAT.
OH, NOT YOU AGAIN!
SO, HAVE THE TWO QUEENS STARTED PULLING EACH OTHER'S HAIR, YET?

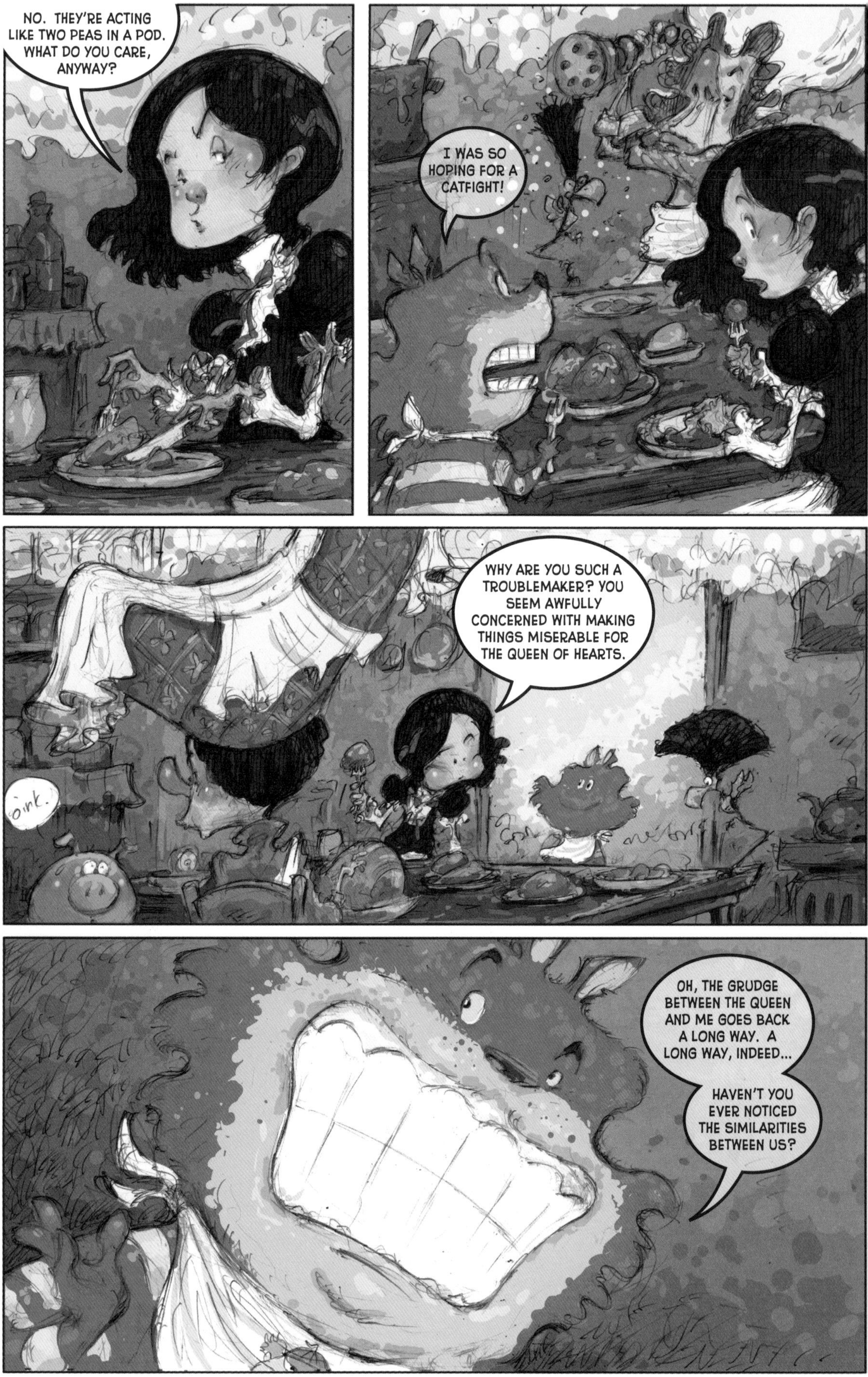
NO. THEY'RE ACTING LIKE TWO PEAS IN A POD. WHAT DO YOU CARE, ANYWAY?
I WAS SO HOPING FOR A CATFIGHT!
WHY ARE YOU SUCH A TROUBLEMAKER? YOU SEEM AWFULLY CONCERNED WITH MAKING THINGS MISERABLE FOR THE QUEEN OF HEARTS.
oink.
OH, THE GRUDGE BETWEEN THE QUEEN AND ME GOES BACK A LONG WAY. A LONG WAY, INDEED...
HAVEN'T YOU EVER NOTICED THE SIMILARITIES BETWEEN US?

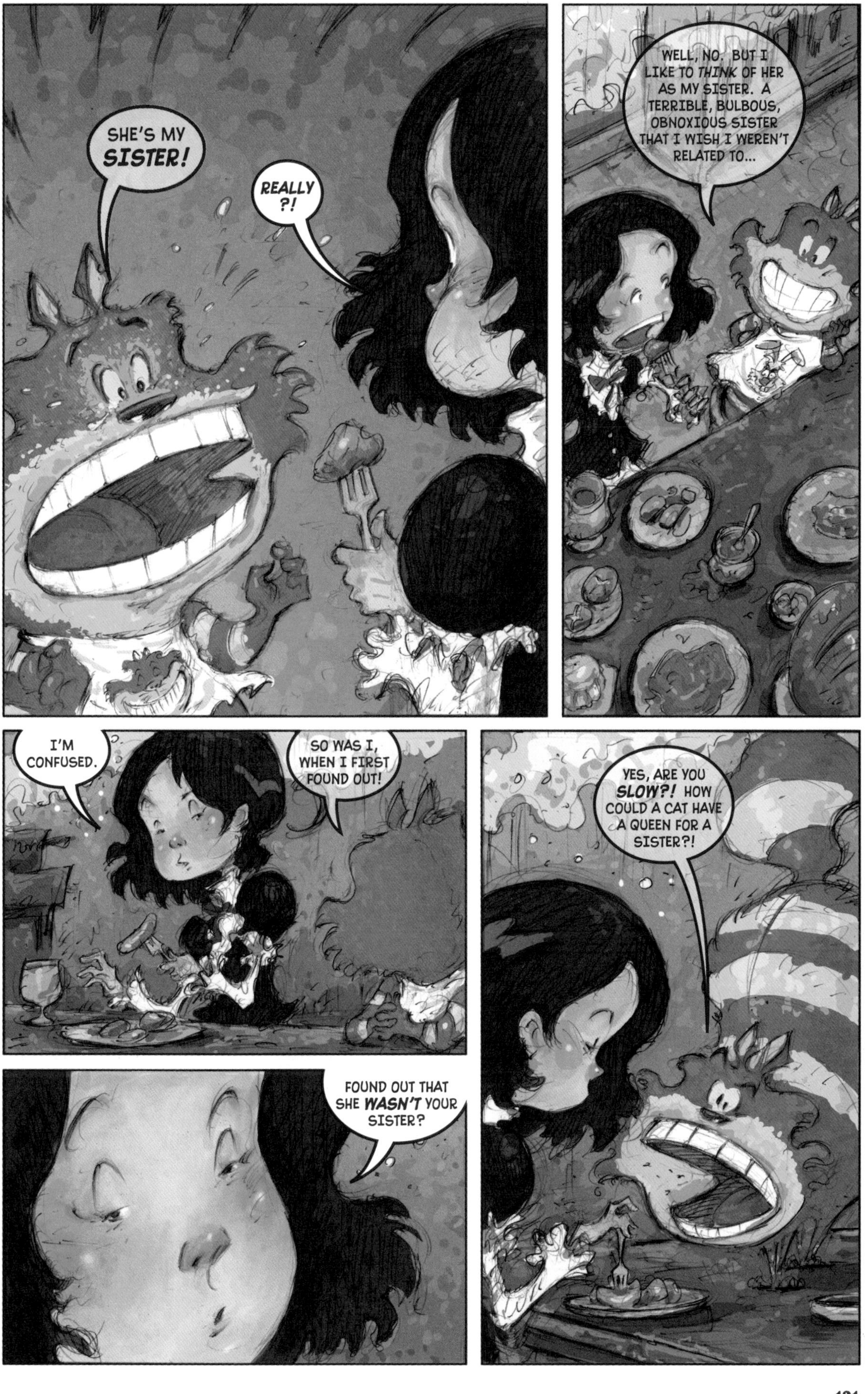
SHE'S MY SISTER!
REALLY ?!
WELL, NO. BUT I LIKE TO THINK OF HER AS MY SISTER. A TERRIBLE, BULBOUS, OBNOXIOUS SISTER THAT I WISH I WEREN'T RELATED TO...
I'M CONFUSED.
SO WAS I, WHEN I FIRST FOUND OUT!
YES, ARE YOU SLOW?! HOW COULD A CAT HAVE A QUEEN FOR A SISTER?!
FOUND OUT THAT SHE WASN'T YOUR SISTER?

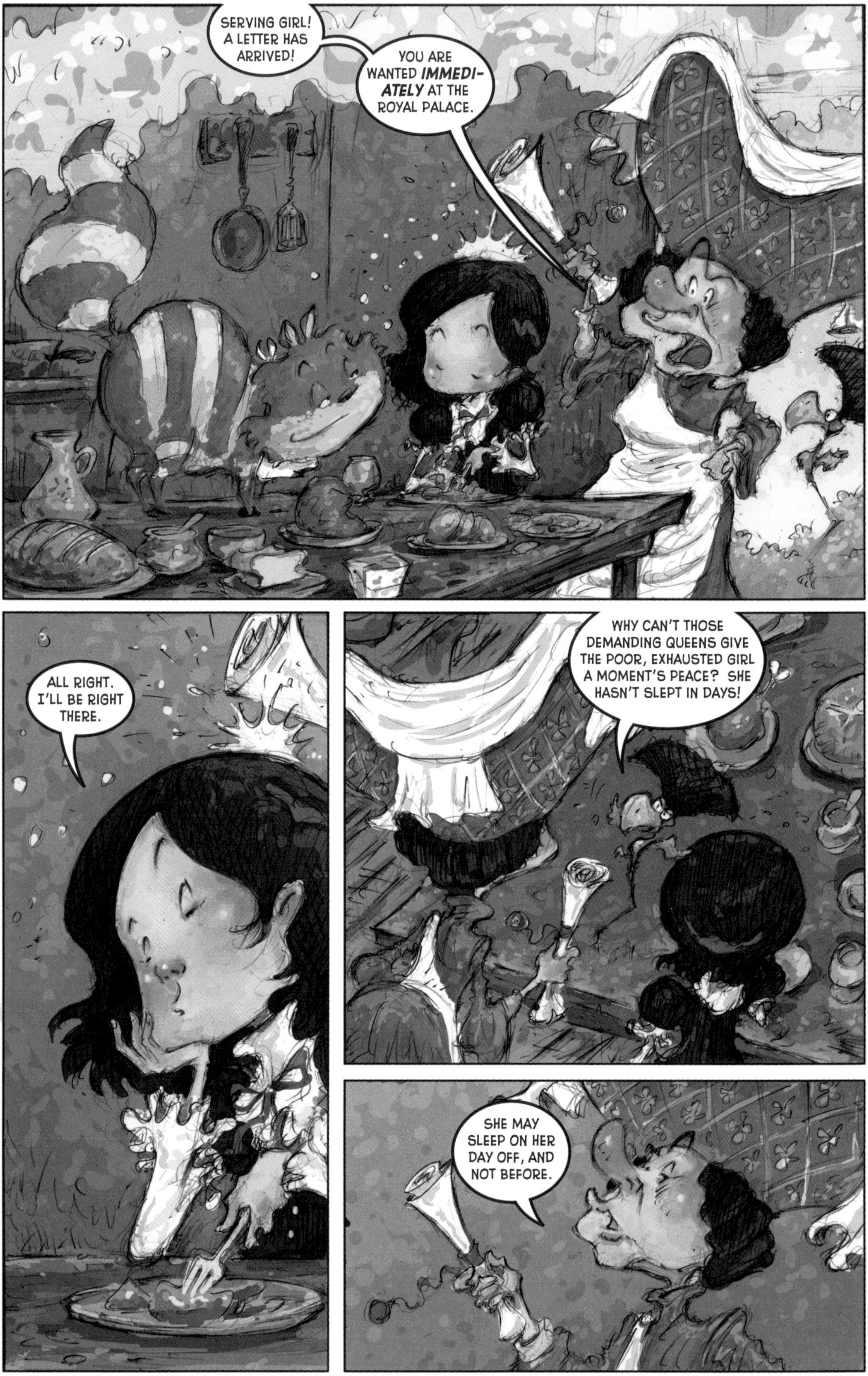
SERVING GIRL! A LETTER HAS ARRIVED!
YOU ARE WANTED IMMEDI-ATELY AT THE ROYAL PALACE.
ALL RIGHT. I'LL BE RIGHT THERE.
WHY CAN'T THOSE DEMANDING QUEENS GIVE THE POOR, EXHAUSTED GIRL A MOMENT'S PEACE? SHE HASN'T SLEPT IN DAYS!
SHE MAY SLEEP ON HER DAY OFF, AND NOT BEFORE.

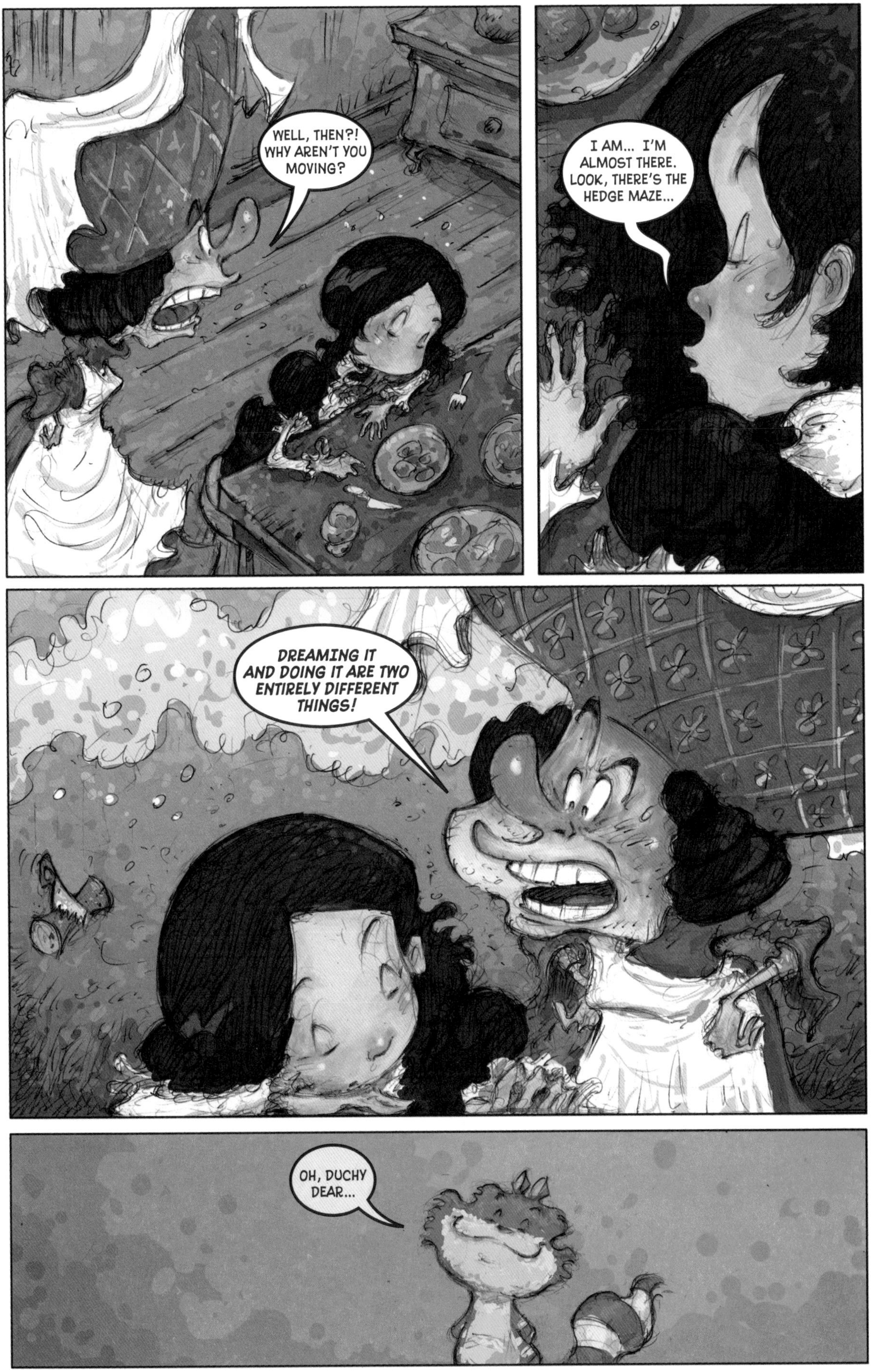
WELL, THEN?! WHY AREN'T YOU MOVING?
I AM... I'M ALMOST THERE. LOOK, THERE'S THE HEDGE MAZE...
DREAMING IT AND DOING IT ARE TWO ENTIRELY DIFFERENT THINGS!
OH, DUCHY DEAR...

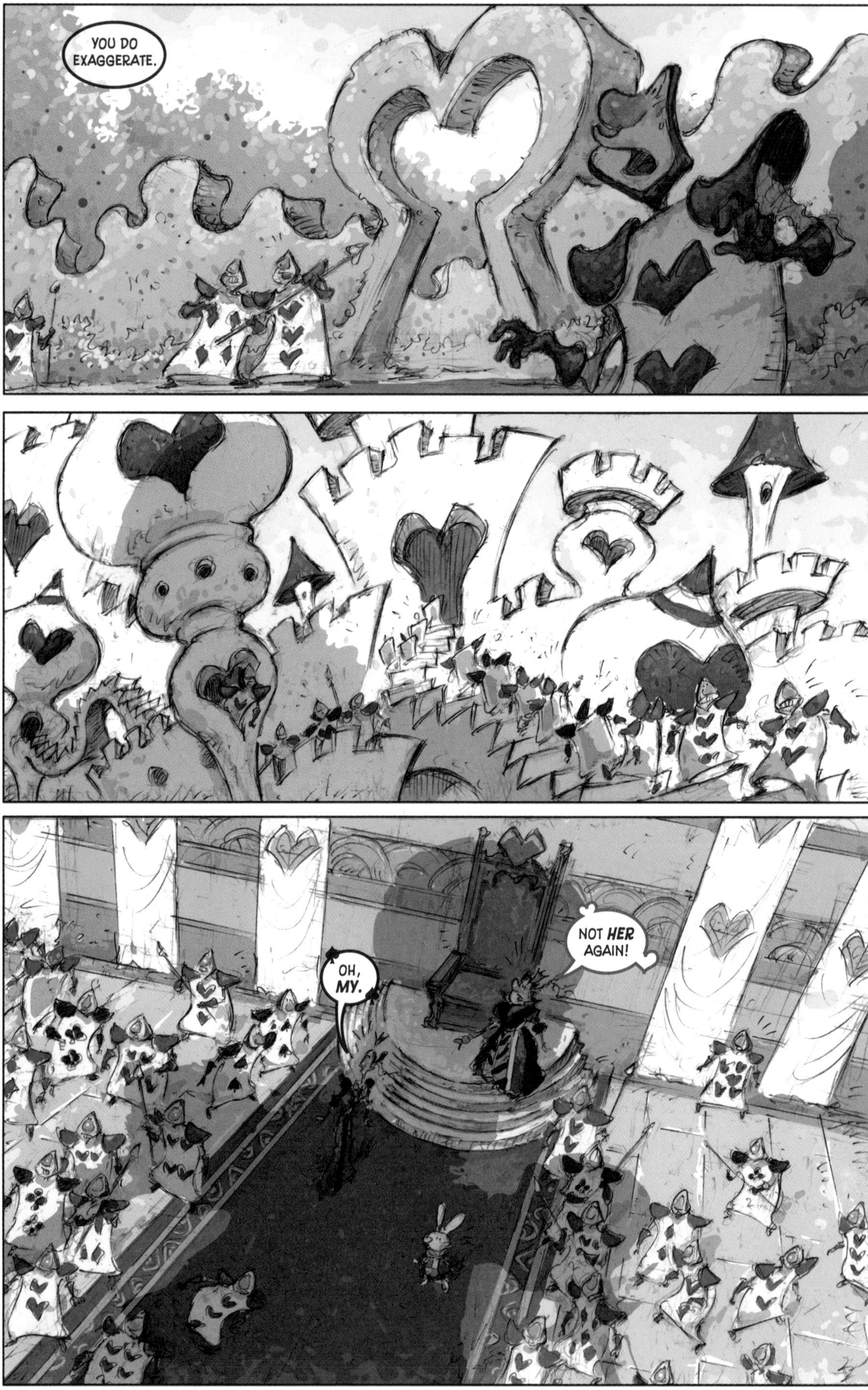
YOU DO EXAGGERATE.
OH, MY.
NOT HER AGAIN!

Chapter Six

Cut The Deck!

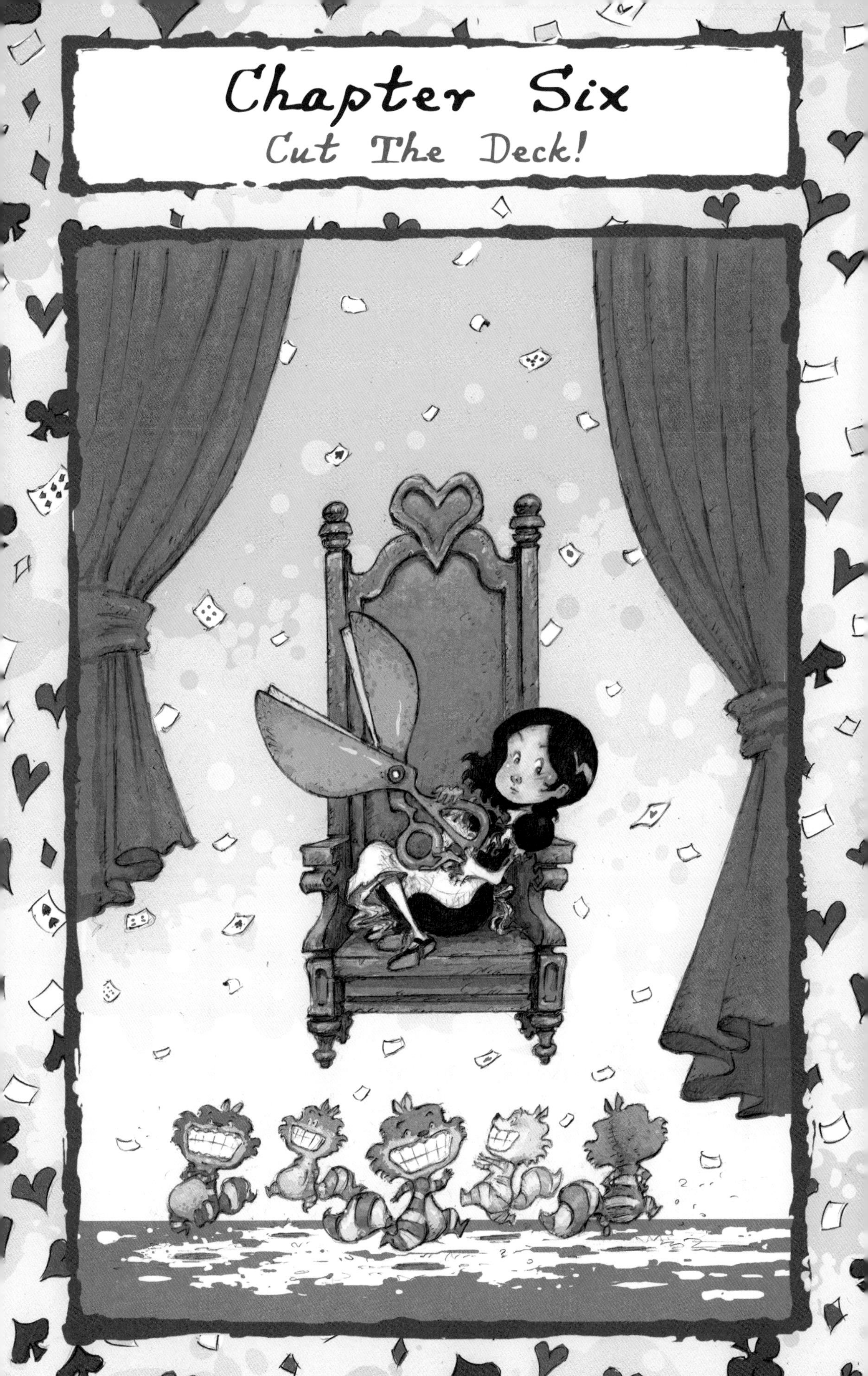

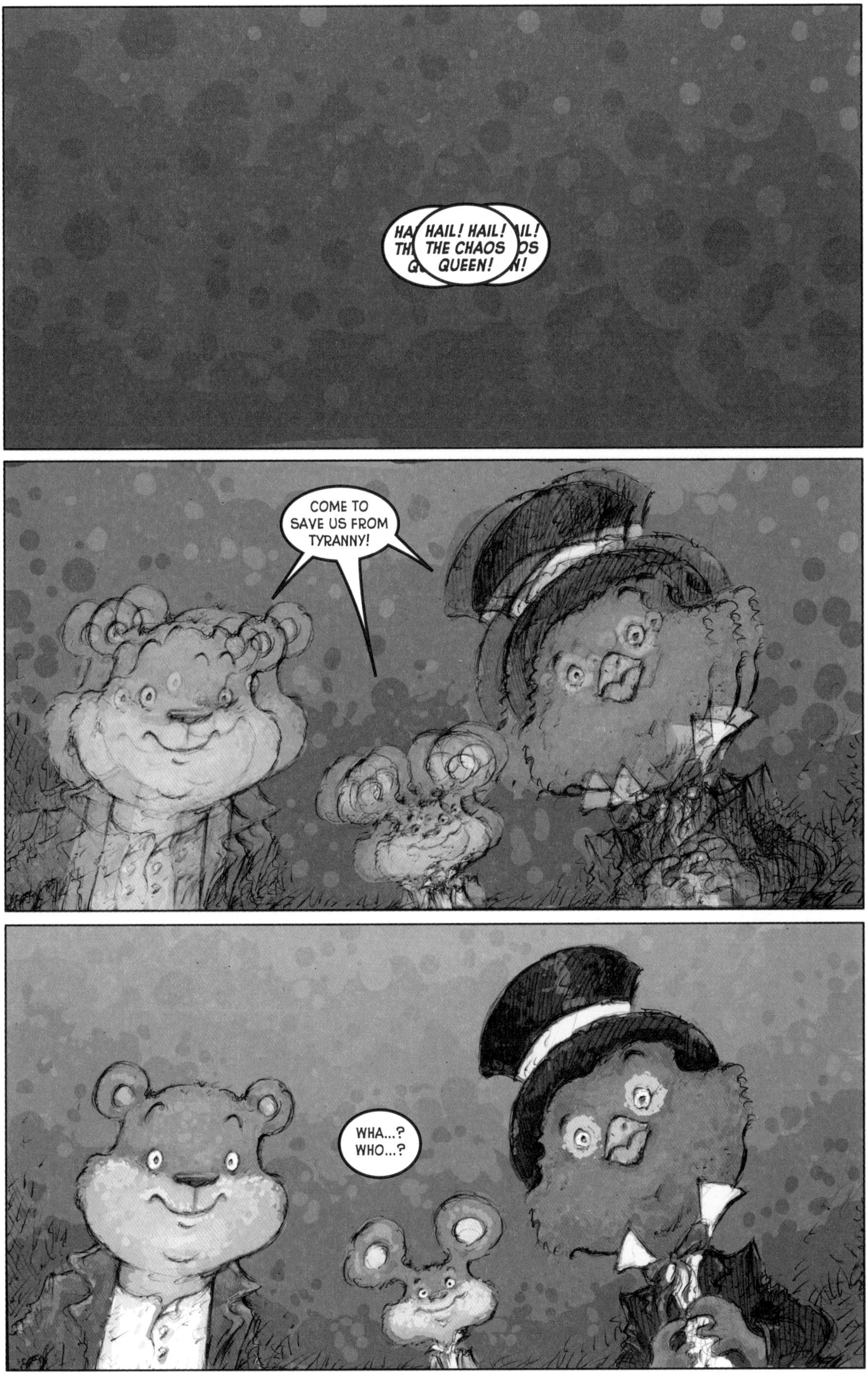
HAIL! HAIL! THE CHAOS QUEEN!
COME TO SAVE US FROM TYRANNY!
WHA...? WHO...?

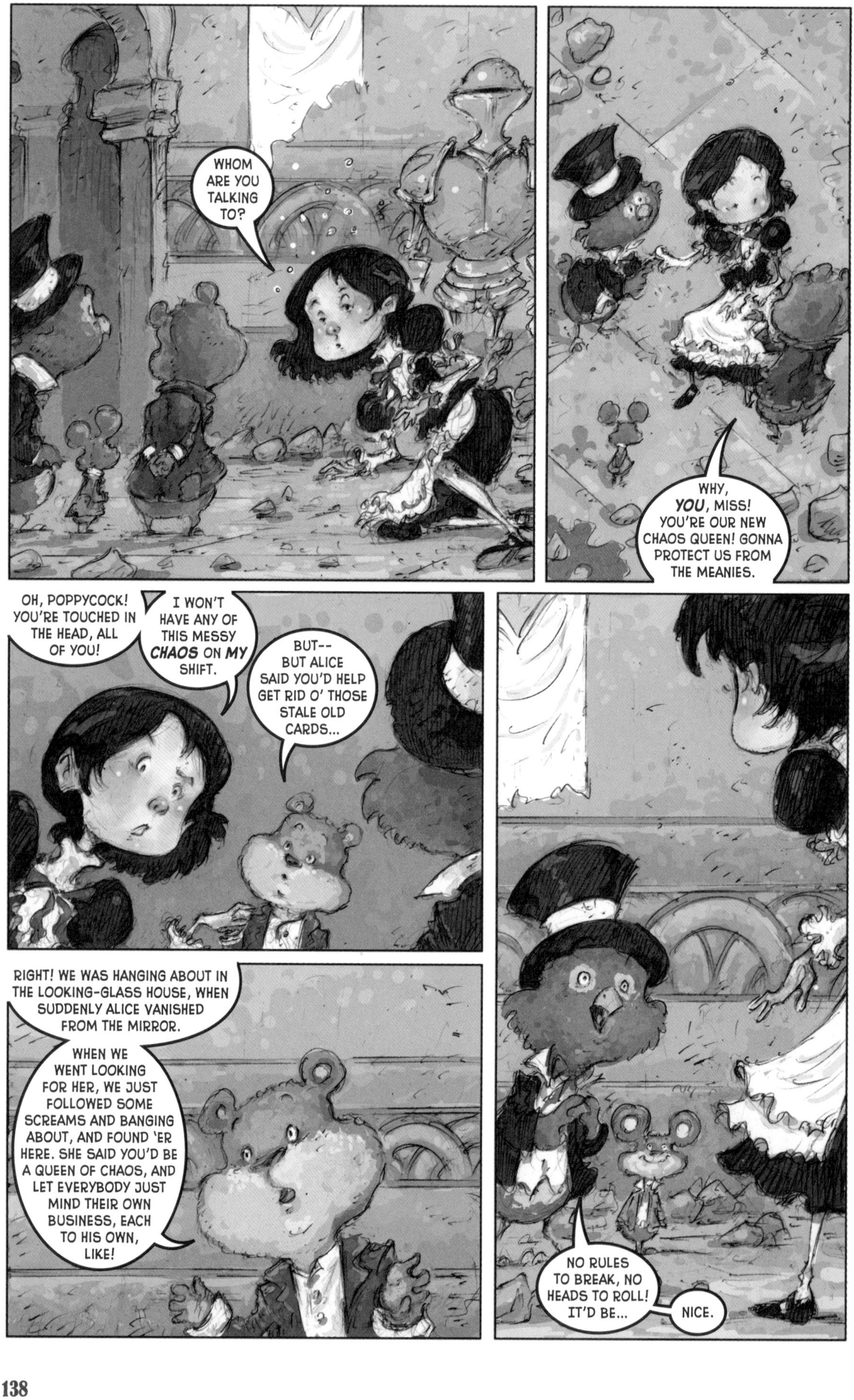
WHOM ARE YOU TALKING TO?
WHY, *YOU*, MISS! YOU'RE OUR NEW CHAOS QUEEN! GONNA PROTECT US FROM THE MEANIES.
OH, POPPYCOCK! YOU'RE TOUCHED IN THE HEAD, ALL OF YOU!
I WON'T HAVE ANY OF THIS MESSY *CHAOS* ON *MY* SHIFT.
BUT-- BUT ALICE SAID YOU'D HELP GET RID O' THOSE STALE OLD CARDS...
RIGHT! WE WAS HANGING ABOUT IN THE LOOKING-GLASS HOUSE, WHEN SUDDENLY ALICE VANISHED FROM THE MIRROR.
WHEN WE WENT LOOKING FOR HER, WE JUST FOLLOWED SOME SCREAMS AND BANGING ABOUT, AND FOUND 'ER HERE. SHE SAID YOU'D BE A QUEEN OF CHAOS, AND LET EVERYBODY JUST MIND THEIR OWN BUSINESS, EACH TO HIS OWN, LIKE!
NO RULES TO BREAK, NO HEADS TO ROLL! IT'D BE...
NICE.

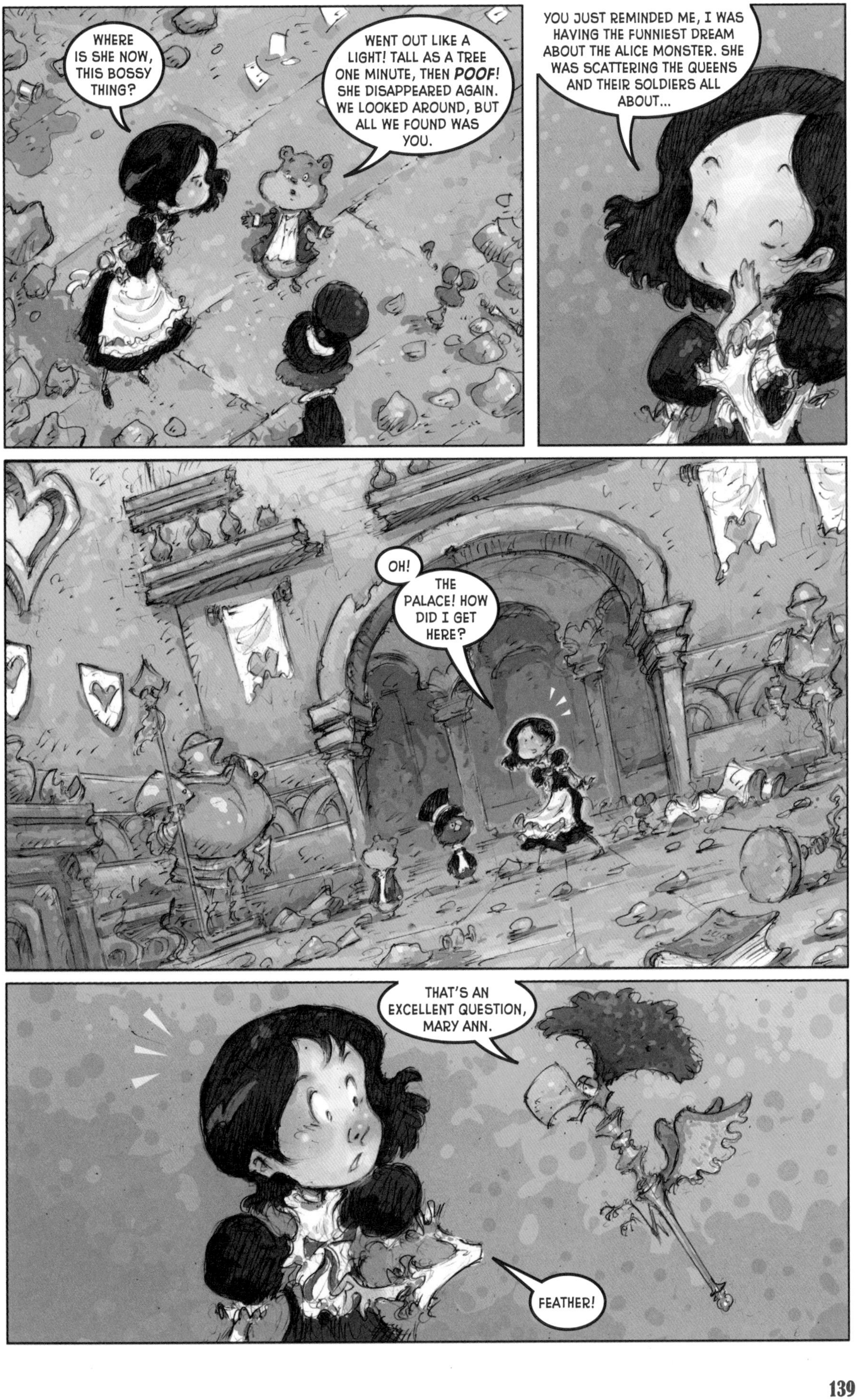
WHERE IS SHE NOW, THIS BOSSY THING?
WENT OUT LIKE A LIGHT! TALL AS A TREE ONE MINUTE, THEN *POOF*! SHE DISAPPEARED AGAIN. WE LOOKED AROUND, BUT ALL WE FOUND WAS YOU.
YOU JUST REMINDED ME, I WAS HAVING THE FUNNIEST DREAM ABOUT THE ALICE MONSTER. SHE WAS SCATTERING THE QUEENS AND THEIR SOLDIERS ALL ABOUT...
OH!
THE PALACE! HOW DID I GET HERE?
THAT'S AN EXCELLENT QUESTION, MARY ANN.
FEATHER!

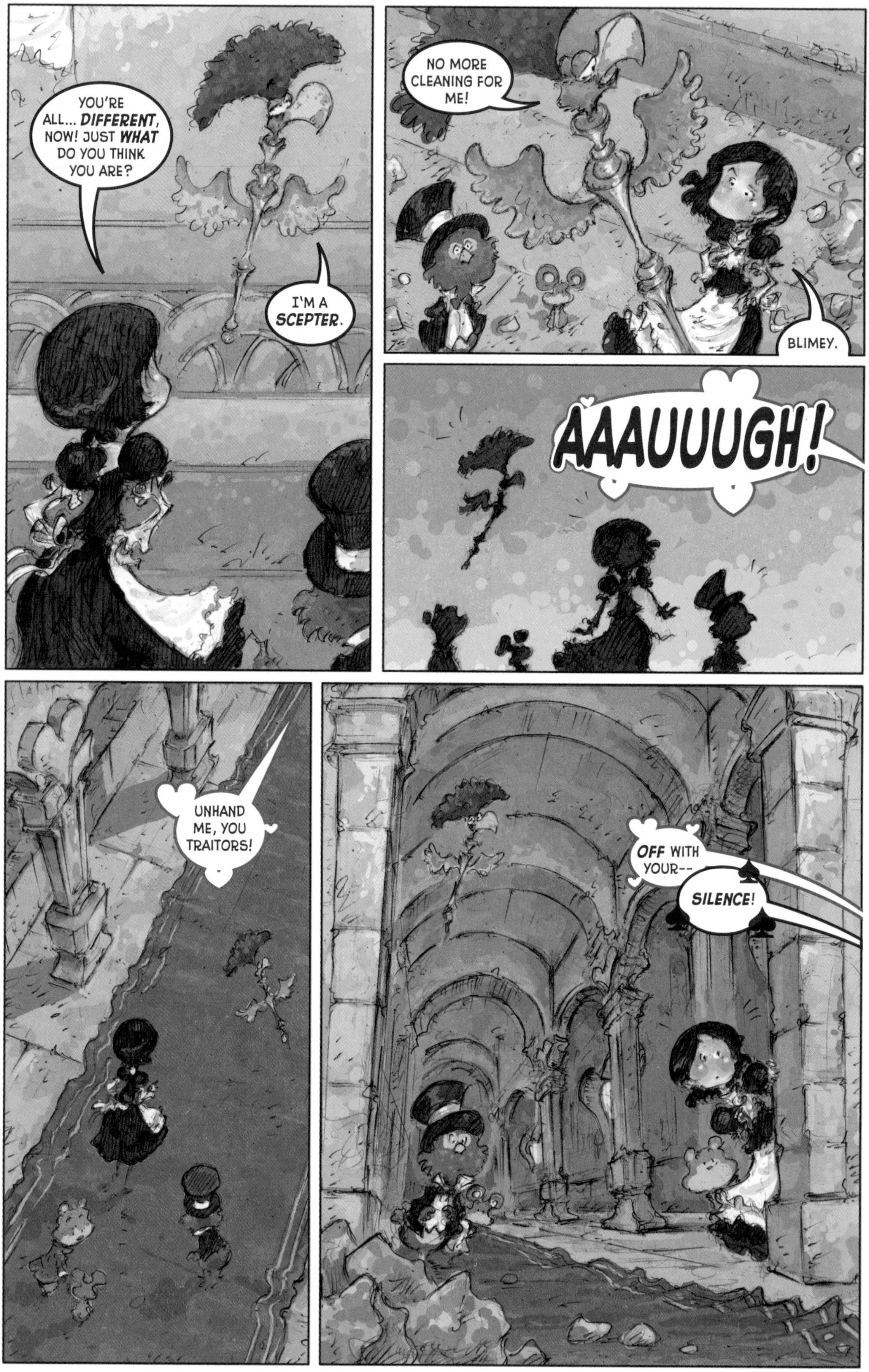
YOU'RE ALL... **DIFFERENT**, NOW! JUST **WHAT** DO YOU THINK YOU ARE?
I'M A **SCEPTER**.
NO MORE CLEANING FOR ME!
BLIMEY.
AAAUUUGH!
UNHAND ME, YOU TRAITORS!
OFF WITH YOUR--
SILENCE!

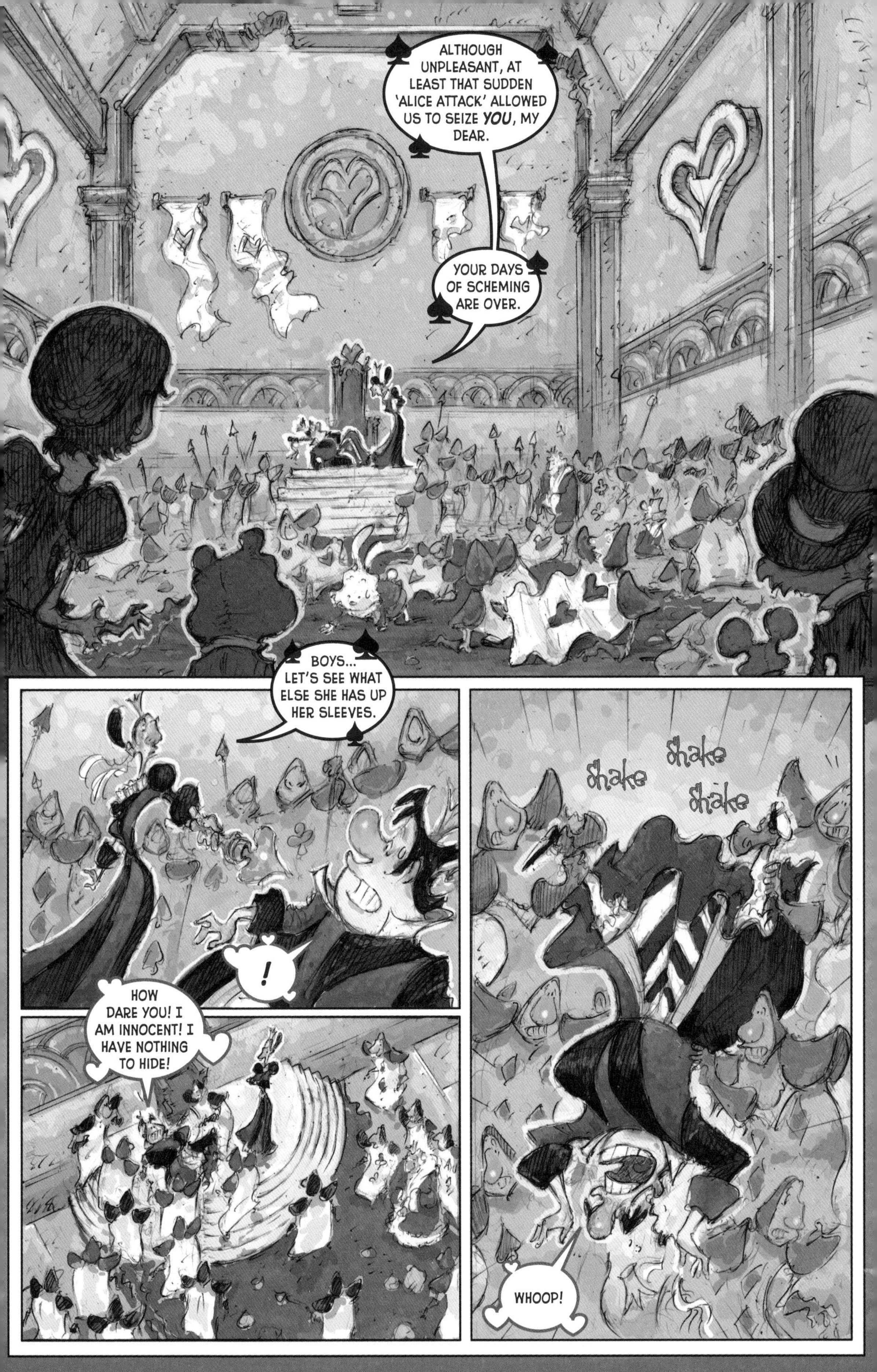

ALTHOUGH UNPLEASANT, AT LEAST THAT SUDDEN 'ALICE ATTACK' ALLOWED US TO SEIZE *YOU*, MY DEAR.
YOUR DAYS OF SCHEMING ARE OVER.
BOYS... LET'S SEE WHAT ELSE SHE HAS UP HER SLEEVES.
!
HOW DARE YOU! I AM INNOCENT! I HAVE NOTHING TO HIDE!
Shake
Shake
Shake
WHOOP!

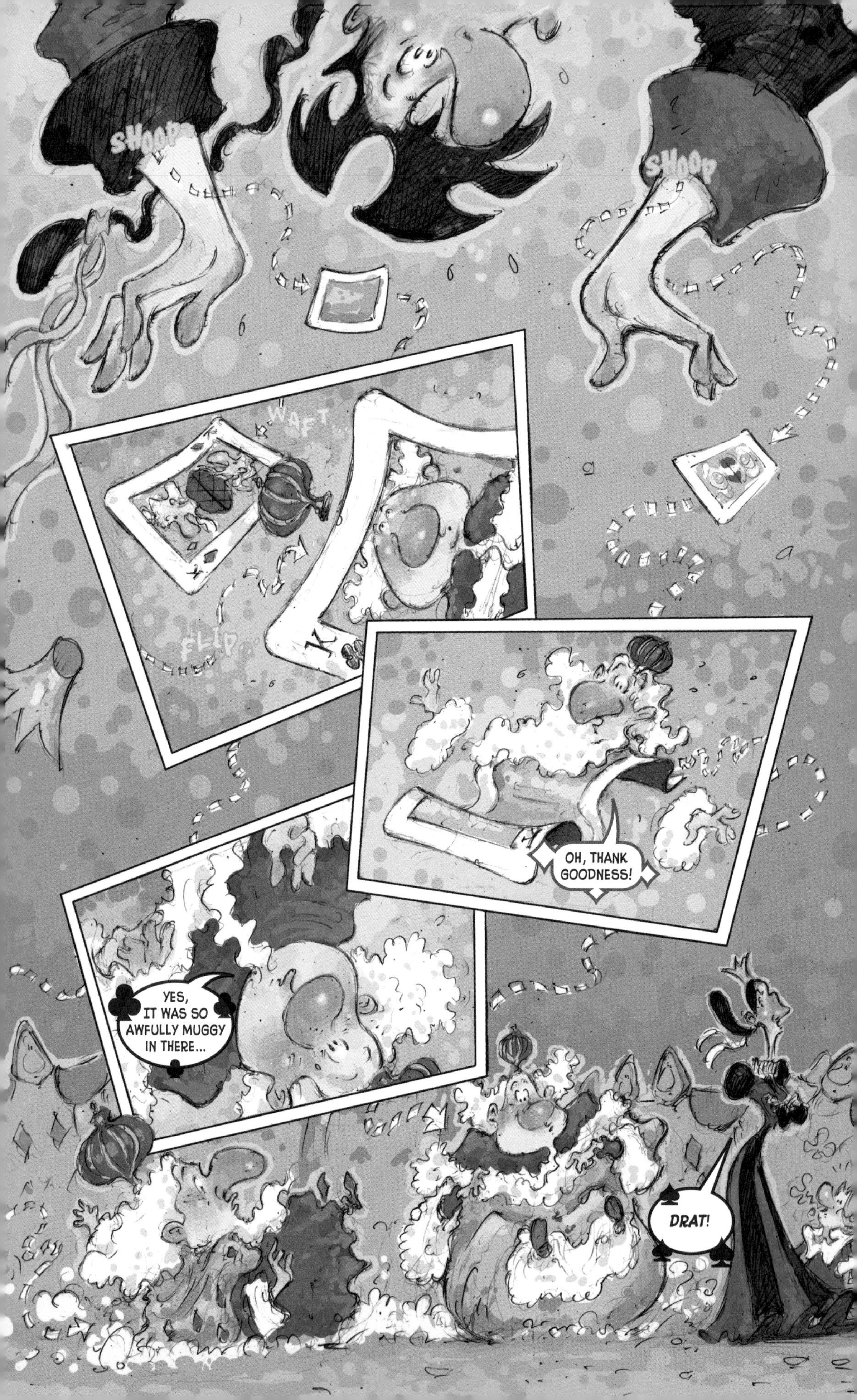
SHOOP
SHOOP
WAFT
FLIP
OH, THANK GOODNESS!
YES, IT WAS SO AWFULLY MUGGY IN THERE...
DRAT!

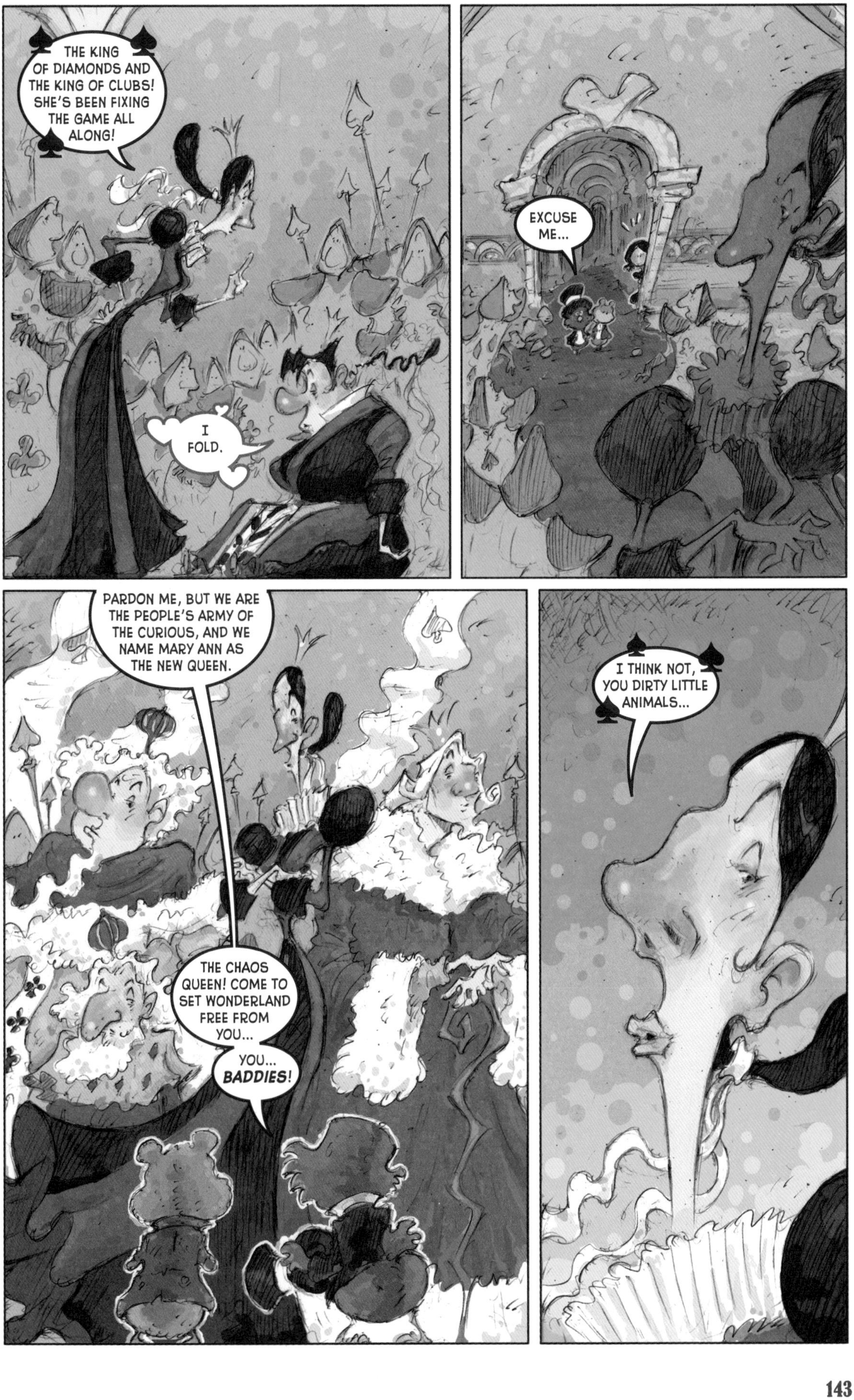
THE KING OF DIAMONDS AND THE KING OF CLUBS! SHE'S BEEN FIXING THE GAME ALL ALONG!
I FOLD.
EXCUSE ME...
PARDON ME, BUT WE ARE THE PEOPLE'S ARMY OF THE CURIOUS, AND WE NAME MARY ANN AS THE NEW QUEEN.
THE CHAOS QUEEN! COME TO SET WONDERLAND FREE FROM YOU...
YOU... ***BADDIES***!
I THINK NOT, YOU DIRTY LITTLE ANIMALS...

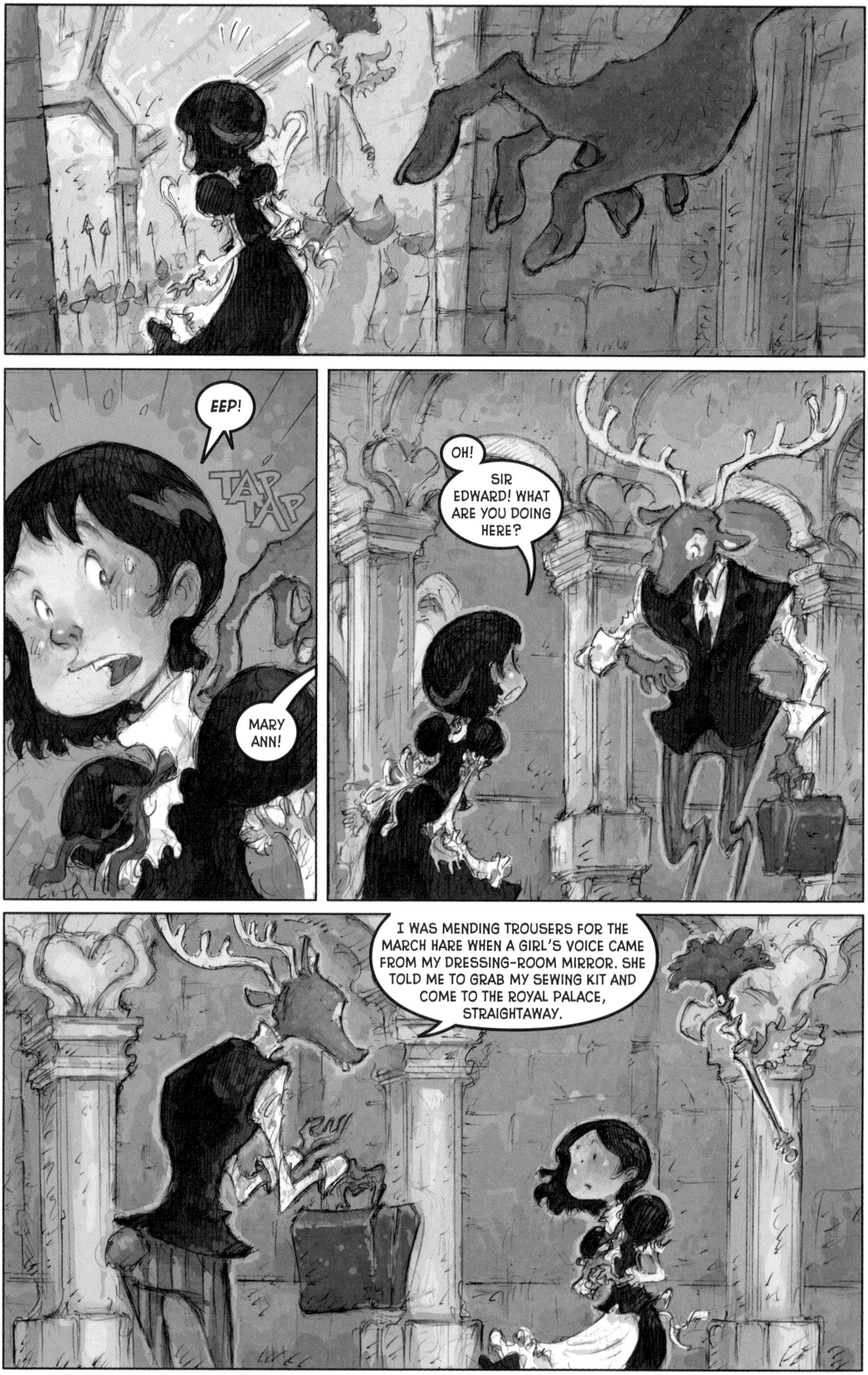
EEP!
TAP TAP
MARY ANN!
OH!
SIR EDWARD! WHAT ARE YOU DOING HERE?
I WAS MENDING TROUSERS FOR THE MARCH HARE WHEN A GIRL'S VOICE CAME FROM MY DRESSING-ROOM MIRROR. SHE TOLD ME TO GRAB MY SEWING KIT AND COME TO THE ROYAL PALACE, STRAIGHTAWAY.

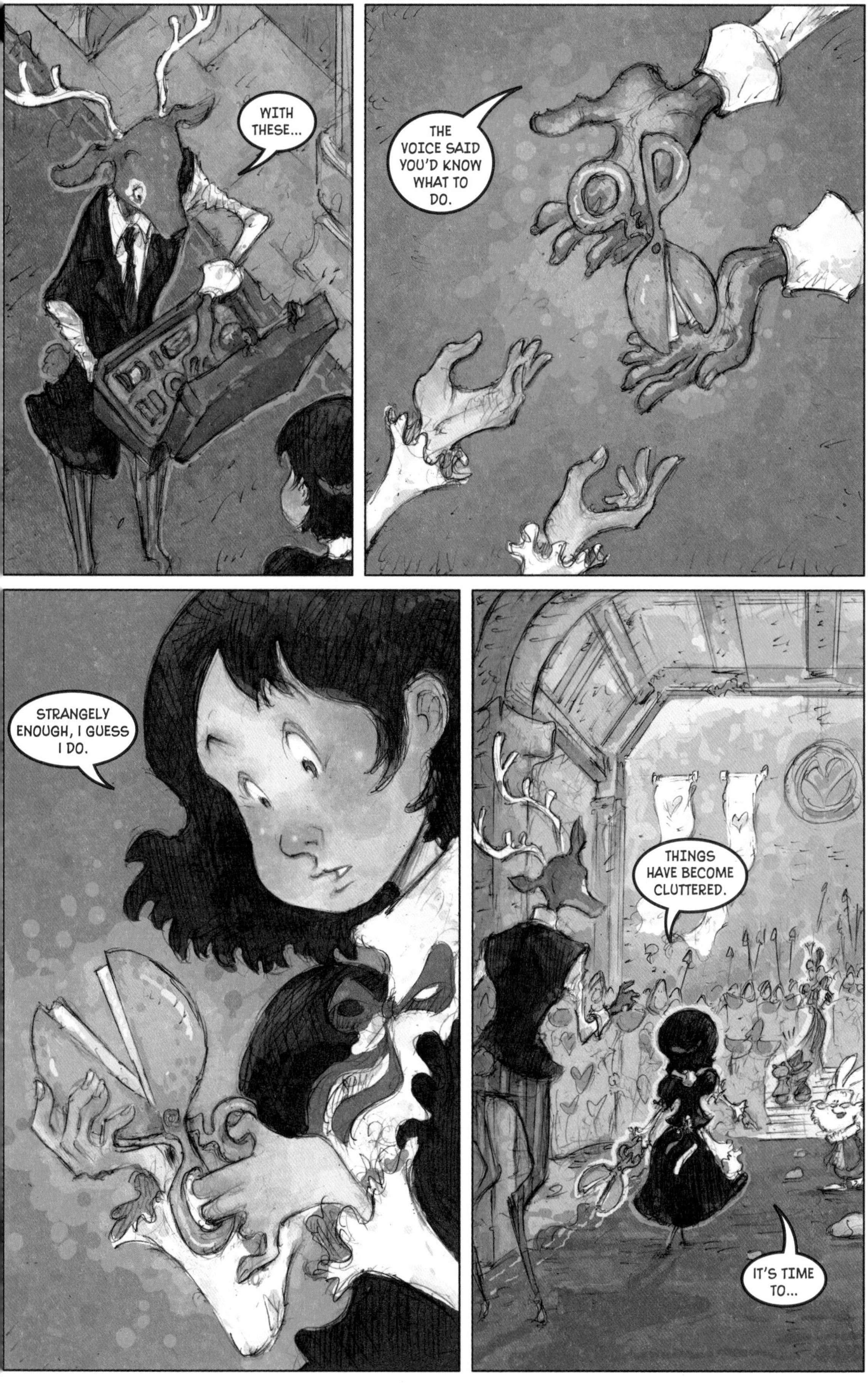
WITH THESE...
THE VOICE SAID YOU'D KNOW WHAT TO DO.
STRANGELY ENOUGH, I GUESS I DO.
THINGS HAVE BECOME CLUTTERED.
IT'S TIME TO...

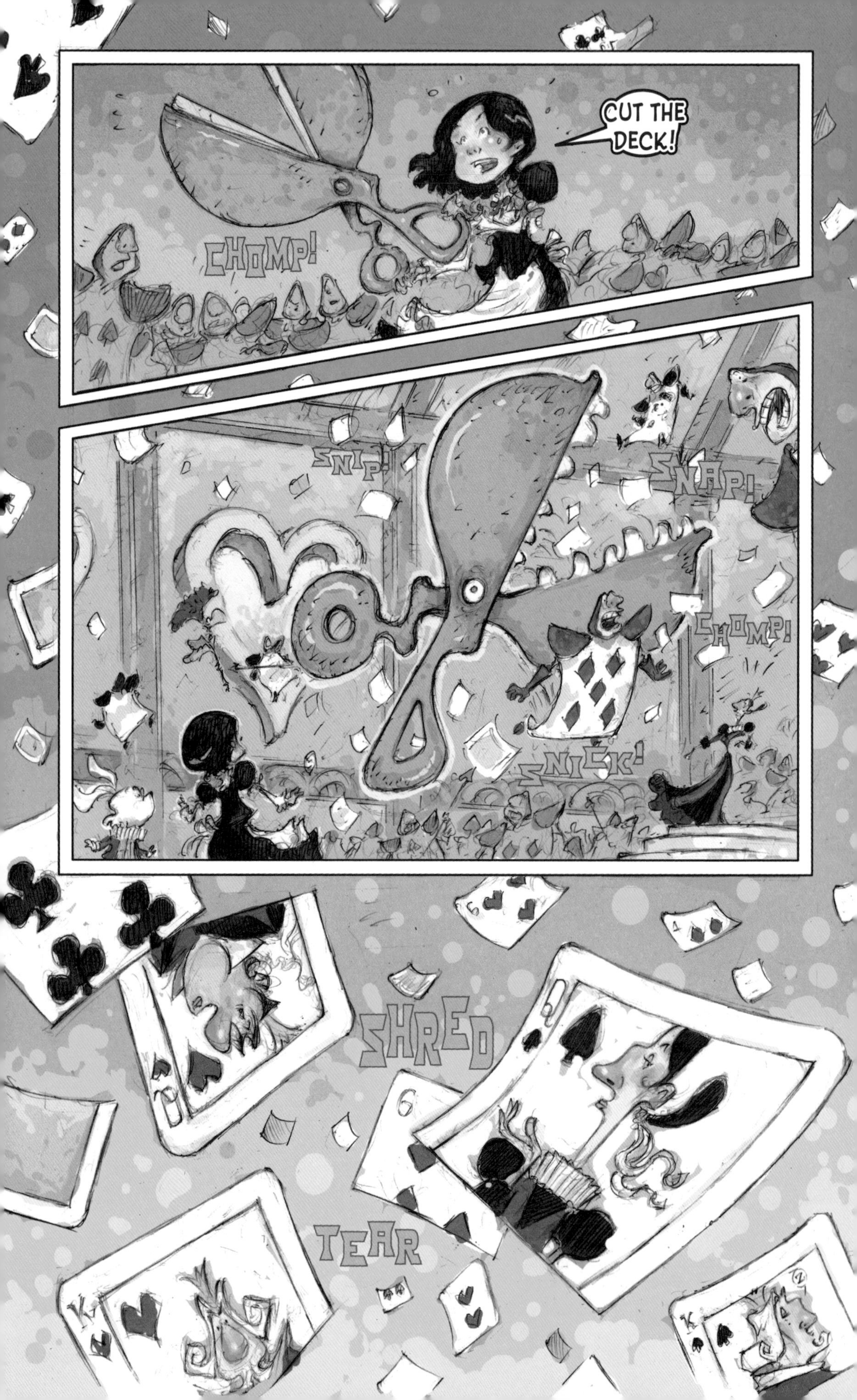
CUT THE DECK!
CHOMP!
SNIP!
SNAP!
CHOMP!
SNICK!
SHRED
TEAR

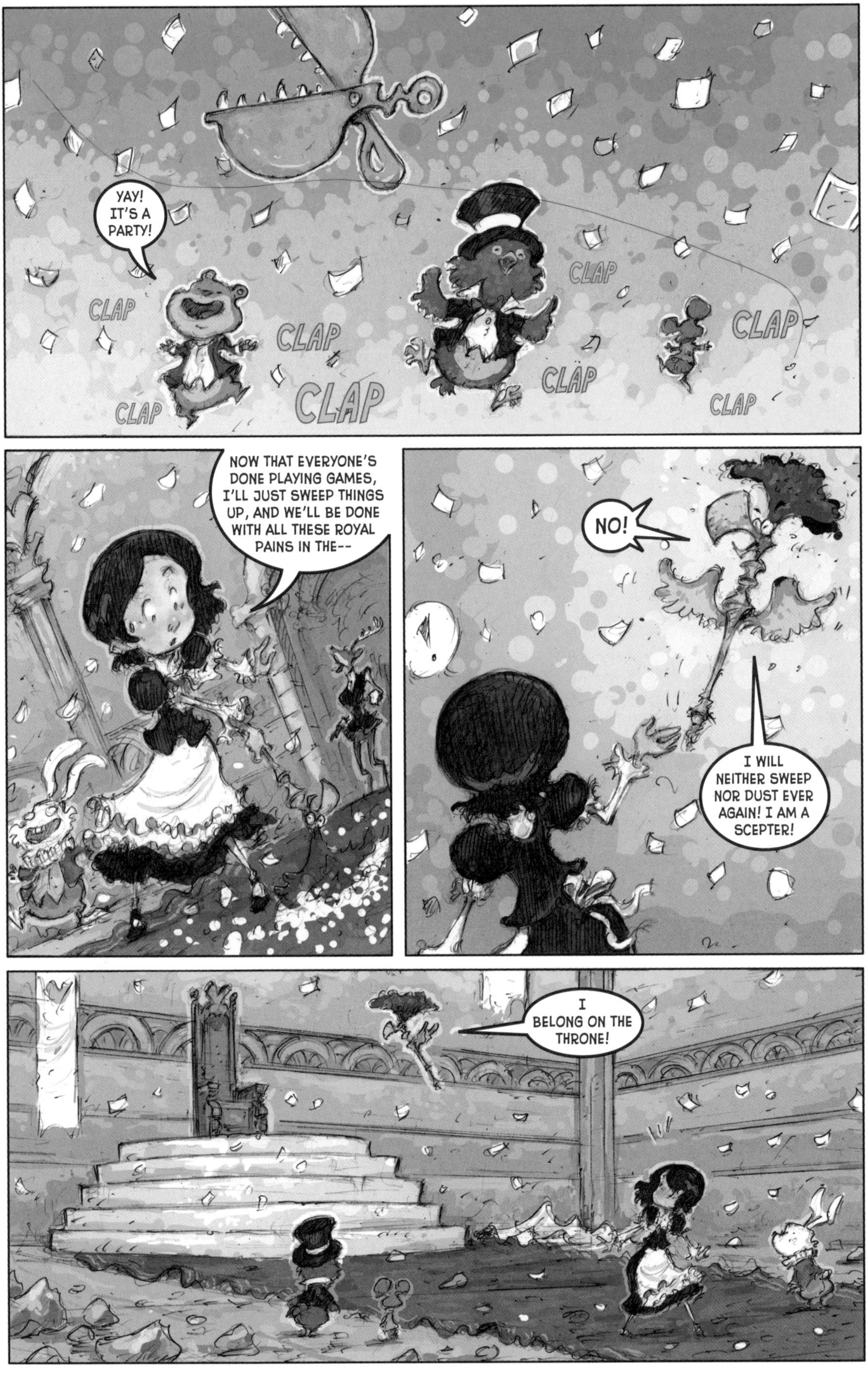
YAY! IT'S A PARTY!
CLAP
CLAP
CLAP
CLAP
CLAP
CLAP
CLAP
CLAP
NOW THAT EVERYONE'S DONE PLAYING GAMES, I'LL JUST SWEEP THINGS UP, AND WE'LL BE DONE WITH ALL THESE ROYAL PAINS IN THE--
NO!
I WILL NEITHER SWEEP NOR DUST EVER AGAIN! I AM A SCEPTER!
I BELONG ON THE THRONE!

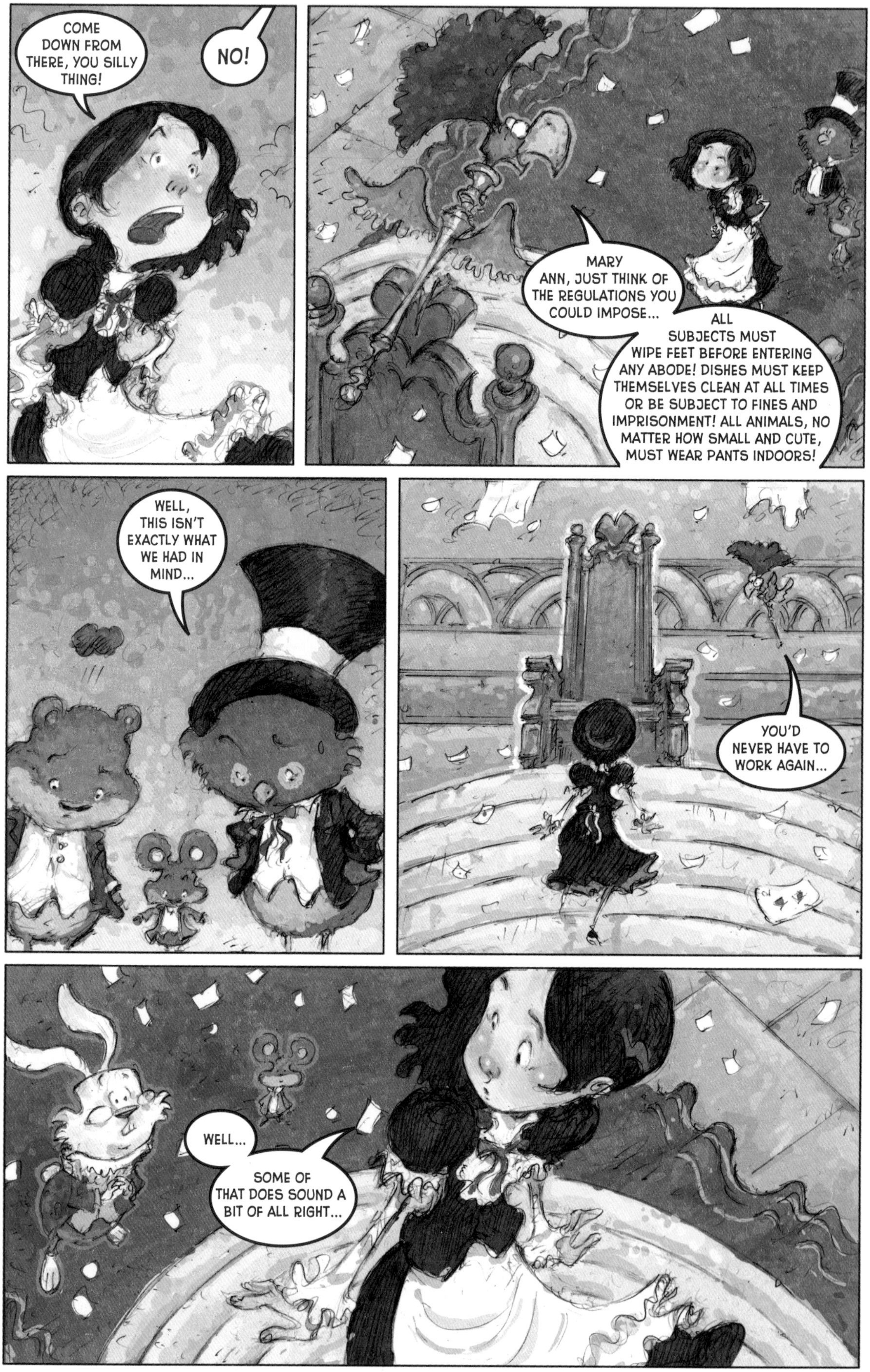
COME DOWN FROM THERE, YOU SILLY THING!
NO!
MARY ANN, JUST THINK OF THE REGULATIONS YOU COULD IMPOSE...
ALL SUBJECTS MUST WIPE FEET BEFORE ENTERING ANY ABODE! DISHES MUST KEEP THEMSELVES CLEAN AT ALL TIMES OR BE SUBJECT TO FINES AND IMPRISONMENT! ALL ANIMALS, NO MATTER HOW SMALL AND CUTE, MUST WEAR PANTS INDOORS!
WELL, THIS ISN'T EXACTLY WHAT WE HAD IN MIND...
YOU'D NEVER HAVE TO WORK AGAIN...
WELL...
SOME OF THAT DOES SOUND A BIT OF ALL RIGHT...

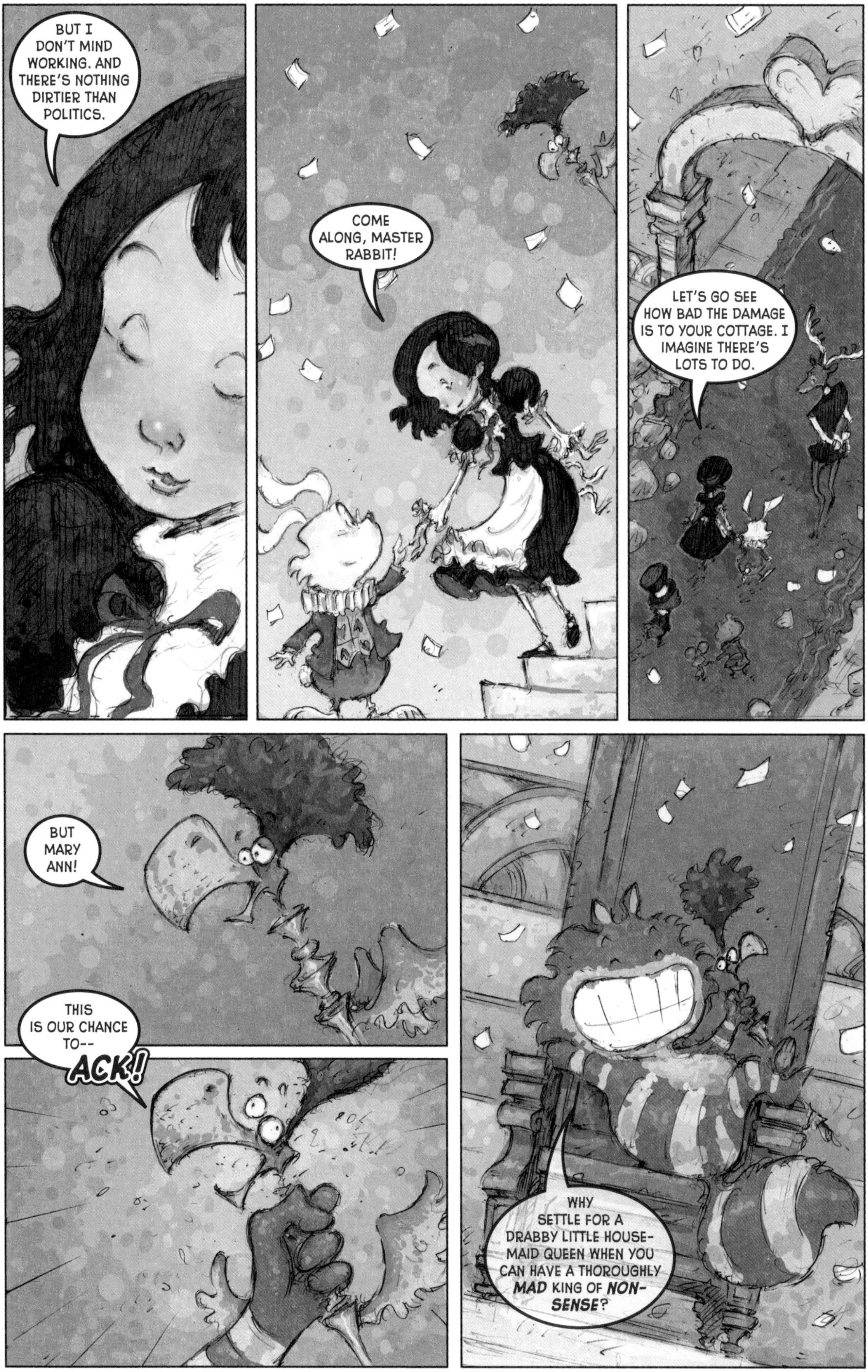
BUT I DON'T MIND WORKING. AND THERE'S NOTHING DIRTIER THAN POLITICS.
COME ALONG, MASTER RABBIT!
LET'S GO SEE HOW BAD THE DAMAGE IS TO YOUR COTTAGE. I IMAGINE THERE'S LOTS TO DO.
BUT MARY ANN!
THIS IS OUR CHANCE TO--
ACK!
WHY SETTLE FOR A DRABBY LITTLE HOUSE-MAID QUEEN WHEN YOU CAN HAVE A THOROUGHLY *MAD* KING OF *NON-SENSE*?

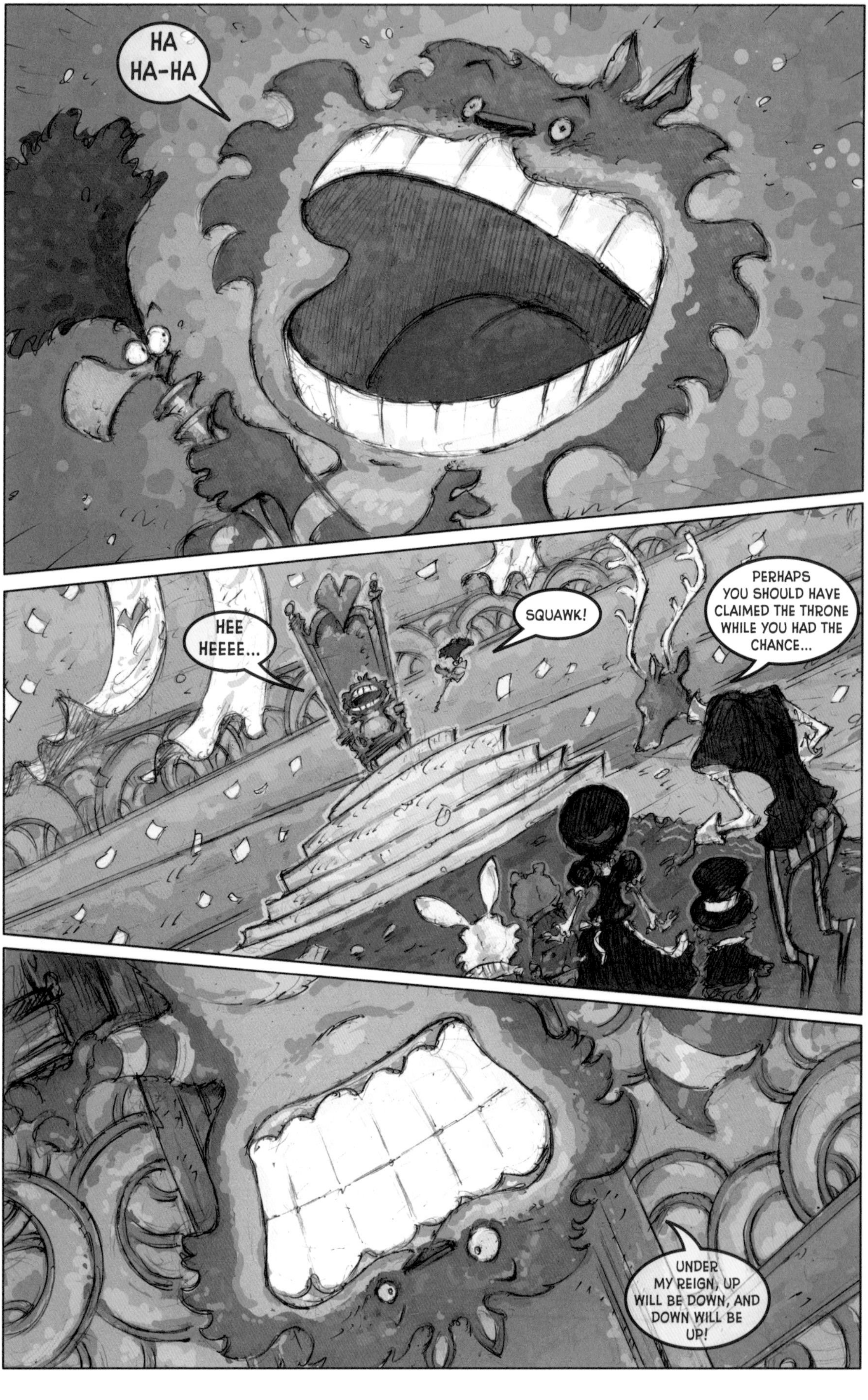
HA HA-HA
HEE HEEEE...
SQUAWK!
PERHAPS YOU SHOULD HAVE CLAIMED THE THRONE WHILE YOU HAD THE CHANCE...
UNDER MY REIGN, UP WILL BE DOWN, AND DOWN WILL BE UP!

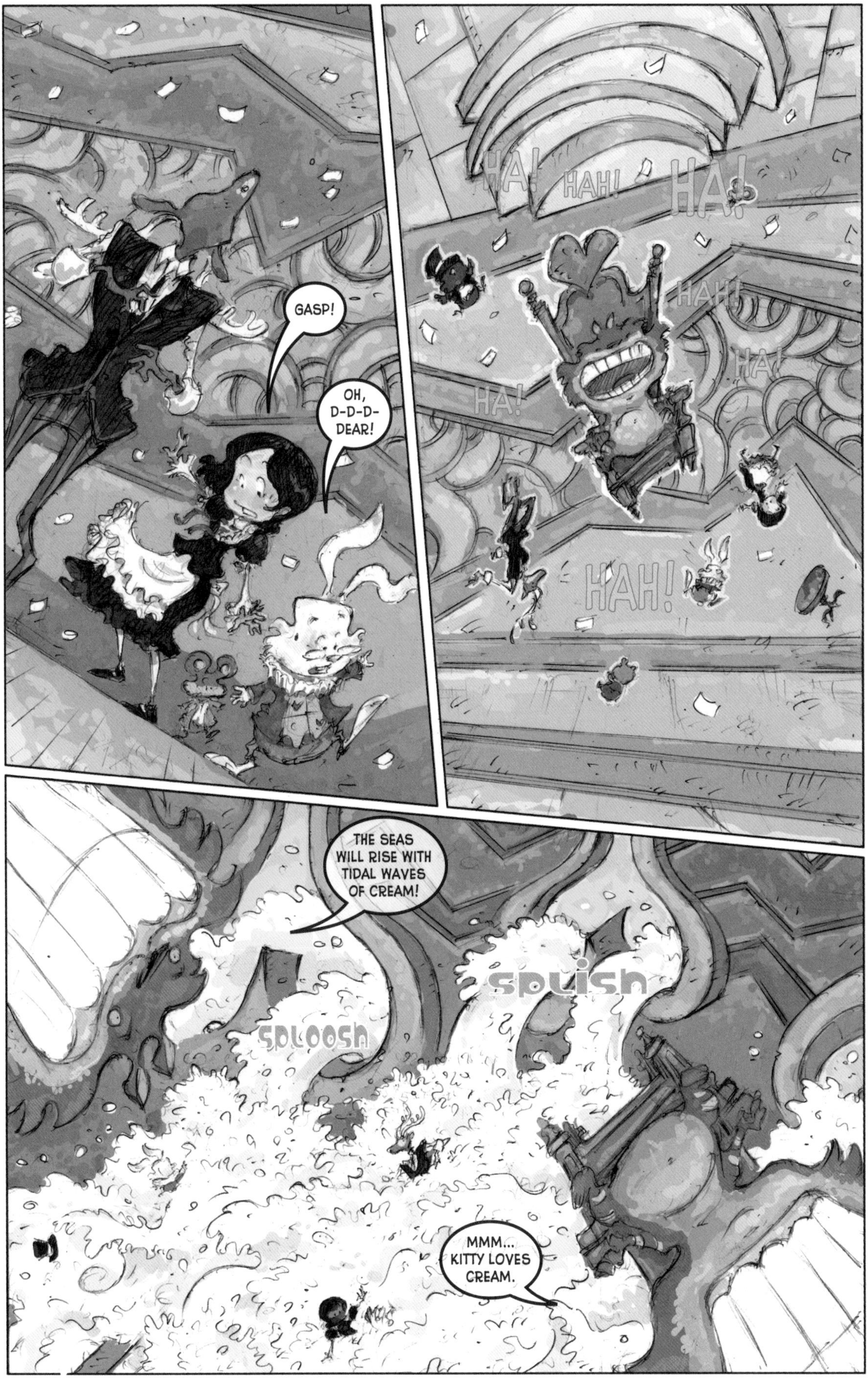
GASP!
OH, D-D-D-DEAR!
HA! HAH! HA!
HAH!
HA!
HA!
HAH!
THE SEAS WILL RISE WITH TIDAL WAVES OF CREAM!
SPLISH
SPLOOSH
MMM... KITTY LOVES CREAM.

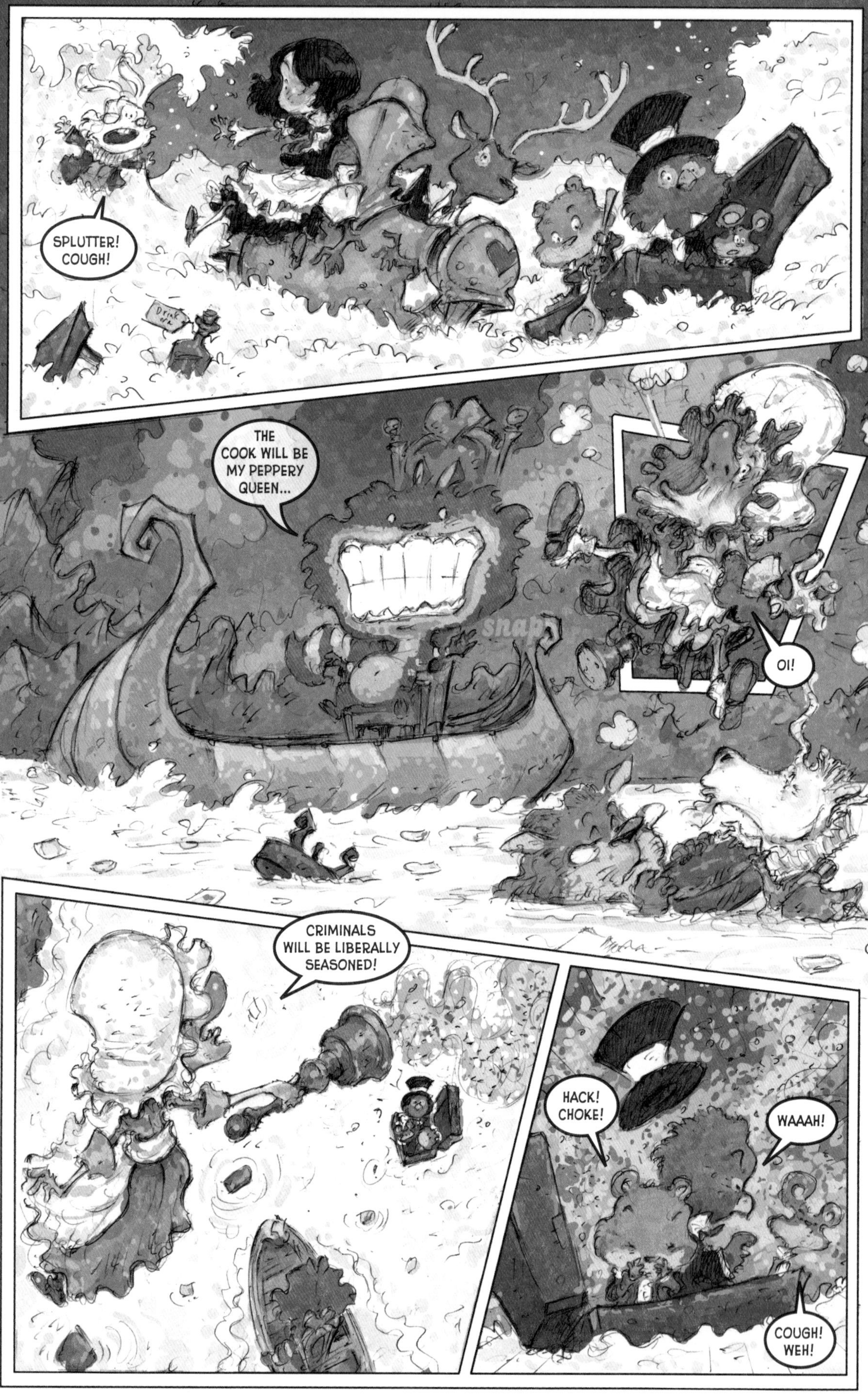
SPLUTTER! COUGH!
THE COOK WILL BE MY PEPPERY QUEEN...
snap
OI!
CRIMINALS WILL BE LIBERALLY SEASONED!
HACK! CHOKE!
WAAAH!
COUGH! WEH!

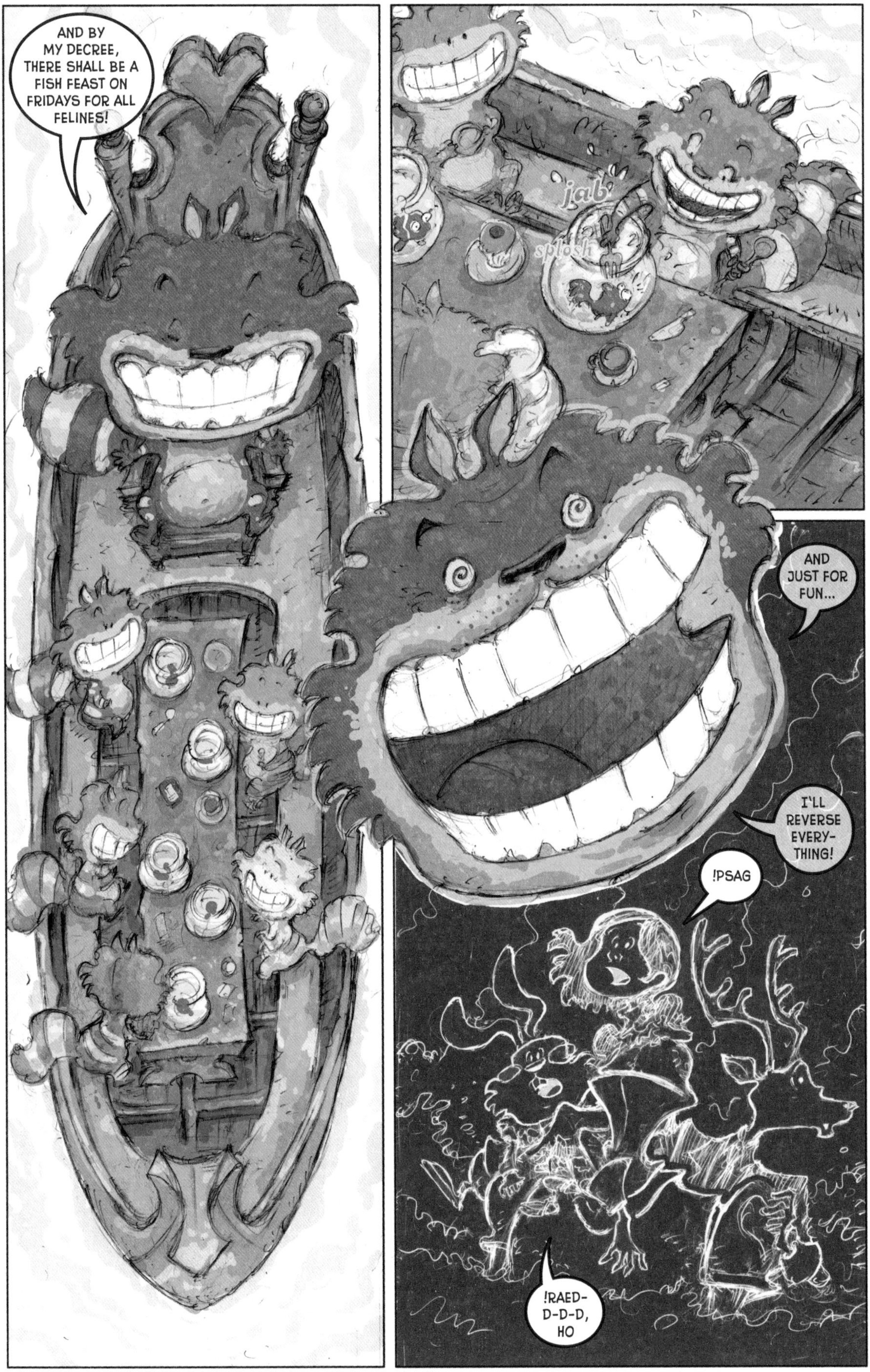
AND BY MY DECREE, THERE SHALL BE A FISH FEAST ON FRIDAYS FOR ALL FELINES!
jab
splosh
AND JUST FOR FUN...
I'LL REVERSE EVERY-THING!
!PSAG
!RAED-D-D-D, HO

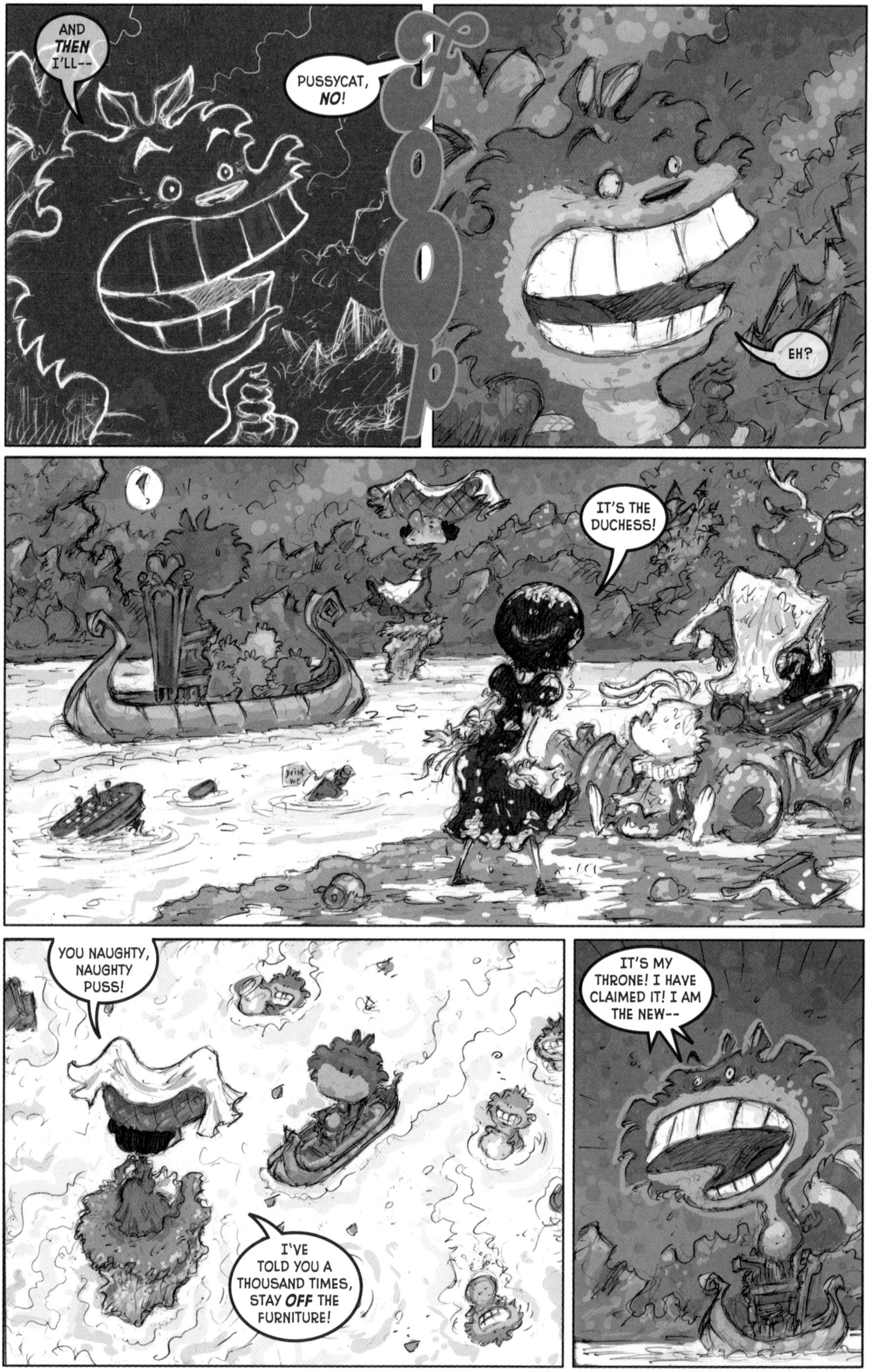
AND THEN I'LL--
PUSSYCAT, NO!
Foop
EH?
?
IT'S THE DUCHESS!
YOU NAUGHTY, NAUGHTY PUSS!
I'VE TOLD YOU A THOUSAND TIMES, STAY OFF THE FURNITURE!
IT'S MY THRONE! I HAVE CLAIMED IT! I AM THE NEW--

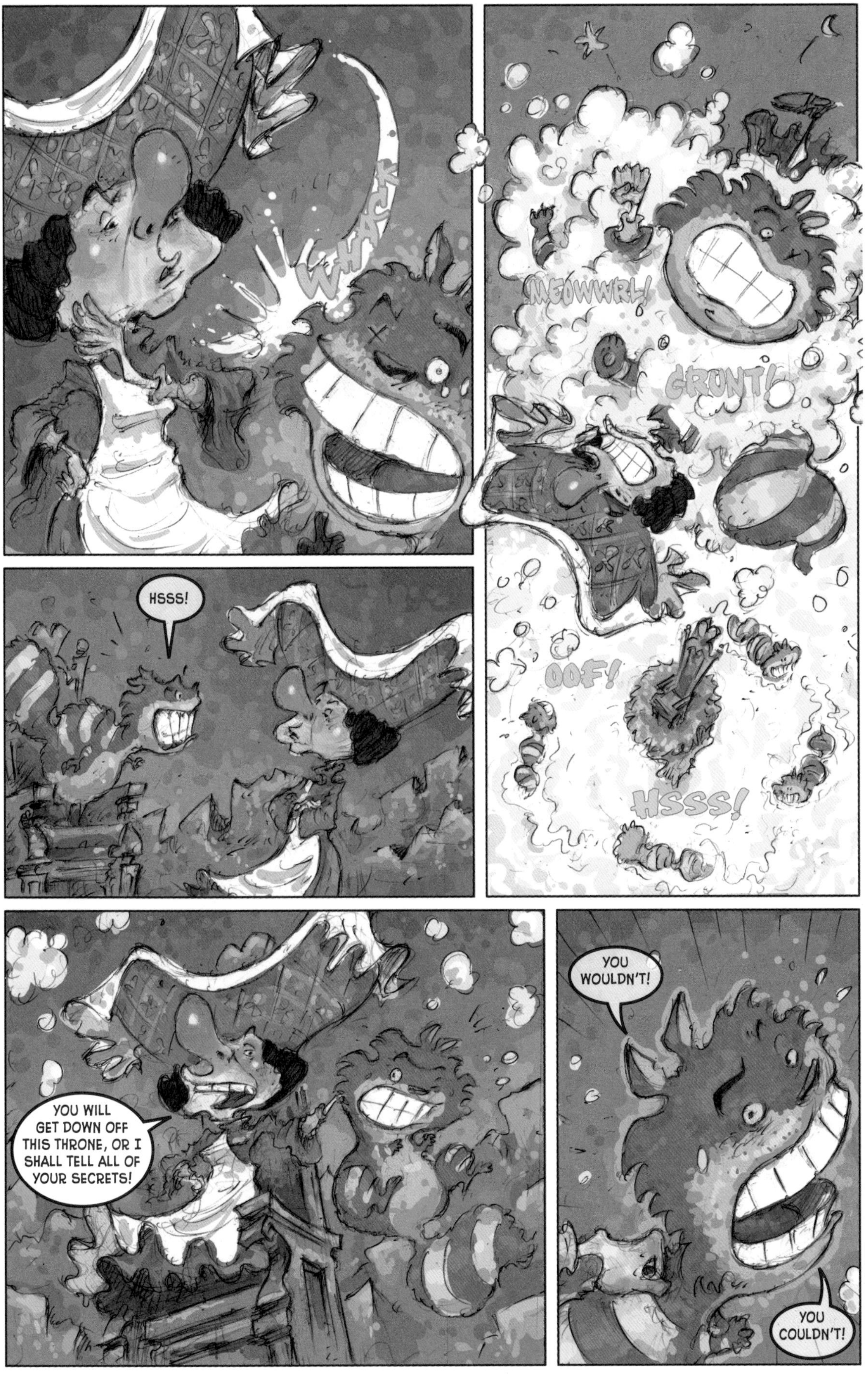

WHACK
MEOWWRL!
GRUNT!
OOF!
HSSS!
HSSS!
YOU WILL GET DOWN OFF THIS THRONE, OR I SHALL TELL ALL OF YOUR SECRETS!
YOU WOULDN'T!
YOU COULDN'T!

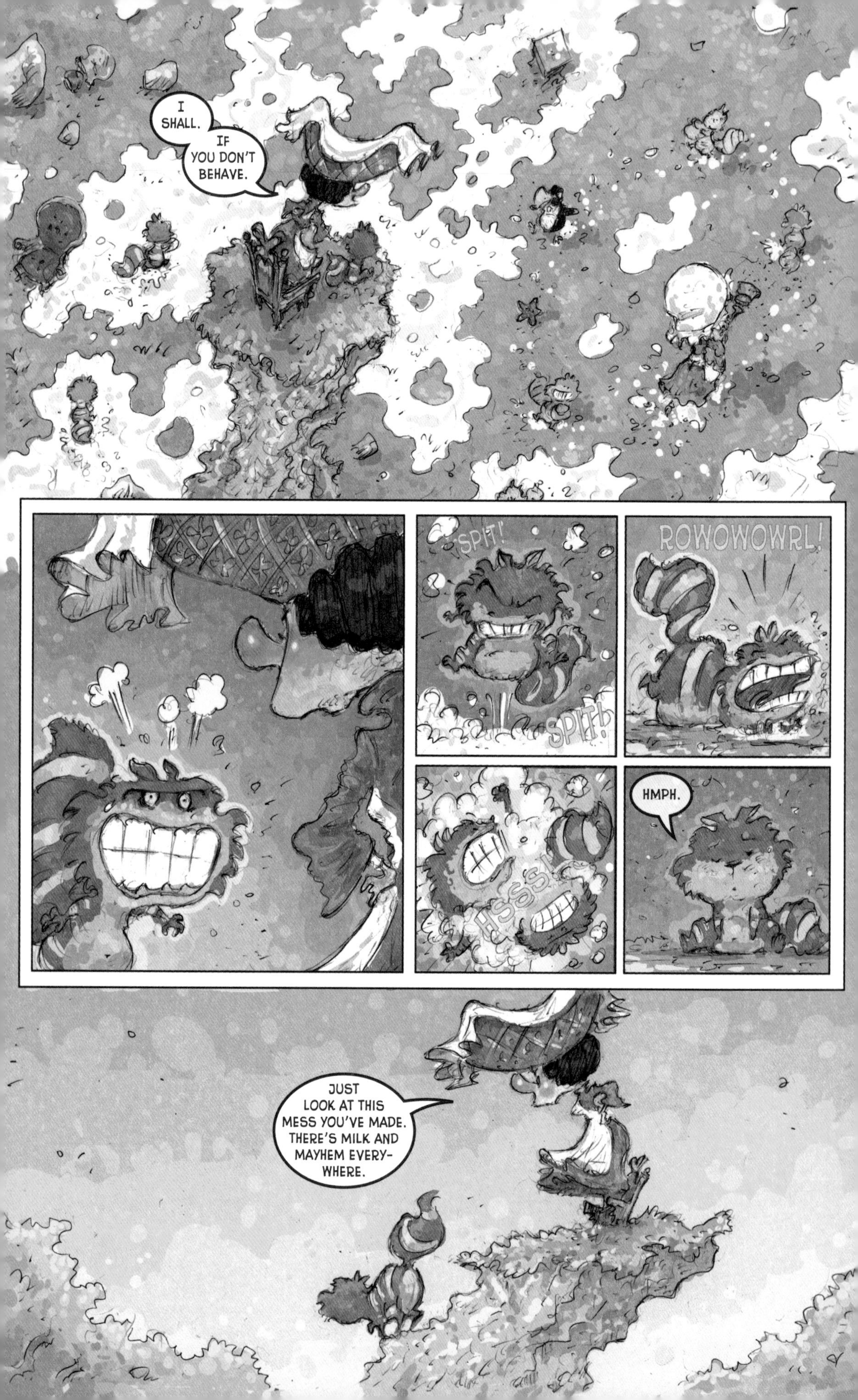
I SHALL.
IF YOU DON'T BEHAVE.
SPIT!
SPIT!
ROWOWOWRL!
HSSS!
HMPH.
JUST LOOK AT THIS MESS YOU'VE MADE. THERE'S MILK AND MAYHEM EVERY-WHERE.

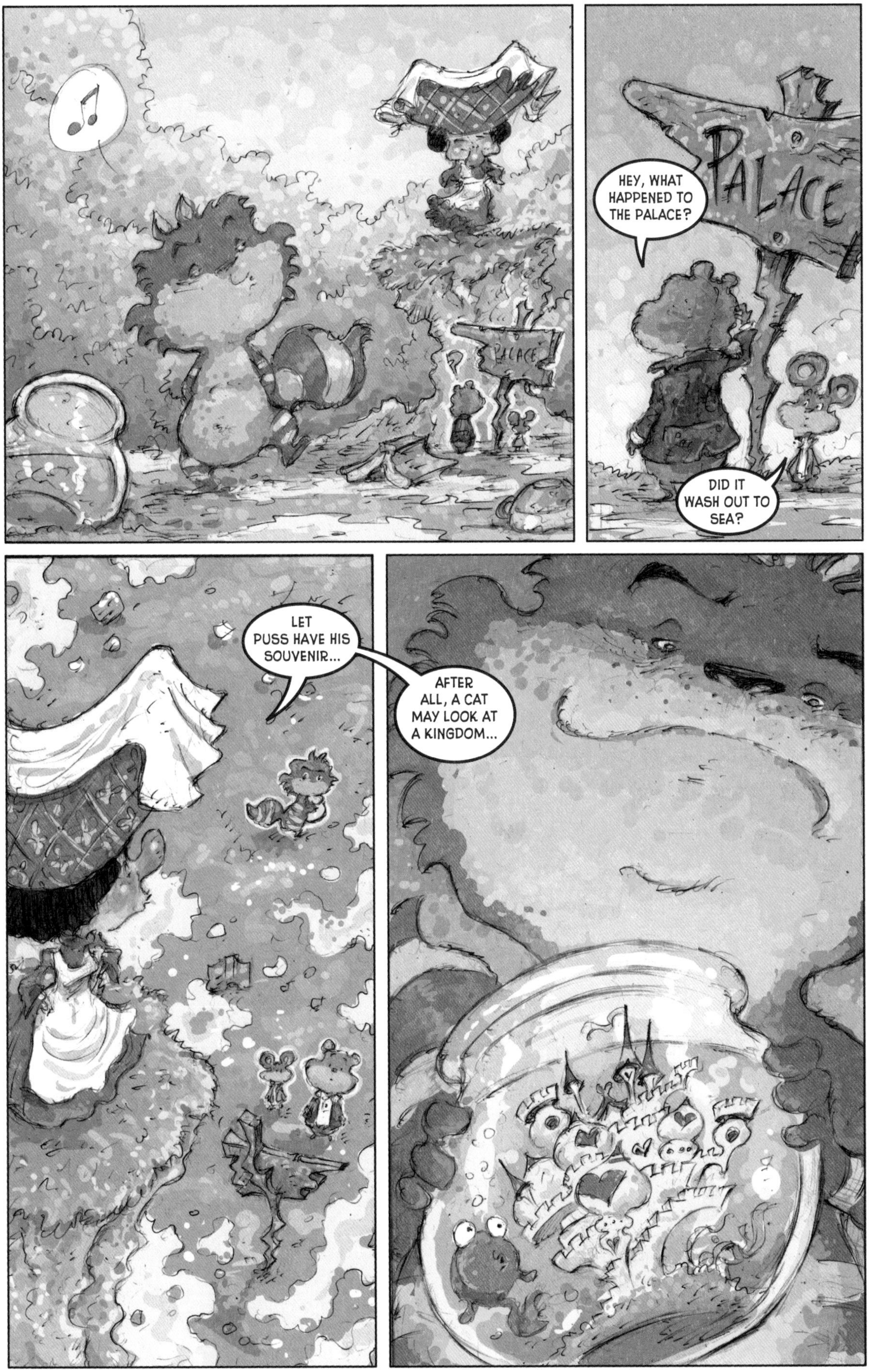
HEY, WHAT HAPPENED TO THE PALACE?
PALACE
DID IT WASH OUT TO SEA?
LET PUSS HAVE HIS SOUVENIR...
AFTER ALL, A CAT MAY LOOK AT A KINGDOM...

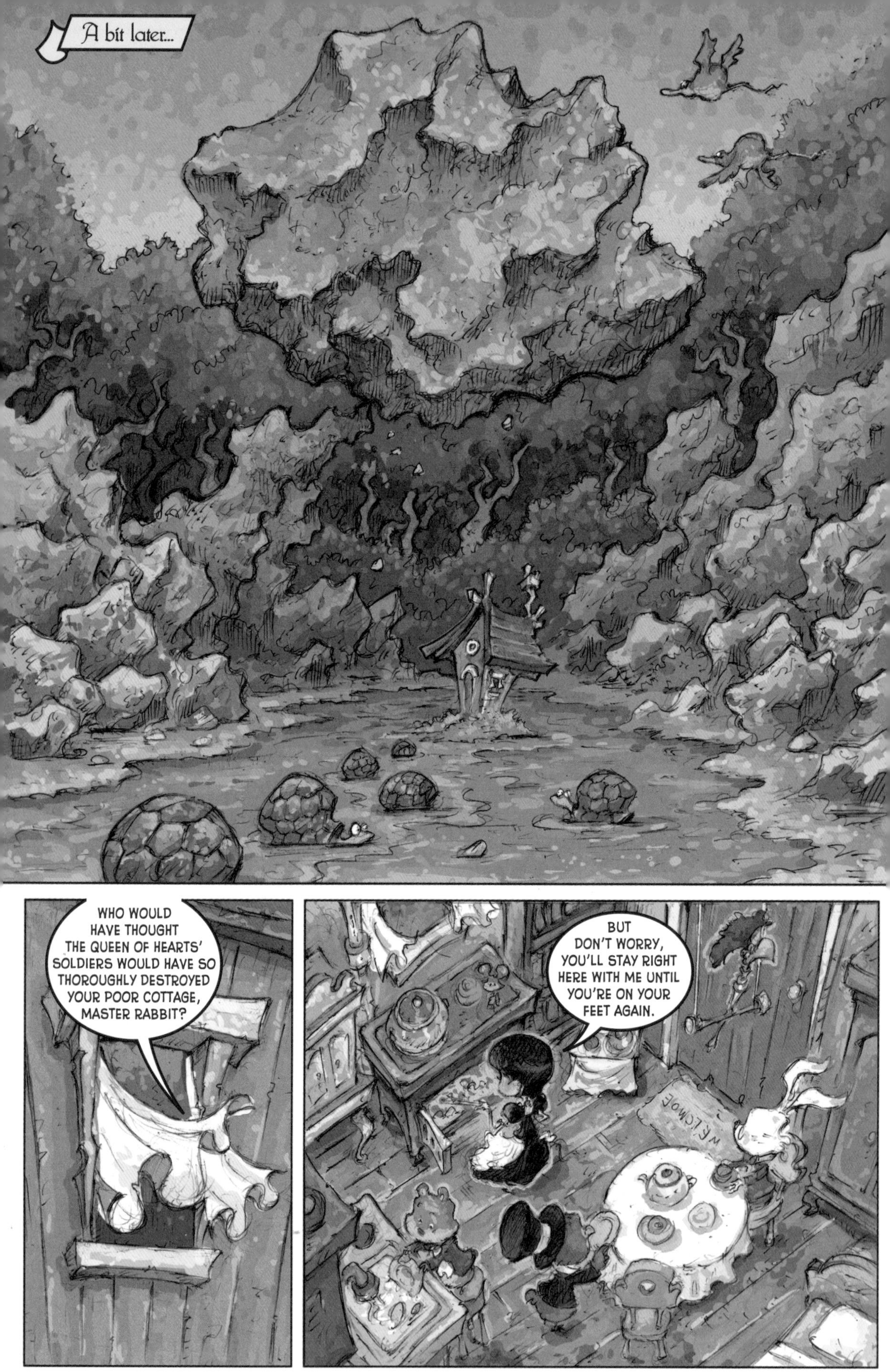
A bit later...
WHO WOULD HAVE THOUGHT THE QUEEN OF HEARTS' SOLDIERS WOULD HAVE SO THOROUGHLY DESTROYED YOUR POOR COTTAGE, MASTER RABBIT?
BUT DON'T WORRY, YOU'LL STAY RIGHT HERE WITH ME UNTIL YOU'RE ON YOUR FEET AGAIN.

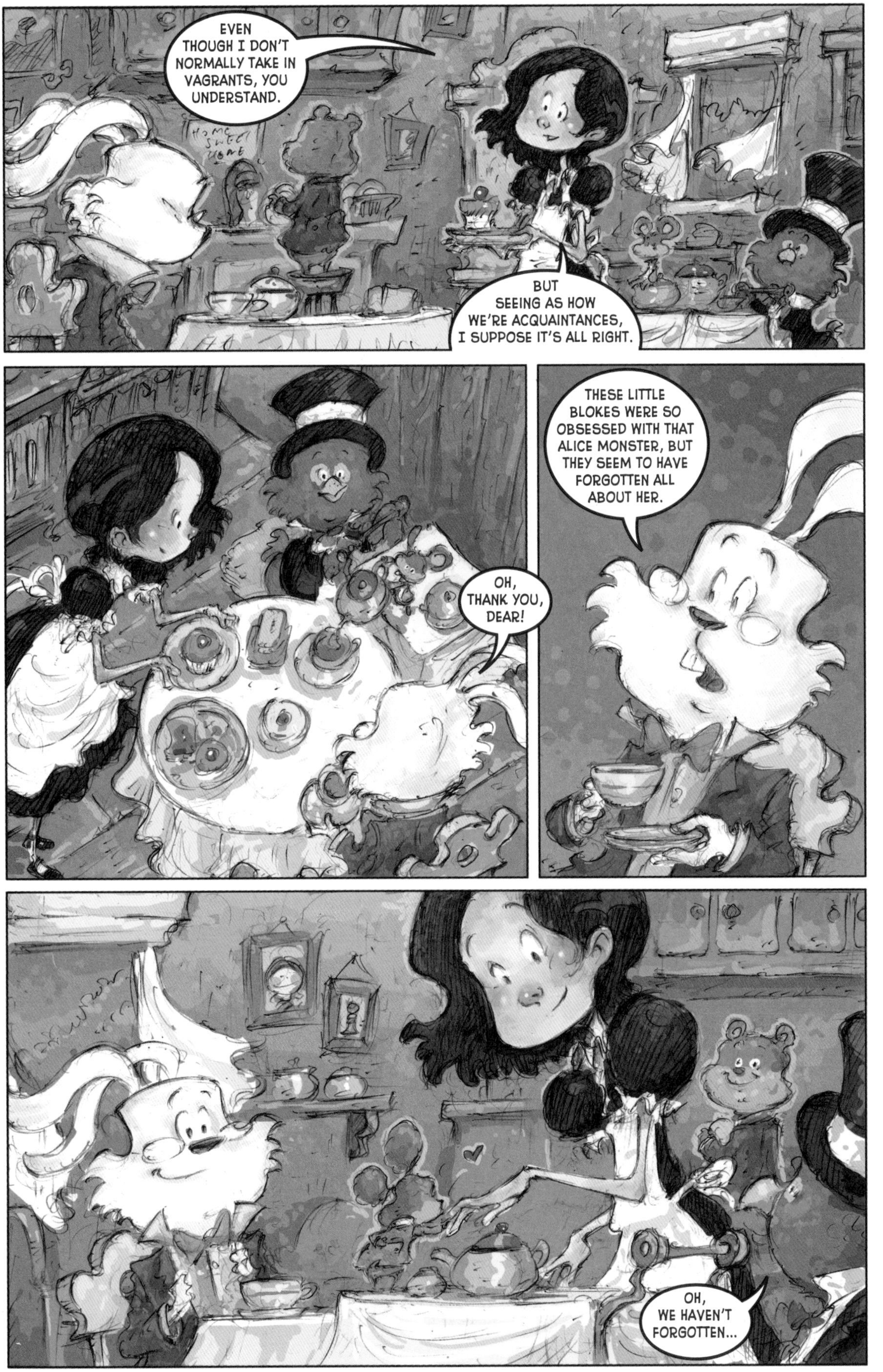
EVEN THOUGH I DON'T NORMALLY TAKE IN VAGRANTS, YOU UNDERSTAND.
HOME SWEET HOME
BUT SEEING AS HOW WE'RE ACQUAINTANCES, I SUPPOSE IT'S ALL RIGHT.
OH, THANK YOU, DEAR!
THESE LITTLE BLOKES WERE SO OBSESSED WITH THAT ALICE MONSTER, BUT THEY SEEM TO HAVE FORGOTTEN ALL ABOUT HER.
OH, WE HAVEN'T FORGOTTEN...

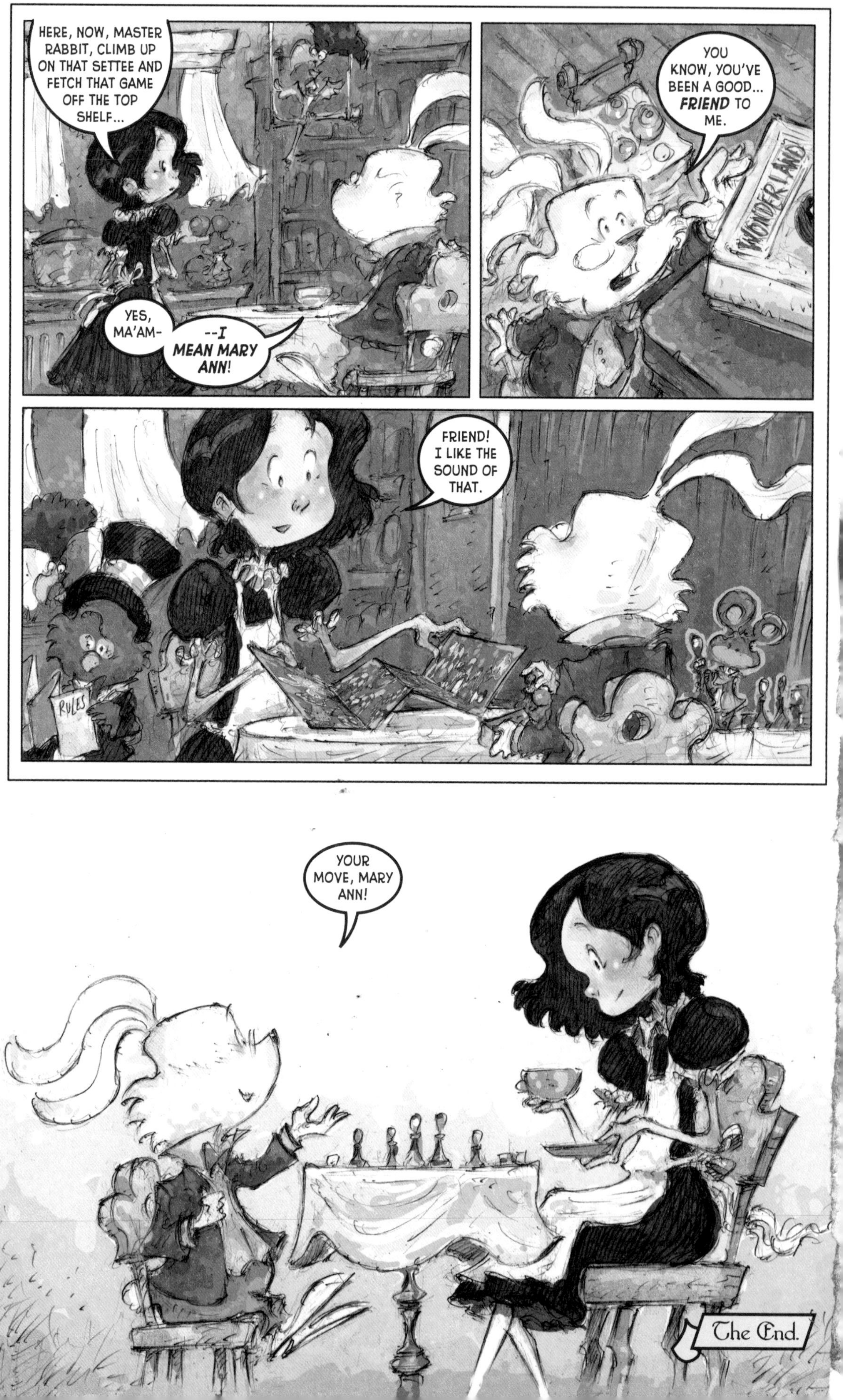
HERE, NOW, MASTER RABBIT, CLIMB UP ON THAT SETTEE AND FETCH THAT GAME OFF THE TOP SHELF...
YES, MA'AM-
--I MEAN MARY ANN!
YOU KNOW, YOU'VE BEEN A GOOD... FRIEND TO ME.
WONDERLAND
FRIEND! I LIKE THE SOUND OF THAT.
RULES
YOUR MOVE, MARY ANN!
The End.